Praise for the Novels
of Lacey Alexander

What She Needs
Winner of the HOLT Medallion Award

"Lacey Alexander has created a book which literally 'wows' the reader. Buckle up and hold on tight. Impossibly hot!"
—Fallen Angel Reviews (5 Angels)

"One very hot, sexy, and erotic book. Full of sexual fantasies that will have you flipping the pages to see what will happen next!"   —Fresh Fiction

"Prepare to be swept away on an erotic journey of sexual awakening! The imagery and attention to detail will thrust you right into the sensual fantasies and erotic adventures. . . . *What She Needs* is very sensual, erotic, and will open your mind to infinite possibilities!"   —The Romance Studio (5 Hearts)

"An ultraheated erotic romance. The heat is on."   —The Best Reviews

"This book sizzles. . . . Ms. Alexander explores the spectrum of the human sexual experience without embarrassment or ridicule."
—Erotic Romance Writers

"Each sex scene is more varied—and hotter—than the last in this delightful read. Fans of heroes with tragic pasts will swoon over Brent."
—*Romantic Times* (4 Stars)

The Bikini Diaries
Write Touch Award Winner and Colorado Award of Excellence Finalist

"Hot, sizzling, and sexy! Lacey Alexander definitely will scorch your senses."
—Romance Junkies (5 Blue Ribbons)

continued . .

"Ms. Alexander sweeps away her readers in a sinfully erotic yet surprisingly nongratuitous manner." —*Sacramento Book Review*

"With intriguing characters, [a] fast-paced story line, and tight writing, plus a host of naughty sexual adventures, Ms. Alexander delivers a powerful story." —*Love Romances & More* (4½ Hearts)

"Truly a phenomenal book. Lacey Alexander is a remarkably gifted author who writes exactly what I want to read, pushing boundaries with titillating sexuality, but never going beyond what's tasteful. . . . Do yourself a huge favor and buy everything Lacey Alexander has ever written. You won't regret it." —*TwoLips Reviews* (5 Lips)

"[The] most erotic book I have read. Lacey Alexander has written a no-holds-barred romp of sexual delights . . . a profound book." —*Joyfully Reviewed*

"I loved this book. Each sexual act was well written and done extremely well." —*Night Owl Romance* (5 out of 5, Lifetime Keeper)

"I was completely swept up in Wendy's journey. . . . Lacey Alexander is certainly the queen of what I fondly call 'romantic kink'!" —*Wild on Books* (5 Bookmarks)

Seven Nights of Sin
Write Touch Award Winner

"Lacey Alexander's books bring out the good little bad girl in all of us. Unforgettable in an '*Oh, yeah, do that again, please*' sort of way." —*Michelle Buonfiglio, myLifetime.com*

"Thoroughly tantalizing, with magnetic characters, a sizzling plot, and raw sensuality, this book will have you fanning yourself long after the last page!" —*Romantic Times*

And for Lacey Alexander

"Ms. Alexander is an exceptionally talented author who, time after time, takes us on extremely erotic journeys that leave us breathless with every turn of the page. . . . This author pens the most arousing sexual scenes that you could never imagine."
—Fallen Angel Reviews

"Lacey Alexander has given readers . . . hot, erotic romance with no holds barred."
—Romance Junkies

"Ms. Alexander is probably one of the most talented, straightforward, imaginative writers in erotic romance today."
—The Road to Romance

"Lacey Alexander just 'wowed' me! Incredibly hot!"
—Romance Reader at Heart (Top Pick)

"Lacey Alexander is a very talented writer."
—The Romance Readers Connection

"Lacey Alexander is an intoxicating erotic writer using sensual and sexual prowess to embrace your inner passions and desires. Sexual discovery at its best."
—Noveltown

"Lacey Alexander's characters . . . are so compelling and lifelike."
—Coffee Time Romance

"Sooo romantic and sexy!"
—Cupid's Library Reviews

"Lacey Alexander takes blissful hedonism to a whole new level in this blazingly brazen, passionately erotic love story!"
—Ecataromance

Bad Girl by Night

A H.O.T. COPS NOVEL

Lacey Alexander

A SIGNET ECLIPSE BOOK

SIGNET ECLIPSE
Published by New American Library, a division of
Penguin Group (USA) Inc., 375 Hudson Street,
New York, New York 10014, USA
Penguin Group (Canada), 90 Eglinton Avenue East, Suite 700, Toronto,
Ontario M4P 2Y3, Canada (a division of Pearson Penguin Canada Inc.)
Penguin Books Ltd., 80 Strand, London WC2R 0RL, England
Penguin Ireland, 25 St. Stephen's Green, Dublin 2,
Ireland (a division of Penguin Books Ltd.)
Penguin Group (Australia), 250 Camberwell Road, Camberwell, Victoria 3124,
Australia (a division of Pearson Australia Group Pty. Ltd.)
Penguin Books India Pvt. Ltd., 11 Community Centre, Panchsheel Park,
New Delhi - 110 017, India
Penguin Group (NZ), 67 Apollo Drive, Rosedale, Auckland 0632,
New Zealand (a division of Pearson New Zealand Ltd.)
Penguin Books (South Africa) (Pty.) Ltd., 24 Sturdee Avenue,
Rosebank, Johannesburg 2196, South Africa
Penguin Books Ltd., Registered Offices:
80 Strand, London WC2R 0RL, England

First published by Signet Eclipse, an imprint of New American Library,
a division of Penguin Group (USA) Inc.

First Printing, June 2011
10 9 8 7 6 5 4 3 2 1

SIGNET ECLIPSE and logo are trademarks of Penguin Group (USA) Inc.

LIBRARY OF CONGRESS CATALOGING-IN-PUBLICATION DATA:

Alexander, Lacey.
    Bad girl by night: a H.O.T. cops novel/Lacey Alexander.
        p.   cm.
    ISBN 978-0-451-23323-3
    1. Women—Sexual behavior—Fiction. 2. Identity (Psychology)—Fiction. 3. Michigan—Fiction. I. Title.
    PS3601.L3539B33   2011
    813'.6—dc22   .   2011003178

Set in Centaur MT
Designed by Alissa Amell

Printed in the United States of America

PUBLISHER'S NOTE
This is a work of fiction. Names, characters, places, and incidents either are the product of the author's imagination or are used fictitiously, and any resemblance to actual persons, living or dead, business establishments, events, or locales is entirely coincidental.
    The publisher does not have any control over and does not assume any responsibility for author or third-party Web sites or their content.

Bad Girl by Night

Risk! Risk anything! Care no more for the opinions of others, for those voices. Do the hardest thing on earth for you. Act for yourself. Face the truth.

—Katherine Mansfield

Chapter 1

She knew how to do this.

She got out of the car, body humming, the mere click of her heels over asphalt somehow adding to her anticipation. Was it from the audible evidence that she was moving, getting closer to her destination after two long hours in the car, or was it the reminder of the shoes themselves, the fact that she wore her sexy strappy heels for one purpose and one purpose only?

The hotel sat along the water in Traverse City—a busy tourist town on Michigan's west coast—and the architecture said "modern yet warm" with stone pillars and lots of dark wood to remind you where you were: the great outdoors, the "north woods." Yet boating and hiking were the last things on her mind as she stepped inside and looked around, her gaze homing in immediately on the big oak doors that led to the hotel bar.

As she walked into the Lodge, curious eyes swept over her dress—red and silky, clingy. Like the rest of the building, the décor was warm, woody, the walls hung with things like old snow skis and hunting vests. A large mural depicting a family of bears spanned the long wall behind the bar, where she calmly, confidently eased up onto a stool. She didn't mind the eyes she felt watching her—in fact, it heightened the tingle of expectation, the eagerness now stretching through her in a slow-flowing river of heat.

The gaze of the good-looking bartender, in his late twenties, held no judgment as he said, "What'll ya have?"

"A white wine spritzer, please." Once, she'd started out with cocktails and discovered they made her too drunk, dulled her senses too much. And even simple wine possessed the power to leave her tipsier than she wanted to be right now—watering it down with a little Sprite made it just right. And that was the key to her trips here every few months—making sure everything was *just right*. "Goldilocks Does Traverse City."

The thought should have made her smile, but it didn't. Nothing about this amused her.

Acclimating to her surroundings, she glanced around—without being obvious—to get an idea of the bar's patrons. She spied a creepy-looking old guy watching her from a booth and immediately blocked out the ick factor his gaze delivered. Loads of masculine laughter echoed from a darkish corner somewhere behind her, and the sound heightened her senses. Three college boys ogled her, too, from the end of the bar. Too young. But at least flattering. And if there were other females in the room, she didn't notice—they were invisible to her right now.

She could move on to another bar if she had to, but she'd give this one a while first. This was like . . . hunting. And north woods girls understood about hunting—that the best hunters were patient, quiet, still. They let their prey come to *them*. And then they struck. She knew how to do this.

Once upon a time, the endeavor had made her nervous—she'd questioned her every move, analyzed everything around her; it had all taken an enormous amount of courage and concentration. The act of walking into a bar, meeting a man, leaving with him, had been accompanied by grave fear. *Valid* fear. She knew the kinds of bad things that could happen to a woman.

But each time she drove from Turnbridge to Traverse City, the two-hour commute transformed her even more than it had the time before. She became no less smart than usual, yet she was more in control; she was self-possessed; she was the one who orchestrated the events, ran the show. Fear fell away to be replaced by power. And now, at thirty-two, she could barely remember the fear of those early years—it had disappeared completely. Now the moves came naturally. They took little more effort than breathing.

The night, the darkness, protected her. So did the low-cut dress, which showed her curves and flashed too much cleavage. Cleavage that made a promise. The shoes, too, were like sexual armor—they turned her into someone tall, willowy; they also made her into a woman unafraid of her needs, bold enough to take what she wanted. Heavily painted eyes provided one more shield, as did her hair. Long honey gold shot through with warmer strands—she normally wore it straight, tucked behind her ears or pulled back into a ponytail, but when she came to Traverse City, she used hot rollers to change it into something wild and tousled.

The whole ritual, most of it taking place before the mirror above her dresser, made her feel like one of Pavlov's dogs—the very act of preparation exciting her hours before her goal would be reached. Somehow the long, detailed process—and the rising fever of expectation that came with it—made the whole thing more satisfying in the end.

A few sips before her glass was drained, another appeared before her on a napkin. She looked up to meet the bartender's eyes and he gave her a small smile. "From the guys at the end of the bar."

She tossed only a cursory glance in their direction. The college boys. One of them was attractive, probably a football star or something equally as ego-building, judging from the arrogance in his pointed gaze. But in addition to his being too young—which generally meant selfish and clumsy in her experience—she didn't like him. A little arrogance was one thing, but this guy was overrun with it; it was the most obvious thing about him. "Tell them thanks," she said to the bartender, "but that I'm meeting someone."

The bartender, suddenly her confidant, raised his eyebrows in curiosity. "Are you?"

"I'm sure I will eventually," she replied, all smooth voice and unwavering self-control.

His grin said he liked her style—then he headed back to break the news to her youthful admirers.

She heard the football star mutter, "Shit." She'd cost them five dollars, after all. And a minute later he and his friends left, clearly seeking greener pastures.

When a highball glass was plunked down next to her from behind, she turned to see—oh, hell—the old guy. Though he wasn't as old as she'd first thought—early fifties, maybe—he appeared grizzled, tired for his age. "You look lonely," he said.

She knew she looked far more *ready* than lonely, but that aside, what man thought that was a good pick-up line? "I'm not," she assured him sharply.

"Damn, girl—I just came over to say hi, get to know you a little." He sounded angry, offended. She didn't care. This was how the game was played—you didn't have to be nice. She had the idea he'd been drinking for a long time already.

"I'm meeting someone," she told him. It was a tried-and-true excuse, easy to remember, and not even technically a lie, since, as she'd told the bartender, she *would* eventually find the guy who was just right for the night. She always did. She'd never gone home unsuccessful. Not even back in the beginning when her hunting expeditions had also held all that uncertainty and worry. She knew how to do this.

"You been sittin' here half an hour," he pointed out. "You ain't meetin' nobody."

She met the man's glassy eyes, stared right through him. Any other time, any other place, she'd feel stupid right now, embarrassed maybe, caught in a fib. But her armor protected her. *"It's really none of your business who I'm meeting or*

not meeting." She spoke pointedly. Knew she sounded a little scary. Enjoyed it
and sensed it making her nipples a bit harder than they already were.

The graying man with the tired eyes just swallowed, then moistened his
lips as if they were dry. "Whatever," he finally said—then picked up his glass
and turned to walk away, muttering, "Bitch," as he went.

"Sorry about that," the bartender told her as he approached, apparently
having heard at least the last part.

But she just gave a short shake of her head. "No worries." In her normal
life, such an insult would wound her. Here, it was nothing.

Just then, a good-looking guy with dark hair approached the bar, a few
feet to her left. "Can I get a couple more beers?" Sounding good-natured,
friendly, as he addressed the bartender, he lowered two empty longnecks
to the smooth wood counter. Then he glanced her way and offered a short
"Hi."

She smiled back without planning it. "Hi." And the insides of her thighs
warmed.

She watched him then as he chatted with the bartender—he wore stylish
jeans, a button-down shirt with the sleeves rolled up. His hair was black as
coal, soft, thick, and he was due for a trim. He was the self-assured sort of
guy who cared about his appearance but didn't go overboard. What did he do
for a living? He looked like . . . an airline pilot, or . . . maybe a photographer.
He was smart, focused, professional—but not a suit-and-tie guy.

How he made his living didn't really matter, though—it was just a game
she played with herself sometimes. What mattered was that he was hot,
handsome, and old enough—early to mid-thirties—to know what to do.
And that he had a nice smile. Not lecherous, but not prim. She knew, even as
quick as their exchange had been, that he'd caught a glimpse of her cleavage
and admired it, but he didn't think she looked lonely. Or desperate. Which
was good. Since she wasn't. But she was feeling more *ready* by the second.

When the bartender turned to get the beers, she made conversation, pointing over her shoulder. "Is that you and your friends I hear having such a good time back there?" The deep male laughter had continued, like background music to her thoughts. And her easy flirtation had come out as smooth as always. Because she knew how to do this.

He met her gaze, his eyes a vivid blue that drew her attention. Blue like pictures of the Mediterranean—saturated, rich, captivating. He gave her another smile. "Wow, didn't realize we were being so loud. Sorry."

She shook her head, knowing she looked pretty and confident to him. "I don't mind. Just feel like I'm missing out on the party," she teased.

He shrugged. "You're welcome to join us." But then he lowered his chin, as if rethinking the offer. "Although you might feel outnumbered with about a dozen guys, most of them drunk."

"Are *you* drunk?" she asked, eyebrows lifting.

He thought it over, then held out his right hand, palm down, teetering it back and forth, as if to say he was wobbling on the edge. She liked his measured honesty, that he hadn't simply said yes or no. This one held potential.

So she confided, "Me, too." Yes, she definitely knew how to do this. Sometimes it was so easy it was almost scary.

That was when she cast a surreptitious look toward his *left* hand. Good—no ring. And no tan line indicating he'd just taken one off. Some things she held sacred. Even here.

"So . . . you meeting somebody? A date?" He wasn't shy about letting those blue eyes roam her body a little, and it made her feel even warmer, all over. She wondered if her nipples could be seen through her bra and dress.

"I was. But looks like I got stood up." Like everything else, she said it smoothly, her tone indicating she wasn't too broken up about it. Even in this particular lie, she knew how to sound above-it-all, still possessing the upper hand. No one would feel sorry for her.

The man gave her another bold perusal from his spot at the bar, one that left her inner thighs literally aching. "Guy must be an idiot."

She smiled. "Thanks."

And that was when he moved closer, sat down on the stool next to hers. "Can I buy you a drink?"

She tilted her head, flashing her best flattered, flirtatious, but still fully in control expression. She was *always, always* in control. "Sure. But what about your friends?"

He gave her a look that said, *Get real.* "Let's see—I can hang out with a bunch of hammered guys, or I can sit and talk with a beautiful woman. *I'm* not an idiot—I'll take what's behind door number two."

As soon as the adept bartender set two open beers on the bar, he went about mixing another spritzer.

"What's your name?" her suitor asked. Or would that be her prey?

"Desiree."

"I'm Jake," he said.

Once her empty had been replaced with a fresh drink, her companion lifted his beer bottle. "Should we toast?"

She picked up her glass and said, "To handsome blue-eyed strangers who rescue damsels in distress."

He grinned, clinking the bottle's neck lightly against her glass, even as he appeared a little skeptical. "You don't look very in distress, Desiree."

She took a sip through her straw and confessed, "You're right—I'm *not* a damsel in distress. But you *are* a handsome blue-eyed stranger. And you're suddenly making my night look a lot more promising." Then she glanced toward the room's rear corner. "Unless you decide you want to get back to your friends, after all."

"Aw, *hell* no, honey," he said, and she decided he *was* just a little drunk, but that was okay—even good. People lost their inhibitions when they were drunk. And she wanted him. He was *just right.* Goldilocks knew when she'd hit the mark.

They talked then. About nothing in particular. The warmer than average temperatures for May. The wineries out on Old Mission Peninsula. She was glad he didn't ask her anything personal; she asked nothing of him, either. And when he inquired, "What brings you to Traverse City?" she kept it simple.

"Here on holiday." It sounded European, sophisticated—and vague.

"By yourself?"

A simple nod.

He asked no more. He clearly got the message. She wasn't into sharing.

"Dude, where the hell's my beer?"

This voice came from her right, and she turned to find a good-looking guy staring past her toward Jake—his tone impatient without being angry. Dirty blond hair, a bit shaggier than Jake's, along with a few days' stubble on his chin, gave him the vibe of a surfer. But the clothes—dark jeans, a zip-up sweater over a knit tee—kept him looking well put together.

"This is Colt," Jake said. "He's not usually so rude."

When Colt's gaze dropped to her face, then traveled a little lower, she got the idea it was the first time he'd actually noticed her. But now he *was*—in a big way. "Shit. Sorry. Hi."

She liked his instant repentance. Moreover, she liked the way these guys clearly sensed her confidence, saw her sexuality—yet treated her with respect. Yep, just right.

"Well, *now* I understand what the holdup is," Colt said, still eyeing her appreciatively as he leaned to take the dark bottle Jake reached past her to deliver. The move brought both men closer to her, allowed her to take in the slight musky scent each gave off—and to feel that zing of chemistry, that thing that was either there or it wasn't. And it was there. With . . . both of them, she realized as a strange frisson of heat slowly ascended her spine.

Of course, it was Jake who she'd felt that automatic connection with, Jake she planned to be with tonight. And yet that didn't stop Colt from helping himself to the stool on the other side of her and proceeding to ask her name, ask her teasingly what she was doing "hanging out with *this* guy—when you could have *me?*"

He was drunker than Jake. But he had a winning smile.

So she took the bait. "Could I? Have you?" And she might be flashing a playful grin, but she also knew she'd just taken this to the next level. Colt had made it easy. And she saw little reason to act shy or demure.

Jake's friend drew back slightly, met her gaze. His eyes were green. The green of marbles. Of the foliage in impressionist paintings. "Are you kidding, darlin'? Of course you could." *Darlin'.* It was the first time she'd realized he spoke with a slight drawl—Southern, and bold. A little cocky as well. But not in a bad way.

"Now, wait just a minute here," Jake said laughingly at her other side. She turned back, reminded that he made her feel warm inside. If her first impression of Colt was one of bold excitement, her first of Jake was warmth, the kind that could cover you like a blanket. "You can have *me*, too—just in case I haven't made that clear enough yet. And I was here first," he added with a wink.

She bit her lip, gave a sexy smile, and moved her glance back and forth between the two men. "Decisions, decisions."

Then she took a sip of her spritzer, a big one.

Suddenly, she wanted to be a little more intoxicated, a little *less* in control. That wasn't her normal way, but this suddenly wasn't the normal situation for her, either. And it was moving fast, and she thought if she wanted to keep up, the easiest way might actually be to . . . let herself go a little.

Of course, the whole point of coming to Traverse City was to let herself go—but only while maintaining that unwavering sense of being in command of the situation. It was odd how those two factors worked together so closely. They sounded contradictory, but they weren't. Being in control was the part that made it safe, the part that gave her power. Without that, the letting-herself-go part would be reckless to the point of being impossible.

And yet . . . there was a dark part of her—a darker part than she'd ever even imagined until this very moment—urging her to think the unthinkable. Urging her to let herself go in a whole new way. She couldn't quite get there, though, couldn't quite let herself even *have* the thought wafting about the edge of her consciousness. She couldn't pull it together, make it concrete— something was blocking it out.

So she took another big drink, and her head swam—just a little. Just enough to begin letting that forbidden idea *in*. And it made her stomach pinch. But it also made her pussy weep beneath her dress.

Desire. Add an *e* and you have Desiree. Desire had created her, and it was what drove her. It was the biggest part of her. So she always listened to it— she couldn't *not* listen. And what it was telling her right now was a little hard to believe, but suddenly she didn't quite possess the power to shut it back out, either. Once you let something out of the box, it was out. *Just listen. Open your mind to it. Decide if it's what you want.*

Colt was less subtle than Jake in ways—he talked more about himself, trying to impress. In the next few minutes, she found out he was a security expert and highly paid private bodyguard.

"Lot of bodies to guard up here in rural Michigan?" she couldn't help asking on a laugh.

"I don't live around here," he informed her. "I work in Miami."

"I was guessing someplace different—from the accent."

"Born and raised in east Texas," he told her, adding with a grin, "but I get around."

"I'll bet you do."

Unlike the college-boy football star, she liked Colt despite his arrogance, some of which she suspected had been brought out by alcohol. He kept talking, mentioning some of their other friends by name, and as her head began to spin trying to keep track of it all, Jake eventually interrupted him to explain that they were a group of old buddies who met here every summer "to do the fishing-hiking-drinking thing for a few days."

"Sounds fun," she said, and she meant it. To have that many friends. To be that carefree.

Next to her, Jake shrugged and said, "This is *more* fun." Somewhere along the way, as Colt had regaled her with his guy tales, Jake had begun leaning closer. She took in his masculine scent again, laced with the tang of beer, and her stomach seemed to curl in on itself as his thigh pressed against hers, solid and warm.

When she turned to look at him, his face was nearer than she'd realized. Her gaze drifted from his eyes to his mouth, not more than an inch from hers. And when she spoke, her voice came out lower than usual. "Are you getting fresh with me?"

"Damn straight," he said in a deep timbre. And then his hand eased onto her knee.

She felt the touch in her panties as well as in her breasts. She'd grown so excited that her tits felt swollen. *Tits. Pussy.* They weren't words usually in her vocabulary. Except for when she made her little excursions to Traverse City. They were words she'd picked up from other men over the years—dirty talk while fucking. That was another one—*fucking.* As a fresh wave of intoxication swept over her, the shock of it all hit her fresh. No one who knew her would ever believe it. That she could be titillated by such words. That she could seduce strangers. But she shut the thought out as soon as it came. That wasn't who she was tonight—the woman everyone knew. Tonight she was Desiree. Queen of desire. Lust. Sex. Queen of everything hot and nasty.

When Colt's hand came to rest on her other knee, it was more of an abrupt, attention-getting touch than a sensual one—but she let her eyes linger on how it looked to have two men's hands on her at the same time, just for a second, before lifting her gaze to his.

"Hey, now," he said, "does this mean I'm losing? Just 'cause he met you first?"

She blinked. Did it?

She wanted Jake—he was more her style on such outings, and the urge to rub her body against his, to feel that glorious friction, was mounting wildly.

But . . . she was attracted to Colt, too. If Jake had never appeared, she'd have been more than happy to flirt with sexy Colt, more than happy to let him under her skirt before the night was through.

"Losing what exactly?" she asked.

It was rare to find two men she found so . . . acceptable for her needs, at the same time, same place. And it seemed almost a shame to let either of them go to waste. She had the strange sense, in fact, that if she left with Jake, she'd pine for Colt a little even as she let Jake pleasure her. And she couldn't imagine choosing Colt, either, because Jake turned everything inside her liquid and oozy, like hot fudge melting slowly over a gooey brownie.

Which brought her back to that unfathomable thought. Which she'd finally allowed herself to acknowledge—even if only as something hazy and distant. Now, a little drunker, a little more turned on, she let herself examine it more concretely.

"Losing *you*." Colt's eyes fell half shut as he answered, and the touch on her knee changed—he squeezed lightly, the sensation shooting up her thigh. Suddenly, he appeared as caught in passion as Jake, and it made her look back and forth between them. And consider. The unthinkable.

Two men.

Was it such a far stretch from where she already found herself? In a bar two hours from her small hometown, dressed provocatively, here for sex. Did it make all that much difference whether it was with one guy or two?

Of course it did. She knew that. The *real* her knew it anyway. But she wasn't the real her tonight. She was confident Desiree. She could have what she wanted. For Desiree, nothing was forbidden—it was all just pleasure. There was no guilt, none of society's rules and mores. Her chest went hollow, her throat dry. With the decision she'd just made.

"Does anyone really have to lose?" she asked, her voice coming out huskier than she'd ever heard it.

Neither guy answered right away. And finally, Colt said, "Um . . . what do you mean, darlin'?" Both still curved their hands over her knees, where the silky fabric of her dress had risen slightly higher on her thighs. She parted them now, just a little, on instinct. And her cunt clenched in a longing so intense she'd never experienced anything quite like it.

She swallowed, the stark lust turning her throat thick as she looked to Jake. "Do you have a room here, at the hotel?"

"Yeah," he said deeply.

"Could we go there now?"

"Um—yeah. God—of course."

"All three of us," she said. Not a question this time, but a statement.

It was as if her words had drained all the air from the dimly lit room. The two men stayed still as statues as they absorbed her words. She saw them glance back and forth between each other and her, clearly weighing the proposal, and her heart pounded almost painfully against her rib cage. She'd just done this, started this. And she wanted it. She wanted this experience most women would never have, this forbidden thing. And now that she'd actually suggested it, she harbored no regrets—only a pervasive hunger that echoed through her whole body.

Despite music from speakers somewhere overhead, and more of their friends' raucous laughter from the back of the bar, the proposition hung heavy in what felt like a startling silence—until Colt finally cleared his throat to say, "Sure, darlin'—why not?"

So she looked to Jake, her eyebrows raised, her cheeks flushed and tingling with excitement.

He let out a breath, appearing almost too aroused to speak. And then he replied, "All right. Let's go."

Chapter 2

"Here," Jake said, stopping in front of a door on the second floor. They'd taken the steps, too impatient to wait for the elevator.

She watched him jam a key card in the lock, then push his way inside. He flipped on a light as she followed, Colt hot on her heels, his hands playing about her hips. Then Jake turned and peered at her in the lamplight, eyes glassy with lust.

What now?

Simple. You suggested this, you take the lead. Just follow your instincts. They never failed her. At least not here, with strangers, in hotel rooms.

She stepped forward, pressed her palms to Jake's chest, warm through the thin fabric of his shirt. She met his blue gaze, somehow more vibrant in the room's low lighting, and murmured, "Kiss me."

A low growl left his throat as he closed sure hands over the curves of her waist and lowered his mouth firmly to hers. His tongue pressed between her lips instantly and she surged with wetness below.

Another hot spasm erupted between her legs when Colt's hands snaked up under her arms to smoothly cup her breasts, making her moan against

Jake's mouth. Colt groaned, kneaded her flesh ever so boldly, and she found herself thrusting her chest outward, upward, shoving it more deeply against his touch. God, yes. Whatever brief moments of trepidation or doubt she might have experienced up to now—they all vanished. Following her instincts was going to work just fine.

"I want you both to fuck me *so* hard," she heard herself whisper hotly. The words had come out unbidden.

"Oh baby, we will—we will," Jake promised breathlessly. And then his kisses were dropping to her neck, and onto her chest . . . Colt still massaged her tits, and she simply leaned her head back, surrendering herself to them both. She wanted control—but sometimes, when she got to this part, the control came with choosing to give herself over to the experience, the pleasure.

Behind her, the heat of Colt's body pressed into hers, and then—mmm, God—his hard length nestled against her ass, at the very center. She whimpered at the sensation, yet stayed keenly aware of Jake as he pushed the thin straps of her dress from her shoulders, then tugged lightly—a silent message to his friend to release her breasts so the fabric could fall.

Yet even without Colt's firm hands, her breasts themselves stopped the clingy fabric's natural descent until Jake pulled further, with a little more force than she'd witnessed in him up to now—*appealing* force. She lowered her arms so the dress could come off easily, and finally it dropped, skimming across her skin like one more touch before settling at her hips to reveal a shimmery concoction of red and hot pink, a demi bra that lifted her breasts high while barely covering the nipples. A glance down reminded her how big and full they looked in it—that it gave them the appearance of being barely contained, ready to tumble from the confining lace. "Jesus," Jake muttered, taking in the sight.

"Those are fucking gorgeous, darlin'," Colt rasped near her ear; then he kissed her shoulder as his hands came back to knead them again, eagerly.

She felt almost unsteady, weak with desire, and she wanted her men to start getting undressed, too. So she found the strength to reach up and work at the buttons on Jake's shirt as he ran his hands down her sides, his thumbs spanning onto her slender stomach.

Once his shirt was open, he shrugged it off, and she sighed at the view of his chest and shoulders, finding him sturdy, pleasantly muscular, perfect. A tattoo she couldn't make out resided on one arm. She ran her palms from his chest slowly to the waistband of his jeans, letting her fingertips slip inside as she eyed the prominent bulge in the denim just below—but then she withdrew them because his belt suddenly seemed too difficult a task while Colt continued his firm caress of her tits, making her feel all the wilder. She could only lean back into the hot bodyguard, languorously lifting her arms over her head to run her fingers through his messy hair while she bit her lip, eyes still on Jake's hidden erection.

In response, Jake undid the belt, unbuttoned his jeans, pulled down the zipper—then moved in close to her, hands at her hips, hard-on pressing against her clit. She sucked in her breath. *Two men's hard bodies, mine in between.* Ultimate pleasure. She knew that couldn't be true, that there was much more to come—but she'd never felt anything more delicious than being so tightly sandwiched between two hot guys, two stiff cocks.

Jake moved against her, creating a hot friction that set her pussy on fire, the heat radiating outward. In back, Colt rocked into her now, too, sliding his hardness up the valley of her ass, and she thought she might come, right then and there, like that—until Jake changed things.

He stepped back, just slightly, and lowered his searing gaze to her tits once more. Then he dragged two fingers slowly down the center of her chest until they lodged between the plumped flesh of her breasts—still in Colt's firm grasp—and began to glide them up and down. His voice came low, ragged. "I want to slide my cock right here."

A hot sigh left her at the promise. "I want that, too."

"But right now, I want to suck these gorgeous tits." And with that, he pushed down both thin bra straps, and Colt's hands fell away, and her breasts spilled free. Both guys groaned, and behind her, Colt muttered, "Damn—nice."

A fresh burst of moisture shot through her cunt as Jake reached up, framing her tits with strong hands, leaving the nipples uncovered. He lightly flicked his thumbs across the hard, pointed peaks, making her whimper slightly. And then—oh Lord—he used thumbs and forefingers to pinch, just a little. She got wetter still.

Finally, he did what he'd told her—he bent to close his mouth over one turgid pink nub, pulling deeply. "Oh God," she moaned as the pleasure stretched through her, all the way to her pussy.

She could barely remain on her feet now, and Colt must have sensed that since his arm came around her torso, anchoring her to him as Jake continued his ministrations to her breasts, sucking first one, then the other. Sometimes he backed off a little, using only his tongue, but mostly he drew on her nipple hard and complete—while Colt ran his free hand down over her hip . . . and then under her dress, up her bare thigh.

She heard herself panting, lost in the pleasure of two men, two sets of hands. Soon she would have two cocks, as well, a thought that made her shut her eyes and let out a slow, deep breath. But for now, the hands—and Jake's skilled mouth—were plenty, and seemingly all she could handle, anyway, especially when Colt's fingers slipped into her panties, from the back, beneath her ass, and into her wet folds. "Unh," she breathed—and then he slid two fingers up inside her. "Mmm—oh!" she cried out. The Texas bodyguard didn't waste any time—and that was fine with her.

As he began thrusting those fingers up into her, he nibbled at her shoulder, then her neck, rasping near her ear, "You're so damn wet, darlin'. My fingers are drenched."

"You both . . . excite me . . . so much," she managed, breathless now.

It was then that she found herself grabbing, clawing—using one hand to try to push down Jake's blue jeans, the other to pull at the fabric covering Colt's shoulder behind her.

"Calm down, darlin', calm down," Colt soothed her deeply. "We'll get there."

Her words came in rasps—and didn't completely respond to what he'd just said. "I . . . can barely . . . stay on . . . my feet."

Jake bit lightly at her nipple, murmuring against her flesh, "Then we'd better sit you down." And with that, he scooped her effortlessly up into his arms. A small easy chair sat closer to them than the king-size bed, so that was where he lowered her, then leaned immediately in to kiss her lips, reaching to caress one bared breast again. He seemed ravenous, as if he'd been unable to help himself, making her feel like the most desirable woman on the planet.

And she felt like the *naughtiest* one when Colt began parting her thighs and she let him. Still busy kissing Jake, she didn't even bother looking at Colt as he knelt and moved in between—she just curled her legs around him as she scooted down in the chair.

As she made out with Jake, she touched *him* with one hand, Colt with the other. Colt had taken off his sweater and shirt now, too, so it was the first time she felt his skin, her fingertips caressing his shoulder, arm. She became aware that Colt was pushing up her dress where it still hung around her, shoving it to her waist to reveal the lacy boy short panties she wore—the same red and pink as the bra that still circled her body.

When he let out another low groan, she thought it meant he liked them, and he shored up the suspicion, saying, "Jake, bud—look at these sexy undies our little miss Desiree's got on."

Jake stopped kissing her and glanced down. So did she—just in time to see, and feel, Colt stroke his thumb over her mound. Jake let out an audible sigh—either at the panties or at the sight of his friend touching her, she didn't know which.

"I almost don't wanna take 'em off," Colt said. "But on the other hand . . ." He grinned up at her.

"Those are nice," Jake said to both of them. "But I bet the hot little pussy underneath will be even prettier."

"*Hell* yeah," Colt growled, then told her to lift her ass so he could pull them off.

She complied, watching along with her companions as Colt slowly peeled the lace down her thighs, over her knees, and finally over her shoes. "Unh," Jake breathed. Clearly, he liked that she'd shaved between her legs, leaving nothing but a small thatch of pale brown above her slit.

Colt's eyes on her pussy were heavy-lidded as he parted her thighs once more, perusing her pink folds. She finally shed the bra, and the guys simply studied her, as she now wore only her fuck-me heels with her dress gathered around her waist. She felt a bit like a centerfold, and she liked it. She liked being their dirty little plaything. It was why she was here, after all. It wasn't awful to be a man's sex object if you *wanted* to be, if it made you feel good, if everyone was happy in the end.

"Damn, I wanna fuck you," Colt growled, "but first, I'm gonna lick this hot, pink cunt until you come." Her pussy practically lurched at his words. And she spread her legs a little wider in invitation.

She bit her lip, anticipating the moment when he would go down on her. And then it came, and a moan rose deep from her throat as the sensation delivered by his tongue vibrated through her entire being. "God, fuck, yes," she breathed. The stubble on his chin scratched lightly, but she was so excited it only added to her pleasure. She grasped her own breasts, shut her eyes, lifted her crotch against his face.

"Aw, honey, let me help you with those," Jake said, standing beside the chair and reaching down to slip his hands under hers, massaging her tits.

And she reached instinctively for his open jeans—the bulge she'd been craving was right next to her face now, after all. "I want your cock, baby."

He let out a low groan, still molding her soft, sensitive breasts as she used both hands to shove his jeans over his hips, then reached into his underwear. And mmm, God—his erection was so big and long and hard, springing from his boxer briefs now like some wild thing breaking free. She squeezed it gently in her fist, caressing.

"Shit, that's good," he murmured.

Down below, she still moved her pussy in rhythm with Colt's deep licks, each one heightening her pleasure, making her feel a little more crazed.

"Put it in my mouth," she begged of the cock in her hand, looking up at Jake.

"Aw . . ." he sighed at the demand, but he had to release her breasts and stand up straight to do what she'd asked. And the move allowed her to see the big shaft clearly for the first time. Arrow straight, pink, and engorged, it was solid and large. Just right. On instinct, she held his dick like an ice cream cone and licked at the tip, taking away the pre-come gathering there. "Fuck," she whispered, eyes falling shut in pleasure as the taste on her tongue made her pussy swell.

She bit her lip as Colt licked her harder—then he slipped two fingers inside her, just like before. She looked away from the delicious shaft in her hand just long enough to tell him breathily, "That's so good. Fuck me with your fingers."

He complied, thrusting them in and out, and narrowing his licks to her swollen clit, which jutted prominently from her paler flesh.

"Yes, baby," she purred, "lick that hot little pussy. Lick it good."

After the dirty talk, she returned her attention to what she held in her fist and ran her tongue over the tip once more before swirling a lick around the whole engorged head. Jake's breath came heavy, hot. She noticed his fists clenching at his sides just before he bit off a ragged command. "Suck it for me, honey."

Her face flushed with heat as she lowered her mouth fully over him, going down as far as she reasonably could, testing the feel of him near her throat. Above her, he muttered, swore gently—and she began to move up and down.

Mmm, she could seldom remember a time when she enjoyed sucking a man's cock so much—almost instantly. *Maybe it has to do with the fact that someone's licking your clit at the same time.* Damn, this being-with-two-guys thing had a lot going for it.

Now Colt *sucked* her clit, she thought. The pleasure there rose, expanded. She found herself fucking his mouth with greater abandon and feeling ravenous with Jake's perfect erection. As Colt sucked her harder, *she* sucked *Jake* harder. She lifted her gaze to meet his and relished his eyes on her, reveled in being watched by him, wondered how gloriously obscene she looked. The thought made her take him a little deeper, to her throat—and then she went still on him, just letting him feel the pressure of her mouth from the tip to nearly the base of his penis. Moans escaped him as he watched her, as their eyes locked. *Look how hungry I am for this cock. Look how dirty you make me.*

And then she passed a certain threshold and knew she would come. Within a few heated seconds. She found herself sliding her lips vigorously up and down Jake's stiff length, whimpering around it as she thrust her cunt at Colt's mouth. And then she finally released the hard-on from her lips because she had to, because she had to scream out her pleasure as it rolled through her body in giant waves. "Oh . . . oh God! Oh, fuck, I'm coming! Yes, yes, yes!"

When the pleasure ebbed and she finally quit moving, Colt lifted his face from between her legs. "Jesus, darlin', you taste good," he told her with a wicked grin, the area all around his mouth shiny with her moisture.

Too weakened to respond, she simply let out a replete sigh as she let her head drop back against the chair—and met Jake's eyes. She still held his erection in her hand, and now she ran her tongue slowly across her upper lip. To her delight, he looked just as entranced by all this as she was.

When she glanced back to Colt, she found him shedding his pants, and she watched his naked body from behind as he rummaged in a wallet, finally pulling out a strip of condoms. She'd brought some in her purse, given that she never knew when she might catch a man unawares, but she liked a guy who was prepared.

Turning back to face her, he held up the round disk of rubber he'd just opened and said, "Why don't you do the honors?"

She smiled slightly as she released Jake from her hand and took the condom—then Colt stepped close to the chair between her still-parted thighs, his hard-on at eye level with her. It was perhaps paler in tone than Jake's, with a slight arc, and shone with more veins—a bit different from his friend's, yet just as hard and lovely and masculine. And somehow the close-up sight reminded her just how powerful an erect phallus could be, how forceful, but in a way she thoroughly craved and felt all too ready to experience.

Wrapping both hands around Colt's slightly curved cock, she studied the head, the length, the arch. She touched her tongue to her upper lip as she peeked up at Colt's face, his eyes glazed with lust. After expertly rolling the thin sheath down over the rigid column of flesh, she said, "Fuck me now."

In response, he let out a soft groan, then sank back to his knees on the carpet. The chair sat low to the floor, putting his dick at just the right height. She spread her legs farther, as far as she could, letting her knees rest over the arms of the chair on either side. She wanted to put herself on full display for them. She wanted to be a centerfold again.

Above her, Jake let out a hot sigh.

She sensed him watching, along with her, as Colt positioned himself, then eased his way inside her. She let out a low moan at the filling sensation, shut her eyes, squeezed her own breasts. "Oh God," she purred.

"Damn, you're tight," he said through clenched teeth. He sounded surprised, and she guessed she couldn't blame him—he probably thought she did this every weekend.

She met his gaze, bit her lip, drank in the feeling of him beginning to move in and out of her in slow, even strokes she felt to her core. "Mmm, God, yes," she said.

But she wanted something more at the same time. She couldn't squander this unexpected bounty, after all. So she again reached for Jake's hard cock, squeezing it sensually in her fist, then bringing it back to her lips.

"Ah . . . ah, fuck," he breathed in agonized pleasure as she closed her mouth back over him. Talk about power. Giving one man that much pleasure while taking it from another—it made her feel more in control of her body than ever in her life. She'd never felt so sexually fulfilled and knew she never *would* the normal way. One man, a relationship? Those things weren't for her. And that truth might make her daily life a little less than she'd hoped for as a girl, but *this* . . . *this* surpassed her wildest dreams of pleasure.

Soon Colt fucked her harder in pistonlike drives that made her cry out around Jake's length, even as she sucked him with vigor in the same hot rhythm Colt used below. Her body felt like a receptacle—a receptacle for cock, all the cock she could get.

When finally Jake pulled his length from her eager lips—almost forcefully—saying, "Shit, stop before I come," she hungered immediately for its return. Her mouth felt empty and she clenched her teeth in frustration even as she continued to emit hot whimpers in response to Colt's deep plunges below.

But then Jake knelt beside her, leaning in to take her breasts in his hands, more firm than gentle now, and began to kiss her again like there was no tomorrow. And mmm, it was good to have her mouth back on him, in whatever way possible—good to have that part of her body stimulated once more. When he thrust his tongue there, she instinctively closed her lips around it and sucked, as if it were a replacement for that fine cock of his—she was desperate for the sensation. As Colt continued thrusting into her welcoming cunt, she held Jake's tongue with her mouth and got lost in it all for a long, heady moment, eyes shut, body supremely pleasured.

When she opened her eyes, Jake's were right there—and their gazes connected. And . . . oh God. Given that another man was fucking her, it—without warning—turned into an undeniably, shockingly *intimate* moment.

You're seeing all of me right now. All my sexuality. The best of me. The worst of me.

And she let herself wonder for a brief split second how he really viewed her right now—did *he* think he was seeing the best of a woman? Or the worst? Could a man like him really value this—the darker instincts at her core? Or did he, deep inside, think she was bad now?

Stop this. It doesn't matter. This is about you. *What* you *want. What* you *need.*

And what *did* she need right now? Easy answer.

"I want your cock back so bad," she told him. "I want you to fuck my mouth."

Their faces still close, he shut his eyes, drew in his breath, looked as impassioned as she felt.

But then he gritted his teeth. "When do I get inside that hot pussy? When do I get to fuck your brains out?"

She was breathing heavy now, too. "Don't worry—it won't suddenly close up shop for the night." She pressed a palm against his warm, sturdy chest and told him exactly what she was thinking. "But your cock is so perfect. It feels so good in my mouth. You have to let me suck it some more."

"Shit," he murmured, "when you put it like that . . ." He got back to his feet, peered down on her—his dick stood at attention just above her face. "Of course you can suck my cock, honey. You can suck it all night long if that's what you want."

"Mmm, I do," she promised him.

And again she was filled, to the brim it seemed, with two incredibly hard erections, both pumping into her, making her feel pummeled with utter, raw, dirty delight. Only like this, only as Desiree, could it feel so good, so right, to take such pleasure in the sensation of having her body used by men, so right to leave behind every other part of who she was for a night and give herself over to base, animal instincts and revel in it completely.

And—oddly perhaps—even in all her expeditions to Traverse City, she'd never been the kind of woman who craved cock the way she was craving it, *hungering* for it, right now. Up to now, her sexcapades had always been about the whole experience, every facet of it: the power, the pleasure, the freedom, the touching and grinding and fucking—all of it. But somehow, now, having two hard, perfect erections available for her use at once made her appreciate them in a whole new, intense, and primal way. Tonight, with Jake and Colt, she felt starved—like no matter how much she had, she wanted more. She felt positively crazy for their dicks.

Still fucking her, Colt's hands closed over her upper thighs as his thrusts lengthened, grew more prolonged—and finally he went still, tipping his head back in exhaustion. Then he pulled out, leaning back to rest.

She used her hand to extract Jake from her mouth in order to cast her other lover an appreciative look, even as her cunt adjusted to no longer having something inside it. "That was *so* good, baby," she said to Colt.

He gave her a typically cocky grin and arched one eyebrow to reply, "There's more where that came from, darlin'. Just need to take a break for a little while so I don't explode."

"I'm counting on it," she said, ever bold, ever saucy—and then she looked pointedly to her blue-eyed stranger. She hadn't moved—she still sat sprawled indelicately in the chair, her sex on vivid display. Gaze still on his, she reached down, stroking her middle finger through her folds, then raising the same fingertip over her head to Jake's lips. He parted them, took it inside, tasted her, groaned.

"You wanted my pussy," she told him. "It's all yours to play with now."

Chapter 3

Jake didn't say a word—just kept his eyes pinned on hers as he moved around in front of her and knelt down, his jeans and underwear still around his thighs. His gaze dropped to her slit—open from arousal, pink flesh visible. Then he did as *she'd* done—he ran one fingertip gently down the center of her. It made her shudder. Such a soft touch didn't seem as if it should elicit such a strong response after so much action—but maybe it was the look in his eyes that had caused her to tremble a little. Because something there had changed.

Tonight, as always when she fucked someone, she'd taken the lead, called most of the shots. And Colt—with his cocky attitude—was pushier than Jake, and so Jake had patiently taken what he'd been given. And she knew he'd enjoyed it—but she sensed that now maybe he was *tired* of being patient, tired of letting the other two in this ménage à trois decide how things were going to go. He suddenly looked more demanding than she'd come to expect from him. And it turned her on more than she could have anticipated.

And yet—if she wasn't careful here, she could lose control of the situation. She could lose the upper hand. It was all just a mental game, of course—maybe it didn't matter; maybe she gave her need for control too much power over her naughty trysts. Maybe she should just let Jake *have* it, see what he would do with it.

But old instincts died hard, and she knew instantly she *couldn't* let him have all the power—that power was what made her able to do this. That power was what let her fuck so wildly and indiscriminately.

He used his hands, fingers, to explore her—at times deliciously grazing the soft pale flesh surrounding her cunt, at other moments running his fingertips through her wetness. He kept his eyes on her pussy as he examined it—but then for long, intense moments, he'd lift his gaze to her face instead. He witnessed her every flinch, her every shiver—he could clearly see how much these small, exploratory touches excited her.

When he thrust two fingers inside her, she gasped. Small compared to Colt's dick, of course, but like everything else Jake was doing to her right now, she felt it more than she could make sense of. He watched himself fuck her that way, his fingers sliding smoothly, quickly, in and out, in and out, palm up—then he extracted them and looked boldly at her once more as he lifted them to his mouth and sucked them clean. Her chest went hollow.

"Fuck me," she said. Forcefully. Since something inside her was beginning to feel . . . a little weak, a little dominated. Just from his gentleness. She didn't *want* gentleness right now—she wanted things hard. Suddenly *he* was calling the shots.

"When I'm ready," he replied, not gruffly but with full confidence—and then . . . oh Lord, he thrust his fingers back inside her and bent to kiss her pussy as passionately as he'd earlier kissed her mouth.

Ragged cries of pleasure erupted from her throat and she gripped her breasts tight, just because she needed something to hold on to. "God, oh God," she heard herself murmur. And then—dear Lord—while still kissing her there, he pressed his free hand flat over her belly, just above that remaining thatch of pubic hair, and pushed down. Inside her, his fingers stroked the front wall of her cunt, and . . . oh Christ, it felt good. Crazy good. Especially with him giving her those lush openmouthed kisses all around her clit.

She sucked in her breath, squeezed her tits tighter. Her lips quivered, until finally she bit the lower one to stop it. Her head fell back with a groan and she moved against his fingers, his mouth, unbidden. The pleasure was so strange, intense—like a whole new way of being fucked. It wasn't . . . orgasmic. No, it was something almost . . . deeper. Her whole body pulsed with it.

And then he stopped. Backed off—with mouth, hands. And reached for the strip of condoms Colt had tossed on the table next to the chair.

"Wh-what was that?" she asked as he deftly sheathed himself.

The look he flashed was nearly as arrogant as one of Colt's. "Foreplay," he said simply—and then he thrust his cock deep inside her.

She let out a short cry, adjusting, then told him, "Oh God, you feel good."

On his knees before her, he curled his fingers tight over her inner thighs as he hissed in his breath. "Colt was right—you're tight as hell."

She touched her tongue to her upper lip and said, "Fill me up. Fuck me deep."

And so he did. He rammed his rock-solid erection powerfully into her, again, again—each stroke making her sob with the hard pleasure of it. "Yes!" she rasped at him. "Yes!"

Was it so different from when Colt fucked her? Maybe. It was slower— and, again, harder. She still sensed him having tired of being a bystander in all this and now wanting to take over—if you could call a guy getting his cock sucked so long her mouth was sore a *bystander*.

She absorbed each hard thrust he delivered with a naughty joy that flowed through her like a raging river, and for a few minutes she even forgot that her sense of control suddenly felt a little threatened. Each slick plunge echoed to the tips of her fingers and toes. She looked into his commanding eyes and thought back to the bar, how not very long ago they'd been saying hello, exchanging friendly smiles—and how quickly they'd gotten from there to here. *There* had been nice. *Here* was better. *Here* was what she'd come for. *Here* was what would sustain her another few months until she felt the driving need to do it again.

When Jake stopped, though, and pulled out, she remembered about that sense of control—and she acted. Not only because she wanted control *back*—but also because she wanted to suck his cock some more. Because she needed to have it in her, one way or another.

She sat up tall, grabbed his muscular arms as he began to stand, and shoved him back toward the bed with a lunge she didn't plan but that just happened. It didn't take much effort—she'd caught him off guard, off balance. As his ass came down on the edge of the mattress, she dropped to her knees, grabbed his cock, yanked off the rubber, and went down on him with vigor.

He let out a deep growl of pleasure—and went still on the bed.

When she peered up at his handsome face, she found that challenge to her power still resting in his gaze—but for the moment, the power was hers. She'd subdued him, had him where she wanted him, even while on her knees.

From the corner of her eye she caught sight of Colt—he'd been standing back quietly, watching intently for the last few minutes, but now he came closer, beginning to talk dirty, telling her to suck that cock, telling her what a dirty girl she was. Her pussy flared at the words, at the truth. She had no shame.

The next thing she knew, Colt was moving in behind her, on his knees as well. Her dress, which had stayed twisted around her waist all this time, draped over her thighs now, but Colt slid his hands up underneath, molding them to her bare hips—and his dick bumped against her ass as he tried to position himself. And then—sweet heaven—he was thrusting inside her, letting out a deep groan, filling her back up. She cried out, too, around Jake's erection, and once more knew the ultimate pleasure of two cocks. Would anything less ever feel as good?

The three of them found a steady rhythm together. Her lips began to feel stretched and sore, but she didn't want to stop, *never* wanted to stop. She peered up at Jake as she moved her mouth up and down on him, and he looked . . . astounded, she thought. By the pleasure? By her aggressiveness? She had no idea, but she liked it.

That was when he took her face in his hands, then ran his fingers back through her hair, stroking. "My God, you're amazing, baby," he said deeply. "Damn, you suck me good."

Why did that affect her so? She *knew* she was good, after all. Why did the look in his eyes, and the wonder in his voice, soften her a little inside, make her feel all this a little more? Not in her body, where she *wanted* to feel it, but in her . . . heart, a part of her anatomy that had no role here. No role at all.

When finally she felt forced to rest her mouth, she did what he'd mentioned upon first entering the room—leaned forward and pressed her tits around his hard length. And mmm, she'd forgotten how much she liked doing that or she'd have done it before now. Having it there rivaled having it in her mouth. Another way of fucking him; another way of using her body to pleasure them both. Something about the rawness of the move took away that softness she'd briefly felt. Good.

"Shit, your tits are gorgeous," he told her, shifting his hands from her hair to the sides of her breasts to hug them tighter around his dick. Yes, *yes*.

"Your cock feels so good and hard between them," she purred.

Behind her, Colt continued fucking her—the man had fabulous staying power—and the threesome moved together that way for what seemed a long while. And—no, she decided, nothing would *ever* feel this good again; no single man could. Which made her want to feel all of this even *more*. "Oh God, fuck me," she told Colt over her shoulder.

He only grunted in reply—but she didn't care, since he kept on pounding away at her and she soaked up every ounce of sensation.

A few minutes later, his breath hard in her ear, Colt muttered, "Damn, gotta take another break. You wear me out, darlin'."

But he smacked her on the ass for good measure just before he pulled out, and she let out a sexy "Oooh" over her shoulder and giggled. Then she turned back to look up at Jake, who wasn't smiling at all.

"I want to fuck you again," he said, his voice rigid and demanding. "So hard and deep you scream."

"I want to fuck you, too," she promised him, then got to her feet and slammed him roughly to his back on the bed before he knew what was coming. She wouldn't let him take control again *that* easily. It was time for her to be on top.

She finally shoved her dress over her hips and to the floor, and within seconds, she'd retrieved another condom and was climbing on the bed, straddling Jake's thighs, rolling the rubber down over his hard-on. "Mmm," she sighed, just from the anticipation—and then she balanced herself on the tip and sank down.

They both moaned at the entry—and, as always, she felt it more in this position. But she wasted no time adjusting—she rode him hard and vigorous, her whole body now at a fever pitch that drove her to talk dirty. "Oh God, your cock is so huge inside me. Huge and hot and hard. Fuck me. Fuck me like you mean it!"

And he thrust up inside her—yes, yes, yes—but in this position it was mostly her doing the fucking. She bit her lower lip, pressed her body down on him, again, again. His erection was so deep in her now that it almost hurt—given that she *didn't* do this every weekend, and she was getting quite a workout. But it was a good sort of pain, the kind that reminded her she was alive, that she was a vital sexual being, that she could take as much pleasure in sex as anyone else. And, tonight, maybe even more.

In between her moans and sobs, she talked more about his cock. "It's so deep inside me, baby. It's so big and perfect. Perfect in my mouth, and perfect in my pussy."

Colt, always needing to be the center of attention it seemed, said from somewhere behind her, "What about mine?"

She just laughed, even rolled her eyes. Then she turned to find him watching from the chair. "I love it, too," she promised him with a naughty, teasing grin. "Bring it back here and I'll prove it."

And like a wild man, Colt immediately got to his feet and jumped up onto the bed, standing on the mattress—clearly he knew what she had in mind; clearly he'd noticed she liked to suck cock. The height wasn't exactly right, but close enough—he stood alongside them, his knees slightly bent, allowing her to pull his now unsheathed shaft to her lips.

Just like every time she'd been in a similar position with them tonight, she loved having two glorious erections inside her, and she loved the way they watched her. Colt prodded her with more nasty talk. "That's right, darlin', suck me while you fuck him. Take us both all the way in, real deep. That's it, now. That's it."

As she worked both guys over, Jake's hands lifted to massage her breasts, and Colt gently held her head in his hands. She felt wild, at once powerful yet a little submissive—the world's most carnal being. All of them moaned and groaned together until pleasure seemed to saturate the room, filling the very air around them.

When Colt withdrew from her mouth, announcing that he was going to come, she said, "On my tits," and both men let out deep, lustful sounds.

Running her tongue over her upper lip, she lifted her breasts with both hands to give him an easy target. And he finished himself off with his hand, groaning deeply as she encouraged him, saying, "Come on me, come on me," until hot white semen shot from the tip of his cock in three wild arcs, most of it spattering her breasts, the rest on her stomach and on Jake's, as well.

As she reached boldly for Colt's shaft one last time, licking the rest off for him, she wondered lasciviously if Jake had ever had another guy's come on him before and suspected the answer was no. Then she made a sensual show of rubbing Colt's warm juices into her flesh, massaging it in, looking down to see how it left her skin shiny for their eyes. She'd once been with a guy who'd wanted to come on her, and the truth was, she hadn't liked it much—it had felt like an anticlimactic end to sex—but here, now, with *two* guys, with still more sex taking place, it felt perfect, and hot, and dirty.

So perfect, in fact, that it made *her* come. As she rubbed the last remnants into her breasts as if it were body lotion . . . with both of her men watching her and moaning at the sight—and with Jake still fucking her—she felt it rising quick and hard. She pinched both her still-moist nipples slightly— and then the rush of hot pleasure came in a deluge, forcing thready sobs from her throat as it rocked her body, making her pitch forward slightly until she was clawing at Jake's stomach for purchase.

When he let out a noise, she thought she'd hurt him—her eyes bolted open and she said, "Sorry."

But when he grabbed tight to her arms and she saw the hungry look in his eyes, she realized it was excitement he was experiencing, not pain. "*You're so fucking hot,*" he muttered, teeth clenched—and then he flipped her on the bed, to her back, that quick.

It was startling, and she knew it had shown in her eyes.

Somehow he'd stayed inside her during the brisk move and now she was under him, and he held her pinned to the bed by her wrists as he fucked her with wild abandon. She cried out at the intensity of the strokes, but at this moment she didn't mind feeling a little overpowered, a little shocked, because it also turned her on. And maybe it wasn't like losing her power since she knew she'd driven him to this, she'd gotten him this aroused. Maybe it was just a whole *new* kind of power she'd never known about before.

And yet . . . she was lying to herself a little, working too hard to tell herself she was still in control here. Because his eyes on her as he thrust into her—deep, deep—were as penetrating as his cock. It felt as if they were probing hers, trying to see behind all those shields, all that armor, almost as if . . . as if he knew there was something else underneath.

She didn't look away—she simply tried to look tough, tried to be Desiree through and through. And she was. Everything she *felt* was Desiree—all that heady abandon, all the dirty pleasure coursing through her, body and soul. And yet . . . was there another hint of softness sneaking in, a different sort of surrender?

Even when he pulled out and brusquely turned her over again, tugging her up onto her hands and knees, she still felt it. Even when he could no longer look into her eyes. As he thrust his cock back into her from behind, his fingertips digging into the flesh of her hips, ass, she experienced it again. A sense of surrender.

She'd had sex in this position many times, but always, up to now, this and anything else she did to please a man, or to please herself, had felt like something she'd either orchestrated or at least given her full consent to. She hadn't given her consent to this. And yet, the pleasure, both mental and physical, remained. It was just different. Different in that—as Jake fucked her hard and deep now, as he made her cry out, made her feel out of her head from the hot strokes pummeling her body—she felt . . . a little bit like herself. A little bit like the person wearing all that sexual armor had gotten up and walked out of the room at some sneaky point and left *her*, only *her*, to deal with all this. And pleasure or not, that was just a little bit too much to take.

"Spank me!" she yelled.

Because giving him a command, having him obey it, would turn this all back around, make it right again, make her feel like she was *supposed* to feel. Completely.

"*Spank me,*" she said again, lower, but with force.

"Are you a bad girl?" he rasped behind her.

"Oh, yes! I'm a very bad girl and I need to be punished."

And so he drew back his hand and smacked her ass, and she said, *"Harder."*

And so he did it again, this time harder. And she cried out with an abject rush of pleasure because it had worked—it had given her back that sense of orchestration, of having power over him.

Her blue-eyed stranger, she realized, had rescued her again, unknowingly. Because for one brief moment in their encounter, she'd become what she'd claimed she wasn't: a damsel in distress. She'd dropped her guard, or maybe she'd let him rip it away from her. But she had it back now. And the fact was, the command she'd issued had brought her more than mere control—she *loved* to be spanked, because that extra flare of sensation shot through her like one more naughty delight, and because she *was* a very bad girl.

"Aw, aw shit—I'm gonna come. I'm gonna come in you," Jake groaned behind her, and so she steeled herself, gritted her teeth, and tried her best to stay upright—but as he growled his orgasm, his drives came so hard they pressed her flat to her stomach in the bed.

He collapsed atop her that way—then finally rolled off her.

She was facing away from him and almost turned to look at him—but then decided against it, decided it would be better to just stay quiet, to pretend she'd fallen asleep that fast, the way guys often did afterward.

It wasn't her normal endgame. But she felt . . . more spent than usual. Less like Desiree than usual. She feared the very act of looking at him, right now, would make her more vulnerable than she wanted to be. So she simply closed her eyes and willed sleep to come.

She wasn't sure how long she slept, but she opened her eyes to find herself naked on a bed with her blue-eyed stranger. *No, stop—he's not your anything. He's just a guy you fucked. Like every other guy you fuck.*

Colt lay sprawled, even more naked than her—since she still wore her sexy shoes—in the chair where so much of their sex had taken place. He

...ept, too. The room lay quiet, still. Jake's jeans remained bunched around his thighs.

She studied them both. She'd just had a ménage à trois. Sex with two men.

This part, the after part, was usually surreal enough on its own, yet finding herself with two guys instead of just one made it wildly more so. *But it doesn't matter. It's just one more secret, one more thing nobody knows about you. Tomorrow it'll seem like a dream, just like always.*

Her muscles were tired, achy. It had been strenuous sex. Her mouth still felt swollen, stretched, the area between her legs tender. It would be nice to just sleep here, but that wasn't how her trips to Traverse City went. They had to be short and sweet. Well, short and hot. Short and nasty. It was definitely time to go.

Easing up off the bed, she took pains to be quiet, not shift the mattress. Usually, after sex, she and her partner at least exchanged a few words, said things like, "That was nice," or "That was hot," or "That was amazing." She hadn't done that this time, but she was sticking to the game plan from here on out—which was to leave without further interaction if possible. And it usually was.

Sometimes she suspected the guys she had fucked woke up as she was leaving but pretended to be asleep. That was fine with her. Occasionally one of them would open his eyes, say a friendly goodbye. Also fine. Once, though, to her surprise, a guy had actually acted hurt by her attempt at a silent departure. She still remembered how offended he'd seemed. "You were just going to leave without even saying goodbye?" Like they'd just shared something special. Like they were high school sweethearts or something.

She'd simply looked at him and been scathingly honest. "Yes." No apologies.

"After everything we just did together?" the guy had said.

Geez, was he serious? He was acting like . . . a girl. "It was sex. Good sex.

But just sex," she'd reminded him—since he'd clearly forgotten she'd just picked him up in a bar and fucked his brains out after about five whole minutes of conversation. "Good night," she'd added brusquely on her way out the door—sorry to be a bitch but not willing to let down her guard even an inch.

Which was why it was a little unsettling that somehow she'd let her guard down with Jake. Not with Colt—with him, it had all been what it was supposed to be. Hot, raw mutual pleasure. And with Jake . . . well, it didn't matter now, and she could put those moments of weakness, of *realness*, behind her.

She slithered back into her dress without a sound, pushing back the sad sense of emptiness that sometimes plagued her in these moments. Locating her bra and panties, she stuffed them in her purse. That was another piece of the ritual: Don't waste time putting underwear back on—once it's over, it's time to get out. Her heart always beat a little harder during this part—just hoping she could make a clean escape.

Going home would be the same as always. She'd pull off the road at the same little picnic area she always did, about halfway there, and change into the fresh undies, jogging pants, and tee she'd stuffed in an overnight bag that now sat in the passenger seat of her small SUV. She'd open a wet wipe from her glove box and remove her makeup. She'd run a brush through her hair, pulling out much of the hair spray and curl. And she'd return home with only a little laundry to prove the night had ever happened.

Tomorrow would be mostly normal. Memories, that tenderness between her thighs, and a small load of delicates would make it a transitional sort of day—back to real life—and otherwise, she'd go about her business as usual in every other way. And she'd feel like her real self again.

Then the next day would be *completely* normal, as would every day—until the next time. The next time that dirty need clawed at her. That need she couldn't fill any other way than to drive someplace where no one knew her and engage in a night of hot, casual sex.

Taking careful steps on her heels across the carpet, toward the door, she stopped, looked back. At Colt, then at Jake. She'd been very attracted to them both, but certainly Jake in particular. She suspected that, in real life, he was a good guy. Maybe or maybe not a pilot, or a photographer, but a good guy. Who'd just fucked her brains out. The last part was all that mattered, though—the only memory she'd have of him. He wasn't her first one-night stand and he wouldn't be her last.

One final glance, and then she was out the door, down the hall, down the stairs, soon climbing behind the wheel of her RAV4. A few stoplights and she'd be out of Traverse City and onto the straight, open roads of rural Michigan, where there were no interstates but traffic was light enough that it usually didn't matter.

She'd be home and in her bed soon, above the little shop on Main Street in Turnbridge.

She'd be Carly Winters again. Maker of furniture by hand, the old-fashioned way, just like her father before her. Winner of the pie contest at the Fourth of July Festival three years running. Town sweetheart.

If they only knew.

Chapter 4

Carly appreciated rituals, habits. She generally fell into bed in her apartment above the shop just after the late news at eleven thirty, but no matter how late she might have occasion to stay up—like on those occasional trips to the Lake Michigan shore—she awoke at seven thirty every morning with or without an alarm clock. She meandered to the kitchen, ate a light breakfast of toast or maybe a muffin from Beth Anne's Bakery, said good morning to the big cat who was by then twining around her ankles under the table, then got dressed and made her way downstairs to start work.

The shop didn't open until ten—and noon on Sundays—but she enjoyed those early-morning hours most. She liked knowing she could get absorbed in her work without being disturbed—it was just her and the wood and her tools. She liked the quiet view out the big front shop window—whether it was watching the snow fall on still winter days or the sense of solitude brought by misty blankets of morning fog in spring or fall, before the sun burned it all away. On summer days like today, the mornings were generally clear and bright—she would see other shopkeepers headed into work or maybe someone walking a dog up Main Street. It was the busy season, and Turnbridge was open for business. And while those winter days were more her style, summer was necessary—she earned seventy-five percent of her income between May and September.

This particular June morning was like all the rest—a raspberry muffin purchased yesterday at Beth Anne's made a sweet breakfast, and as she carried her coffee cup to the sink afterward, she bent to pet the large gray angora cat on the floor. "Morning, Oliver."

He was a serious cat, the kind who looked as if he ran the place—but with her, he was a little needy, hungering for her attention when no one else was around. She smiled down at him, pondering how they both sometimes wore . . . disguises.

But the smiled faded as fast as it had come. She didn't like thinking about that. At times—like now—it even turned her stomach a little. She had a love/hate relationship with her secret life, her secret Saturday nights in Traverse City. In one sense, when viewed from a distance, it seemed a grand, exciting, naughty, and wonderful thing. But in another . . . it wasn't exactly a *pretty* secret. Most secrets, she supposed, weren't. It was the sort of thing that, in some moments, she couldn't believe she'd ever done—let alone numerous times—and she wasn't sure why she did it.

Well, wait. That wasn't true. She *knew*. On a physical level. She did it when she needed sex.

But she still wasn't sure why she couldn't find a nice guy and have nice, *normal* sex like other people.

She shook her head, trying to clear it. Then took a quick shower and, afterward, went to get dressed. As she reached toward her underwear drawer, wearing a towel, she noticed a tiny swath of red-and-pink lace sticking out of *another* drawer—her lingerie drawer. She opened it, shoved the panties all the way in, and shut it, quickly. Almost like . . . if she didn't look too closely, the drawer wouldn't exist. How could she take such delight in something that at other times made her feel so . . . shameful?

She gave a little shiver, fetched a pair of more functional undies—cotton, pink with black polka dots—then threw on a plain black bra, a pair of jeans, and a University of Michigan T-shirt. She hadn't gone to school there. She hadn't gone to college anywhere. But her friend Dana had—and the shirt had been a gift one Christmas about ten years ago. As for the jeans, she wore them every day in the shop, even in summer, since her work was messy, dusty, and she could wipe her hands on her thighs without the dirt showing too much. Swiping up a navy blue elastic band from her dresser, she pulled her hair back into a low ponytail, another practical move for work.

She spent the next two hours laboring on an old-fashioned crib. Dana—who'd married Hank Willis, a Turnbridge fireman, and who also worked part-time in her mother's antiques store up the street—was pregnant with her first baby. The crib would be a gift at the shower Carly and Beth Anne planned to throw this fall before the bundle of joy arrived in November.

Hmm. Baby showers. Used to be bridal showers. Carly had thrown or attended more than her fair share.

Yet as she reached for one of her father's old bench planes and began meticulously smoothing a slab of oak, her mind drifted from showers to . . . the particular pair of panties she'd just seen upstairs. To the last time she'd worn them. Two guys. The memory nearly stole her breath. *Concentrate on the wood. Get lost in the wood.*

Just then, someone waving through the shop's front window caught her eye. Tiffany Cleary was fourteen and often came by just to hang out and pet Oliver. Now she passed by the large pane of glass that said WINTERBERRY'S WOOD CRAFTS AND FINE FURNITURE in gold lettering. Carly lifted a hand to wave in return, but then looked back to her work.

Hell, maybe she should have stopped, let Tiffany in, even though it was still long before time to open. If she had, her mind wouldn't have turned instantly back to the events of her last trip to Traverse City, nearly a month ago. The sex had been . . . unbelievable. And a little unsettling in moments because of that Jake guy and her sense that he somehow knew there was more to her than met the eye. But it had come to nothing, which had left only the indescribably hot pleasure of the evening. The problem was—she didn't want to remember it right now.

Sometimes she did. Sometimes at night. When it was dark, when she was in bed, sometimes she reached between her legs and stroked herself to orgasm, and in those moments the extreme memories of her wild night seemed like a supreme victory in her quiet life, and they were just the thing to help her come.

But during the day, in the shop, working in the window, when she was the very epitome of the simple, down-to-earth Carly Winters everyone here knew—she didn't want to think about it then. She didn't even want to be aware any of it had ever actually happened. Had she really put on a sinfully sexy dress and driven two hours to fuck a stranger? Or, in the last instance, more than one?

Fuck. She hardly ever used that word, or others like it, outside of those nights—even in her mind. Why had she thought it just now? Maybe because what she'd done with Jake and Colt couldn't accurately be categorized as anything *but* fucking.

Sex with one guy? She could be pretty damn dirty and aggressive with one lone guy and still, afterward, tell herself it was simply sex. No harm done, free country, woman with needs . . . all that. But there was no making the threesome less than what it was, no matter how much she might wish her brain would let her water it down, sugarcoat it. She'd fucked two guys at once; she'd been crazed and hungry and lusty with them. Nope, that wasn't really something she could just call casual sex. It had been wild fucking, plain and simple.

And even as much as the memory shamed her in her real world, at the same time, it was making her panties wet. Remembering the way she'd sat sprawled in that chair, legs parted as far as humanly possible for them.

Remembering the heat in Jake's blue eyes when he seemed to almost look through her—and the way he'd pinned her to the bed, and then a little later rammed forcefully into her from behind. She let out a breath, glad her T-shirt was loose, since her breasts felt a little achy now and her nipples would surely be visible through anything tighter, even through her bra.

It was actually almost a relief when the ten o'clock hour rolled around and she walked to the door to turn the Open sign toward the window. It was a Tuesday, one of the quieter days of the week during summer, but still, already a few cars were starting to park along the curb outside.

Turnbridge was a rare small town these days. No Walmart or outlet mall had cropped up to lure customers away from smaller businesses, so Main Street remained adorned with a drugstore, hardware store, bank, and more. At the same time, however, Turnbridge was known for its crafts and antiques. Just across the street from her stood a specialty yarn and bead shop in a circa 1920 building, a homemade toy store occupied the old Five and Dime up the block, and Debbie Cleary, Tiffany's mom, had opened a successful scrapbooking store in a small house around the corner on Maple. Farther up Main, storefronts gave way to old Victorian homes, and many of those had also been turned into antiques shops or craft stores, Dana's girlhood home among them. Dana's mother still lived upstairs, but she'd transformed the ground floor into a friendly store, each room filled with wonderful old pieces of furniture, candlesticks, frames, and collectibles.

Carly's shop didn't get as much foot traffic as many of the stores did. Although she created smaller pieces—bread boxes, keepsake boxes, trays, checkerboards—most of her offerings were large, pricy items like tables, chairs, and bookshelves that didn't draw in as many casual shoppers from the sidewalk. But that suited her fine. At the end of the day, she still made enough to keep the business running, and even had a healthy savings account for lean years. So it wasn't as if turning the lock on the door and opening the shop today meant a barrage of customers rushing in—it meant only that she was no longer officially alone in her private world. And most days, that wasn't necessarily a good thing, but today, maybe it was.

At noon, another ritual—she stepped in the back room and made a call to Schubert's up the street. A small, family-friendly restaurant during the day, more of a pub at night, the place served simple fare like burgers and sandwiches. Carly got her lunch there almost every day until winter came, when she started "hibernating" a little more, preferring to go upstairs and grab something from the fridge. Otherwise, she liked the opportunity to get out, take a walk, breathe some fresh air.

"Schubert's," answered Frank Schubert himself, a friendly fifty-something man she'd known her whole life.

"Hi, it's Carly, calling in my lunch order."

"Ham and swiss on white, light mayo?" he asked.

She even tended to order the same thing every day. "You got it." But she didn't mind if that seemed boring. For her, such rituals were a way of giving her life structure, keeping everything in order.

"Ready in five," he said, and she told him she'd be there soon.

After flipping around a CLOSED FOR LUNCH, BE BACK SOON sign in the window, she locked the front door and began her journey up the street. It was hot out—in the eighties—with a bright sun beating down from a clear blue sky. A soft breeze kept the day pleasant, however, and as Carly took her daily stroll up the sidewalk, she saw Beth Anne wave from the bakery window, where she was probably preparing for a lunch break herself. Then Mrs. Castellini, a friend of her mother's, beeped and waved as her big old Buick rolled past. Shoppers dotted Main Street—a few of them heading into the Bear Den for lunch, and the Moosewood Deli seemed to be hopping for a Tuesday, every umbrella-covered table in the small outdoor seating area occupied.

Schubert's sat at a four-way stop, the front facade on the diagonal, as if one corner of the building had been cut off—and the same fading, scripted SCHUBERT'S sign had hung over the door for Carly's entire life. A blast of air-conditioning hit her as she walked inside. A couple of the tables in the small dining area were filled, and a few of the stools at the bar were taken by town cops in navy blue uniforms.

Frank, gray-haired and balding, stood behind the bar chatting with the policemen, so she stepped up between two vacant stools where he'd see her.

He smiled in her direction, reached beneath the counter, and pulled out a brown bag containing her sandwich and a bag of chips. "Four ninety-nine," Frank said, hitting a few buttons on the old-fashioned cash register mounted behind the mahogany bar. And as she reached into her purse, extracting a five from her wallet, he resumed talking to the nearest cop. "Couldn't find a nicer little town than Turnbridge, if you ask me," he said. "Trust me—after a couple months here, you'll never want to leave."

As Carly passed the money to Frank, he said to her, "This here's the new officer the town just hired, Jake Lockhart." And when, two stools away, the uniformed man turned toward her, it took her only a second to realize—he was her blue-eyed stranger.

It was like a punch in the gut that left her light-headed. Jake, looking shockingly staid—even if just as handsome—in a police uniform, tilted his head slightly, appearing a little puzzled even as he clearly began to recognize her, too. Shit. Shit oh shit oh shit.

"Nice to meet you," she said quickly, then glanced away and grabbed up her bag, saying to Frank, "Keep the penny."

She was turning to escape, her heart thudding painfully against her chest, when the new town cop said, "Desiree?"

Double shit. She just stood there, her face going numb.

"No sir, this here's Carly Winters," Frank corrected him. "Runs Winterberry's up the street—you've probably seen it. She makes some beautiful furniture—you oughta stop in, check out her work."

Jake blinked, met her gaze. And if she were a better actress, she could have appeared entirely unaffected, or even bemused, the way someone did when sincerely mistaken for someone else. But the brief window of time for that had fled and she knew, without doubt, he could see in her eyes that he *hadn't* been mistaken, and that she was just a liar—a liar with a very different identity from the one she'd presented to him, a liar who'd fucked two men she didn't know just as easily as she'd walked in here to get her lunch.

She swallowed around the sudden lump in her throat, and his eyes never left hers as he said, "My mistake. Sorry."

She gave her head a light shake, all she could manage just now. "No problem," she replied too softly, barely able to draw breath into her lungs. Then she forced out a quick, "See ya, Frank," and made a beeline for the door.

She couldn't feel her legs, nor the checkerboard tile floor beneath her feet. She leaned on the big wooden door with all her remaining strength and burst out into bright sunlight, wanting to run.

But running would only call attention to herself. And there was nowhere to run anyway. *He was in her town. Where she lived. Where everyone knew her.* This was her worst nightmare come true, the most horrific thing she could imagine. *This can't be happening. It just can't.*

She walked quickly, her stomach churning, her breath still shallow. How the hell had this happened? He was Turnbridge's new police officer? Not a pilot. Not a photographer. A *cop*. She'd been completely off the mark with that. But it hardly mattered. She had much bigger problems to worry about.

He would tell people. *Of course* he would tell people. The other cops. Guys loved to brag, after all. And God knew she'd given him something to brag about. She could almost hear the conversation already. "You know that girl Carly? Well, I met her a month ago, but she claimed her name was Desiree and she fucked my friend and me senseless in a hotel room. Yeah, both of us. Her idea. She couldn't get enough." She feared she might vomit.

God, it was too damn hot out here. The sun suddenly made her woozier than she already was. She stared at the evenly spaced lines in the sidewalk as she trudged onward, trying to keep her balance.

"Carly, you okay? You look kind of . . . freaked-out."

She forced her gaze upward to find Dana's husband, Hank, a tall, burly guy who was as kind as the day was long. She blinked, her throat going dry. "I'm fine, Hank," she lied. "Just . . . a smidge under the weather today . . . and the sun's getting to me. I'll be better once I get back to the shop and eat." She held up her bag as proof she would soon be well.

Still looking concerned, he said, "Want me to walk you?"

"No, I'm good—really," she said, then trundled past him, unable to concern herself right now with what he thought. She'd explain it all away later. For now, she just had to get inside, keep the door locked—screw the customers; this was an emergency—and somehow figure out how to deal with this.

Except . . . there *was* no answer. She already knew that. There was no way to remedy it.

The stranger whose cock she'd sucked to oblivion was now a resident of Turnbridge, and he knew her worst secret. She felt frantic inside, desperate to fix this somehow, to stop the inevitable outcome, but no fix existed. None.

She imagined the horror on Frank Schubert's face when he heard the ugly, unthinkable truth about her. Her mother, Dana, Hank, Beth Anne, the whole damn town. Every person she'd ever known, since birth.

Maybe they wouldn't believe him. He *was* a stranger, after all, and no longer the rescuing kind. And such a tale—that Carly Winters led a secret life as a world-class slut—would be hard to swallow by anyone's standards.

But no matter *who* believed *what*, this would be ugly.

Ugliest most of all, she realized, because it was all true.

Jake tried not to seem like he was rushing off as he hurriedly paid Frank Schubert for his burger and fries. He also tried not to seem weirded out. Because he was. Big-time.

Frank was still talking about Carly. Damn—her name was *Carly*. Not

Desiree. "Everybody loves Carly—she's a sweetheart," the man was saying, even as Jake climbed down off his stool and said so long.

As he pushed through the heavy door out into the sun, he could barely process what had just happened, what he'd just seen. The same girl who'd been with him and Colt last month—but . . . not the same girl at all. She didn't even have the same name. And he wasn't about to let her get away.

Talk about shell-shocked. He couldn't remember a time in his thirty-four years when something had left him so stunned.

The truth was, ever since that night he'd been mystified, intrigued, and a little obsessed with thoughts of her. He'd been sorry to wake up and find her gone afterward—and he'd had a hell of a time getting her off his mind. He hadn't really succeeded, even now, even after a move and starting a new job. In fact, the very notion that he now lived closer to Traverse City had pleased him, as it increased his opportunities to party with his buddies in the area, which increased the chances that maybe he'd run into her again sometime.

She'd been *so* fucking wild, more than any girl he'd ever been with, and it had aroused him more than any other experience in his life. And at the same time, she'd sported an air of sophistication that had left him intrigued.

The girl he'd just been introduced to—*Carly*—didn't seem wild *or* sophisticated.

But her eyes were the same, minus all the makeup.

And she'd been unable to hide her shock at seeing him again. So he knew it was her—no question.

As he jogged up the street, he tried not to call attention to himself and was glad no one here knew him yet and wouldn't question his hurry. After a block and a half, he spotted her up ahead, her long blondish ponytail hanging down her back—one more thing that looked entirely different about her than on the night they'd met. The night they'd fucked. With Colt.

He'd thought he'd had some pretty wild sex in his day, but he'd never done anything like *that* before. And when she'd first suggested it, he'd been a little worried it would be awkward with a longtime friend—but at the same time, he hadn't felt inclined to say no. She was hot as hell, and she'd wanted to get nasty with him and his buddy, and that had been a lure too strong to resist.

She walked briskly, her ass swaying quickly back and forth in old blue jeans that looked naturally sexy, even with a loose T-shirt. But he was in good shape—he had to be for his job—so catching up with her didn't even leave him winded. As he came up behind her, he said, "Carly."

She peeked over her shoulder, her hazel eyes growing wide with fright just before she turned back around and picked up her pace again.

"Wait," he said, and when she ignored him, he came up beside her, took hold of her arm.

She stopped then, looked up at him. And they froze like that for a minute. Both thinking back, he supposed. To the last time they'd touched. To nakedness, and lust, and explosive orgasms. And seeing each other now, unexpectedly, in such a different setting—it was just plain strange. "What's the deal?" he finally asked, lowering his voice.

"Please let go of me," she said, her tone soft but firm, "before people start staring."

Okay, fair enough—he released her.

But in response, she resumed moving forward—so he did, too. "What—you're just gonna walk away and pretend nothing ever happened between us?"

Despite the season and the sun, her face went noticeably pale as she stared straight ahead. "Yes. If you'll just let me, that is."

"I'm afraid I can't do that," he informed her.

After which she stopped again to blink up at him, appearing frantic, angry. "Why not? Why can't you just forget you ever recognized me? Why can't you just let me go on with my life in peace?"

Jesus—what the hell was she so mad about? A long, belabored sigh left him before he said, "Look, it's not like I'm out to torment you here."

"Well, that's exactly what you're doing."

"It's just that . . . when you meet somebody a second time and they seem so . . . uh, different, not even with the same damn name . . . Hell, how can I not want to know what's going on?"

Her breath came thready now, and it made him feel bad, like he really *was* tormenting her. "I don't care *what* you want to know—can't you just be a gentleman and let it go?"

He exhaled an irritated breath. "Don't take this the wrong way, but . . . you didn't seem to want a gentleman the night we met. I never got the chance to *be* a gentleman."

It made her face turn red. Shit. He hadn't meant to embarrass her— but it was a little hard to swallow her request to be a "gentleman" given the things they'd done together on that deliciously dirty night. She started walking again, so he followed behind, coming up beside her once more. "I'm sorry—I didn't say that to upset you. I just want to understand. Why did you lie about your name?"

She seemed to be ignoring him now, digging a key from her purse as they stopped before one of the quaint Main Street shops—like Frank had mentioned, the lettering on the window said WINTERBERRY'S. And she made *furniture?* He was just beginning to process that part. His mind still spun. As she unlocked the door and pushed it open, he started to follow her in, figuring she was just seeking privacy to talk to him—until she turned on him with angry eyes and said, "What do you think you're doing?"

"Coming in."

She blinked, looking as incredulous as if he'd just suggested they have sex again. Maybe that's what she thought he was after. "No, you're not."

"Seriously?"

"Seriously. Please just go away and leave me alone."

Okay, her snotty attitude was beginning to piss him off—because he'd done nothing wrong here and she was acting like he had. "I can't come in

your shop?" he asked a bit more harshly. "What if I want to buy something?"
It was a store, after all. How could she keep him from going inside?

"I'm closed for lunch."

"Shit—can't we just talk for a few minutes? Like civilized human beings?"

When she turned back to meet his gaze this time, though, she was actually trembling. All over.

Aw, hell—snotty or not, it made him feel like an ass.

Now she spoke more slowly, her rudeness laced with a true sense of desperation. *"Look, if you have even an ounce of kindness inside you, you'll forget you ever met me."*

The words, the look in her eyes, made Jake go still, frozen in place on the step below the entryway—as she went inside, shut the door in his face, and audibly turned the lock on the other side.

Chapter 5

J ake stood there for a minute, as if waiting for her to change her mind and open the door. After all, she was right on the other side. Maybe she'd suddenly see reason.

But then he remembered the shocking new fact he was still trying to wrap his brain around. Desiree wasn't *quite* the same woman he'd just met. And while Desiree was the kind of woman who'd open the door, this Carly chick was someone else entirely.

Finally, he stepped down onto the sidewalk and started slowly back up the street, completely baffled as he continued trying to reconcile that the person who'd just locked him out of her store was the same welcoming, aggressive woman he'd met a month ago.

The woman he'd shared with Colt. Sometimes the memory still shocked him—for lots of reasons.

He'd gone through a special hostage ops program with Colt at police academy ten years ago, and while he'd always gotten along with him, they weren't particularly close. If someone had told him an hour before it had happened that he'd be having a threeway with the guy that night, he wouldn't have believed it. It was just dumb luck they'd been hanging out together on that particular evening of their yearly reunion. Colt had taken a business call on his cell as they'd headed toward the bar, and he'd stayed in the lobby to finish it, requesting, "Somebody get me a beer," as the other guys went inside. Jake had complied, and they'd taken turns buying beer for each other all night.

Was he sorry Colt had been involved in his tryst with Desiree? Wait— shit . . . Carly. Her name was Carly; that was hard to get used to. For the past month, Desiree had been giving him wet dreams that had left him waking up in the morning feeling all of thirteen years old. But he didn't feel like a kid when he really let himself remember that night—nope, then he felt about as much like a lusty adult male as a guy could.

And the truth was, he *didn't* regret Colt's involvement. The evening hadn't turned out like he'd initially envisioned it might—he'd never been with a woman so bold, so uninhibited. But it had set his blood racing, drawn him to her in a way that had felt . . . almost magnetic, like he couldn't have resisted if he'd tried.

And then, in the midst of all that sex—he'd begun to see tiny hints, the quickest glimpses, of something softer underneath her lust. And in the midst of all *that* had come his frustration at times that she was so . . . controlling. Of the sex.

It shouldn't have mattered—she'd willingly pleasured them both, and given that he was a red-blooded American guy with an appreciation for a lit- tle kinkiness from time to time, it seemed stupid to care who was in charge. And yet, *he* needed some control, too. At the very least, he needed an even playing field. He wasn't used to being with a girl so aggressive and command- ing in the bedroom—or anywhere else he'd ever fucked someone.

He wasn't oblivious to the fact that, his whole life, he'd picked girls who were just a little bit submissive, or at least not dominant. He'd always had control issues, especially with sex—but he'd always thought he'd handled it pretty capably. Yet now he was forced to realize that . . . well, maybe he'd handled it only by gravitating to girls who weren't so bold—and now that he'd finally been confronted with one who was, that's when he'd found himself consumed with the driving urge to make sure things went the way he wanted. He'd gotten edgy, tense. And then an old, familiar surge of self-preservation had kicked in, along with an archaic compulsion to . . . be a man—a big, strong, masculine man.

There had been those moments when Colt had pulled away and Jake had unwittingly found himself in a weird, silent sort of sexual struggle with her. Partly because he'd ended up pretty drunk by the time she'd invited herself and Colt back to his room, and he'd been acting on pure instinct. But partly because . . . of that need for some control. He'd needed to get her under him. He'd needed to feel a little power over her. And when he'd begun to feel her dominating him, something in him had instinctively rebelled. Finally turning her over in the bed, fucking her the way he wanted to fuck her, had been deeply satisfying.

Now, of course, he knew that he hadn't been imagining those few softer expressions in her eyes. He hadn't realized it at the time, but they'd been like chinks in her armor. And if he'd had the time to chip all that metal away, what he'd have found underneath was . . . *this*. Carly Winters. A girl who clearly tried to look plain, almost tomboyish—but she didn't quite succeed. She couldn't. Her eyes were too large and expressive and pretty, her lips too lush, her body too curvy, even in that T-shirt. A girl who—each time he'd met her—appeared to have something to hide.

So who was she really? The confident bombshell? Or the uncomfortable, nervous plain Jane? Or was she neither of them at all?

What had she come to Traverse City looking for? Sex, obviously. But had there been something more on her agenda? And had she gotten it?

Shit. Maybe none of it matters if the girl wants to shut you out of her life.

He ran a hand back through his hair in frustration, the sun making him too hot in his dark uniform.

Of course, she might want him out of her life, but he couldn't be completely. Turnbridge was a small town. And getting smaller by the second, it seemed.

Maybe most guys wouldn't care so much about what had happened—but Jake was big on honesty. He didn't like feeling misled. Or being treated like a jerk when he hadn't been one. Could be that it embarrassed her to see him again, but damn—why did she have to be so cold? The more he thought about it, wrapping his mind around what had just happened, the more it pissed him off.

Still . . . if she wanted nothing to do with him, if she wouldn't even give him the courtesy of five minutes, what could he do besides leave her the hell alone? He wasn't the stalker type and he wasn't about to start now.

He had some news for her, though. It didn't matter if he left her alone for the next fifty years—he'd never forget that night. He'd never forget the naughty things she'd done to him; he'd never forget the hot pleasures she'd delivered. And he'd never forget the raging heat that had risen in him unbidden when she'd pushed him to the brink and almost made him *lose* control just in order to take some of it back.

Carly ate her lunch in the shop's back room, or tried to anyway. She'd lost her appetite. Oliver circled her feet, meowing up at her, sensing something was wrong. She remained too panicked to think straight.

When she was done, she tried to gird herself. *Just walk back out front, unlock the door for any customers who might want to drop in, and get back to work on Dana's baby crib.*

But she felt too sick to her stomach. So sick that she left the door locked, deciding to take the afternoon off. She wound up back in her apartment, sitting next to a window with a throw pillow clutched to her chest. She kept her eye on the street below, as if watching would somehow inform her if Officer

Jake Lockhart was out telling all the good folks of Turnbridge how she'd shared a wild ménage à trois with him and another guy.

It probably wouldn't happen *today*, of course. He wouldn't just blurt it out. But as he got friendly with the other policemen, it would come up somehow. They'd be talking about women, or sex. Or even just the shops on Main Street. Or he'd mention needing a kitchen table and someone would kindly recommend he look at Winterberry's, and then the story would somehow tumble out.

The one thing sitting by the window *did* tell her was that he didn't come back. She could have reopened the shop without facing him, but she just wasn't ready to face *anyone* yet. Because her world had just changed. Irrevocably.

Even if he never told anyone, her life would never be the same. Because she would never again be able to see a Turnbridge police officer or squad car—one of which patrolled Main Street hourly—without being reminded of the things she'd done. That she lived a lie. That she wasn't the good girl everyone believed her to be, *wanted* her to be.

Somehow, when it had been her secret alone, it had been . . . almost like a thing she'd just imagined, made up in her head, or dreamed. When a tree falls in the woods and there's no one there to hear it, does it make a sound? When a girl fucks strangers in Traverse City and no one else knows about it, did it really happen? Now that someone knew about it, someone who would now know all the same people *she* knew, her secret became much more . . . tangible. Almost a thing you could touch—like a photograph or a diary. The fact that someone else *here* now shared the same memory she did made it feel like so much more than a dream. And maybe that feeling of it being only a dream was the thing that had allowed her to do it. If no one else knew, there was no aftermath. Now there would always be the threat of consequences. Even if she never did it again.

And what made it all even worse was—God, when he'd touched her, grabbed her arm on the street, sensation had shot all through her. *Lust.* The same hot desire she'd felt upon meeting him. Which meant that every time she saw him, not only would she suffer the worry and shame of her secret, she would also suffer the same raw, stark need she'd experienced that night. It seemed a horrible combination of things to feel all because of the presence of one mere man.

That night, she barely slept. She tried to tell herself this would all be okay, that whatever happened, it wasn't the end of the world—but that wasn't entirely true. Her world was small. It didn't take much to mess it up.

The next day, however, she got up as normal—ate her breakfast, petted the cat. She got dressed, started work, opened the shop. And nothing bad happened. Jake Lockhart didn't show up or even pass by. No townsperson came dashing in to tell her the horrible rumor the new town cop was spreading. It was a regular day.

At lunchtime, she even managed to place her normal order at Schubert's. Of course, on the walk there, she felt herself wanting to look over her shoulder the entire time, and she literally held her breath as she stepped inside—but only a couple of guys who worked at the drugstore sat at the bar eating lunch today.

And she'd just breathed a big sigh of relief when Frank Schubert handed over her lunch, saying, "Weird, wasn't it, when that new policeman thought you were somebody else?"

Her throat threatened to close up, but she managed, "Yeah, weird."

"Desiree," Frank mused aloud. "What kinda crazy name is that?"

It's desire with an e on the end. But of course she didn't explain that. Or that she'd thought it sounded exotic, classy—things she wanted to be. She just shook her head and quietly mumbled, "I don't know."

"Normally, I probably wouldn't even remember what name he called you," Frank went on, making her sort of want to slug the nice man, "but it was so unusual, guess it stuck with me."

She just nodded. Handed Frank a five. Said, "Keep the penny." Refrained from saying, *It's only that unusual if you've never left Turnbridge.*

"Anyway, strange, ain't it, to think somewhere out there, there's somebody who looks like you enough to confuse him that way? 'Cause he seemed pretty certain at first."

For God's sake, let it go, Frank. "Yeah, strange," she said.

"Next time I see him, maybe I'll ask him where he knew this Desiree person from. Maybe she's some long-lost relative of yours that you don't even know about."

Christ. "No, Frank, don't." She hoped she hadn't sounded too forceful, or startled, but she couldn't help it. Trying to act more normal—which was the word, the *goal*, of the day for her—she said, "I mean, it creeps me out a little to think there could be someone somewhere who looks like me, so . . . I'd rather just forget about it. Okay?"

Easygoing Frank shrugged. "Sure—whatever you say."

"See ya, Frank." *And please, please don't go around telling people the new cop thought he knew me and called me Desiree.*

That afternoon, Carly sold a bread box and a tray, just before a customer who'd ordered a custom dining room table of ash came by with a pickup truck to get it. She spent the rest of her day working on the crib.

Most of Carly's work mimicked the Shaker style. While her father had built more intricate pieces featuring lots of curves and carved designs, she herself favored clean lines, found beauty in a straight edge and in the simple symmetry and flow of a flat plane. The crib was in keeping with her usual look, other than the necessary curves required to make it rock, as well as one across the top to echo those below—and the work kept her fully absorbed until closing time.

And somehow, merely reaching the end of the day, and having done it without thinking about Jake Lockhart *or* Desiree for the past few hours, made her feel, well, exactly what she'd been striving for since this morning: normal.

That was when the door burst open and she looked up to see Dana. Uh-oh. Grabbing the sheet she used to hide the project while not working on it, she covered the crib and smiled at her pregnant friend. "Hey—what's up?"

Dana didn't smile back. "What's going on that you haven't told me about?"

Carly just blinked. "Huh?" Oh, God. What did Dana know? What had she heard? Had Jake Lockhart betrayed her already? Her heart began to pound. "What do you mean?"

Dana reached up to shove a lock of short red hair behind her ear, then took on a suspicious look. "My husband tells me you seemed completely rattled yesterday—right before he saw you being chased down the street by the new town cop. Who I got a look at just this morning, by the way, and oh my, is he hot! Hank said it all looked very dramatic—that you had words with him, and that he left here looking completely put out. But Hank also said it was like sparks were flying between the two of you, so he thought it had to be something romantic going on. And I said, 'That can't be, Hank, because I've known Carly since the first grade, and I'd know if there was anything romantic happening in her life.' But on the other hand, I would *love* for there to be something romantic going on, so I hope I'm wrong—but no matter *what* the case, you owe me an explanation, because clearly *something* is going on here that I don't know about."

She'd held her pooching belly the whole time she'd spoken, and Carly figured that was good, since otherwise the nonstop talking might have sent the unborn baby fleeing. Dana had always been gifted at chatter, never even stopping to take a breath, and pregnancy had somehow seemed to exacerbate the trait.

The only *good* thing about it was that the long diatribe had given Carly a chance to conjure a reply. Which was a lie, of course, and she hated lying to Dana. But she had no choice. And it wasn't even a *good* lie—but it was better than nothing and she only hoped it wouldn't come back to haunt her.

"I just met the guy yesterday," she claimed, "at Schubert's." So far, so good. "He followed me out, and up the street—and . . . he asked me out."

Dana gasped, smiled. "Lucky you!"

"But I turned him down."

Then she scowled. "Why on earth would you do *that*?"

"Um, because I don't know him?" Carly pointed out. "And he seemed . . . pushy. He didn't want to take no for an answer. That's why we were, you know, sort of arguing."

As Carly had spoken, Dana's mouth had dropped open, and she now stood gaping at Carly. "Know, schmoe. Who *cares* if you know him? He's a god, Carly. In a uniform. How on earth could you possibly turn down a guy who looks like *that*?"

Carly just blinked, sighed. Damn it. "He . . . didn't do that much for me. I didn't find him all that attractive."

Dana responded by giving her head a little shake, as if she couldn't have possibly heard Carly right. Carly understood that, of course—the man *was* a god. But on the other hand, Dana had tried to talk Carly into going out with *lots* of guys over the years who Carly had *also* claimed she hadn't found attractive, so her response shouldn't come as a surprise. Even if it was hard to believe *any* woman wouldn't find Jake wildly handsome.

"Are you kidding me?" Dana asked.

"No," she lied.

Dana just crossed her arms over her pregnant belly and rolled her eyes. "Why on earth do you have to be so picky about guys?"

"I can't really think of a better thing to be picky *about*," she replied. And that was the first true thing she'd said in a while, but it was actually beside the point. The point was that she couldn't date anyone in Turnbridge because she knew what that would lead to. And she couldn't date the new town cop . . . for oh-so-*many* reasons. The first of which was that he hadn't actually asked her out. And the last being that he knew her horrid secret and must think she was the strangest person on earth. And a host of others lay nestled firmly between those two.

As for her being the strangest person on earth, maybe she was. At least when it came to sex. And back when her sex problems had started, back when she'd thought she hated it, maybe she should have told Dana—but Dana had been so damn sexually healthy and well-adjusted that the whole thing had just embarrassed Carly and made her feel like a loser.

"You're missing out on life," Dana said.

Tell me something I don't know. That's why I go to Traverse City—to grab what little of it I can, even if it's only temporary, and only physical. But she swallowed back the real answers, feeling bad inside again, and said, "Well, I guess that's *my* choice."

Swell. So much for feeling normal.

Jake sat staring at his monitor, rapidly pushing the arrow keys, playing a computer game. "Shit," he muttered. Lost again.

Not that he really gave a crap about the game, but he was trying to distract himself from the hard-on in his shorts. And there was plenty else he could be doing. He'd just moved from an apartment in Detroit to a small house, so he needed some furniture and some lawn stuff—like a mower, to start with. But he only had an hour before his evening shift and was attempting to do something—*anything*—besides get himself off to thoughts of *her.* Desiree. Carly. Whatever her name was.

He let out a sigh as his cock stiffened a little further. He might have decided to leave her alone, but that hadn't exactly gotten her off his mind. And memories of their nasty encounter had been permeating his brain enough *already* before yesterday. Now—now that she was surrounded by mystery, now that he'd seen what he supposed was the *real* her—his lust was somehow heightened. Maybe it should have been a letdown to discover confident, seductive Desiree didn't really exist, but instead . . . hell, despite himself, all the mystery around the woman was making him hotter for her.

He couldn't explain it to himself—didn't even try, in fact. Because he'd told himself yesterday he would forget about her and he'd meant it. But apparently his penis hadn't gotten the memo.

Taking a deep breath, he tried the game again—a challenging and advanced variation on Tetris, an old favorite from when he was a kid. And . . . damn it, he lost again, that quick, because he couldn't even concentrate on the little shapes on his screen—in his mind he kept seeing her looking up at him with those big, hazel eyes while his cock was buried deep in her warm, wet mouth. He kept hearing her whimper and moan when Colt had been licking her, or fucking her. He kept feeling how tight and hot her pussy had been when finally he'd gotten his turn there. Shit—no wonder he couldn't concentrate on a stupid game.

Time to give in. To his baser needs.

Not that there was anything wrong with a little masturbation, so maybe he shouldn't consider it "giving in." But after she'd pissed him off so badly yesterday, he'd wanted to make a clean break from her. She'd come off as a bitch, and he just . . . aw hell, maybe he simply didn't like feeling as if she was *still* controlling his sex. Even from a distance now, which seemed even worse.

Nonetheless, he needed to take a shower before work anyway—so he headed in that direction. Within moments, he stood under the warm spray, eyes closed, soaping up his body . . . soon concentrating on soaping up his hard cock.

He imagined his hands were hers. She'd had damn good hands. Then he imagined his hands were her mouth—God knew she'd liked sucking him, so it was easy enough to fantasize that she was in the shower with him, on her knees before him, sliding those moist lips over his erection. Sliding up and down. Looking up at him, just as she had that night.

Only now . . . since they were in the shower, she looked . . . a lot more like Carly than Desiree. Sucking him. Sucking him until he bit his lip, let out a groan. Sucking him with that same wild abandon and enthusiasm. Sucking him longer, better, than any woman ever had. He envisioned his hands in her wet hair, around her head, pulling her to him, again, again. Glancing down to see that she loved it. Wanted more. Wanted him to come in that hungry little mouth of hers. Wanted him to shoot straight down her throat.

Aw—hell yes. He was coming. Between her pretty lips. And she was swallowing it without a flinch, drinking it, even sucking him dry.

Finally, he opened his eyes, let out a long sigh, leaned back against the tile wall of the shower.

Shit.

He wanted her again, too damn much. He wanted to know her story—*also* too damn much. He knew there was more to her now, and he couldn't seem to stop aching to find out what. Was it a game she'd been playing? Or was she leading some kind of double life—cheating on a husband or a boyfriend?

He closed his eyes again, this time trying to shut it all out, make it go away. Surely there would be other girls in town to date. With a little time, he'd lose interest in this one—he'd quit caring what her story was and eventually just chalk the whole thing up to being one of those occasional bizarre occurrences in life. After all, whatever the situation was, there was drama involved, and he hadn't come here for drama. He'd left the city because he was *tired* of drama.

As he dressed in his new navy blue uniform, checked his weapon, and strapped on his gun belt, he felt better, almost convinced that he would tire of fantasizing about little miss Carly soon enough. He had a new life here, a new job, and that was what he needed to focus on. And meeting some other single girls would help.

So far, his shifts for the Turnbridge Police Department had all been about training, and this one was no different. He was going out on night patrol with another cop around his age, Tommy Gwynn.

As they rode along in Tommy's cruiser, he showed Jake the route they covered hourly and pointed out the few homes and other places where disturbances had occurred in the past, explaining at the same time that it didn't mean they were likely to occur there again. "But we don't get much trouble here, and I gotta show ya *somethin'*, right?" he said with a laugh.

Jake had known life as a small-town cop would hold less action than his work down in the Motor City, but he was beginning to realize it might be a *lot* less.

After Tommy told him about a few law-related scuffles that had taken place here over the years, talk turned to more personal things. Jake learned that Tommy was married with two kids, ages ten and eight, and he'd grown up in Turnbridge but had done a stint down in Saginaw for a few years when his children were little. He'd liked working in a larger city, but his wife had missed her family and wanted to come home when it was time for their oldest to start school.

"I won't lie to ya," Tommy said, "it's a quiet job mostly, but there are good people here, and when they need ya, it feels good to help 'em out. What I'm sayin' is—we might not get many calls, but when we do, I think it matters a little more because the person on the other end is usually somebody you know—your neighbor, or the guy who cuts your hair, or the woman who poured your coffee yesterday. Know what I mean?"

Jake nodded. "I think so." Tommy was saying it was impossible to be a cop here without getting to know everybody. And Jake imagined—to his duress—that included the shopkeepers on Main Street, too.

"So," Jake ventured, "are there any single girls in this town? Or do I need to go somewhere else if I want to have a love life?"

Tommy cracked a grin. "Eh, there are a few. But if you're lookin' for a little love connection on a Saturday night, there's a watering hole over in Cherry Creek I can recommend."

Why did that answer disappoint him for some reason? "What about Carly Winters?" Aw shit, where had *that* come from?

Tommy slanted him a look. "What about her?"

Jake tried his best to sound casual. "Just wondering what her situation is. Is she dating anybody?"

"Her? No way." Tommy laughed. "And sorry to break it to ya, partner, but she won't date you, either."

Jake lowered his chin, curious. "How do *you* know?"

"Carly doesn't date *anybody*. Ever. I asked her out once myself back in the day, before I started seeing Tina. Turned me down flat."

Now *Jake* let out a chuckle. "And if she won't date *you*, that means she won't date anybody?"

"Let's just say," Tommy began, undaunted, "that her last name suits her."

Jake raised his eyebrows in Tommy's direction, wondering what that meant.

And Tommy said, "You know. Winters. Frigid."

It left Jake positively speechless. Carly Winters might be a lot of things, but frigid sure as hell wasn't one of them. "Uh, what makes you think so?"

"A good friend of mine, Chuck Gardner, was her high school sweetheart. They dated for two years, and it was serious—they went to the senior prom together, she gave him her virginity afterward, and they were talking marriage. But what it boiled down to is—she just wasn't into sex, and it caused problems."

It was all Jake could do to keep his jaw from hitting the floor. "Really? She wasn't into sex?"

"Chuck didn't give me every detail or anything, but . . . I got the idea she ran hot and cold—like she'd act all hot and ready, but when they actually did it, she was a cold fish. One time she even cried and wouldn't tell him what was wrong, and it made him feel like a jerk, like he was hurting her or something. He was crazy about the girl, kept trying to make it work, but she finally broke up with him. After that, she dated a couple other guys, but not for long—and as far as I know, she hasn't gone out with anybody since she was about nineteen or twenty. We're talking, like . . . twelve years or some crazy-ass amount of time like that. Some people in town think she's a closet lesbian."

"Nope," Jake said before he could stop himself.

Pulling to a stop at the one traffic light in town, Tommy turned to look at him—and Jake regretted sounding so sure. "How would *you* know?"

"Uh, I just don't think so," Jake fudged. "I mean, have you seen the way her jeans hug her ass." That was hardly a good reason not to think she was a lesbian, but it was all he could come up with at the moment.

"You don't *want* to think so," Tommy said, as if he were the voice of wisdom, "but trust me. I've known the girl all my life and she's just not into guys. Might not be into girls, either—I have no idea—but she's definitely not into guys."

That's what you *think.*

As the police cruiser rolled slowly up Main, Jake's eyes were drawn unwittingly to the dark, brick, two-story building that housed Winterberry's. A dim light burned in a second-floor window.

"Where's she live?" he asked Tommy absently, eyeing that light.

And Tommy pointed, conveniently enough, to the window Jake was already watching. "Up there. Inherited the business from her dad when he died about seven or eight years ago—and she turned the second floor into an apartment."

Good to know.

"But I wouldn't waste my time if I were you, bud."

You're not me.

But actually, Tommy Gwynn was right—he shouldn't waste his time. He'd already decided not to, after all. So what the hell was he doing asking about her in the first place? Finally, to shore up his decision, he said, "Sounds like good advice."

"Hey, maybe some weekend night when we're both off, I'll get a boys' night out together and we'll head over to Cherry Creek."

"Your wife won't mind?"

He shook his head. "We both take a night out on our own every now and then. And just 'cause I can't touch don't mean I can't look," he concluded with a wink. Then he said, "If it's all the same to you, I'm thirsty and this is about the time of night I tend to stop in at Schubert's for a root beer."

Actually, getting out of the car sounded good to Jake. In Detroit, he'd been a motorcycle cop, and spending so many hours in the car would take some getting used to. "Let's do it," he said.

Although after Tommy pulled to the curb and they both got out, Jake said, "I'll catch up with you inside in a few minutes. I need to stretch my legs, take a walk or something." It was the truth.

"Sure thing, man," Tommy said, and they headed off in separate directions.

Jake liked Gwynn, thought he was going to be easy to work with and would maybe be his first real friend here. But he wasn't thinking much about friends as he traveled the Main Street sidewalk in the cool summer night air. Instead he was wondering why the hell Carly Winters hadn't dated anybody since she was twenty. And why, instead, she turned herself into someone else to have wild sex with guys she didn't know. He could see how maybe a girl might want to dress up, go someplace new, get lucky, get laid. But why the fake name? Why the whole different personality? The more he learned about this woman, the less sense she made.

Unless . . . naw, he didn't want to go there, didn't want to think those thoughts.

Even if, when he added what he'd just learned to the whole Desiree conundrum, it seemed like . . . a big warning sign. And Jake knew something about warning signs.

And yeah, he'd just reminded himself—again—that he was done with her, that her issues were none of his concern, but that didn't stop his feet from leading him the few blocks to her building. He stood across the street, just looking up at the window, at the light, trying to catch sight of her. He had no idea why. And damn, he *was* beginning to feel a little like a stalker.

Still, even that sobering thought didn't tear him away—at least not just yet. Standing beneath a streetlamp, he realized that if she happened to glance out, she'd see him, too.

Shit, stop this. Go back to Schubert's. Drink a fucking root beer and get to know the locals. Talk about good advice.

"Okay," he murmured, actually answering himself out loud, then turned on the sidewalk—to find himself face-to-face with Carly Winters.

Chapter 6

She looked as surprised to see him as he was to see her. Clearly, he wasn't the only one taking a quiet walk in Turnbridge tonight.

"Carly," he said, soft, deep.

She sucked in her breath as if surprised to hear him call her by name—or at least by the *right* name.

She looked like she might dart at any moment, so he said, as gently as he could manage, "Please don't run away from me."

His eyes locked on hers, which shone beneath the streetlamp as big and expressive as ever. She wore her long hair loose tonight, falling around her shoulders, messy, pretty. She'd tied a long cardigan sweater over her top and blue jeans, wearing something plain and dark underneath. So simple looking, this girl. And yet . . . so damn complicated.

And as he stood there, probably three feet away from her, he still wanted her. No matter how simple. No matter how complicated. He didn't like it, but he couldn't deny it, either. The same chemistry that had drawn them together so easily that night in Traverse City flowed between them now, hot and palpable. The same but different. *Very* different.

Would she be surprised to know he thought she was prettier like this than on the night they'd met? She'd been a knockout as Desiree, but in all truth, that night she'd been the kind of woman you thought of fucking, not spending time with. Here, now, she looked like the kind of woman he wanted to be with, talk with . . . and yeah—fuck, too. But again, it was so very different from the first time.

He swallowed, trying to find words. "Listen, I—"

"I'm sorry—I have to go," she said quickly, then stepped down off the curb and moved briskly across the street before disappearing inside her building.

Jake stood silently watching, torn inside. In too many different directions.

He burned to know what made this woman tick. He ached desperately to take her to bed. And he knew it would still be a hell of a lot smarter to just walk away and leave it all alone.

So walk away he did, on a sigh, back to Schubert's, where he drank a root beer and indeed chatted with more of the locals and started to feel, bit by bit, as if he were beginning to fit in here, becoming a part of this town.

But *would* he leave it alone? Leave *her* alone? That part he wasn't sure about yet.

He should. But the hell of it was . . . he wasn't certain he *could*.

The two chocolate cream pies Carly held carefully on one of her hand-made cherrywood trays were both perfect, just like every year. The recipe had come down from her grandma to her mother and was now hers. But her mom claimed Carly's meringue was even taller and fluffier than when she baked it herself, and Carly couldn't disagree. She wasn't an outstanding cook or baker, but there were a few things she made well, and chocolate cream pie was one of them.

Now she stood in line at the pie baking booth on the Fourth of July, waiting to enter the annual contest—even if she was having second thoughts about it this year.

"Well, hello, Carly."

She looked up to see Mary Reinholdt, who ran the contest, ready to take her entry, as she placed the pies on the booth's plywood counter, painted red.

"Your signature chocolate cream, I see," the older lady said with a smile as she assigned the pies a number, which she taped onto the tin plates. "Given the heat, we'll get these in the fridge until judging and auction time, of course. Good luck!"

In accordance with a Turnbridge tradition that went back at least seventy-five years, the second pie would be auctioned off after the contest, the baker sharing the first two slices with the person who bought it. Once upon a time, it had been a romantic frivolity—and it was well known in the community that Carly's parents had first dated after her father bought one of her mother's chocolate pies. Now, however, the tradition felt pretty obsolete—last year Carly had ended up sharing her pie with Tiffany Cleary, who'd made a point of outbidding everyone because her dad loved chocolate pie. In other years, Carly had eaten pie with Frank Schubert and also one of her mother's bridge partners. Some men made a point of buying the pie baked by their wife or girlfriend, but the romance of the tradition was mostly a thing of the past and the "sharing" part seemed silly to Carly at this point.

And the sharing part was also what had almost made her not enter this year—just in case the new town cop decided to show up and bid. Since he'd seemed so intent on talking to her ever since they'd met—the second time.

But while eating lunch one day outside the deli with Dana and Beth Anne, Carly had mentioned that she might not enter and her friends had nearly gone crazy.

"You *have* to enter!" Beth Anne insisted. "Everybody loves your pie, and besides, if you don't, that harpy Julie Marie Steinberg might win, and I'd hate that." Julie Marie Steinberg's apple pie had, in fact, won the year before Carly's pie had begun taking the top honor, and the woman—a fairly recent transplant to Turnbridge—was always insinuating that her baked goods were better than what she bought at Beth Anne's. "And if my peach pie were to do well, too, we might shut her out of first and second place altogether this year."

"And besides, why *wouldn't* you enter?" Dana asked.

Carly had hesitated, the faint taste of bile rising to her throat.

"Well?" Dana persisted.

At which point Carly had sighed, felt stuck, and given an honest answer. "Okay, maybe this is stupid, but I guess I'm afraid that new cop will buy my pie."

Dana just blinked her disbelief. "Yes, that *is* stupid."

"Wait, what did I miss?" Beth Anne asked, looking back and forth between them.

After which Carly had been forced to tell the same fib to Beth Anne that she'd told Dana a few days earlier. And then they'd both lectured her on being a stick in the mud, and Dana had said, "How could you not want to go out with him?" and "You *are* baking pies this year, if I have to stand over you with one of your scary woodworking tools to make it happen. And I hope he *does* bid for your pie so you're forced to spend a little time with the guy and give him a chance."

Then, of course, Beth Anne had had to chime in with, "Really, Carly, don't take this the wrong way, but we worry about you." Never dating, she meant. They'd had this conversation before.

Finally, she'd just agreed to enter the stupid contest to shut them up and end the discussion.

And actually, she hadn't seen Jake since that night she'd nearly run right into him on the street. God, the way he'd been standing there staring up at her window . . . Something about it had nearly made her heart stop when she'd come upon him like that in the dark. And when he'd turned to her that very moment, his eyes had sparkled beneath the streetlight.

But maybe he'd finally gotten the message and would leave her alone now.

Damn, she wished that little sidewalk meeting had never happened. Well, she wished *none* of this had ever happened—she wished she'd found someone *else* to have sex with that night, or that Jake had never moved here, or that even if he *had* moved here that he hadn't recognized her.

But the fresher problem was: Before she'd found him staring up at her apartment, she'd been angry with him—yet ever since . . . oh hell, those sparkling eyes of his had heated her up inside. And the mere memory of the moment turned her on, every time he came to mind, even despite the horrible fears she still suffered about him.

And—oh God, it was just plain difficult to face him. In the beginning, the shock had been the problem, and of course the fear. But by that night, she'd graduated beyond the surprise and worry to stark embarrassment. How could she *ever* see him anywhere in town without knowing he was recalling all the dirty, dirty things she'd done with him and Colt? How could visions of those obscene acts—which had excited her so much then and horrified her so much now—not pop into his head every time he saw her, or even passed by her shop or heard her name? What on earth must he think of her? And why had he been so intent on talking to her after she'd asked him to leave her alone?

Of course, maybe she'd handled all this the wrong way. Maybe if she'd just come clean, just talked to him in the first place and asked him, from one imperfect human being to another, to please never tell anyone, maybe that would have been smarter—maybe it would have given him whatever it was he was seeking from her now. But the trouble with that was—the very idea of having an actual conversation with him about it made her want to hide, bury her head in the sand. It wasn't only him she didn't want to face—she didn't want to have to face *herself*, either. She didn't want to face the reality of the things she'd done in the dark of night and then tucked away so neatly along with her sexy lingerie. She didn't want to have to admit, out loud, that any of it had ever happened.

Now here she was at the Fourth of July festival and Officer Lockhart was bound to be here somewhere—if not yet, then later. But maybe he wouldn't even be present for the pie auction on Main Street, shut down to traffic for the day. Maybe, in fact, she'd become completely paranoid about this.

Yet how could she not be? It still felt as if he held her entire fate in his hands.

Stepping away from the pie booth as other ladies handed over their entries, she glanced around at the people milling about. At the red, white, and blue streamers draped overhead, crossing the street from one telephone pole to another. At smiling faces, at well-tended flower boxes lining windows, at tidy storefronts and T-shirts sporting the American flag. Life in this little town was all she knew. Being loved and respected by the good people of Turnbridge mattered to her, deeply. If Jake Lockhart took that away, if he even tarnished it, her life would never be the same.

When a hand closed over her arm, she flinched, but looking over, found only Dana. Thank God. "It's almost Hank's turn in the dunking booth at the fire station—let's go watch," she said with a smile.

Carly smiled back, or tried to anyway, and let her friend lead her in that direction.

But she kept her eyes open for the new town policeman at every turn—and felt a little more thankful, and a little more relieved, with each passing minute she didn't see him.

Jake leaned against the brick wall of the bank building along with Tom Gwynn, taking in the Fourth of July festivities. And taking in Carly Winters. Today she wore a fitted red tee with cute white shorts that reminded him how silky and long her legs were—legs he'd once seen spread lasciviously wide. Her hair was pulled into a high ponytail with some sort of fluffy red-white-and-blue elastic doodad. She looked cute as hell, and—he was tempted to point out to his new buddy—not the least bit like a closet lesbian.

Of course, she didn't exactly look like a girl who would invite two guys she'd just met at a bar to have raunchy sex, either.

She stood with another woman—a pregnant redhead—and a big guy who he'd bet was the redhead's husband. A large crowd had gathered in front of the pie stand—Tommy had told him the pie contest and auction was the biggest draw of the day until the fireworks after dark. Tom had also explained how the auction worked, adding, "So I gotta pay attention when they sell Tina's apple pie. If I don't buy it, I'm a dead man. Last year, she had to eat a slice with Barlow Jones—he's that old geezer you see driving up and down Main in that yellow Cadillac. He's eighty if he's a day, he's always on the make for women less than half his age, and Tina says he even smells weird, too."

Jake just laughed, then listened as an older lady announced the winners of the contest. Third place went to Julie Marie somebody, who looked smug and put out as she approached the stand to take her white ribbon. Second went to Beth Anne somebody, who actually squealed a little when her name was called and ran up to snatch the red ribbon from the emcee lady's hand. "Beth Anne owns the bakery," Tommy told him.

"And first place, for the fourth year in a row," the woman said, smiling with pride, "goes to our dear Carly Winters for her scrum-dilly-icious chocolate cream pie."

A few people in the crowd cheered and the rest applauded, all looking genuinely pleased for Carly. Frank Schubert was right—people loved her. Jake just couldn't quite figure out *why*, since she had yet to be anything other than rude to *him*. Carly appeared gracious and even a bit shy as she wove her way through the crowd to accept the blue ribbon, and the woman squeezed both Carly's hands in hers—one more show of affection for the hometown girl.

As she took her place back with her friends, the woman with the microphone said, "Thank you to all the ladies who entered this year. And now we all know what comes next—our annual pie auction! Proceeds go to the Turnbridge Festival Committee, so be generous, folks, so we can keep having all our wonderful events each year." Then a man standing behind her passed her a card to read as he held up a pie for the crowd. "First up, we have this delicious apple pie baked by Tina Gwynn."

Jake elbowed Tommy. "You're up, dude."

In response, Tommy started to bid, but hesitated, and Jake sensed him trying to choose an appropriate amount that wouldn't offend his wife but also wouldn't break his bank. By the time he was ready, an old man yelled out, "Seven dollars," and Tommy growled under his breath, letting Jake know it was the old guy in the Caddy.

"Ten!" Tommy called.

Four bids later, Tommy was at twenty dollars and looked to Jake like he was starting to sweat. When no other bids came, the lady with the mike finally declared, "Going, going, gone—an apple pie to Officer Gwynn for twenty dollars," concluding with a big wink since the pie had come from Tommy's wife.

And Tina herself delivered the pie a minute later, saying, "My hero," with a pretty smile as she nestled against her husband—who then introduced her to Jake.

As Jake watched them, thinking they fit well together, he began to realize Turnbridge was rife with couples. They were all around him at the festival, and he was pretty sure he was the only single guy at the police department. Back in the city, he'd never thought much about the idea of getting married, settling down, but here, it was clearly the thing to do. *Hmm. If I stay here, will I become one of those settled down married guys buying his wife's pie, going over to Cherry Creek to happily look-not-touch like Tom? Could I be into that?*

He didn't know, but it was way too early to be asking those kinds of questions, anyway—especially since the one single girl in town he knew hated his guts for reasons unknown and clearly had a few problems of her own anyway.

And right now he was far more caught up in looking at Carly Winters' long, lithe legs than in thinking about all the happy couples around him.

But—huh—did *Carly* want that? Did she see all these cozy couples and wish she was one of them? And why the hell wasn't she? Was it really possible *she*—of the infinite blow job—had really broken up with her first love because she didn't like sex with him? Given where Jake had been with her, he just didn't see how that was possible. The mysteries around his hot one-night stand just seemed to multiply.

Barlow Jones, Jake soon realized, bid on *most* of the pies. "Maybe he just likes pie," he told Tom and Tina with a shrug.

But Tina lowered her chin derisively. "No, what he likes is *girls.* The old bastard kept trying to touch my leg under the table last year."

"So, does anybody but me think this is a *really* outdated tradition?" Jake asked. He'd heard stories about such things back in his grandparents' time, but not since then.

Tina nodded. "Everybody does—but we all keep entering our pies anyway. For the life of me, I don't know why."

"People like traditions," Tommy said, putting on his voice of great wisdom. "Nobody likes to see one die, especially in a place like this where old-fashioned ideals are appreciated."

"Next up—" The microphone lady paused. "Oh, look here—it's our beautiful contest-winning chocolate cream pie by Carly. Now, what do I hear bid for *this* wonderful pie?"

True to form, Barlow opened with a bid of seven dollars.

On the other side of the crowd, Frank Schubert went to eight, and then the guy standing with Carly and her pregnant friend raised it to ten. "That's Hank—he's married to Dana there," Tom said, pointing and confirming Jake's assumptions.

Then Barlow took the bid to twelve.

And that's when Jake yelled out, "I'll go twenty."

Tommy and Tina just stared. "What happened to this being an outdated tradition?" Tina asked.

"And what happened to taking my advice?" Tom chimed in.

But Jake couldn't reply because old Barlow had upped the bid to twenty-two, and Jake decided not to fool around here, so he said, "Thirty-five," and the crowd gasped.

And he met Carly's horrified gaze across the way.

Next thing he knew, she was elbowing her buddy Hank, clearly prodding him to bid higher, but he was looking at her like she was crazy, and the pregnant woman between them, for some reason, appeared elated by the whole situation.

"Well then," the emcee lady finally said, sounding a little sly, "looks like Carly's winning pie goes to our newest police officer, and for a very fine price, too. You two enjoy yourselves, now."

Next to him, Tommy murmured, "I'm tellin' ya, pal, not only are you wasting your time, but you just wasted thirty-five damn dollars, too."

Jake, his eyebrows raised, drew his gaze from Carly to ask his friend, "What—the pie's no good?"

And Tommy just laughed. "Oh, I'm sure the pie's good, but you didn't pay all that money just for pie." Then he peered down at his petite wife. "Jake here's got his eye on Carly."

Tina's brow knit as she cast him a look of doubt. "Oh, Jake," she said, her tone one of pity. "Carly's a real nice girl and all, but . . . she just doesn't date."

"That's what I hear. But no worries, since I didn't ask her out on one. All I did was buy a pie." Then he eased upright from where he'd been leaning against the brick to say, "And now, if you'll excuse me, my shift just officially ended, so I'm gonna go claim my prize."

Carly just sighed—as Beth Anne joined Dana and Hank beside her on the street to smile and elbow her like something wonderful had just taken place, and as Officer Jake Lockhart wove his way to her through the crowd, pie in hand. "This is all your fault," she muttered to Dana and Beth Anne through clenched teeth.

"And it's exactly what I'd hoped might happen," Dana chirped cheerfully.

Of course, she couldn't expect her friends to understand why she wanted nothing to do with him. She could only imagine the looks on their faces if she blurted out the truth right now: *I had a very nasty threesome with him and his friend one night, and now I'm mortified every time I see him.*

And no wonder her friends wanted her to find a nice guy to date. They didn't know her other truth, either: *I can't seem to have good sex with anyone except strangers.* Maybe if she lived in a big city where everyone didn't know everyone else's business, she would have done something like see a therapist by now, to try to figure out the problem and work through it—but as it was, she'd just suffered alone in silence her whole adult life, and now here she was, paying for it.

Jake greeted her with a big, sarcastic, animated grin, saying, "Hi there, *Carly*"—but only she knew he was actually reminding her he'd once known her by another name. "I bought your pie. It came with everything we need, too," he said, holding up paper plates and plastic utensils.

Her stomach dropped a little further. Because the sight of him with her pie, right in front of her, brought home the fact that this was real and she had to deal with it. "So I see," she said. She didn't return his smile. She tried to look emotionless, in fact, because all her friends were watching, and other townspeople, too, and she felt as if she were on a stage, with everyone taking in her every move, expression, and response.

"And that means you have to eat it with me—right?" he asked, eyebrows raised.

"Just a slice," she pointed out.

"Whatever. Come on," he said, then shoved the forks and knife into his pocket, freeing up one hand, with which he boldly grabbed onto hers and began to walk, tugging her away from her friends. And unfortunately, no one stopped him. Unfortunately, her friends mistakenly thought this was the best thing that had happened to her in years—when it was actually among the worst.

"Where are we going?" she asked as they walked, the crowd around them growing thinner.

He barely bothered to look at her as he said, "I don't know. Just some-where away from the festival."

She sighed and admitted reluctantly, "I know a quiet place." He'd started up Maple, the street that made a T with Main right next to her building, so she pointed up the slight incline. After a rise of two blocks lay the railroad tracks, running parallel to Main, along with a park bench that faced away from the tracks, toward town.

They walked the whole way hand in hand, and she hated how warm that mere touch made her feel inside, the way she felt it *everywhere*, even in her panties.

As they reached the tracks, Jake said, "Funny place for a bench."

"Not really. Look the other way."

Letting go of her hand, he turned to see that the slope had led them higher than he'd probably realized, providing a bird's-eye view of the mead-ows and tree lines beyond the town. Much of the general area was flat, so the view made it worth putting a bench here. "Hmm—nice," he said, his manner making it clear he was still more interested in her and the whole pie-eating thing than in the landscape.

As they took a seat, Jake did the honors, using the plastic knife provided with the pie to cut a couple of pieces, and she held the plates as he maneuvered the slices onto them. God, this was weird. Weirder than weird. *A month ago we're going at each other like rabid animals—today we're eating pie two blocks from my home.*

Finally, he set the pie plate aside, handed her a fork, and stabbed his own down through the fluffy meringue sprinkled with dark chocolate shavings to the soft pudding mixture below. "I'm sure you're pissed I bought the pie, but I just want you to talk to me," he told her. He sounded resolute and a little irate, like a man determined to have his way. And looked like he was getting it, despite her best efforts.

"Why?" she asked. Because the answer could be . . . so many things. She really had no idea why he was bent on talking with her. Did he just want her to own up to what had happened between them? Or was it something more?

"Maybe I don't like being lied to," he replied, looking her in the eye. His tone caused her fork to stop in midair. "Maybe I'd feel better if I just knew what that was about."

She let out a long sigh, thinking, considering her options—few as there were.

God. Maybe it was best to just tell him. To just . . . humiliate herself a little further and spit out the truth.

Here goes. As he finally shoveled a bite of pie into his mouth, she dropped her gaze to her own slice. "All right, you want to know? Here it is. I wanted sex, and there's no one around *here* I wanted to do it with, so I went some-place else. Happy now?"

"Good pie," he said—then raised his eyes from his plate to her. "But no. I'm not happy yet. Why the fake name?"

She took a deep breath, let it back out. More truth. Even if it was embar-rassing. She didn't like admitting this, but the truth was all she had now, and if she gave it to him, maybe he'd finally leave her alone. "It just . . . makes it easier. If I sort of . . . act like someone else." Her face flushed with warmth at the confession.

He ate another bite and flashed her a matter-of-fact gaze. "For the rec-ord, I'd have been just as happy to have sex with the *real* you."

The words made her flinch slightly; she blinked as she gathered her thoughts. And she glanced down at herself, feeling . . . plain. Like the small-town girl she was. She thought of that night—how handsome and together he'd seemed, how she'd pegged him as a pilot. He might *not* have been a pilot, but he'd felt like someone who was completely out of her league in real life, a guy who could get any girl he wanted. So she wasn't sure she believed him. "I'm not exactly as alluring as Desiree," she pointed out.

"You're just as pretty," he told her without missing a beat, still seeming serious and annoyed. "Maybe not as nice—the jury's still out on that one. But damn, you're nothing if not a woman of mystery, and trust me, that lures me more than I want it to." After another forkful of pie, he said, "Where'd you get the name?"

Crap. Even before she answered, another hot blush climbed her cheeks. "It's . . . desire, with an *e* added on. I guess I thought it sounded exotic, foreign or something, not so . . . small town."

"And why couldn't you tell me all this before now, the other times I tried to talk to you? Why did it cost me thirty-five dollars to make you be civil to me?" He glanced back to his plate again. "Although I'll admit this is damn excellent pie."

Carly released yet another sigh, thinking back, wondering why he couldn't figure this part out himself, why he had to make her say it out loud. "The first time I saw you here, in Schubert's, I was too shocked. Mortified, actually. *Horrified.* I've been living in fear ever since that you'll tell everybody and ruin my life."

"Why would I want to ruin your life?"

"Because I'm sure I don't have to tell you that what you know about me is a pretty juicy secret, and because guys are . . ."

"Dogs? Yeah, a lot of the time we are. But I wouldn't do that to you, no matter how snotty you are to me."

Wow—*that* was a relief. A big one.

But that hadn't been the only problem. "And even now, it's . . . hard to face you. It's hard to know you live here, for God's sake, and that I have to see you on a regular basis."

He looked truly perplexed, giving his head a short shake. "Why?"

She let out an irritated breath. "My God—think about it! Think about that night." But—oh hell—she wished she hadn't said that, since now they were *both* thinking about it. How wanton she'd been—craving those two rock-hard erections like they were sustenance, like they were giving her life. She'd never been more brazen. "I can't imagine what you think of me."

"In what regard?" he asked calmly, but his voice came a little deeper, and she knew he was remembering how dirty she'd been, too—and maybe it was even exciting him a little.

She swallowed around the lump now swelling in her throat. Christ, this was horrible to talk about. And God, how she wished she could make it all go away. "Morally," she told him, her voice coming too soft, like a sinner confessing in church.

He just looked at her for a minute, and she felt it *all*—the lust, the sin, the regret. Until he said, "Who am *I* to judge, honey? I was there, too."

"But I was the one who . . ." Oh damn, her voice was getting shaky. She'd had to bring this up, hadn't she? "The one who . . . suggested it, and who was with . . . you know . . . two people of the opposite sex." By the time she managed *that* part, it was getting hard to breathe.

"The truth is," Jake said, his eyes a little kinder now, for the first time, "I thought you were amazing."

Carly just blinked, not sure what to think, how to take it.

"You were so damn smooth, confident. Not a girl who cared what I thought of her morally, either," he pointed out.

"Well, that was Desiree," she explained. "Not me."

His brow knit. "So it's not just a name? You're like . . . a whole different person?"

God, he thought she was weird. And she probably was. She swallowed, hard.

"Something like that," she managed. "When you grow up in a small town and everyone has this set idea of who you are, and it's someone who's *perfect* . . . it's just hard to let anything else out. Anything . . . sexual, I mean. Until I got the idea of making myself look different. And then came the name." God, her biggest secret, being spilled between them on a park bench as simply as if they were discussing the weather. No one else knew this stuff—*no one*. Lord. Now, not only did she have sex with strangers—she told them her deepest secrets, too.

"So this wasn't the first time you've done it," he said.

"No." Another shameful admission. And none of his business really, yet she'd gotten used to answering him now and the response had just come out. "But it was the only time I was with more than one guy," she said. It seemed an important distinction to her.

"I'm still not judging you, by the way."

"People here . . . *they* would judge me."

He nodded. "I know."

"They're good people, but . . . well, that's the problem here, I suppose— *they're good people*. With a pretty particular sense of right and wrong."

He just nodded, then gave her a sideways glance. "In fairness, since you're telling *me* stuff, I feel like I should tell *you* something, too. So—just so you know—that night was . . . the best sex of my life."

"Really?" The fact was, she knew she was good. Guys told her. Frequently. But still . . . she figured someone's *best* came . . . not with a stranger.

He gave a firm nod, his eyes still meeting hers, and she sensed them both remembering again. More of it. And not the parts with Colt. No, now it was the parts with just the two of them rolling hot and heavy through their minds. She didn't know *how* she knew that, but she just did. Images bit at her. How she'd ridden him on the bed. The way he'd held her down and she'd liked it. The spanking she'd demanded.

Embarrassed even more now, she bit her lip, lowered her gaze, finally forked a bite of her pie into her mouth. It was getting warm, not as good to her as when it was fresh and cool. Still, she chewed the crust, swallowed, and ate another bite—to pass the time, to keep herself busy with something besides memories and awkwardness.

That's when his hand rose, when his fingertip moved to the corner of her mouth. "You have a little . . ." She drew back slightly as his touch came, gentle but direct, until she realized—just as he held it up to show her—that he was wiping a little blob of chocolate filling away.

God, why did looking at the gooey chocolate pudding on his finger feel . . . sexy? Why on earth was it turning her warmer than she already was?

When he moved it to her lips, though, she knew. It was sexy because she wanted to suck the chocolate *off* of it.

Still, she hesitated. When she was Desiree, she knew exactly what she was doing—but when she was Carly, she hadn't the faintest idea how to . . . *be* sexy.

Yet when he applied just a hint of pressure to her lips, her chest went hollow, achy, and she felt herself parting them, letting him slip his finger inside.

Oh Lord. The very act of something, a piece of him, sliding slickly into her mouth ignited familiar stirrings. Instinctively, she closed her lips around it, gingerly used her tongue, tasted the sweet pudding. Then she sucked it away. Mmm, God. Her breasts tingled. And the spot between her legs spasmed. Just from that.

He began to draw his finger out—but then he brought it back, sliding in again, and she let him, and she would have sworn it got hotter outside. Their gazes stayed locked the whole time and her stomach contracted as he watched her. Nervousness warred with arousal inside her and she could stave off neither.

And when finally he extracted his warm, sticky finger all the way, he said to her, low and deep, "No one's ever sucked my cock as good as you did, honey."

The words jarred her, yanked her out of whatever slow sense of seduction she'd been experiencing.

And before she could weigh it, she followed her next instinct: She drew back her hand and slapped him across the face. Because no one had ever said such a thing to her! Not *her*, Carly. Not *here*, in *Turnbridge*. It was unthinkable.

Fresh heat—this time from simple anxiety—warmed her skin as Jake lifted a hand to his cheek and glared at her, clearly as stunned by her actions as she was. "What the *hell*?"

"You can't talk to me that way," she snapped, tense, defensive.

He lowered his chin, pinned her in place with those sparkling blue eyes. "You didn't seem to mind it that night. You seemed to like it. You seemed pretty good at it yourself."

She remained silent, horrified all over again, then shook her head. "Don't you get it? I'm not her."

"Her?"

Had he already forgotten everything she'd just so painfully admitted to him? "Desiree. I'm not that person."

He was back to looking angry again. "So let me get this straight. Desiree is hot and sexy, and Carly is a bitch?"

She gasped. No one had ever called her a *bitch*, either. Now fresh anger rose inside *her*, too.

"Well, you just hit me, damn it!" he reminded her. "Right when I thought we were starting to get along."

Get along. God, what had she been thinking? She couldn't *get along* with him. She couldn't have *any* sort of relationship with him, let alone one that had him putting his finger in her mouth, making her as wet in her panties as he had the first time they'd met.

So she pushed to her feet, incensed, and more than ready to end this. "I liked you better in Traverse City," she told him.

Finally letting his hand drop from his cheek—notably pink now in the bright sunlight—he peered up at her, his eyes turning darker than usual. "I feel the same way about you, trust me."

"Go to hell," she said, then turned to march away. Down Maple Street. Back toward the festival. And her real life. Toward the people who knew her, loved her, got her.

But then, no one really got her. No one in the world understood. Hell, if she was honest with herself, not even she understood.

All she knew was that Jake Lockhart was possibly the worst thing that had ever happened to her. Because he threatened everything she knew about herself. And he was making her look too damn hard at all of it. And because—goddamn it—even now, trudging away from him with her heart beating too fast, she ached for his touch, on her breasts, between her thighs.

And there for a moment, he'd made her feel like Desiree. Dirty, and happy to be that way. Ready to wallow in it. He suddenly made the line between Carly and Desiree appear frighteningly thin.

Even as she walked away, she wasn't sure which side of that line she was on right now.

Carly hated him and thought he was a pig for what he'd said.

And Desiree wanted to drop to her knees and do it to him all over again.

Chapter 7

Jake had thought about throwing the rest of the damn pie away, out of frustration, but he'd taken it with him. It was good pie, blue ribbon pie, and it had cost him thirty-five dollars. Now he sat eating it at his kitchen table. Feeling angry. He'd been annoyed at her before, pissed at her attitude, irritated by her lying. But after the incident by the railroad tracks, he was *mad*. She'd fucking slapped him! And not lightly, either.

He'd been worried the red handprint would still be there this morning, but thank God it had faded overnight, meaning he hadn't had to explain at work what the newest town cop had done to make a woman hit him.

Shoving another sweet, chocolaty bite in his mouth, he examined that— her hitting him.

He'd told her she sucked his cock good. He'd thought—hell, he'd *known*—they were both getting turned on, and he'd followed the simple urge to expand upon that. And besides, it was true—he'd been paying her an honest compliment.

And yeah, sure, if he'd just met her, of course he wouldn't have said anything that vulgar. But given that they'd already spent a night talking dirty to one another, letting it heighten their excitement, he hadn't even questioned the words as they'd left him. He'd thought it was just more of what they'd already shared.

God, talk about a complex woman.

It had kept him tense, his chest tight, all day. When he'd seen Tom at the station, and his friend had looked up with a knowing grin to say, "How'd that pie-eating date go for ya?" Jake had almost wanted to punch him in the mouth.

But then he'd remembered that none of this was Tommy's fault. "About like you predicted," he said without meeting the other cop's eyes. He'd opened a file cabinet, begun looking for a folder. "And it's a mistake I won't make again."

"Don't worry, bud—like I said, we'll get over to Cherry Creek one night and you'll forget Carly ever even caught your eye."

Huh. As if he could ever forget the things that had taken place between him and Carly. And he was beginning to see her point in a way—he no longer liked the idea that they'd be running into each other from time to time, either. But this idea of finding chicks in Cherry Creek was sounding better to him every minute. "Good. The sooner, the better." *So long as they don't use fake names and have weird hang-ups.*

Of course, the very thought of her had made his dick feel as tense as the rest of him. At the realization, he'd just rolled his eyes and tried to will it away, tried to concentrate on the information he was looking up, finishing paperwork on an auto accident he'd handled last week.

After getting home a few hours ago, he'd attempted to keep busy and not think about how pissed off he remained. He'd unpacked a couple of still-unopened boxes of books and CDs in his living room. He'd reheated some supermarket chicken and mashed potatoes for dinner. He'd hooked up his DVD player.

When he went to the refrigerator for a beer, he'd seen the pie sitting there on the shelf and pulled it out instead. Only he didn't bother cutting a slice— he'd just grabbed a fork and started eating straight out of the tin.

Sex and guilt. For some reason, people always wanted to cram those two things together. Sometimes for good reasons. But sometimes for completely stupid reasons, like now. He knew about sex and guilt, from way back, but he'd gotten past all that—and he didn't like being made to feel guilty.

Aha! *That* was the problem here—why he was so mad. She was making him feel like he'd done something wrong with her, or *to* her, and he hadn't. And given what he knew about sex and guilt—son of a bitch, he wasn't gonna let some insecure woman foist her idiotic guilt onto *him*, no fucking way. He didn't even like that she was *trying* to. And the more he thought about it—about how selfish that was, about how . . . fucking irresponsible, how careless—the more pissed off he became.

He'd eaten a sizable chunk of the pie, leaving a jagged, angry-looking edge in the plate, when he found himself pushing to his feet, then grabbing up his car keys from the dish where he kept them by the back door. She might not want anything to do with him, but she was going to have to listen to him, one last time, and then he'd leave her the hell alone—forever. She might have her hang-ups, but that didn't give her the right to go around blaming other people for them, pulling them into her sick, twisted problems—whatever they may be—and he was going to set her straight on that.

The last hints of a sunset burned on the western horizon as he started the car, but by the time he made the few twists and turns it took to get from his house on Pinecone Avenue to Main Street, the night was inky black.

As usual at this hour, the lights upstairs glowed bright, but the shop below was dark. He had no idea if she had some separate entrance to her apartment, so he went to the shop's front door—the same she'd shut in his face not long ago—and rang the buzzer. It lit up when he pressed it, and he could hear it from outside, so he knew it was working.

When no answer came, he pressed the button again, and this time he held it down, his irritation—his entire sense of injustice—escalating as the annoying sound bit through the air, even out on the sidewalk. "I'll stand here holding this thing down all night if I have to, damn it," he muttered, at the same time lifting a hand to bang on the door's large window. He was sick and tired of her deciding when and if she would acknowledge him, and he wasn't willing to wait for the next pie contest. She might want him to be a gentleman, but he'd taken a stab at that and it hadn't worked, so screw it—he could act like an ass as well as she could.

He'd pressed on the buzzer for a few long minutes when he finally heard movement inside—the sound of footsteps on a staircase and then stomping toward the door. Had he pissed her off? Good—he was tired of being the only one who felt persecuted here.

He was ready to tell her he was sick of her making him feel he'd done something wrong. He was ready to say she had no right to foist her useless guilt on him. He was ready to yell at her, get all the frustration and anger she'd caused him off his chest, once and for all.

She yanked open the door, glaring up at him. "What the *hell* do you want?"

And he glared back, ready to let her have it.

Except . . . she clearly had no idea how prominently her nipples jutted through the thin creamy yellow pajamas she wore. Nor could she know that the streetlight across the way shone on the loose, silky fabric to outline her curvy silhouette underneath. His cock, which had been twitchy all day at thoughts of her, went immediately hard in his blue jeans at the sight. Shit.

He was so damn fed up with her, so damn mad. But equally as aroused now, too. And that was the part of him that took over his body, his brain, all at once, in a way it never had before.

He never said a word. Or even made the decision to reach for her. He was simply aware of his hands closing greedily over her waist, his body pressing into her softer one, his mouth coming down on hers as he pushed her back, back, deeper into the shop's darkness. His head swam with lust and pleasure as her startled gasp subsided and she clutched at his T-shirt. He heard the door shut behind him, closing out the night as his hard-on nestled against her abdomen.

He kissed her hard and hungry, needing to drink her in, have her in any way he could. Anger remained only on the fringes of his brain now as his whole being gave way to what was happening. After weeks of strange longing and confusion, of heat that flowed between them on sight, he was going to have her again—completely.

She never spoke, either, or tried to make him stop—thank God. She kissed him back just as wildly, her breath coming in ragged gasps as he finally pressed her into the shop's back wall, next to the stairs. He freed one hand from where it was buried in the slickness of her pajamas to yank at the pants, digging his fingers inside the waistband. Her arms looped tight around his neck now, her tongue in his mouth as he tugged the pajama bottoms over her ass, panties with them, and let them drop to her feet.

Then he deftly released the button on his jeans, and pushed at the zipper until his erection sprung free, even if still confined by underwear. He felt frantic to get inside her again—as if nothing would be right until he was buried in her warmth, as if the world would come to an end if he didn't fuck her as soon as humanly possible. And still they kissed—rough, hungry, raw. He cried out when she scratched his neck.

And then his cock was out, hard and warm against her belly, and she was whimpering hungrily in his grasp, and he knew bliss was almost his—almost, almost. Grabbing onto her bare bottom, he hoisted her upward against the wall, and her legs curled around his hips, and the tip of his aching shaft was warm, wet with her, in just the right spot, so he thrust hard, driving deep. She cried out, her head dropping back in pleasure, and he felt the moist warmth envelop his dick at last, tight as a hot, slick vise that wouldn't ever let go.

His scalp tingled with heat as he resumed kissing her, and she moved against him, fucking him, riding him, and his breath came in hot gasps and growls as he thrust at her, again, again.

They moved like that together for a few raw, feral minutes until her response began to change—until she was releasing hot, thready whimpers, her undulations slowing, growing more jerky, and he knew a powerful orgasm was about to flood her senses.

He held on to her tight as she let out high-pitched cries, her head again dropping back, eyes shut, lips beautifully parted.

And when she lifted her head, met his gaze in the dark, he kissed her hard—once, twice—trying to let her recover a little but still feeling the primal animal urge to fuck her brains out.

With rough movements, he carried her to the nearest flat surface among the pieces of furniture—a small dining table in the middle of the room—and as he laid her back on it, his mind only barely registered that she'd made it herself. Still inside her, he thrust wildly, over and over, needing her to feel him to her very core, needing to force all his hunger out and into her. Moving inside her, he closed his hands over her breasts through the thin fabric still covering them. He wasn't gentle—he couldn't be right now. He squeezed and molded them; he played roughly with her erect nipples, pinching, pulling, making her moan and sob as the coarse pleasure echoed through them both.

Finally, he yanked at the buttons holding the pajama top closed. He heard one of them land somewhere across the room and couldn't have cared less. All he wanted was to get to those gorgeous tits at last, and then they were in his hands, flesh to soft, pliable flesh, and he massaged them in rhythm with his hard, wet plunges.

She cried out, moaning and sobbing, the sounds mixing with his own deeper ones. And when he bent over her, still fucking, fucking, fucking, to suck one beautifully engorged nipple into his hungry mouth, he groaned around it, tugged on it hard, and felt her heels dig into his ass as if to pull his dick deeper inside her. But that was impossible—he was buried to the hilt with each pounding drive. He sucked her tits with wild abandon, showing no mercy, no softness. Neither of them wanted anything soft right now, he knew.

When he hauled her up into his arms again, she wrapped back around him and it felt so damn good, just for once, to have this woman cling to him a little, make him feel like she wanted him. But that didn't soften his raw instincts—she'd probably kick him out after this was over, after all. He felt like he had to take all he could get of her, right here, right now.

He needed a bed, or a couch, something that wouldn't be hell on their knees—because he wanted to take her from behind now, as he had in Traverse City. But when she began kissing him again, he stalled in place—couldn't see, couldn't really walk—and the next thing he knew he'd stumbled into the stairs. They both went down with a thud, fell against the bottom steps together, on their sides; his erection left her for the first time in a long, ecstasy-filled while.

Their eyes met once more, the only light in the room coming from streetlamps outside, and her gaze remained as heated as he felt. They still didn't speak—and on any other night, he'd have asked if she was okay from the fall, but he didn't want to break this hot spell, give her a chance to start a fight. Instead, he reached for her hip as he rose up—and he firmly turned her over on her hands and knees on the steps, and she let him.

As he moved in behind her, though, he found himself wishing he'd gotten her out of that long pajama top completely—he yearned to have her naked body in front of him right now; he wanted to see the arch of her back, the curve of her ass, the muscles in her shoulders. So he found himself running his palms over her round bottom, up under the shirt, feeling the valley created by her waist, the smooth rise of her back following the slant of the stairs. He heard her sigh, just from those simple touches, and it sent a warm tingle down his spine.

But he wanted inside her again too much to linger, so he grabbed onto her backside with both hands, positioned his cock, and slid it in, smooth, deep. A guttural moan left her, and he felt it in his chest. And then he began to thrust again.

This had started as mindless, reckless fucking, but now he was able to think more, to feel. Every hot drive of his dick sent a burst of pleasure through his abdomen, up into his solar plexus. Low groans left him with each stroke as he drank in everything amazing about the moment: from her gorgeous body to her shockingly welcoming attitude, from the way the shadows fell across her form to the knowledge that they were doing it in a dark room without ever even having exchanged a word.

He gritted his teeth as he fucked her harder, harder, made her cry out with each intense thrust. He soon got lost in the pure, driving pleasure, lost in the hard, rhythmic plunges into her hot flesh. And then he was letting out low cries in time with hers, gripping her ass, hammering relentlessly, again, again, again—until . . . aw God, there it was, it was rising inside him, unstoppable, yeah, yeah . . . A ferocious growl sprung from his throat as the orgasm blasted through him, as rough and jagged as the sex itself, nearly rocking him off his foundations as he exploded in her sweet cunt. *God, yesssss.*

In front of him, she went still, and he slumped over on top of her.

Everything was quiet but for the ticking of a clock somewhere. Then a car passed by on the street. They *weren't* the only two people alive, after all, even though it had strangely felt that way for a few minutes.

Damn. Jake had thought what they'd done with Colt was intense, but this . . . this was somehow more; this was the most intense fuck of his life.

Finally, he forced himself up off her—he turned to sit on one of the steps, leaning back to balance his elbows on a higher one as he returned to himself, got some strength and brains back.

When she rolled to her side on the steps to face him, he waited for her to say something. And when she didn't, he asked, "Aren't you gonna tell me to leave or go to hell or something?"

A small breath escaped her. Then possibly the softest voice he'd ever heard left her lips. "No." Just that.

"Are you okay?" He didn't mean it in a smart-ass way—he sincerely wondered if she was all right.

"Yeah," she whispered.

"Just so you know, I didn't come here to fuck you."

"What did you come here for?"

"To yell at you."

She raised her gaze gently to his in the dark. "Fucking's better than yelling."

The surprising reply made him grin. "Damn straight."

Finally, she sat up on the same step as him and began to pull her pajama top around her.

He touched her knee. "Don't." When she stopped, looked over at him, he explained, "Your body's beautiful and you don't need to hide it, not with me." Then he sighed, feeling a little guilty as he added, "And I don't think you have buttons anymore anyway. Sorry about that."

"I'll live."

He didn't quite know what was going on here, but he liked her new attitude.

"So . . . why do you suddenly seem like you don't hate me anymore?"

She sighed. "Remember how you said the sex in Traverse City was the best of your life?"

"Yeah."

"Well, I think *this* is the best sex of *my* life. And it happened when you didn't think I was somebody else. So it's hard to be very mad."

Carly wasn't sure what had just happened to her. Except for the best-sex-of-her-life part. It had been entirely contrary to what usually worked for her—she hadn't had the least amount of control. She could conclude only that the strange, stark hunger had finally built up so much that it had over-ridden her need for that with him.

"What were you going to yell at me for?" she asked.

"Mainly for . . . imposing your guilt on me, I guess. I really never did anything wrong to you, you know."

She nodded quietly. And couldn't deny it anymore. "I know." Then she took a chance, one that probably felt riskier than it was, since to be turned down now, after all this, would be pretty devastating. "These steps are hard. You want to go upstairs? To my bed?"

She caught his small grin in the shadows. "Yeah—that sounds nice."

It felt at once awkward and comfortable to retrieve her pajama pants, go lock the door, and then lead him up the stairs to her place. Not the least of which was because no guy had ever been in her apartment. It was a studio—kitchen at the far side, bed against the back wall, living area set up at the nearest end beside the steps.

She'd been reading a book in bed when all the buzzing had begun, and it lay open, facedown, on rumpled covers. Funny, this was her home, but after what had just happened, it felt as if she'd been away from it for much longer than just fifteen minutes—something in her had changed since she'd gone down those steps.

Ah, the best sex of her life—that was it. Something inside her felt re-freshed, renewed, even elated—despite how uncertain she remained about him, and about herself and all her strange sex issues.

And then—oh boy. She'd been aware for a while now—since standing up, actually—that something felt . . . unusual between her legs, moister, stickier, than usual. And now, as wetness rolled down her inner thigh, she finally realized: It was semen. God.

She turned to meet his gaze. "Um, at the risk of bringing up an unpleas-ant subject, we didn't use a condom."

He shut his eyes, gritted his teeth. "Jesus. I was . . . overcome. Which is no excuse, but . . . that's all I got. Sorry."

"Are you . . . overcome often?"

He gave his head a firm shake. "The last time I didn't use protection was . . . probably about five years ago, the last time I had a serious girlfriend." He paused, sighed, then said, "You?"

This shouldn't be embarrassing, but for some reason it was. "This is the, uh, first time I've *ever* not used one." It made her feel inexperienced or something.

"Wow. That's impressive," he said as she walked to her bedside table for a tissue and tried to subtly take care of the messiness with her back to him. Then he murmured, "No wonder it felt so damn good."

And it made her wonder . . . Was *that* why it was her best sex ever? Because there was no thin barrier of rubber between their bodies?

But no—that wasn't it. It was more than that. Way more.

"Something to eat? Drink?" she asked, tidied up now and ready to change the subject.

She turned to him in time to see him shake his head. "I'm good. I just gorged on chocolate cream pie before I came over."

She bit her lip, studying him. She was mostly naked, but he remained fully dressed—even having zipped up his jeans. So even despite his comment about wanting to look at her body, now that they were in the light, she went to her dresser, slipped on a pair of pastel striped undies, and shed the debuttoned shirt, exchanging it for a tank top.

When she turned back around, he'd made himself comfortable on her bed, laying propped up against the pillows, hands behind his head. "Did you build this bed?" he asked.

She nodded.

"It's beautiful," he said.

"Thanks."

"So, you make furniture for a living. That's unusual."

She nodded once more. "The craft was passed down to me from my dad."

"Do you do it because you love it or because it's one of those family things you got pushed into?" He was so blunt, no beating around the bush.

"Both," she replied, joining him on the bed, lying on her side. Chilly beneath the ceiling fan, she reached for the quilt she kept draped across the end of the mattress and pulled it over her legs.

"Any regrets about it?"

"I find a lot of satisfaction in the work. So if I have any regrets, I guess it would be not taking a break and going to college before committing to the business. I haven't . . . seen much of the world outside Turnbridge."

Their eyes met, and he said nothing, but she could easily read his thoughts: *That's part of your problem, isn't it?*

And of course it was.

But she knew plenty of people who'd lived their whole lives in Turnbridge who were still capable of having normal relationships, normal sex. So it hardly explained anything.

Just then, Oliver came trotting up the stairs. Unlike Carly, the cat wasn't shocked by the sight of a man in the bed—he was too used to seeing people come and go in the shop. "Big cat," Jake observed.

"Jake Lockhart," she said, "meet Oliver J. Cattenstein."

"Big cat with a big name," he said, the corners of his mouth turning upward slightly.

She smiled softly herself, at a memory. "When he first came to live here at the shop, my friends teased me, said he was my business associate, and we decided he needed a professional yet catlike name."

When Oliver jumped up onto the bed to nose around Jake, Jake absently reached out to pet him.

"So you don't hate cats or anything?" she asked.

He flicked a glance to her. "No. Should I?"

She shook her head, pleased. "But some guys do."

"Well, I'm not *some guys*," he said, and the words resonated. Indeed, she was starting to think there was nothing very average about Officer Jake Lockhart at all. From his sexiness to his determination.

"So," he said, his tone more cautious, "are we . . . friends now?"

She raised her eyebrows, a little surprised by the word, all things considered. "Friends?"

"What I mean is . . . if I ask you something personal, are you going to get mad and throw me out?"

Carly took a deep breath. Part of her wondered why he had to spoil this, this one moment since Traverse City when things felt almost comfortable between them. But then . . . the way they'd met, the encounters since then—she supposed it was inevitable that he wasn't just going to stop being curious and let this go. He was a cop, and she'd known enough town cops to know they were naturally inquisitive, always trying to get to the bottom of things. "I won't get mad. I can't promise I'll answer or be happy, but I won't get mad."

Next to her, he took a deep breath, and he looked a little sad before he said, "I know there's more."

She just blinked. "More?"

"Look, honey, you don't become somebody else to have sex unless . . . you think there's something wrong with the person you *are*."

The words nearly knocked the wind out of her, and she was glad she was lying down. She barely knew how to respond. Talk about blunt. Maybe that was a cop thing, too. To her surprise, it *didn't* make her angry at him—but it made her feel a little pathetic. And not very sexy. "That was a statement, not a question," she replied.

He met her gaze. "All right. Why do you have to become someone else in order to fuck?"

She sat up, leaned against the headboard, staring absently at the quilt now pulled to her waist, and nibbled on her lip.

She knew the answer. Maybe. Sort of. But she didn't ever think about that—she simply didn't let herself. She'd never wanted to fully examine how she'd gotten from point A to point B. So she said, "I don't know. It's just always been this way."

"Define always."

She swallowed. "Since high school. Since my earliest sexual experiences. I . . . just couldn't do it."

Now he rolled onto his side, facing her. "What do you mean?"

"I . . . had the urges"—God, had she ever had the urges, as intense as *any* teenager's—"but whenever I tried to fool around with a guy, even a guy I really cared for . . ."

"What happened?"

She thought back to those awful, almost paralyzing moments. "I . . . froze up, felt dirty, felt sick. I . . . couldn't let the *good* kind of dirty out of me, couldn't let anyone see it or even know it was there. It was like there was some invisible wall between the me everyone knows—the town sweetheart and all that—and the sexual part of me. For some reason, I just couldn't let anyone who knew me see that side. No matter how I tried. It was awful. Painful." She sighed, remembering *all* of it. "I hurt someone I loved."

God—Chuck. She hadn't thought about him—in that way—in a very long time. And she hated remembering it now.

"Chuck was my first—well, my only—love. And everything I just told you is what he had to put up with. I wanted to be with him, but like I said, I just froze up, time after time."

"So . . . you had sex with him, or it didn't get that far?"

"Sometimes sex. But it was . . . unpleasant." She stopped, shuddered, remembering—it had felt . . . like rape. Though she'd never been raped, so she shouldn't know such a feeling. And it hadn't been his fault. "It was like there was some heavy weight clamping down on me, making me go completely still, and stiff, when the actual touching and sex happened. It was the worst feeling I ever had. And . . . for the record, that's kind of how I felt yesterday, up by the tracks when I slapped you," she added on a thick, nervous swallow. "It . . . it wasn't logical. It just . . . was."

He only looked at her, and she couldn't read his expression, so she decided it was easier to simply keep talking. "But . . . back to Chuck—the guy was a saint, frankly, but I was too caught up in my own issues to realize it at the time. Finally, I broke up with him because I figured if I couldn't have sex with him the right way, it must mean I didn't really love him. Only I know now that I did—that the problem really *was* just the sex. Because whenever I started dating other guys after him, the same exact thing happened."

"Are you still in love with him?" Jake asked.

She shook her head. "But it took a while to get over it. It broke my heart. Especially since it was *my* stupid fault."

He shrugged. "Sounds like you couldn't help it much."

"Anyway, he's married now, with a daughter, and he runs the canoe livery outside town. When I see him, it's fine—we wave, or say hi, and occasionally even chat for a few minutes. The whole love thing is long in the past. I just wish it had ended for a different, better reason."

"What happened after that? I mean, when did you . . . start the Desiree thing?"

She was still embarrassed that he knew her most personal and shocking secret—and yet, the answer to his question made the base of her scalp tingle, just remembering it. Because, like everything related to Desiree, it felt a little shameful—yet exciting. "My best friend, Dana, went away to the University of Michigan, and one weekend when I was twenty-one, I went down to Ann Arbor to stay with her. We went to a party, I got drunk for the first time in my life, and I had sex with a guy I met there. And I was *able* to. I mean, I *enjoyed* it, for the first time ever. I was able to let go, finally let that part of me out. It was . . . liberating.

"And afterward, I realized it must have been because the guy didn't know me, and so he wouldn't judge me, at least not as harshly as someone from Turnbridge would. He had no preconceived notions of who I was."

"You're really hung up on people judging you," Jake pointed out. "Mind if I ask why?"

She kept her gaze on the quilt, studying the point where four triangles met. "I don't know."

"So . . . any idea why you were able to have really hot sex with *me* a little while ago? We're in Turnbridge, after all. And I know you're the town sweetheart."

She finally looked at him again—and it reminded her how handsome he was, the sensation fluttering all through her. "Maybe it's because you met that side of me first. The Desiree side."

"Then maybe it's good it happened that way," he pointed out.

"Maybe." She wasn't sure. She wasn't sure of anything anymore. Jake Lockhart had turned her world upside down.

When he sat up, announcing he had an early shift and should probably take off, she felt equal parts disappointment and relief. She didn't really want him to go just yet, but it would be easier, safer, once she was alone again, back in her own private little world where no one was trying to make her think too hard about her problems or get to the bottom of them.

"Can I come back and see you tomorrow night?" he asked before standing up.

She almost lost her breath, not having expected that. In fact, she'd thought maybe the intensity of the sex they'd just had might have . . . gotten her out of his system or something. And that their talk just now might have answered all his questions, given him whatever sense of closure or explanation he'd been seeking from her.

So she bit her lip, feeling unaccountably nervous. "I'm not sure."

God, she hated how docile she felt with him tonight. The aftermath, she supposed, of letting him fuck her brains out, of letting him see how much she'd liked it. And even admitting it, too. It had left her . . . vulnerable.

"I want to make us both feel good again, honey," he said, his voice deep, seductive, seeming to reach down inside her and wrap around her beating-too-fast heart. "Can I take you out to dinner somewhere? Or . . . we could do anything you want."

She sensed he was walking on eggshells now, trying to figure out how to please her. Which was . . . nice. Undeniably so. For a guy who hadn't *seemed* very nice since that night in the bar, it was a welcome change that softened everything inside her even further.

"No," she said anyway, though, explaining, "I'd rather not have people talking about us any more than they already are after the pie auction."

He tilted his head. "I'm not sure why it matters."

"Me neither. But that's the way it is." *That's the way it is, and yet . . .* was she really telling him no, this man who'd given her the most outstanding sex she'd ever experienced and who'd gone to such lengths to see her again? This man who was turning her inside out? "But . . . you can pick up a pizza from Angelo's on the way if you want."

His eyes took on a gentle warmth as he said, "Deal."

Chapter 8

"Tina's making a big lasagna for dinner tonight," Tommy said, stopping at Jake's desk. "Said I should tell you to come over for a home-cooked meal when your shift ends."

Jake raised his eyes to Tom. "I appreciate the invitation, man, but I've already got dinner plans. Next time, though—and thank Tina for me." Lasagna sounded good, but Carly sounded better.

As Jake might have suspected, Tommy narrowed his gaze suspiciously. "*What* plans? You don't know anybody here."

He hadn't intended to tell Tommy about this, but . . ."I've got a date."

Tom's eyebrows shot up. "With who?"

"Carly."

Tommy's jaw dropped. "You shittin' me?"

"Nope."

His friend just gave his head a pointed tilt, still flashing a look. "How the hell did that happen?"

Inside, Jake was reeling from the memories, and the sensations they delivered—but on the outside, he just shrugged. "Turns out that pie led someplace good after all," he said, then peered back at the paperwork before him, not wanting to extend the conversation.

"Huh," Tommy said, still clearly shocked. Then he lowered his voice so no one else in the station house would hear. "Well, bud, good for you, but . . . don't go gettin' your hopes up about Carly Winters. I mean, don't expect much. Like sex, I mean."

Jake simply let out a long, slow sigh. He liked Tommy, but he suddenly didn't like Tommy talking about Carly and sex anymore. She'd confided so much in him, and even though he didn't fully understand her hang-ups, he was starting to feel a little protective of her. "How about you just let me worry about that, okay?"

Tommy blinked, clearly catching the slight edge in Jake's tone. "Uh, sure, bud," he said, backing off and making a clear effort to sound easygoing and cheerful. "And we'll give you a rain check on the lasagna."

Carly still felt as if she'd unwittingly stepped into some bizarro world version of her own life. After closing the shop at six, she went upstairs to shower and dress. But she couldn't remember the last time she'd had a real date and had no idea what to wear. Or what to do with her hair. Given that until yesterday she'd been trying to avoid Jake, it was a strange switch in her thinking to care what he thought, to want to please him now. But she did. That was another thing she could barely remember—caring about pleasing a guy, wanting him to really like her.

She decided on jeans and a pale pink tank top with a band of lace at the hem—after all, they were only having pizza at her place, not going to the opera. She left her hair down, letting it dry on its own so that it curled slightly at the ends. Then she looked in the mirror and wondered how she'd gotten here, with him. Why had she confided in him so much? Why had she become this sweet, trusting girl with him?

Wait. That's the real you, who you really are. Sweet. Trusting. So maybe it wasn't so much that she'd "gotten" somewhere with him—she was actually just being *herself.* She simply wasn't used to doing that with guys, and certainly not when it came to talking about sex.

When the buzzer rang at eight, her stomach swam with nerves. She felt as if she were sixteen again, as if it were Chuck on the other side of the door, as if all this was new and mysterious to her. But maybe it *was* new and mysterious. If you took Chuck out of the equation, at thirty-two she had less dating experience than the average high school student. *Blegh—don't think about that. Just answer the door.*

Something about the sight of Jake standing on the front steps in faded jeans and a distressed tee, holding a pizza box in his hand, nearly took her breath away. *I want him. I want him like crazy.* She experienced the wild urge to forget the pizza and rip his clothes off right now. To make it like last night, hot and intense and needful. "Hi," she murmured, heart fluttering in her chest.

Maybe that instant craving was normal after what had happened last night. But it was definitely more than she was used to feeling, even on nights in Traverse City. Because now they'd talked. She'd told him personal things. And he hadn't passed judgment on her, just as he'd promised he wouldn't.

"Pizza delivery," he said with an easy smile as she stood back and let him inside.

Of course, she *couldn't* rip his clothes off. She wasn't Desiree. Having the desire and doing the deed were two different things. Carly had *always* felt desire—she'd just never been bold enough to act on it unless she took on that other persona. Just sharing a pizza with him would be challenging enough.

As she led him upstairs, she said, thinking out loud, "I should have picked up some beer, darn it. Sorry."

But he sounded completely easygoing about it. "I'm not picky. Whatever you've got is fine."

She walked to her fridge and inspected the shelves. "Let's see—I have Coke, some Sprite, water, and a bottle of white wine."

"Let's go with the wine," he said, and she thought: *Good choice.* It would help her relax a little.

She'd put on some music to fill the air in moments when they weren't talking; mostly what she thought of as "mellow alternative" from the nineties. At the moment, 10,000 Maniacs were telling her these were days she'd remember, days when something would grow and bloom in her. And she almost felt that. Maybe because something was growing and blooming already. Just seeing him tonight made last night's strange, stark, wild intimacy feel warmer than it had at the time. They'd shared something. And whether or not it was the sex or the things she'd admitted to him afterward, she already felt a strange, invisible bond stretching between them now. It was thin, tenuous at best—but on the other hand, it was the most profound connection she'd experienced with a man in her entire adult life.

She gave Jake a couple of yellow Farberware plates and instructed him to open the pizza box on the coffee table; then she poured two glasses of wine and joined him. *Here we go. A date. Breathe.*

They ate. Made small talk. He asked her about a few of the townspeople he'd met—he thought someone might have introduced him to her mother outside the bank yesterday, but he was losing track, meeting too many people too quickly. She asked him how he liked Turnbridge, how his new job was going. At one point, Oliver approached and curled up on the floor beneath the coffee table, as if listening to their conversation.

"So I know you built your bed," Jake said, peering over at it. "What else up here have you made?"

She looked around. "Um, the kitchen table. Those bookshelves." She pointed. "The coffee table and end tables. And the trunk at the foot of the bed."

"Wow." He sounded truly taken aback and said, "I admire that. Being able to make things that'll last. I envy your skills."

"Thanks," she said after swallowing a sip of wine. "But it's really all I've ever known. I started learning when I was little."

"Maybe after we finish eating, you'll show me some more of your work downstairs."

She nodded, smiled. "Sure."

He lifted a second slice of the pepperoni-and-sausage pizza from the box onto his plate, asking, "Where'd the name Winterberry's come from? I mean, since it's *like* Winters, but different."

"When my dad opened the shop, my mom thought the name Winters sounded too harsh and cold to be appealing. So she came up with Winterberry's to make it feel warmer and more quaint. And my mom loves winterberry, too, which grows in the wild here. We have some in the woods behind the house my mom still lives in."

Jake tilted his head. "I don't know much about plants," he said. "What exactly *is* winterberry?"

"A common version of holly," she explained. "But its leaves fall off the branches in winter, leaving only the red berries. It's a tough plant, thrives through cold spells and stays just as bright and pretty."

He nodded thoughtfully, saying, "It's a nice name."

And she was being reminded that *he* was nice. Just like that night in the bar in the hotel. And that they could talk about other things besides sex and her issues surrounding it.

"So what were you doing in Traverse City?" she asked, curious and trying to be bold by not letting memories of that night stop her from asking.

"I grew up there," he replied between bites of pizza. "My family moved there from Ann Arbor when I was five. And I went to the police academy near there, too. That particular week, I was at an annual reunion with the guys I went to the academy with."

She raised her eyebrows. "All of them?" Not that she knew how many guys attended the police academy each year, but it seemed like it would be a lot.

"Actually, it's only about a dozen guys from the class—we were put in a special program together and we got close. And we've pretty much stayed that way, all this time. Friends come and go, but these are the guys I can call up in the middle of the night from anywhere, and if I need them, they'll be there. And I'd do the same for them."

"What kind of special program?"

"We all showed an aptitude for dealing with high-pressure situations, so we received special training for handling hostage situations. We were called the Hostage Ops Team, H.O.T. for short."

"Wow," she said, duly impressed. But she couldn't resist pointing out, "Although . . . somehow I don't feel they were training you to end up in a place like Turnbridge."

"Nope," he replied. "They were training me for a place more like Detroit, and that's where I've been since I graduated . . . until now."

She blinked. "And what on earth brought you *here*, Officer Lockhart?"

He stopped eating, let out a sigh. "I worked in the inner city. Lot of shootings there. And stabbings. And even the occasional hostage situation."

She tilted her head. "Isn't that your specialty?"

He lowered his gaze, then lifted it back to hers. "Yeah—but it wears on a guy after a while. So I decided to make a change, try someplace quieter—and here I am." He sighed, took a drink of wine. "Though just between me and you, I'm already starting to get a little worried."

Wow. Now *he* was confiding in *her*. Maybe it wasn't the same as sharing your most personal problem, but it still made her feel a little more connected to him. "About?" she asked.

"I felt like I did some good in Detroit, helped people in rough situations who needed it." He paused, shook his head. "Here . . . well, things are even quieter than I thought they'd be. So quiet that I'm not entirely sure I'm even . . . needed."

Carly drew in her breath, let it back out. Then took a sip of wine for courage. Because she couldn't attest to whether the Turnbridge Police Department could really put his skills to the best use, but . . . "Maybe you've already helped somebody here and you don't even know it. Maybe there's more than one way to help someone."

When she shyly lifted her eyes to his, their gazes met, held, and she knew he was reading her loud and clear. Though he softly said, "I . . . can't believe you think I've done anything to help you."

She swallowed, feeling nervous again, but wanting so badly not to be. She wanted to tell him how she felt, regardless of how personal it was, of how sexual. "Last night was . . . *big* for me. Because it was . . . different. From usual. Because I was just me, not anybody else, like you pointed out. And because I didn't freeze up or fall apart. I just . . . *wanted* it. In a way . . . in a way where I couldn't stop. I've never had sex like that before, sex that . . . urgent."

He kept his eyes on her the whole time, listening, watching her, and finally asked, "Then . . . why do you look scared right now?" Plates sat forgotten on their laps, wine abandoned on the table.

"Lots of reasons," she told him. She wasn't thrilled to hear she looked afraid, but she wanted to keep going, keep sharing this bold honesty she was learning to have with him. "Because I don't even know how to go on a date with a guy. Because I don't know how to have sex the normal way. I don't know how to be me and how to be sexual at the same time." *And because I don't know much about caring for a man, either, not since Chuck, but I'm starting to fear I could care about you*—and to mix caring with sex, for her, somehow seemed like the ultimate risk.

Slowly, Jake set his near-empty plate on the coffee table, then reached to set hers aside as well. Then he slid his hand into hers where it rested on her knee, gently caressing her skin with his thumb. His voice came low, seductive. "I can help you figure all that out, honey. It's not so hard, I promise."

"*How* can you help?" she asked, his simple touch sending ripples of sensation up her arm, into her breasts.

"Like this," he told her, leaning nearer.

She caught her breath. And then he kissed her. Gently. Sweetly. Deeply.

In the hotel room, they'd kissed hotly. Last night, they'd kissed urgently. But they'd never before kissed like this.

She kissed him back without thought, instantly intoxicated by him. His mouth was firm yet tender on hers, silently coaxing her to let go of her inhibitions and just follow her instincts. She tried, hard. *Turn off your thoughts. Your fears. Turn off every old feeling. You already know you can be with this man, and he's pretty perfect, so just be with him.*

She raised her palm to his cheek, felt the rough stubble there. Without quite intending to, her lips parted, inviting his tongue into her mouth, and the move saturated her whole body with warmth, especially when a low moan left him, letting her know that . . . mmm, he felt it just as much.

When finally they stopped kissing, their foreheads touched and she absorbed his very nearness, bit her lip, let out a sigh. Then his hand slid softly up her side, stopping at the swell of her breast, and she trembled.

"I want to touch you," he whispered. "Like last night. But slower."

It became difficult to breathe then, both from desire and nervousness. Yet she said, "I want that, too. I want . . . all of you."

Lifting a hand, he gently brushed back her hair and spoke in a rasp. "I'm gonna give you everything you want, Carly. Everything you can take."

She sucked in her breath. She wasn't used to that, being called by her name during sex. But he clearly thought the response was just another heated reaction, and she was glad. She didn't want to do anything to break this spell, this passion growing between them right now.

Especially when he laid her back on the couch and began kissing her again—just kissing, caressing. Lord, it reminded her of a very long time ago, with Chuck. But this was better. Because she wouldn't say no to what was coming; she wouldn't suddenly feel sick and scared and paralyzed by it all. So she kissed him back with sweet abandon, and when their legs intertwined, she let out a soft moan.

They began moving together, the friction thick and delicious as her body lifted against his almost of its own volition. He'd grown hard, and his erection pressed alluringly against her hip as his hands kneaded her waist and then began to ease up under her top.

"Can we take this off?" he whispered.

She managed a nod, working against her very "Carlyness" and trusting him, trusting him to make this so good that she'd forget everything bad that had ever come before it.

"Lift up your arms," he told her, and she did, letting him smoothly remove the tank.

Underneath she wore a pale pink bra—part mesh, part lacy flowers that lined the upper edges of each cup. She knew her nipples were visible through the sheer fabric, and Jake let out a low groan at the sight. Then he met her gaze, lids heavy with lust. "That's so pretty, baby."

She bit her lip, her cheeks filling with heat, and felt a little like Desiree but also a little like herself. "I'm glad you like it."

"I'm in love with it," he murmured, then let his hands curve around her outer breasts before he stroked both thumbs over her taut, beaded nipples.

"Unh," she breathed as the sweet, hot pleasure echoed through her.

And then he lowered his mouth there, kissed the tip of one breast through her thin bra, making her shudder, making the crux of her thighs spasm. She wanted more of him, too, so she pulled at his T-shirt until he rose to strip it briskly off and toss it across the room, the move leaving him sitting up, straddling her hips now.

His chest, his stomach, were perfect—well-muscled yet lean, sprinkled with dark curling hair that narrowed into a line leading down into his blue jeans. And for the first time, she finally got to look at the tattoo on his arm: a badge with the words PROTECT, SERVE, and HONOR on it. She reached up to touch it with one fingertip, and he glanced down at it but said nothing.

Then she pressed both palms flat against his chest, exploring the firmness of his muscles as his hands closed back around her breasts, making her flood her panties with moisture. He squeezed and caressed, teased the stiffened peaks with his fingertips, pressed his erection against her mound, all while she slowly moved her hands downward over his stomach.

Her breath became labored as the heat built inside her. This wasn't so hard. In fact, it was pretty damn easy at the moment. Even being under him, seeing him tower over her—just like when she became Desiree, as long as she felt in control of the situation, it was fine.

She wanted . . . oh God, she wanted to undo the button on his jeans, then the zipper. But she began to feel shy. Carly-shy. Damn it.

But Jake must have sensed her hesitation because that's when he released her breasts and ever so gently took her hands, her fingers, and helped her undo the button, even as she trembled a little. Then the zipper, too.

And after that, he rose up, scooted back a little, and undid *her* jeans, the slide of her own zipper making her shiver. "Lift up," he whispered, so she did, letting him tug the denim down to reveal yellow bikini panties dotted with pink flowers, a rim of pink lace edging the top. He released a hot sigh and ran one fingertip lightly along the lace border. "So fucking pretty," he murmured, and the words moved all through her like warm liquid.

Fuck me. If she were in Traverse City and he were a stranger, she would say it right now, demand it. It's what she wanted, and those were the words that came to mind.

But it was still hard to reconcile that part of her with the woman everyone knew, so she simply sucked in her breath as she let Jake remove her jeans completely—and then he stood up next to the couch in order to push his down as well. Underneath, he wore gray boxer briefs that clung pleasantly to his thighs, and to the sturdy bulge in front.

"Take those off, too," she told him, the words coming out unplanned. Easier than *fuck me*, she supposed, but still bold for Carly Winters.

"All right," he said smoothly, then pushed them down.

When her eyes dropped to his erection, her heartbeat kicked up. Need lurched within her, hunger coming out. *Fuck me. Feed it to me. Fuck my tits.* These were things she might say if she was having sex with a stranger in Traverse City. And for some reason, she still couldn't say those things any other way. Even with a man she'd already said them to once before. So she just bit her lip and ached wildly inside for his hard, lovely cock, her whole body craving it, craving more of him.

But that's when he dropped to his knees and bent over the couch to lower a kiss right between her legs. "Oh God," she whispered, taken aback, and her focus shifted from his body to hers.

"I want to kiss this sweet pussy," he murmured against it, making her shudder for more reasons than one. Excitement. And . . . and . . . Lord, why should that word shock her? She'd heard it, said it herself, during sex, dozens of times. And yet it caught her off guard, made her clench her teeth lightly. Carly didn't *do* dirty. That was Desiree's department—and Desiree wasn't here. And so she didn't reply, but she still refused to let old, backward responses make her freeze up, inside or out.

When Jake tugged at her panties, she lifted, let him pull them down. Like always when she knew she was going to have sex, she'd shaved herself there, but she almost felt a little embarrassed now by the rawness of it, by how very on display it put her.

As if reading her mind, Jake rasped, "I love that you're so bare here. Excites the hell out of me."

And apparently *that* excited the hell out of *her* since the very spot he spoke of tingled at his words. And did so even more when he gently grazed the soft, pale flesh there with his fingertips.

Finally, he parted her legs—and she let him. He gazed down on her open slit, just as he had on the night they'd met. Things had ended up seeming weirdly intimate with him that night—but *this*, *this* was intimate. *Sharing yourself with a man you know is so much more powerful than sharing yourself with a stranger.*

When he began to stroke his fingers down through her pink folds, she let out a whimper. And when he smoothly slid his fingers inside her, a short cry escaped her throat. Shock. Pleasure. Welcome invasion.

As he lowered his mouth to the juncture of her thighs, she bit her lip, shut her eyes, sank into the blinding lust of it all. *Yes, yes,* it felt so good! He thrust those fingers firmly into her wetness, over and over, as he licked the swollen nub above. Throaty cries escaped her—at some point, without thought, she lifted one leg, balancing her ankle on the back of the sofa, giving him even easier access. And she began to absently clutch at her own breasts—as Desiree would, because they needed some attention, too, and because she knew it turned guys on.

Even when she realized it, she didn't stop—she squeezed them in her hands, tenderly pinched her nipples. She wondered if he was watching, if he liked it. And that gave her the courage to finally open her eyes.

Jake *wasn't* watching her—at the moment, his eyes were closed and he looked completely entranced and hot as hell. She soon found herself reaching down with both hands, running her fingers through his thick hair, and almost pulling him closer, pressing his face into her wet crotch. She looked at herself—sprawled there in the light of her apartment, with her sexy pink bra lifting her breasts high and her flowered panties strewn on the coffee table—and she realized: This particular lingerie, in this particular place, was so not Desiree. And it *was* so truly her. This was *her*, Carly, having her pussy eaten by a man, getting into it completely, being open and excited and naughty—and it was good.

I can do this. I am *doing this.* A burst of elation rushed through her. And the awareness, the acceptance, came with a fresh surge of arousal that made his every lick hotter, made every sensation stretch more wildly through her body. "Oh God," she heard herself murmur as the pleasure rose. "Oh . . ." And then it reached that peak, that point of no return, when she knew orgasm was imminent, just a few heartbeats away, and she clenched her teeth, made fists in Jake's hair—and tumbled into the hot abyss of ecstasy, moaning, sobbing, and then biting her lip, trying to quiet herself, vaguely aware that anyone passing by on the street outside might hear through the open window.

But she didn't let that part worry her much—she was too in the moment, and too into Jake Lockhart and the glorious pleasure he'd just brought washing over her. And she wasn't pretending to be anyone else.

Her eyes had fallen shut again at some climactic point, and when she opened them she was almost a little embarrassed to find herself still spread for him, his face wet with her juices as he looked up at her. But then he cast her a sexy grin, eyes shaded with masculine pride as he asked, "How was that, honey?"

"Good," she breathed. Which seemed like an understatement given what she'd just experienced, but she was weak, and she had a feeling the expression on her face told him everything she couldn't right now. *You're changing me. Changing what I'm capable of. How I can see myself. You're making it all better.*

Slowly, Jake pushed to his feet, his look edging from pride back into hunger as he let his hand drift to his erection, stroking it lightly in a way that excited her to the very tips of her fingers and toes. And then he leaned near, his cock still in hand, and his voice came in a low rasp as he asked, "Can I put it in your mouth, baby?"

Chapter 9

Carly drew a gulp of air into her lungs. She wanted to just say yes. God knew she wanted to suck him, pleasure him. She wanted to be the same bold girl who'd just come for him so hard. But for some reason she hesitated—and just as quickly realized that maybe it was the position. She was lying down. And it would give him so much power—and her so little. If it had been her suggestion, it would have felt different, but she knew that somehow it would be easier if . . . "Um, let me . . ." *Let me what?* She sat upright, then instructed him, "Lie down."

He didn't argue and, in fact, seemed totally cool with that, simply lying back at the opposite end of the couch from her. She watched him, admiring his cock, so big and upright, and almost immediately, her breasts began to ache and her pussy to yearn.

Positioning herself on her hands and knees between his legs, she reached out, wrapped her fist around his erection, then lowered her lips over it. And . . . mmm, just like the night they'd met, having him in her mouth fulfilled her in a way going down on a guy never had before. At the time, she'd thought it had to do with having both him and Colt inside her at the same time, but now she was forced to realize this went deeper. Maybe it was just the strong chemistry between them—who knew?—but whatever the case, she felt just as hungry for it now, just as satisfied to have that part of him in her mouth, just as satisfied to take him as deeply as she could and to know how much enjoyment it brought him.

"Aw, aw . . . baby, yeah," he murmured. "That's so damn good. So damn good."

His deep voice fueled her, his delight creating still more of it for *her*.

"Aw, honey—look up at me while you do that. Let me look in your eyes."

She'd done that in Traverse City, too—she'd even taken dirty delight in imagining how obscene she appeared to him. Now she responded, meeting his gaze as he filled her mouth, but it was so raw—hot, but *too* raw—that she looked back down again, even closed her eyes again.

Above, Jake just groaned his pleasure and told her she was beautiful, and within a few seconds, she'd forgotten how brazen it had felt to peer up at him that way and she refocused on her own pleasure, at how primed her body felt as she delivered her hot, generous ministrations, at how strangely pleasing it was to work over him this way, to feel that hardest part of him within her soft lips and the tender confines of her mouth. It all made her suck him more vigorously—it made her want more of him in every way.

So when finally her mouth tired, she released him but instantly lowered her breasts over that magnificent erection. She still wore her bra, but the plump inner curves arced from the tight fabric to blanket him, wrapping softly around his hard length.

"Oh God, that's so hot, honey," Jake growled. "God, yeah—fuck me with those gorgeous tits."

And though the briefest hint of a familiar revulsion swirled to life inside her, mostly his dirty talk heightened her pleasure, made her feel alive and desirable and excited. And then he sat up a little, just enough to strain, to reach over her back and unhook her bra until it fell away, off her shoulders, off her breasts, making her feel all the more intimate with him given what they were doing right now. She hugged the soft mounds of flesh around his cock as he slid it between them, all the while telling her she was beautiful and amazing.

Having at last lost most of her inhibitions, she followed the urge to lean over and lick the tip of his erection again, even as it lay nestled between her tits—she licked the pre-come away looking into his eyes; she ran her lips around the head as he whispered still more hot words of encouragement. Again, pleasure had overcome those old bad feelings, and again she was getting a wonderfully naughty taste of the woman she could really be. With Jake anyway.

Finally, her lover rasped, "I want inside you now. I want to fuck you. Let me have you, Carly."

And like before, it stunned her a bit to be called Carly—but not as much as it had the first time. And she moved quickly past it because she was ready for this, so ready for it, all of it.

They both sat up then, Carly on her knees, Jake with his legs still parted around her. Pulling her to him until they'd resituated and she straddled his thighs, he asked, "Do you want me to wear a condom?"

She let out a soft breath. Then whispered, "No. I mean, since we've determined that we're both . . . you know. And because . . ." *Say it. Just say what you mean.* "I want to feel you, really *feel* you. With nothing in between us."

He nodded shortly, looking almost weakened with passion. "I want that, too, baby."

Glancing down at his cock, she felt frantic to have it inside her, and so she lifted, took his erection in her hand, balanced herself on the tip.

"Slow," he told her. She wasn't sure why—maybe he sensed how hungry she was for him. And frankly, going slow was the last thing on her mind right now—since they'd already *gone* slow and now she was ready for fast. So she simply remained still, not quite sure how to react.

That was when he put his hands on her hips and ever-so-gradually impaled her on that rigid shaft.

"Ohhhh." The word came deeply, from her gut, with the prolonged entry that resonated to her very core. She bit her lip, feeling somehow more full with him than ever before.

And then he began to move, to set a pace for them, and just as he'd promised, it was slow, lingering, a rhythm that forced her to feel every inch of every stroke, every inch of every protracted slide of his thick cock against her slick inner walls.

Her very breathing slowed in response—but came labored and shaky, too. She looked into his eyes naturally as they moved together—suddenly, now, it didn't occur to her to look anywhere else. His gaze drifted to her lips, sometimes to her breasts, but it always came back to her face, and when his amazingly slow thrusts reached their deepest point, that was when the pleasure was deepest, too—that was when low moans erupted from her throat.

They moved that way for a long while, no words between them—no words *necessary*—until finally she whispered, "I've never . . . had sex . . . like this before."

Like hers, his breath was audible, filling the space between their words. "Like what?"

"So . . . slow."

Still they maintained that tempo. His hands gripped her hips so that it wasn't quite the same as her riding him—he was fucking her, sliding all the way in and all the way back out at a pace he set, orchestrated. His breath still came heavy. "Do you like it?"

She nodded, but felt as if all the blood had drained from her face due to the depths he was reaching inside her, due to the utter intensity of it all. When she spoke, her voice was as breathy as before. "I . . . like it . . . the other ways, too . . . but this is . . . pretty amazing."

"I know."

Somehow her pleasure was intensifying—not in her clit, but deep within her. "I feel . . . every inch of you. I mean . . . really feel it. Deep. Sliding."

"I feel . . . every inch of you, too. So tight on me. So fucking wet. So fucking perfect."

"Fuck me," she whispered, peering needfully into his eyes, trembling with the reality that she could really do this, really say these things.

"Oh baby, I am . . . I am. I'm fucking you so deep . . . filling you up so much."

"Yes," she breathed. That was all. Just yes.

"Lean back," he told her. "Just a little."

She didn't know why he requested that, but she did so without question, holding on to his shoulders, and he further instructed, "Try to . . . tilt your pelvis. Try to . . . flatten it a little, as if you were . . . flattening it against my thighs."

Again, she didn't question him, even if what he asked took more thought than she was in the mood for right now. She tried to do what he'd said, tilting, situating her ass against him in such a way that her lower abdomen lay more flat than upright, putting more actual space between their torsos.

And then he pressed one palm firmly against her there, on her belly, just above where their bodies met, and she asked, "What are you—?"

"Shhh. Shhh—just feel it."

She quieted. And . . . felt it. Oh. Ohhhh.

She began to understand as the strange pleasure filled her. It was familiar but new, a deepening of the sensation a woman got when a man was inside her. And she remembered then that he'd touched her this way back in Traverse City, too, but only his fingers had been inside her then. That had felt good, different, powerful—but this was . . . more. She met his gaze as the strange, engulfing pleasure spread inside her. What . . . ? What was . . . ? But she couldn't even form questions. She just bit her lip and began to moan.

Her head dropped back. And the sensation spread outward—almost infinitely, she thought. It seemed so simple, and yet she'd never experienced anything like it before. Wild sex, hard sex, fast sex—she'd had all of that and loved it, but now, this agonizingly slow, simple sex was taking her to unforeseen heights of pleasure that echoed through her whole body.

Soon her moans turned to low sobs. Thought left her completely. All that existed was sensation and response. It was as if her body had been electrified from the inside out. Like the similar touches on the night they'd met, this wasn't orgasmic exactly—it wasn't going to make her come—yet it was a deep, permeating pleasure buffeting her entire body, making her feel as if her whole being was getting thoroughly, deeply fucked.

"Oh God. Oh God, more," she heard herself whimper, beg. "I—I can't take it anymore. Please fuck me harder, faster! Please!"

A quick groan left Jake's throat before he responded by driving up into her harder, just like she'd asked. She cried out and he did it again, again—and then he finally wrapped his arms around her and moved to lay her down on her back and begin plunging into her in earnest. He kissed her mouth hard and her arms twined around his neck. She felt him everywhere—in her, on top of her, around her, and soon her legs circled his waist, too.

They fucked that way for a few long, blissful minutes when Carly knew nothing but the sense of connection with him, the sense of him moving in and out of her, taking the inexplicable pleasure of a few minutes before and turning it hotter, harder, into something familiar she could grab on to. Until finally he went still—tired, she supposed—and lay atop her, lowering a few kisses to her neck. His breath warmed her skin there. She turned to face him so that his kisses found her mouth again, and they were slow, sweet— sometimes his lips simply lingered over hers, barely touching, yet she felt it tingling all the way down her spine.

When finally he pulled out of her, raising back up onto his knees, she let out a gasp at suddenly being empty, unhappy, and peered up at him in shock.

"Relax, we're not done," he told her, then reached for her hands to pull her up as well. "Turn over, on your knees."

And like in Traverse City and again last night, she didn't mind. Surrendering to him a little. After all, when she thought about it, she'd surrendered to him *a lot*—and nothing but pure pleasure had resulted.

So she faced the rear of the couch on her knees where he positioned her, resting her elbows on the back—then realized he was standing up behind her, on the floor. "Arch your ass," he told her—and he smacked it once, the sensation echoing all through her—then grasped firmly onto her hips and slid his hard cock back inside.

They both let out low sounds of pleasure—and then he began to pound into her, hard. She curled her hands around the top of the backrest, holding on, crying out at each deep drive he delivered. *Yes, yes.*

And then she realized she was . . . peering out the window behind the couch, on the side of her building that faced Maple. She was looking west up Main Street, past Beth Anne's and the drugstore, beyond Schubert's, and into a golden pink sunset. Dusk was falling over another summer night in Turnbridge, and she was in the apartment above her shop having her brains fucked out by the hot new cop in town, and anyone who happened to be out and glanced up just then might well see her illuminated in the window—and she didn't care. Not enough to stop anyway. Not enough to stop soaking in the hard delight he sent reverberating through her body over and over again. She still cried out with each powerful stroke, and like so many times with Jake already, the pleasure held more power than her fear.

And then he leaned in closer—the front of his muscular male body warming her ass, her back. And his hand snaked around her hip and between her thighs and—*oh God*. It was the cherry on top of the deliciously sweet and gooey ice cream, and just what she needed—to come again. It happened in only a few short moments—she was biting her lower lip, sobbing and moaning, finally saying, "Now, now, now!" as the second orgasm exploded through her, fiery hot, rocking her whole body, causing her to pitch and jerk forward.

"Aw fuck—me, too," he groaned, and then pounded into her harder,

harder, practically taking her knees out from under her—but now his arms were both anchored around her waist to keep her where he wanted her.

After his final, long, well-pleasured sigh, they collapsed onto the couch together, Carly on her back, Jake alongside her, half on top of her.

They stayed quiet, resting, until she said, "What the hell *was* that?"

"That?" he asked. "*That* was a really good fuck—something I'd think you'd recognize by now."

"No, the first part," she explained.

And Jake tipped his head back slightly in understanding. "Oh, *that*. I think it was your G-spot."

"Oh," she said, still a little amazed as she thought it over. "But . . . I thought if you found your G-spot you came—from the inside, I mean, like in some different way than usual. I didn't come until . . ."

"Some women come from it, some don't," he said. "But either way, most love it."

She slanted a glance up at him. "And you know this from . . . ?"

"Experience," he said simply.

So confidently that she raised her eyebrows at him.

"What?" he asked. "It's just something I discovered on accident once, and so I've . . . kept it in my repertoire."

And she laughed out loud.

He smiled. "*What?*"

"You have a repertoire," she repeated, amused by the thought.

"We *all* have repertoires."

"Not me."

"Of course you do. Or Desiree does anyway."

And when she started to protest, Jake interrupted to say, "Don't tell me she doesn't. You have certain things you do, things that work for you, and other things you know guys like."

Carly sighed, then admitted, "Okay, true. I just never thought about it before, I guess. Or maybe I just find it funny to think of it as a repertoire."

He lowered his chin, his look pointed. "You oughta be *thankful* I've developed a repertoire."

She offered up a small, honest smile. "I am. It's got some good stuff in it."

"So does yours. Carly." The words seemed designed to remind her that she and Desiree were the same person deep inside, whether she liked it or not.

And . . . maybe it was time she got that through her head, quit the silly game of separating them so much in her mind. It was time she faced the simple truth about that, even if it was still hard for her to accept.

"What do you like in my repertoire?" she decided to ask him. If they were discussing repertoires, after all, why not?

Propped up more on his side next to her now, he absently ran his fingertips over her stomach. "Tonight? Or the night we met?"

Don't shy away from this. You are *her. Quit running from that.* "Anytime."

"I love when you fuck me with your tits," he told her without hesitation. "And when you massage them—that's hot. And you know how good you suck my cock. And . . . I nearly lost it when you told Colt to come on you."

It was the first time they'd discussed that night in any truly frank, honest terms since he'd discovered how sensitive she was about it.

"That last one isn't really part of my repertoire," she admitted, thinking back.

"No?"

"It was the first time for that—an impulse. Because I . . ."

"You what?"

She swallowed, sorry she'd stopped. So she reminded herself how easy he was to talk to—maybe because he was so honest himself—and explained. "Remember I told you last night that I'd always used a condom before?"

He nodded.

"So I just . . . haven't had many dealings with, um, semen. I've never, um, let anyone finish . . . you know, in my mouth. And once, a guy wanted to do what Colt did . . . come on me"—she realized she was blushing, but ignored it and moved on—"and I didn't like it much. It wasn't a very satisfying end for me. But that night in the hotel . . . I was curious about it, how it would feel under different circumstances."

He looked down at her. "And how did it feel?"

"I liked it better. Because you were still inside me, so it wasn't over. That made it pretty . . . hot."

"Damn straight it did. Like I said, I nearly came, too." He bent to lower a soft kiss high on her breast and leaned close to her face to say, "Honey, if you're curious about semen, I can, uh, help you out with that. It's in you right now, you know."

She gasped lightly. "I'd forgotten." She really had—she just wasn't used to it. She'd been aware right after he'd come, but since lying back on the couch with him, it had slipped her mind.

She said nothing when he got to his feet, walking around the coffee table, and returned a minute later with his T-shirt in hand. Kneeling next to her, he touched her hip and said, "Lift," and then slid the shirt under her on the couch. "I don't want to make a mess," he told her with a grin. And for all she knew, *she'd* already made a mess, but she'd deal with that later.

Next, he dipped his middle finger deftly between her legs, stroking her there, making her sigh—then coming up with wet fingers, definitely more wetness than she emitted on her own. He dabbed it on one of her still-taut nipples, then rubbed it slowly in while they both watched. She sucked in her breath, bit her lip. And for some reason liked the idea of having him leave part of himself behind. The emotion came from somewhere deep inside, somewhere primal that she couldn't quite understand.

He stroked between her thighs once more, again coming up with a wet, whitish substance—and this time, he held his finger to her mouth.

Like before, she drew in her breath—but then she parted her lips, slowly let the tip of her tongue come out. He brought his finger closer still—until she licked the tip. The taste was somehow sweet yet earthy.

"How is it?" he asked.

She bit her lip. "Sweet, kind of." Then she smiled. "Like you."

"Knock it off," he told her teasingly, and she realized maybe a cop didn't want to be sweet. But he was. Sometimes demanding, sometimes pushy as hell. But at his core, he was clearly a good man.

The intimacies they'd shared tonight felt . . . almost impossible to her. Two days ago, after all, she'd wanted nothing to do with him. And now, well . . . thank God he'd come into her life. Because he was making it so much better. He was helping her blend Desiree into the rest of her, something that had felt hopeless until now. She felt so . . . normal tonight. Like a normal woman having normal sex with a guy.

Only—wait, no, that wasn't really true. Because the fact was—there was nothing normal about the sex she'd had tonight. It was . . . mind-blowing. Beyond incredible. And profoundly intimate.

"I have to work in the morning—I should go," he said then. And she was immediately disappointed, but she understood. And she wasn't sure she was ready for a sleepover just yet. She'd come a long distance in a short time, but she couldn't do it all at once. So as he found his underwear and put it on, she just nodded quietly.

"Doing anything Friday night?" he asked.

She shook her head against the couch pillow.

"Want to get together?"

Another silent nod.

"Dare I suggest we eat in a restaurant or will that totally freak you out?"

His exaggerated sarcasm made her grin. "Quit acting like I'm weird."

He grinned back. "You *are* weird. But I like you anyway."

She lowered her chin as if challenged, but continued smiling, and said, "Fine. Pick me up at seven and we'll go out."

Chapter 10

Jake sat eating a turkey melt for lunch at Schubert's bar on Thursday with Tommy, when his friend swiped a napkin across his mouth and said, "So you never told me how your date was the other night."

Jake gave him a sideways look, lowering his sandwich to his plate. "I'm surprised you managed to go this long without asking."

Tommy ignored the sarcasm and flashed a grin. "Well?"

"It was good," Jake answered casually, then crunched down on a potato chip.

"That's all you're gonna tell me?"

"Yep," Jake said. "Hate to break it to ya, but I'm not sixteen."

Tommy made a face at the remark but remained undaunted. "So is it like I told you? Is she . . . ?"

Jake lowered his voice as he turned to Tommy. "Is she frigid? No." Not that he really wanted to talk about Carly's sex life with anyone, but he thought it was high time to put that particular rumor to rest.

Tom sat up a little straighter, his eyes registering his surprise. "Really? How *is* she?"

"She's normal," Jake said. And that wasn't strictly true, but that was none of Tommy's business. "She's a normal woman. So let it go already."

"Fine, whatever you say," Tommy agreed—then resumed eating his burger and fries for a minute until he suggested good-naturedly, "Maybe whenever you take me up on that lasagna offer, you can bring her. We'll make a night of it, play some cards after dinner or something."

Jake appreciated the change in Tom's tone. "That sounds good," he replied. And it did. Not exactly as exciting as his *last* two nights with Carly—but life wasn't always about sex and excitement. Jake believed a healthy balance in all things kept a person happy. Some nights it was wild G-spot sex, other nights it was gin rummy—and that was okay.

Since his two nights with Carly, he'd thought about her a lot. Not only the good parts, but the parts he couldn't just gloss over in his head—the whole Desiree masquerade. He hadn't wanted to pry any more than he already had—he just wanted to enjoy seeing her transform, enjoy helping in the process. He didn't want to become her self-appointed psychiatrist. And yet . . . what had happened? Because *something* had. You just didn't get that hung up about sex if everything had been right in your life.

Still, maybe I should let it go. Maybe I know too much. As a cop, there had been plenty of times when it had actually been beneficial that he could sometimes recognize such problems in people, when it had allowed him to assist someone in getting the help they needed. But maybe in everyday life it was a curse to realize, to know, something bad had to have happened to Carly. Maybe something she didn't even remember. *Maybe it's just enough to know you're helping her overcome it.* He hoped he was anyway.

Just then, as he heard the front door open behind him, Frank Schubert looked up with a smile. "Hi, Carly."

Jake turned to see her hair pulled back in a low ponytail, and she wore a Michigan Wolverines baseball cap, a simple yellow gold tank, and jeans. But she might as well have been in that pink bra and those flowered panties from the other night—because just the sight of her warmed him, and made him start getting hard, too. He was glad to be sitting down.

And as they exchanged smiles, he began to wonder exactly what kind of panties she *did* have on. Because, okay, sometimes it *was* all about sex and excitement. So far, her underwear had ranged from hot and classy to cute and sexy, and it kept him curious about what was hiding under her simple clothes. And feeling rather privileged to know the sides of Carly no one else did.

After she said hello to Tom and paid Frank for her lunch, Jake said, "Why don't you grab a bar stool—eat here with me." And it had nothing to do with pushing her out of her comfort zone—he was simply glad to see her.

"All right," she said quietly, even if she looked a little uneasy about sliding up onto the leather-covered stool beside him.

Across the bar, Frank looked surprised and said, "Guess it's true."

"Guess what's true?" Jake asked, reaching down for another chip.

"Heard you bought her pie. I missed the auction this year, but everybody in town was talkin' about it."

At this, Carly simply raised her eyebrows at Jake as if to say, *See?*

But he only replied with a shrug, as if to say, *So what?* "Yeah, I bought her pie."

"Heard you paid thirty-five dollars," Frank went on. "That's outrageous."

To which Jake only grinned. "Kind of, yeah."

"So was it worth it?" Frank asked.

"Every penny," Jake told him, then gave her thigh a quick squeeze under the bar.

"Well, I think it's nice," Frank said. "'Bout time our Carly kicked up her heels a little."

And this time it was *Jake* who raises his eyebrows at *her*. *See?*

"Well, enjoy your lunch," Frank told them, wiping his hand on a towel. "Bon appétit—or whatever it is they say."

Turnbridge wasn't exactly a mecca of fine dining, but the Grizzly Grill, just a block east of Winterberry's on Main, served good home-cooked meals, boasted a dark, warm décor, and offered tall, somewhat secluded booths. Not that that kept anyone from finding Carly and Jake on their Friday night date. One key thing Carly had forgotten was that anyone going out to dinner in Turnbridge on the weekend was likely to show up at the Grizzly.

They had just ordered their food when Dana and Hank spotted them and came over to say hello. "Introduce us," Dana insisted with a big smile, so Carly did.

"Nice to meet you," Jake said, coming off as perfect as he had the very first time Carly had seen him. No, even *more* perfect. Because this wasn't a man after only sex. This was a man who wanted to spend time with her. This was a man who respected her in spite of everything he knew about her. There was no denying it: This man went *way* beyond perfect.

After small talk about Dana's impending baby arrival and how Jake liked their little town, the other couple departed, but not before Dana gave Carly a big wink that both annoyed and embarrassed her in front of Jake. And by the time their food arrived, they'd seen Tiffany and her parents, Frank Schubert's wife, and a handful of other Turnbridge residents who had known Carly her whole life and were clearly amazed to see her out on an actual date with a man.

"This is exactly why I wasn't too wild about going out on the town together," she told him across the table, voice low.

"To avoid having people see you commit the horrible act of eating with someone?" he asked teasingly.

"To avoid being the talk of the town," she corrected him. "Since, as you can see, people seem inordinately interested in who I'm out with."

He just gave his usual shrug. "It's because I'm new here. And because they care about you."

"And because I'm the girl who never goes out on a date."

From Jake, yet another shrug. "And now you do." Then he pointed to her plate and changed the subject. "How's your meat loaf?"

"Just as good as I told you it was. Here, try a bite. You're gonna regret not getting it." She cut a chunk off with her fork and held it across the table for him to sample.

After she eased the fork into his mouth, his expression transformed into one of pure pleasure—and then he admitted, "My God—this is the best meat loaf in the freaking universe."

"Told ya."

"We might have to trade," he suggested, looking down at their plates. "I mean, the pork chops are good, but . . . damn."

"Nope, no way—I *told* you to get the meat loaf. Maybe next time you'll listen," she scolded playfully.

And it was that easy.

To be with him. On a date.

And yeah, maybe everyone she knew *was* talking about it, but she was beginning to see—with Jake's help—that it was really no big deal. Maybe it was even a *good* thing. She'd just never felt so darn . . . normal before, so she wasn't used to it. But it was nice.

"Dessert?" he asked when they were done.

"No," she said quickly.

His eyes widened. "*That* was decisive."

"And you're not having any, either."

He gave his head a derisive tilt. "Wait a minute here."

"Trust me," she told him quietly. "Don't have any dessert and I'll make it worth your while."

At this, Jake flashed a lascivious look. "Okay, with talk like that, you're starting to sway me a little more. In fact, now that you mention it, I think I'm ready for the check."

"All right, honey, make it worth my while," Jake said once they'd gotten back to her place, and he didn't bother trying to hide his lecherous intent. He liked her a lot, but he also liked *fucking* her a lot, and by the time they'd chatted with a few more people on the way out, paid the bill, and walked back up the street to her place, he had a hard-on the size of Detroit's Renaissance Center—or that's what it felt like anyway.

So as soon as they reached the top of the stairs, passing by the big, quietly sleeping cat at the top, he playfully pushed her back onto the bed and pinned her there, one eyebrow arched as he waited to see what she had in mind for him.

That's when she bit her lip and let out a little laugh.

"What's funny?" he asked.

"I, uh, may have given you the wrong idea when I said I would make it worth your while."

Now *both* his eyebrows shot up and he flashed an accusing look. "Is that so?"

"Let me up," she told him, "then close your eyes."

Jake rolled to his back on the bed, thinking her cute as hell despite how eager his penis was to get down to business. He supposed they'd get to sex soon enough. "This better be good," he teased, eyes shut.

A moment later, the mattress shifted as she rejoined him there, and she said, "Okay, you can open 'em and see your surprise."

She sat cross-legged beside him, holding a fluffy-looking meringue-topped pie—she'd also brought over two small plates, some forks, and a knife.

He sat up and smiled. "Chocolate cream, I presume."

And she nodded. "You seemed to like the last one so much that I thought you deserved another one—for free this time. As a . . . thank-you."

"For what?" he asked, leaning a little closer—although maybe he already knew.

She met his gaze and said, "Being patient. And not thinking I'm the freak from hell."

He shrugged. "Well, I was probably more demanding than patient, but . . ."

"Whatever," she told him, giving her head a quick, happy shake. "Either way, you've made me feel pretty damn normal the last few days. And that's kind of monumental for me. So I made you a pie."

As he leaned in to give her a kiss, saying, "I can't wait to dig in," he realized that, more and more, he was seeing in her what the people of Turnbridge saw. She really *was* a sweetheart—nothing in that was any sort of an act. She was just a sweetheart with a really naughty side she'd never been able to let out, and to his way of thinking, it was the best of both worlds. It still nagged at him a little to wonder why, to wonder what had kept that hot, sexual side of her caged up for so long—but he told himself again that it wasn't his place to worry. Maybe his only duty here was to keep enjoying setting her free.

Almost as if reading his mind, she bit her lip, cast a sheepish smile, and said, "Sexy lingerie and some Desiree-style seduction probably would have been better, huh? See? If I don't become someone else, I have no idea what I'm doing."

Jake started cutting the pie as he formed a response. "Lingerie and seduction are nice. But so is pie. I'm a fan of both. And either way, I'm gonna have you naked soon enough, so we can start with dessert." He concluded with a wicked grin, still feeling his hard-on, but at the same time also looking forward to the pie. And as they sat on the bed eating, he was reminded that the pie committee didn't give her those blue ribbons for nothin'—it was good stuff. "Damn, this is almost *as good as* sex," he told her on a low chuckle.

She laughed in reply and said, "I wouldn't go *that* far, Officer Lockhart."

"Well, it might be a close second," he conceded. Then pondered further, saying, "Put the two together and it would be heaven on earth."

After which he looked at her, watching as she forked a bite of the fluffy, creamy pie into her mouth—the same sweet, soft mouth that worked such miracles on his cock—and . . . shit, that was all it took.

He didn't know why, but something about the simple act of watching her eat suddenly made him crazy for her. Crazy in a way that wouldn't wait for pie anymore. Maybe his erection was through being ignored. But whatever the case, she was wrong about him being patient—when it came to her, he was the most *im*patient man alive.

So he picked up the pie and set it on the bedside table, along with his empty plate. Then he took her plate and fork from her hands without a word of explanation, setting them aside, too.

"What are you doing?" she asked, wide-eyed.

"I've had my dessert," he told her. "Now I'm having *you*."

When he pinned her to the bed this time, it was much more passionate than playful. But when his first deep kiss elicited a moan from the girl beneath him, he knew she was into it, too. Thank God. As he sank onto her body, melding his harder, muscular parts with all her softer, curvier ones, it was like descending into bliss. As his hands found her breasts, she let out a heated sigh, and there was a part of him that simply wanted to mold and caress those two alluring mounds all night—but the bigger part of him was the impatient part, the part between his legs that wanted to get her clothes off.

So he wasted no time stripping off her fitted pink top over her head, then removing the cute capri pants below, finding more scintillating undies underneath. Tonight a lacy lavender bra hugged her round breasts and her panties were transparent lavender mesh sporting little pale green bows at each hip. One glance at them nearly made his cock lurch from his pants.

A lot of guys he knew couldn't care less about lingerie, but Jake appreciated "the wrapping," as he thought of it. Not to mention the anticipation it built. Yet since he'd already had enough anticipation tonight, he peeled those pretty panties right off, following with the bra to leave her completely bare.

As always, the sight of her breasts elicited a low groan from his throat, and he framed them with his hands. "Will you slap me if I say you have spectacular tits?"

She gave her head a quick shake, her eyes heavy-lidded, lips parted. Thank God. They'd come a damn long way since last weekend when it had cost him thirty-five dollars just to talk to her.

"Good," he murmured, caught up in studying her rosy nipples, beautifully stiff and ready to be sucked. "Because they *are. Fucking spectacular.*" And then he lowered his mouth and feasted on her.

He loved her hot sighs, the feel of her fingers in his hair, her nails making his scalp tingle as he licked and suckled one sumptuous peak before moving on to the other. Damn, he could get lost in this. And yeah, his dick ached for her, but suddenly he realized he didn't want to rush now that they were in the thick of the passion. Getting her naked was helping to restore his patience, making him want to take his time enjoying every inch of her pretty body. And that's what prompted him to say, "I can only think of one thing that would make these beautiful nipples any tastier."

"Um . . . what?" she asked in a breathy whisper.

"This," he said—then he reached over and indelicately jabbed two fingers into the remaining pie, scooping out both pudding and meringue, and smeared it across the peak of one sumptuous tit.

She sucked in her breath at the sensation, eyes wide at what he'd done.

Then he unceremoniously licked and sucked all the pie away, letting out a deep "Mmm" of satisfaction as he worked.

When he met her gaze, her wet, now-sticky breast between them, her breath trembled.

"Like I said," he told her, "heaven on earth."

She said nothing, but she didn't have to—her eyes, dark and impassioned, told him how hot she thought it was. So he said, "Lift up and let me pull down the covers. I don't want to get your quilt messy."

"Okay," she whispered, helping him get the quilt and top sheet down, and apparently not caring much about the sheet beneath her or she'd have said so. Good to learn a little kinkiness was more important even to good girl Carly Winters than getting chocolate on her sheet.

They used their feet to shove the covers completely off the end of the bed while Jake hurriedly shed his clothes at the same time—then he reached for another glob of pie, this one bigger than the first. Smearing it on both her lovely breasts, this time he used the fingertips of both hands to rub it in circles, to make sure she felt the gooey stickiness from her erect nipples outward, and because it felt good to him, too—so slick on top, so soft underneath.

Soon enough, he bent to lick and suckle the chocolate and meringue away once more, the sweet taste only adding to the lush delights of swirling his tongue around her nipple, then taking as much of her breast into his mouth as he could. His face was getting sticky from the pie, but he didn't care, and when he'd almost licked her chocolaty tits dry, he ran his index finger through one remaining glob of chocolate and held it to her mouth—just like he'd done the first time they'd eaten pie together, but oh so different.

She parted her lips, took his finger inside. Sucked it dry. Then moved to sit up and reach for the pie herself, coming back with chocolate-covered fingertips.

He'd risen to his knees, straddling her thighs, so when she sat back up, she was face-to-face with his hard cock. Below him, she bit her lip, looking just slightly shy, and God, it turned him on even more—maybe because she was so very "sweetheart Carly" in that moment, but he also knew what was coming, and that it would come from the *other* side of Carly, a side he equally appreciated.

She wiped the messy pie onto the head of his dick, then used her finger-tips to spread it around, and down onto the shaft. He sucked in his breath at the messy pleasure, and when she took his pie-slathered erection in hand and peered demurely up at him, his stomach contracted.

She licked her way up his length, to the very tip, where she swirled away the pudding and nearly made him lose his mind, the sight and sensation wrenching a groan from his gut. And when she sank her whole mouth over him, he had to shut his eyes, lean his head back. She slid her lips up and down, up and down, making him wetter and wetter, sucking the chocolate-and-meringue mixture away until he began to feel crazed with the pleasure. "Aw baby, that's so good, so fucking good," he murmured.

After a minute, she scooped up more pie and this time simply used her fist to put it on him, working his cock in a slow, heated massage as the pud-ding oozed between her fingers. And then his dick was between those slick, sumptuous breasts, sliding wetly, hotly—she used her hands to press the soft flesh around his rigid shaft. And they moved that way together, in perfect, torrid rhythm, until—aw, Jesus—she resumed sucking him again. Yes. God, yes. Ah, damn, she was masterful at this—and when she looked up at him, his hard cock filling—stretching—her mouth, her face messy with pie now, the same as his had become . . . shit, he had to kiss her. He loved the way she sucked him, but he needed to feel her mouth under his, *all of her under him.*

After that, it was just plain messy—sticky hands roaming each other's skin, sticky wet body parts rubbing together—but it excited them all the more. They traded feverish, chocolaty tongue kisses as he slid his moist cock against her bare slit. At times like this, her shaved pussy was *especially* appealing—he could feel how smooth she was there against his erection.

"I want to make your pussy taste like chocolate, too," he rasped in her ear. And she murmured a breathy, "Mmm, God."

He slid immediately down her curvy body, grabbing another handful of the now-demolished pie as he went. She parted her legs wide, and he adored her for it as he smeared the chocolate and meringue there, slathering the bare white flesh as well as the pink inner folds.

And then he ate her, using both tongue and mouth to lick and slurp the gooey pie away. But he did it slow and thorough, making sure he tasted every fold and crevice, enjoying every sexy sigh and moan. He ran the tip of his tongue around her clit over and over, then licked the swollen pink nub as if it were a lollipop. Even long after the pie was gone, he could still taste its remnants mingling with her more pungent flavor.

Her messy hands were in his hair, holding his head there, and he liked it, liked her letting him know she wanted his mouth on her, licking her clean. She began pumping against him, fucking his face, and he let her. Yeah, he wasn't wild about giving up control, but this didn't feel like that—this just felt like a different way of being fucked by her, so he latched onto her sweet clit with his mouth and sucked inward.

Her cunt jolted against his face and she let out a cry that made him dig his hands into her ass, pull her even closer. And then she was whimpering, thrusting, and a glance upward revealed her clutching onto both tits, which only made him crazier, made him drive his cock against the bed a little—and then she was screaming out, fucking his mouth hard, hard, hard, and he knew she was coming.

His skin prickled with heat as he let her ride it out—then he finally backed away, but not before gently bestowing one final parting kiss to her rosy folds.

He wanted to fuck her—he wanted to fuck her brains out. But . . . he also wanted to keep right on getting messy with her.

He'd never had sex this messy before—he'd never really seen the appeal—but there was something about the gooey glide it provided, for hands, for other parts of their anatomy, that had him heated to a fever pitch, and he wasn't ready to be done with that yet. He felt the compulsion to do *every-thing* with her, everything two people could do, maybe things he hadn't even thought of yet. Until twenty minutes ago, after all, he'd never thought of rubbing pie on a woman's body, and look at them now, both drenched in sticky sweetness and aroused beyond all comprehension.

So even as much as one part of him wanted to ram his raging erection into her, he instead placed his hand on her hip and gently rolled her over in the bed, to her stomach.

"What are you doing?" she asked. He was pretty sure *she* wanted to fuck, too.

"I'm gonna eat pie off your sweet little ass. Can you hand me the plate?"

She reached toward the table and grabbed onto what remained of the pie, passing it back to him as he said, "Do you know how good your ass looks in a pair of blue jeans?"

"Um—really?" she whispered.

"*Hell* yeah," he told her. "And now I'm gonna find out how good it looks in chocolate pudding."

She laughed a little and wiggled her butt, inviting the playfulness, so he gave it a light smack. And then he bent to kiss it. Just once. And it made her sigh. Like that had probably felt better than she'd expected.

So he kissed her there again, this time earning a small moan that tightened his cock all the more. Damn. She was so responsive. And it was a crying shame she'd spent so long *not* responding to guys, and then not even *trying* except for her outings to Traverse City. Maybe that was why he wanted to do *everything* with her. Because she needed it. She deserved it. He wanted her to feel every good, hot, sensual sensation there was to experience.

Situating himself between her legs, he reached back into the pie plate he'd set on the bed next to them and grabbed out two handfuls of pudding and meringue, smearing them unapologetically across her ass. They'd come this far—there was no worrying about delicacy or messes at this point.

He licked it off with vigor, tasting the chocolate, which was somehow made better by having been spread over her flesh. While he worked, he used his hands to continue rubbing the pudding around wherever he wasn't licking.

At one point, his hand snaked instinctively back between her legs, just to make her feel good there, too—to keep her hot and wet. And then his fingers made their way inside her—so moist and slick, from both the pie and her natural juices.

"Lift your ass up, baby," he said on a heated breath—because he wanted to see, wanted to watch his chocolaty fingers go in and out of her, the pudding melting and oozing now, the sight weirdly exciting to him. Extracting his fingertips, he licked them clean—then once she'd pulled her knees up under her, raising her bottom higher, he pushed them in again, fucking her that way, making her sigh and pant.

The lust that overtook him now was a primal one—about fucking and instinctive exploration, about wetness and loss of inhibition. Still watching himself touch her, fuck her, he eased his fingers back out and slid them upward, gliding across the narrow bit of skin between her cunt and asshole. A strange, impassioned noise echoed from her throat, and her anus contracted, puckering ever so slightly. Jake followed the urge to slip the tip of his middle finger inside.

Her reaction was instant and unmistakable. "Unh." The sound came deep, guttural. He felt it in his chest, sensed the profound and unexpected level of her pleasure. So he didn't hesitate—he slowly, smoothly pushed his finger all the way in.

In front of him, she sucked in her breath—he heard it, and this time it was her whole body that seemed to contract. In response, so did his. He wanted to fuck her this way, wanted to make her feel it, wanted to make her crazy with the heat of it.

He began to move his finger in and out—thrusting, thrusting—and she began to whimper and sob in a way he'd never heard from her before. He became vaguely aware of her clawing at the sheets beneath her, wild and uninhibited—and so he fucked her ass harder, as hard as he could manage with just a finger.

"Oh God, stop, stop!" she sobbed.

He went still. "Not good?" Shit, had he misread her response?

"No, it's . . . it's : . ." She sounded breathless, finally managing, "It's amazing. I . . . I can't even understand how amazing it feels. But it's so good that . . . I almost can't take it."

Fresh heat flooded his body, warmed his cheeks. No, he *hadn't* misread her. But he kept his finger mostly still as he said, "You've never had anything in that spot before."

She shook her head where it now rested against a pillowcase. "No."

"Some girls don't dig it," he told her, "but some do."

"Um, guess you can put me in the do category."

God, she was amazing to him. Not only the way she loved sex, but the way she was getting freer and freer about it with him.

A thought which turned his mind back to primal urges, possibilities. The desire to pleasure her in ways she'd never been pleasured before. The desire to slake his own needs. His voice came in a low, gentle rasp. "Do you want my cock there? Do you want me to fuck you that way?"

Chapter 11

Her voice came soft, breathy, unsure. "Will it hurt?"

His chest tightened with the full measure of lust and tenderness he felt for her. "I'll be as gentle as I can and we can stop if it's too much."

She looked over her shoulder at him. Their eyes met. And she whispered, "Okay."

A quivery breath left him. At her trust. At the intimacy of the moment. At the strange burst of masculinity vibrating through his muscles as they tensed with the responsibility he'd just accepted: be gentle enough not to hurt her; be rough enough to make it feel as good as humanly possible.

As he reached for the pudding now—it was no longer pie—he simply saw it as lubricant, as what would make this work for her. He generously slathered his erection with it. And then he positioned the head of his cock at the tiny fissure of her ass and wondered how this would go. Taking his cock in hand to guide it, he pressed slowly inward.

She let out a cry through clenched teeth—but then quieted, sighed.

"Is it okay?" he asked, his heart beating slow but hard against his chest as he held back.

Her breath trembled. "I . . . I think. It's . . . so strange."

Jake swallowed back his fears and pressed his length deeper, sliding, easing slowly inward until he was mostly inside her ass. Aw God, it was *so* fucking tight.

"Oh . . ." she moaned.

"Good?" he asked, hoping like hell. His face felt hot, flushed.

"Uh-huh." It came out whimpery and high-pitched.

Now his chest went warm, too. Thank God. The news led him to begin moving, in and out, fucking her ass in a slow, gingerly glide. He'd felt strangely close to Carly before now—somehow tied to her, by secrets, by lust, by the overpowering need that had risen between them. But he'd never felt quite as intimate with her, quite as connected to her, as he felt in this moment, listening to her pretty, heated sighs fill the air, watching the feminine sway of her back below him, the curve of her round ass, and the spot at the center where his dick was so sweetly, snugly buried.

Carly clenched her teeth lightly, her heart pounding; her very pores seemed to vibrate with the nearly overwhelming pleasure permeating her being. It wasn't only in her nether regions—it radiated outward to the very tips of her fingers and toes. Her scalp tingled hotly—hell, her entire *body* tingled, each thrust in her ass wrenching fresh perspiration from her. She heard her own whimpers and moans, but everything was involuntary now—being wrung from her.

She'd never imagined, never dreamed, doing *this* could feel so good—even while utterly consuming her. So strange, like a whole new way of having sex—and it was perhaps the only time in her life that having so little control had at the same time felt so amazing, so impossibly intense. There was little room for thought—about control or anything else—it was simply sensation, sensation, sensation. She'd never felt so thoroughly fucked before.

Or . . . did any of that feeling have to do with this being Jake, the only man in her adult life whom she'd ever begun to feel any remote attachment to? The only man . . . who'd ever been patient enough, determined enough, to break down the invisible walls surrounding her all these years and keeping her from really connecting with a guy.

Right now, this minute—there might be little room for thought, but there remained room for emotion, and she had the oddest inclination . . . that she was falling for him. Really falling.

But she couldn't even examine that right now—too much power echoed from his rock-hard cock through her ass, her pelvis, out into each of her limbs. Enough power to make her crazy. She cried out, sobbed, moaned. She felt herself thrashing about, but wasn't sure why. Behind her, his groans came heavy, deep, and she sensed him getting as swept up in this heady brand of sex as she was. She'd never been this physically excited, this pushed to the edge of such intense pleasure, without coming. And as each plunge of his erection drove into that tiniest of orifices, she felt as if it was almost enough to make her come with no other stimulation. *Almost.* That was the part making her thrash around, wild with a pleasure that needed to peak and wouldn't quite. "God oh God oh God," she heard herself whimper—desperately pleasured but on the edge of a hot, wild agony she couldn't quite comprehend.

She parted her legs, even though they were drawn up beneath her—not a decision, but a physical instinct, her clit begging for attention. She thrashed a little more, crying out, screaming—oh God, what hot, strange pleasure!—until finally Jake's hand came, between her thighs, where she was so deeply in need.

She thrust against it automatically, shamelessly—and in a few short seconds, the powerful orgasm was rocking her body, jerking her mercilessly, overwhelming her with the hardest, most jagged ecstasy she'd ever experienced.

She was drenched in sweat. Not to mention pie. Oh Lord. She lay in a heap, coming down from it—when behind her Jake said, "Oh fuck, honey—me, too. Here I come." Those last strong thrusts shook her all over again—and reminded her: *Oh God, he's fucking me in the ass.* It was at once strange to her that she'd never experienced this as Desiree and even stranger that she was experiencing it *now*—when her darker, dirtier self was nowhere in sight.

Except that . . . maybe they were becoming one. Finally. Maybe as she'd acknowledged once before, she was learning, with Jake, to let herself feel those darker, dirtier desires—without masking them behind a slinky dress and a fake name. Maybe she was finally learning to be who she really was. Because of him.

A fter they both recovered and lay together in a heap for a few minutes afterward, Carly opened her eyes and began to look around. At the sheets. At their sticky bodies. At the remains of the mangled cream pie in the bed with them. And then she cracked up laughing.

Jake appeared a little alarmed at first, like maybe he feared she'd lost it—but when his eyes found the pie plate as well, he joined in the laughter. "God, it's weird what some people will do in the midst of lust," he said, and it made her laugh even harder.

After they shared a sensual shower together—Jake washing his hair and then hers, his fingertips making her scalp tingle as much as the sex had— they stripped the sheets from the bed and put on new ones, then flung themselves down on them, exhausted.

"Okay, the next time I go using pie as lubricant, remind me it's a big mess to clean up afterward," Jake told her.

She rolled to face him on her pillow and mused aloud, "It's not something I'd want to do every day or anything—but . . . it was pretty hot."

Jake's blue eyes sparkled in the low light. "So you don't mind that I demolished your pie?" Then he flashed a playful grin. "I mean, it's a blue-ribbon winner, after all."

"It was for a good cause," she replied, smiling. "A *weird* cause, but a good cause. I think." She scrunched her nose slightly.

And that was when he rolled toward her, too, clean and naked and beautiful, to draw her into a loose embrace. "*Definitely* a good cause, no thinking about it. I think *thinking* too much is probably what gets you into trouble, so knock it off. And anything that makes you feel good is a good enough cause for me, sweetie pie."

Yet another laugh burbled up from her throat. "Sweetie pie?"

He offered up a self-deprecating smile. "That just came out. Because I'm a dork. Or maybe because I just got intimate with a pie."

She nuzzled against him. "Don't worry, I still like you anyway. And you can call me sweetie pie whenever you want."

They both eased onto their backs then, relaxing, still recovering from what had turned into a tiring night. That was when his eyes seemed to catch on something, and he used his toes to pluck her long-forgotten panties from where they lay draped over the bed's footboard. "So, do you always wear such sexy undies, little miss Carly?" He sounded pleased by the notion.

"Mostly," she told him, adding quietly, without much forethought, "They're another one of my secrets."

"A *good* secret. I look forward to finding out what you have on under your clothes every time I see you now."

"I like having you see them," she admitted, swallowing past the nervous lump rising in her throat. It wasn't the usual sort of conversation for her, so just discussing panties, even after what they'd done tonight, still made her blush. But on the other hand, it seemed silly to hold anything back from him at this point. That was probably why she barreled ahead, saying what was on her mind even if it didn't pass her lips with total ease. "I mean, no one ever *has* before. Well, except for . . ."

"Desiree nights?" he asked.

She nodded, still sheepish about that. She was glad he knew her truth—it was freeing in a sense—yet it still embarrassed her in a way she couldn't get over in just a couple of days.

"Why do you wear them, then—when no one's going to see?"

Ah, he was back to the panties. Good—that was easier than discussing Desiree. "I guess it was . . . a private way to feel a little bit sexy, even when no one thinks of me that way."

"*I* think of you that way," he promised her.

And her heart warmed. "I'm glad."

They drifted into silence for a moment—a moment in which Carly let herself begin to really sink into this, feel comfortable with this . . . this *thing* with him. What was it? An affair? A . . . relationship? That didn't matter right now, though—not as much as the fact that it was the first time she'd really started to feel like this was all okay. She had a lover. Maybe even a . . . boyfriend. And she was starting to care about him. And that's what people did. They dated. They cared for one another. They had sex. Maybe not with cream pie all over their bodies, but that was beside the point.

She was beginning to feel normal. And happy.

"Speaking of secrets . . ." Jake began then, but he trailed off.

And her stomach churned a little. *Uh-oh—that's what you get for feeling happy.* He suddenly seemed more serious, and maybe hesitant, and she considered not even replying. But she couldn't quite bring herself to ignore him. "Yeah?" she asked softly.

He turned again to face her in bed, and when their gazes met, his looked probing—and kind of sad. "What happened to you, honey?" he whispered.

"Huh?"

He pressed his lips together, appearing to choose his next words carefully. "Something happened to you," he said. "Something that . . . messed you up inside, about sex. What was it?"

Carly said nothing—because she wasn't sure what to say. She wasn't sure of the answer herself.

"I don't meant to pry, I really don't," he went on. "It's just been on my mind—I can't seem to shake the question. It keeps coming back to me, worrying me."

Her stomach contracted slightly. "I worry you?"

He sighed. "Can't help it."

She wasn't sure how to take that. Was it sweet concern or . . . "I don't want to be like . . . some needy girl, some charity case for the big-city cop who helps people."

He tilted his head against the pillow, reached out to rest one hand on her bare hip. "Don't worry, I don't do sexual charity. And this has nothing to do with being a cop. It's that I'm sleeping with you, and I like you, and . . . I just hope you're okay, honey."

She let out a breath—one she hadn't realized she'd been holding. Okay, it was sincere concern, his worry. And maybe that meant . . . there was something worth worrying *about*?

She blew out a tired breath. She'd just . . . always refused to let herself examine this very much. And when she did . . . well, there were things that came to mind, but they were sickeningly unpleasant, so she usually just shut out the thoughts, the memories, and switched her focus to something else. "Are you sure something had to have *happened*?" she asked, still not quite wanting to go there. "Maybe . . . this is just the way I am. Maybe it's . . . random, happenstance."

And somehow, when he shook his head and appeared so very *sure* about it . . . damn. It made it hard to deny that there were things inside her that hurt, things she'd never let out—ever. And . . . hell. If no one else had these problems, there must be a reason she *did*. It was one thing to avoid thinking about this on her own—but to deny the issues out loud, now that someone knew about her private sex life, made her feel a little dumb, like someone in denial.

So as memories mixed and swirled inside her, she plucked one out. Kevin.

"Maybe it was . . . this thing that happened when I was eleven," she ventured, hating the pinch in her gut that came with the recollection. God, she hadn't thought about this in so long. Because it was just wrong. That it had happened. And that it had made her feel so bad inside, so bizarrely guilty. She could see that now, that the guilt shouldn't have been hers—and yet, somehow she'd been made to feel at fault.

Jake's blue eyes on hers were wide, patient, understanding—and it gave her the courage to tell the story. She'd told Dana—at the time. But only now, years later, could she see the full measure of how truly creepy it had been. "My family had a big Labor Day picnic at our house, with the whole extended family. My uncle Troy brought a friend with him, this guy named Kevin. Kevin was . . . completely charismatic—he was cute, funny, polite, helpful, and the whole family just gravitated to him instantly." She'd gravitated, too. She'd never met someone who so effortlessly cast a spell on everyone around him.

"So I and my female cousins instantly had crushes on Kevin, and he was so nice to us, actually paying attention to us in a way you wouldn't expect an older guy would with little girls. We were flattered when he played badminton with us, and when he sat with us to eat. And we were all sort of jockeying for attention with him and . . ." She stopped, bit her lip at the irony. "And I . . . won."

"Won?"

Her breath caught in her throat and a strange frisson of disgust fluttered through her midsection. "He started paying more attention to me than the other girls. Flirting. And even touching me—hugging me, putting his arm around me, holding my hand."

Dark suspicion edged Jake's voice when he asked, "How old was this guy?"

"Twenty-two," she said, still shocked by that herself.

She saw Jake's jaw set. "And you were *eleven*?"

She nodded.

"What happened?" Jake asked then, more softly. "What did that bastard do to you?"

"Nothing," she answered quickly, wanting to allay his worst fears. "Just the things I told you. But . . . somewhere along the way I realized it had gone beyond just being friendly—I'd wanted his attention, but I'd never expected to really *get* it. Not like *that*. And . . ." She stopped, swallowed uncomfortably. "And I . . . felt things. You know—girl things, sexual things, a response. And I began to realize he was, too, and how wrong that was—and I didn't see that coming, and it just felt so ugly inside."

She slowed down, took a deep breath—it surprised her that she could still feel it all so freshly, as if she hadn't had lots of very grown-up sex since then, as if she were eleven all over again. "And around the time I started to feel uncomfortable," she made herself continue, "my cousins got jealous and went to my mother—they told her I was flirting with Kevin and hanging all over him. Even though it was much more the other way around. I mean, I was *eleven*. I'd never done any more than talk to boys in school—I didn't know *how* to hang all over someone.

"So my mother and grandmother came to me about it together . . . in a way that made me feel I'd done something wrong. Looking back, I know I didn't—I *couldn't* have. Like I said, I was so completely innocent then. And *he* was the freaking adult—the one who had control of the situation. And I suppose my mom and grandma were just alarmed, and maybe they were more concerned with finding out what was going on than with how their approach would make me feel. But in the end, I felt terrible. Like I'd done something to be ashamed of. But all I did was talk to him. I swear."

"You don't have to defend yourself to me, honey," he assured her firmly.

"I *know* the guy was wrong. I know an eleven-year-old girl isn't responsible for something like that."

"And—and once it started, I didn't know what to do, how to stop it. I'd actually gone into the house and into my room, just to get away from him, by the time my mother came to me."

"Good for you," he said, nodding staunchly, and then he hugged her. Tight. Just held her for a long minute. And finally he murmured, "Do you know whatever happened to the guy?"

She shook her head. "No. We never saw him again. I don't think he was from around here."

"That's probably good. Because if I knew where he was, I might have to hurt him."

She drew back just enough to look into his eyes. "That's very chivalrous— but remember, even as icky as it was, he didn't actually *do* anything to me."

"He would have if he'd gotten the chance. And a guy like that very likely did things to some other little girl along the way."

Again, he sounded so certain, not an ounce of doubt. "How do you know?"

"Because that's how people like him work. That's just how it is."

She said nothing, not wanting to believe he was right, not wanting to remember how . . . *dirty* the incident had made her feel. At eleven. She sighed, her stomach tightening just slightly.

"I guess," Jake began a moment later, "that could explain why you fear people will think badly of you if you . . . have any sort of sexual identity whatsoever, why you care so much what people think. The first time in your life anyone ever saw you being attracted to a guy, the people you cared most about made it seem wrong."

Still in his embrace, she let out a sigh. She truly hadn't ever let herself think through this so carefully until now, yet maybe that made sense. Because God knew she'd never wanted to feel that way again. And it had always made her feel ashamed if anyone—even Chuck—thought she really *wanted* sex, really *felt* those kinds of feelings.

When Jake peered into her eyes, she was surprised to find him still looking . . . uncertain, unconvinced. "But is there . . . anything else, honey?" he asked.

She blinked. "Why?"

"Because what you just told me sucks, but . . . I think there's gotta be more."

More. Lord. The simple word suddenly felt like a chisel chipping away at her flesh. Because she'd thought maybe the story about Kevin would . . . be enough. To explain things, to satisfy him, to make sense of it all to both of them. But it wasn't, and the rest of it played at the edge of her brain now— the really bad stuff. The unfathomable stuff. The stuff no one knew because it was too awful for anyone to believe. *She* didn't want to believe it.

So she pushed it away, like always—just shoved the vague memories and hideous feelings toward the back of her mind.

Only . . . they wouldn't quite go this time.

She'd never had anyone trying to pull this out of her before, trying to *make* her dredge it up. Shit. Her stomach churned painfully now. Shit, shit, shit.

"What is it?" he asked.

Hell, he'd clearly seen the look on her face.

"Nothing." She glanced down, at his chest.

And he used one bent finger to tenderly lift her chin, to make her look at him again. "Something," he whispered.

And her throat swelled and everything in her felt as if it were curling in upon itself, as if her very body were disintegrating bit by bit.

She thought about trying to say it—this awful thing on the fringes of her mind—to put it into words. But how? And . . . should she? Could she? She trusted Jake—at this point, she trusted him an insane amount for someone she'd really just met. But did she truly want another human being on this planet to know about the revolting thing darting about the jagged outskirts of her memories?

"You can tell me, Carly, whatever it is. I promise."

And she followed the instant instinct to throw her arms around his neck and say, low, close to his ear, "I'm afraid you'll think I'm bad."

He drew back slightly, blinked, and she realized what she'd done, how little sense it made in the context of everything else. "I could never think you're bad—I swear."

"Why?" she asked around the swelling in her throat.

"Because . . . I know you. I mean, I know we just met, and under odd circumstances, but all that aside, I *know* you, Carly. I understand you—better than you think. And I *care* about you. A lot. I want to take away the things that hurt you. But I can't if you don't tell me what they are."

God. That was . . . sweet. And it made her feel safer than . . . wow, maybe safer than she'd felt since she'd been a little girl. Back when there *was* no sex. Only innocence. Good things.

And when he hugged her tight and placed a kiss on her temple, it also made her *braver* than she'd ever been—even in a red dress in Traverse City. Because compared to *this*, that was nothing.

Chapter 12

She bit her lip, found herself burying her face in Jake's chest, then whispered, "Um . . . when I was fourteen, my mom got adult mono, and it's contagious for up to two months. And when she was diagnosed, my parents decided my dad shouldn't sleep with her. So . . . since I had a double bed, he came in my room and slept with *me*."

Her throat felt like it was physically closing up as she spoke, but she'd started this now—she'd started it, so she had to get through it. "And, um . . . he would, um . . ." Her voice was shaking. "He touched me."

When she said no more—her stomach clenching now—Jake gently added the rest for her. "In ways he shouldn't have."

She let out a sigh, and her answer came small, childlike. She pulled back a bit to motion toward her breasts, saying, "Here." Then pointed downward. "And there." She swallowed hard, the memories at once vague yet searing, her body tensing just as it had on those hideous nights.

"It always started in the middle of the night. It would wake me up. And I was so . . . completely *shell-shocked* . . . that something in me just froze." She swallowed past the thickness in her throat, remembering a sense of paralysis taking over her body. "I just . . . lay there, pretending I was asleep. And then

I'd roll away, still acting like I was sleeping, but . . . he'd start again. And it . . . it didn't seem possible that it was really happening. Because he was my *father*." God, it was hard to breathe as she spoke. She'd never said these words before. Not even in her own mind. She'd always known it had happened, but she'd just refused to let herself think about it for more than the second it took to push the bad thoughts away. If she didn't think about it, it didn't have to feel *real*, like a thing that had really taken place.

"Maybe . . . maybe that doesn't seem so bad," she went on, "because, I mean, I know lots of people endure worse. But it was . . . awful. It made me sick. I . . . didn't know what to do."

"No, honey," Jake soothed her, his voice deep, warm. "It . . . it *is* bad. But *you're* not bad. That never should have happened to you. Ever." And he hugged her to him and she simply lay in the comfort of his arms, hating the memories, hating the way her entire body had clenched in response to them.

After that, they talked more. It came in bits and pieces—gentle questions from Jake that forced her to dig deeper into the pain of the past. It horrified her, and it was agonizing to go back to that strange, almost surreal time, to push past the protective mental walls she'd put up around it—but once the first piece of the wall had come down, it seemed necessary to demolish the rest. And even as strange as it felt to share her worst, most repulsive memories with Jake, he was so understanding that she found herself telling him . . . more and more.

Maybe . . . it needed to come out.

"I'm not sure how many times it happened—I just know it was more than once, because I have a few different, distinct memories about it. And I remember . . . lying in bed afterward, still wide-awake, my skin crawling, still in that weird state that felt like . . . panic or something . . ."

"Shock," Jake suggested, and she nodded.

"I'm not sure if I ever slept at all those nights. I remember just waiting, praying morning would come because I couldn't stand lying there next to him. Maybe . . . maybe I even left the bed and slept on the couch or some-thing." She shook her head. "I don't know. The details are foggy."

"Did you ever confront him?"

She shook her head. "No, never. I . . . couldn't even face the fact that it happened. I'm not sure I've ever really let myself believe it *did* happen . . . until right now." Her stomach plummeted all over again. "I mean, he was my dad. The man who was supposed to . . ."

"Protect you," Jake finished for her again, sounding as sad and broken as she felt inside.

"I never let myself think about it—any time it entered my thoughts, I just instantly pushed the memories away. Maybe that's why the memories are so foggy in ways. Mainly, it would come to mind when I was with Chuck, or with other guys I dated—they would start touching me, and even though I was aroused, at the very same time I'd feel disgusted. I guess it felt . . . like *him* touching me. And I guess when I became Desiree . . ." She stopped, thought through it. "Then it wasn't *me* being touched anymore. It was . . . someone with no past, no bad memories. It was . . ."

"Someone who'd never been abused that way," Jake said quietly.

Abused. Wow. She'd never thought of herself like that. It was such an ugly word. It sounded so much like someone you'd see on a TV talk show. "Was I?" she wondered aloud. "Abused? Because . . . I mean . . . he was a good father in every other way. He taught me to ride a bike. He read me bedtime stories. And . . . he taught me my craft, what I do for a living. He taught me woodworking . . ." Again, she swallowed past the lump in her throat. "He taught it to me *lovingly.* Because we both valued it and he wanted to pass it on to me."

With his arms still loosely around her, Jake gave her a markedly sad look. "I'm so sorry, honey. But yeah—that was abuse. It doesn't matter what else he did or didn't do—it doesn't make *those* actions any less wrong. Just please know there's no shame in it. Not for you, I mean."

And that was when Carly finally lost it, when it all finally came spilling out of her—nearly twenty years of anguish. Tears rushed forth and she clutched at Jake's chest, pressing her cheek there. His gentle touch soothed her, along with his soft, deep voice, whispering that it was okay to let it all out. And finally, finally, she let herself really feel the pain of what had happened to her—and she cried for a very long time.

When at last the tears started to abate, she sat up, reached for some tissues, wiped at her eyes, blew her nose. She noticed that Oliver had quietly joined them on the bed and she reached out an absent hand to stroke the side of his neck. Her head still spun, though. How was it she'd always known—in the back of her mind—that these things had happened, yet she'd never truly admitted it to herself? How was it that these old truths felt so painfully fresh and new?

She sighed, trying to wrap her head around it all. "He's been dead a long time now. And I loved him. Even though I also always harbored some . . . resentment toward him that I never really could explain, probably because of this." She shook her head. "I—I'm not sure how to feel about him now."

"You acknowledge your right to be angry at him. Outraged. And then, after you let yourself feel that—you try to forgive him," Jake said simply—and again, he sounded so very sure. "You take some time, work through it in your head, and you eventually forgive."

Forgive? Given Jake's clear anger throughout the conversation, this part surprised her—enough that she asked, "What do you mean?" After all, forgiveness seemed to contradict everything else he was telling her.

In response, he simply gave his head a short shake, now looking as tired as she felt. God, it was probably late—she had no idea how long they'd been lying here talking. At some point, they'd pulled the fresh covers up over their naked bodies and it made her feel . . . a bit protected somehow. "Look," he said, "I'm oversimplifying this, big-time—it's complicated as hell. And maybe I'm jumping ahead too fast—trying to give you the remedy when you're just getting the diagnosis. But . . . in the end, you gotta try to forgive the person who hurt you. Not for their sake, but for yours. You just gotta get it out of you. You get it out, you let it go as best you can, then you start to move on."

As they'd talked, she'd assumed he knew about such things due to being a cop, due to all the drama he'd seen on the job, all the different people he'd had to deal with from all walks of life. And yet . . . there was something in his voice now, a certain passion, a sharp and biting edge, that made her lift her gaze to his—and try to look deeper into it.

Because suddenly she grasped that there was something more going on than she'd understood up to now. "Why do you know so much about this?" she whispered.

Jake's face went numb as he realized he'd said too much.

But hell—she'd bared her soul to him, in every possible sense. Maybe somewhere along the way he'd forgotten he had his *own* secret to keep.

Maybe now it was only fair to tell her *his* truth.

He let his gaze narrow on her, felt his jaw tightening as he sought the right words. *Just say it, damn it—just tell her.*

"It . . . happened to me, too."

She flinched in his arms, her pretty eyes bolting open wider.

And he went on. "Not the same way. Nothing about it was the same. But . . . I was molested when I was a little kid."

He watched her carefully, maybe because she was so much nicer to focus on than those ugly recollections. He saw her swallow heavily; he read the pure astonishment in her eyes. Of course, he'd long since become desensitized to his past, to what had happened—he supposed telling her was tripping him up only because he hadn't thought about it much recently, and he'd never told too many people about it.

"Wh-what happened to you?"

"I was seven," he said. "And I was walking to school. Usually, my mom drove me, or my older brother or sister walked with me—but they all stayed home sick that day. A neighbor was supposed to take me, but I was waiting outside and she never showed up, and my dad had already gone to work, so I decided to just act like a big kid and walk myself. It was only a couple of blocks, and it didn't seem like a big deal. And then . . ." He stopped, swallowed. Saw images behind his eyes. The navy blue parka he'd worn on a cold March day. The lines in the sidewalk beneath his tennis shoes. Yeah, he was desensitized, but he was reliving the sad moment that had defined a huge part of his life. "Then a man pulled up next to me in a green station wagon and asked me to help him look for his dog."

The light gasp that echoed from Carly's throat told him that this particular ploy in child abduction and molestation had become so well-known— almost to the point of being clichéd—that it had reached even places like Turnbridge. He closed his eyes for a moment. "Man, I look back on that moment and just wish I'd been . . . wiser. Smart enough, *distrustful* enough, to remember everything my mom and dad had ever said about talking to strangers and all that, but . . . I liked dogs, you know? And the guy seemed . . . nice." He shook his head, disgusted all over again that any human being would be so deceptive in order to hurt a little kid.

When he met her gaze, her eyes looked glassy again, and he pulled her close and whispered, "Honey, don't cry for me. I'm okay, I promise."

She met his gaze and nodded, but didn't look convinced.

So he said, "I'm only telling you because you asked, and because . . . given the stuff *you* just told *me*, I think it's fair, and I want you to know you're not in this alone. All right?"

Another nod, but she still appeared frightened for him, and all he wanted in the world in that moment was to take care of her.

But first he needed to finish telling her—now mainly to make her understand that, even as sick and awful and damaging as abuse was, it didn't have to destroy you. You could take control of it if you tried hard enough.

And so he told her about that day and how the man named Larry Downy had lured him into his car, driven him to his apartment, taken him inside and touched him, and then made Jake touch him, too. "Then he dropped me off late at school and said he was gonna go look for his dog some more, like nothing ever happened.

"The only saving grace," Jake went on, "was that I had a really great family. The kind who had taught me I could come to them with anything, and even though I was confused and scared shitless by what had happened, I told my dad about the whole thing. He went to the police, and it took them a while to track the guy down from what I could remember about his car and his apartment, but they eventually identified him and found out he'd been tried but not convicted of child molestation before.

"Only, by the time they got a name on him, he'd cleared out. His apartment was a dive—a rent-by-the-week kind of place. I'm pretty sure he moved around a lot, to get away with what he was doing to kids. But the most important thing—for me—is that my mom and dad got me the help I needed right away."

"What kind of help?" she asked.

"I saw a therapist named Dr. Jim—for years." Another image entered his head: the kind man with the big mustache who'd put him at ease from the start. "Saw him a lot when I was little—less frequently later on. But it wasn't until the end of high school that I quit seeing him altogether. And don't get me wrong, by the time I was sixteen, I was pissed to be going to therapy, making up fibs about it to my friends, especially when it didn't seem like there was anything wrong with me. But the idea was for him to make sure I stayed in good shape through the time I started dating and having sex, you know?"

"Well, it must have worked, because you seem . . . *fine*. You seem incredibly well-adjusted. Unlike me," she added.

"What happened never goes away completely. But thanks to Dr. Jim and the fact that my parents didn't run from the problem or pretend it didn't happen, I . . . at least *understand* myself most of the time. I understand my reactions to certain things—I understand my urges, all that. So . . . mostly, yeah, I'm pretty well-adjusted. And in retrospect, I'm thankful I put up with all those years of seeing Dr. Jim."

"So what did Dr. Jim do that made things so much better?"

He thought back, tried to put it into words—words that might help *her* the same way they'd helped *him*. "He taught me, from almost the moment I met him, that it wasn't my fault, that I didn't do anything to make it happen. He taught me the difference between healthy sexual responses to things and unhealthy ones, and he even encouraged me to make my own decisions about when it was right to act on my desires and when it wasn't. Mostly, for me, in the end, I decided it's all good as long as it's consensual and doesn't hurt anybody or take advantage of them in any way."

Since Carly had looked pretty freaked-out as he spoke, it surprised him when a small smile formed on her pretty face. "So what would Dr. Jim think about using a pie as a sexual aid?"

A grin stole over him. "Probably that for all his hard work, I turned out pretty kinky." He let out a laugh, then got more serious. "But like I said, if everybody's into it—and old enough and sane enough to consent—it's all okay."

Her cheerful expression faded as she asked, "When . . . when we were with Colt, did it freak you out when he came on me? I mean, when . . . you know . . . some of it got on you?"

"No, baby," he said, eager to put her at ease. "I've told you before—the whole thing was hot. And if I have any issues left at all . . ."

"Yeah?"

"They're about control."

She bit her lip, clearly understanding where he was coming from. "That's why I ended up feeling like you were almost fighting me that first night."

He nodded. "If I decide to give up control, that's cool. But when some-body decides *for* me, that's harder. Even when it's all in the name of good sex."

Her eyes widened. "Exactly! It's completely the same way for me." But like before, her sudden brightness dimmed. "Do you have any idea whatever became of the man who hurt you?"

He shook his head. "It eats at me sometimes. Because I figure he's proba-bly hurt a lot of other little kids, too. Even now, I occasionally check around for his name, on the Internet, or in criminal databases, but he's never there. I'm not sure if that's a good thing or a bad one, you know? Whether it means he faded off into the sunset—or that he's still out there doing bad stuff and getting away with it. He was a fairly young guy when he molested me— around thirty—so chances are he's still out there living and breathing . . . somewhere."

"Did you do what you told *me* to do? Did you forgive him?"

"Dr. Jim made me understand that something hideous had probably happened to the guy to make him that sick of a human being. And that didn't excuse it, but it might at least explain it. That helped. Some anyway. So, yeah, more or less, I learned to forgive him."

He rolled to his back in bed, staring at the slow whirl of the ceiling fan overhead, still holding Carly's hand under the covers. "Listen," he said, "I don't want to go all psychiatrist on you, but . . . at the very least, you oughta get yourself a few good books on this subject and read them. You can't shove this back into the closet, you know? It's a lot healthier to deal with it, and just learning about it might help you out a lot."

"So you aren't gonna tell me I should seek professional help?" she asked, sounding surprised.

He supposed he must have come across as a huge therapy devotee. "If you're up for it, sure. But most people aren't. I wouldn't have been if I'd had a choice—but I was a kid and it was forced on me. And it was the best thing that could have happened to me, too. But you're an adult—you get to make your own decisions. Just doing some reading about it to start out will make you feel less alone."

"*You* make me feel less alone."

"I'm glad, Carly," he said, turning his head on the pillow to look at her. Then he squeezed her hand tighter. "And I'm here if you want to talk more about it, okay?"

"Okay," she whispered. Then . . . "Is this why you became a cop?"

He shrugged. "I just always felt the urge to . . . protect people." And he'd never particularly connected what had happened to him when he was seven with his career choice—but now that she mentioned it, it made sense. *Sometimes it's a lot easier to dissect other people than to dissect yourself.* "So . . . probably, yeah."

Tired of talking about all this—tired in general because it was late—he tried for a small grin and asked, "So, it's the middle of the night. Are you gonna kick me out or can I sleep over?" He hadn't stayed overnight up to now because she'd been so skittish about him—he hadn't wanted to freak her out any more than he already had. Things between them had been crazily intense, and yet at moments there had remained a lot of distance between them—the kind you couldn't measure but could only feel. And now, tonight, that distance seemed to have closed completely.

She shook her head against the pillowcase. "No—you can stay."

"Good." Partly because he didn't particularly feel like getting himself up and dragging his ass home this late. But partly because his heart was kind of . . . filling up with her. Because sure, it hadn't been his dad who'd hurt him, or even anyone he knew—but he understood something about what she'd been through . . . and now the whole way they'd met made sense.

Life was funny. *If her father hadn't hurt her that way, I'd never have met her. She'd be happily married to Chuck. I'd be the new cop in town and she'd just be pretty Mrs. Gardner who won the pie contest. And she and her husband would laugh over how much he'd had to spend to save her from eating pie with Barlow Jones.*

She'd be happy—and I'd be missing out on this amazing connection with her.

But . . . maybe none of that mattered because maybe he wouldn't feel such a strong bond if they hadn't both been through something similar. He wondered, deep down inside, if he hadn't worried, from the moment he'd met her here in Turnbridge and figured out she had issues about sex, that someone had hurt her this way. He supposed he just hadn't wanted to jump to conclusions, to assume that anybody with hang-ups had been molested.

Yet now that he knew, he felt all the more tied to her, like what had started out as a tiny string of chemistry between them in Traverse City had thickened, strengthened, transformed into a big, solid, twisting rope entwined with wild-growing vines.

And he didn't want to break away from that. He just wanted to take care of her. And he wanted to make her strong. He wanted to show her that she could free herself from all this—that anything Desiree could do, Carly could do even better.

Over dinner at the Grizzly Grill, Jake had told her he was leaving the next day for Chicago. Before accepting his job with the Turnbridge Police Department, he'd asked for this time off to visit his parents, who'd moved to the Windy City around the time Jake had gone to the police academy. His brother and sister were coming, too, and bringing their families; they planned to spend the week celebrating his father's sixty-fifth birthday and retirement by playing golf, fishing, and having quality time together.

And even as attached as she felt to Jake now, Carly thought maybe it would be good to have the coming days all to herself—so she could process what she'd finally acknowledged about her past.

Jake had stood with her on Saturday morning, kissing her goodbye and sweetly asking if she was okay. She'd just nodded. She felt a little numb, a little strange, but underneath all that, she had the strong sense that, "I'll be all right—I promise." And then she'd kissed him some more before finally sending him on his way.

After which she had called Tiffany Cleary, who was always up for odd jobs, and asked if she wanted to make some summer money by manning Winterberry's for a few days.

By noon, she was driving to a bookstore in Cherry Creek—God knew she couldn't check out the books she sought from the Turnbridge Public Library, if they even *had* such books—and she soon found herself thankful for the store's large selection when she discovered exactly what she was looking for: a book on sexual abuse, and another on incest.

An ugly, ugly word, but she supposed that was what she'd suffered. As she'd acknowledged when talking with Jake, she'd simply never permitted herself to think about those horrible nights long enough to give them a label. After all, who wanted to accept that they'd been abused?

Carly then spent the following days up in her apartment reading. She even did some exercises the books suggested. As a first big step, she went to her father's graveside and talked to him. Only in her head, but before it was over, it began to feel . . . healing.

Then she followed instructions from one of the books to write a letter to her abuser, addressing what he'd done, and then forgiving him for it. It wasn't something meant to be delivered—it was more like getting it off your chest and onto paper. Just as Jake had told her, the book explained that the forgiveness was for *her*, not her dad—it would allow her to let go of the tremendous hurt inside her as much as possible and move on.

Continuing as the book directed, she read the letter out loud. She'd cried during the process, but she supposed that was to be expected. Then, after the shop was closed Thursday night and Tiffany had gone, she walked out to the little patio in back where she kept a picnic table and grill, and she burned the letter. And though that part had sounded completely cheesy to her, she felt exactly what the book had promised she would—as if all those bad, heavy feelings were burning up, too, then drifting away as the breeze carried the ashes up Maple Street.

"There you are! What's going on? We've been worried about you."

She flinched then, looking up to see Beth Anne rounding the corner to the patio, eyes wide with concern. Had she seen Carly setting a piece of paper on fire in the grill?

But before she could formulate an answer, her friend went on. "Tiffany said you asked her to watch the shop this week, but she didn't know why. Is something wrong? Are you okay?"

All right, good—Beth Anne hadn't seen her burning her letter. According to the book, it was entirely her choice whether she chose to tell anyone about the abuse, and she'd decided to keep it to herself—and Jake. The important part, she'd learned, was just dealing with it in some way.

"Well?" Beth Anne asked.

Crap. Maybe it hadn't been the wisest thing to disappear for days without telling anyone. But it had made sense at the time, and she could handle this. "I'm . . . fine," she replied, and it was only as that word left her that she realized she truly *did* feel fine. She wasn't suddenly perfect inside, and maybe she never would be—but the fact was, she felt far more fine than she could ever remember.

Beth Anne, however, just looked all the more alarmed. "Then what's the deal?"

And whereas Carly normally felt nervous and on the spot when her friends expressed concern about her, now she found herself responding in a shockingly calm manner. Maybe that came with feeling fine. "I'm just . . . taking some 'me time.' I don't do that enough."

"As in never," Beth Anne pointed out, and then wiped her hand across her forehead. "*Whew*, now I can be relieved. And I'm glad you're doing something good for yourself for a change. But, uh, what's the occasion?"

Carly just shook her head, smiling lightly, still feeling surprisingly in command of the situation. "Nothing in particular. Just realized I never take a vacation, so I'm taking one *here*, now. I'm using the time to sort of . . . clear my head on some stuff. I'm doing some reading." Which was the truth. "And taking some bubble baths." Also true, because she had. It had been part of one of the exercises in her books.

"You know, after seeing you out last Friday night, Dana had this crazy theory that maybe you were holed up in your apartment having sex with the new town cop for days on end, because no one's seen him around this week, either." The sigh Beth Anne released this time was less happy than the last. "But looks like that was just wishful thinking."

"No," Carly said, the word leaving her with alarming ease. "I *have* been having sex with the new town cop. *Amazing* sex, in fact. He's out of town right now, but I'm guessing when he gets back, we'll have *more* amazing sex."

For someone who wasn't usually comfortable talking about her sex life—or the usual lack thereof—Carly even enjoyed it when her friend's mouth dropped open. She couldn't quite believe it, but it was actually fun to shock Beth Anne. She smiled and went on, brimming with a brand-new inner confidence. "I bet you guys thought I never *have* sex, huh?" she asked, suddenly feeling the need to share her new sense of normalcy. "Well, surprise—I do."

Once Beth Anne got over her shock—she broke into an enormous grin. "Praise the Lord! You have no idea how happy this makes me."

After which Carly couldn't resist teasing her even further. "But be careful when you go running to tell Dana. I don't want to be responsible for sending her into premature labor."

Chapter 13

When her front buzzer sounded the following evening around nightfall, she opened the door to find Jake standing on the other side. He looked beautifully rugged and unshaven in a T-shirt and jeans.

"Hey," he said, voice low, blue eyes sparkling in the light of streetlamps just starting to illuminate Main Street. That quick, her heart nearly pounded through her chest.

"Hey," she replied softly, just drinking him in, wanting him. She'd never met a man who brought out such a visceral reaction in her, a craving that felt bigger than both of them each time she saw him.

"How are you?" he asked—and given the gravity of their last encounter, the question held more weight than usual.

"I'm good," she said, her simple answer feeling equally as noteworthy.

His eyes widened slightly, hopefully. "Really?"

"Yeah."

That was when he lifted both hands to her face and kissed her.

She sank into it, let it sweep her away, curled her fingers around his wrists to make sure she didn't melt into a puddle right there on the front steps of her shop.

"Missed you," he breathed when the kissing finally came to an end.

"Come in," she told him, taking his hand.

From there, they lay on her bed catching up, and they ordered pizza to be delivered from Angelo's. It was strange to be talking about golf and birthday cake one minute and the letter she'd written and burned the next—but in another way, it was easy, because Jake made it that way.

After the empty pizza box was set aside an hour later, Jake pulled her to him, closing his hands over her ass through the khaki shorts she wore, and pressing his hard-on to the crux of her thighs. Mmm, God, he felt so good. And after a week of looking inward and examining unpleasant things, she realized again just how ready she was to resume living.

"I want you," Jake murmured, eyes heavy-lidded with lust, yet then his eyebrows pinched together lightly. "But only if you're into it. I mean, maybe sex seems weird to you right now."

And he was sweet as hell to be concerned, but she said, "Are you kidding? If you don't rip my clothes off in the next two minutes, I'm going to lose my mind."

"Thank God," he said, then reached for the bottom hem of the tank top she wore.

Within mere seconds he was rolling her to her back, parting her legs, and pushing into her. Whispering how hot and wet her pussy was. Kissing her neck, her breasts, thrusting hard and deep. And in the end leaving her just as sated as always. As she slinked away to the bathroom afterward, returning to find him asleep in her bed, she wondered how she'd had the strength to walk away from him in Traverse City.

But it was simple. She'd been a different person then. Or as close as she could come to being one. Now everything was different.

*   *   *

On Monday morning, she resumed her normal schedule, back in the shop at eight a.m., refreshed and full of energy, Oliver by her side.

When she called Schubert's to place her lunch order, she stopped Frank from making her usual ham and swiss and instead ordered chicken salad on a croissant. And when she returned to work later, getting back to Dana's baby crib for the first time in a while, she decided the piece actually looked plain—and she wanted to give it more flair. She still appreciated the simple beauty of straight lines, of course, but at the same time she felt her artistic perspective shifting, just a little; she found herself wanting to create something with a few more curves, with a greater sense of movement and flow.

And when she woke up on Tuesday, instead of throwing on the nearest old T-shirt for work, she drew from her closet a bright yellow fitted tee that hugged her shape a little more and made her feel a bit prettier. It was still practical for the shop, but it was more cheerful—like she was beginning to feel inside. And rather than pull her hair back into its usual ponytail, she changed things up by grabbing a big clip from her dresser and twisting her hair up into a cute, messy knot like Tiffany sometimes wore.

When Winterberry's front door opened just before lunchtime, she looked up to see Dana—who was beaming. She said to Carly, as if Carly might not know, "You're having sex with Officer Lockhart!"

"I can't believe it took this long for the news to reach you," Carly said with a grin, glancing up from sanding a small heart-shaped keepsake box— she'd just designed it herself this morning, and it would make a great, reasonably priced gift item.

"I can't, either—I wanted to kill Beth Anne when she told me she'd known since last week. And I kind of wanted to kill *you* for not telling me, too," she said, "but I'm too happy to be mad. And wow, you even *look* different, too. You're all . . . glowy or something."

And that was an apt description, Carly decided, for how she felt, both inside and out.

Thanks to Jake, everything inside her was changing, in big and wonderful ways.

That was when Dana's eyes dropped to the heart box. "Wow, that's gorgeous. I want one."

Most people thought of Jake as a pretty strong, capable guy. Some people would even call him tough. He was a cop, after all. Back in Detroit, he'd taken down plenty of bad guys. He'd dealt with criminals from all walks of life. Not a whole lot scared him.

But what had happened that morning when he was seven years old walking to school—not many people knew about that. It was his kryptonite. In some ways he thought it had made him stronger, *forced* him to be stronger. Yet no matter how he sliced it, it was impossible to think of that defenseless little kid walking down the street, getting coerced by a stranger, and not feel a little weaker for it.

And yet, he'd told Carly without blinking an eye. He'd barely even weighed the decision. Once she'd shared with him about her father, telling her had felt . . . natural. And that was a first.

He'd told other women in his life, years earlier. But even as caring as his old girlfriends had been, there was something much more comfortable, much more *right*, about telling someone who really *understood*—in a way you just *couldn't* if you hadn't been through something similar.

The walk between his place and Carly's was about a mile, but the sun was setting, cooling the air, and he'd felt like getting outside, taking his time, leaving the car behind. Walking, he'd always found, helped him think.

The calendar page had just turned from July to August—it had been a month since he'd bought Carly's pie. The changes in her since that time amazed him. Not only the ones he alone saw—in bed—but the changes in her everyday life, too. She dressed differently. And though she'd seemed invested in her work before, now she appeared truly enthusiastic, often showing him new pieces and new ways she was altering old designs. She'd finished the crib for her friend Dana, and to Jake, it looked entirely different from the piece she'd first shared with him a few weeks ago.

As for their relationship . . . well, that was what it was now—a relationship. He felt closer to her all the time. They ate lunch together most days—either meeting at Schubert's or eating on her back patio. And, of course, the nights were even better.

He continued to push her sexually, just in small ways now, and she welcomed it. She'd even started getting into the same sort of dirty talk they'd exchanged in Traverse City—she'd finally figured out that she could be as wild as she wanted with him and he'd still care about her afterward. Somewhere along the way she'd completely lost her inhibitions; she shied away from nothing he suggested. Damn, she'd melded her sweet self and Desiree nicely.

Sometimes they talked more about what each of them had been through when they were young, but most of their time together was spent just being a regular couple—eating out, eating in, talking, laughing, and having lots of hot sex.

And that was probably best, Jake had decided. He wanted to be there if she needed to talk, but the more attached to her he began to feel, the more he wondered . . . if it was a good idea. For two people with their particular backgrounds to be together. They ignited such profound passion in each other sometimes that . . . hell, was that healthy?

You knew it all along, though. You had to.

After all, from the moment he'd found out Desiree wasn't really Desiree, hadn't he, deep down inside, suspected why? He might not have *wanted* to think it, or believe it, but he knew what abuse—of any kind—could do to people, how badly it could fuck them up.

And maybe knowing it—knowing it gut-deep even if he hadn't quite admitted it to himself—maybe that was what had drawn him to her so intently, so ravenously, even when she'd wanted nothing to do with him.

Maybe he'd wanted to save her.

Or maybe he'd wanted to be with someone who could understand him completely.

But if he'd still been seeing Dr. Jim, he was pretty sure his old confidant would have told him that this was a *bad* idea, that two people suffering from the same wound couldn't heal each other, and that you couldn't save anybody anyway—that people had to save themselves.

Yet maybe she had. Saved herself. It sure as hell seemed that way.

In a way, it made him feel . . . fucking heroic. He'd made her face her past, helped her start moving beyond it.

But in another way . . . hell, he'd never felt this tied to a woman before. Let alone after only a month. Maybe this was a dangerous bond to share.

And yet he kept walking, just as eager to reach her as he'd been from the first time he'd chased her up Main Street.

As he rounded a corner onto Main just now, Turnbridge felt like a much different place to him. People greeted him or lifted a hand to wave. He'd started feeling comfortable here. He still wished his new job was a little more exciting, but he'd left Detroit because he'd *wanted* a quieter existence, right?

His heartbeat actually sped up in anticipation as he neared Carly's shop, ringing the buzzer when he finally arrived since it was past closing time. A moment later, she whisked open the door with a smile, her honey-colored hair falling in gentle waves around her face.

"Hey," he said in a low rasp.

"Hey yourself," she said, then lowered her gaze from his eyes to his hand. "What's this?"

Damn, he'd been so lost in thought that he'd practically forgotten he was carrying the potted plant he'd picked up at a greenhouse outside town. "It's a winterberry bush," he said, then glanced at it a bit skeptically. "Or it will be. Eventually."

She smiled, taking it from him, as he explained, "You mentioned wanting to put some plants in that little green space by your patio and I figured this would be a good start. I was picking up a few things for my yard when I saw it."

She tilted her head, raising her gaze back to his. "Jake, that's so sweet. Thank you."

"And I didn't get it just because of the store name and all that," he went on. "After I read the tag and talked to a guy at the greenhouse about it, it was more that it kinda . . . *reminded* me of you. I mean, he told me, just like you did, how hardy it is, even in harsh conditions. And I was thinking you're way that way, too. Strong, and tough, and beautiful, despite *your* harsh conditions." Then he let out a breath. "Damn, that sounded a lot less corny in my head."

"Are you kidding?" she said, wide-eyed and gorgeous. "That's possibly the best thing anyone's ever said to me."

"Yeah?" he asked, still not feeling quite as cool and secure as he generally did.

"Definitely. And I love the winterberry bush."

"'Cause . . . I figured the best thing anyone had ever said to you was when I called you sweetie pie," he joked.

"Now, *that* was corny," she informed him. "Even if I'm weirdly starting to like it a little, too."

And there was something about her eyes just then—or maybe it was her whole demeanor, the way she now balanced honesty with the simple unassuming confidence he was still getting accustomed to in her—that made him say, "I know we planned to walk down to Schubert's for burgers, but can we go upstairs first?"

She raised her eyebrows. "What for?"

"Because I need to be inside you. Like . . . now." He'd been aroused *enough* on his walk here, but this was something beyond that, beyond normal—edging closer to what he'd felt the night he'd come banging on her door and ended up fucking her senseless against the back wall. And on the stairs. Somehow the utter purity he saw in Carly, mixing with the bright new sparkle in her eyes, drove him a little wild.

"Um . . . okay," she said breathily, and her eyes said she was turned on now, too, that fast.

Once in her apartment, they fell on the bed together, exchanging instantly hard kisses and tugging at each other's clothes. He murmured that he had to sink his cock into her hot, wet pussy before he lost his mind. She closed her hand around his erection like a warm vise and whispered, "Fuck me, Jake. Please fuck me hard."

And then he was pushing her to her back, pinning her to the bed as he plunged inside her. And they were both moaning, groaning, thrusting. Until the moment when he least expected her to do what she did—roll him, shove him, over onto *his* back.

And then *he* was the one who was pinned, his wrists caught in her small fists as she hovered above him, grinding, undulating, so hot and beautiful. She was actually pretty damn strong for a girl, but he could have overpowered her at any moment. And he . . . wanted to. Damn, how he wanted to—every fiber of his being urged him to get her back under him. But he didn't.

Because she was going to come soon—he could tell. And God knew he didn't want to stop *that.*

And because . . . he knew he had to let her have *some* control.

The truth was, over time, she'd mostly let him take the lead; she'd become somewhat submissive to him in bed. But then moments like this always came, reminding him that—deep down—they both had that same need to be the one with the most power, the one who ultimately controlled the sex. And they both always would. *That's exactly why Dr. Jim would tell me this is a bad idea.*

Yet when she climaxed, crying out, clawing the tips of her fingernails into his skin to send an extra ribbon of heat rippling down his spine, he forgot about all that. For a few hot, satisfying seconds anyway.

When finally she collapsed on his chest, breathing hard, nestled against him, his arms closed around her and he found himself threading the fingers of one hand through her hair, gently stroking, caressing—and trying to hold back. Just long enough to let her recover from her orgasm.

Until he couldn't anymore, and then he flipped her over, taking back that blessed control, and pounding his aching cock into her hot, slick cunt, just like she'd asked him to, until he was no longer thinking about anything at all—he was just fucking her, like an animal, like the animal they each became with the other. Her deeply pleasured cries, along with strangled-sounding words like "Yes!" and "God!" fueled him, and he rammed himself into her over and over, every pore of his body wild with it, until finally he toppled over the edge, too, biting off, "Fuck yes, now, now," as he began to explode in the tight glove of her sweet pussy.

And then it was *him* crumpling against *her* pliant body, lost in sated exhaustion, melting into the warmth of her skin as he tried to come back to himself.

Finally, she whispered, "That was better than hamburgers."

And he let out a laugh against her shoulder as dusk began to slowly fall across Main Street outside the windows, dimming the air around them.

Jake didn't know how much time had passed when Carly said, "Do you ever hate that you've gotten involved with me, with so much drama?"

He lifted his head from where it rested on her plump breast, blinking down at her. "Where did *that* come from?"

She shrugged against a pillow. "I was just thinking. That this hasn't exactly been a . . . normal sort of relationship, has it?"

He let out a sardonic chuckle. "Not exactly, no. And . . . at first, I was telling myself to avoid you because, after Detroit, I thought I was ready for a drama-free life." Then he rolled to his side next to her, propping up on one elbow to peer down at her. "But hey, we've all got drama, right? Hell, things are so quiet in Turnbridge that maybe I even *need* a little drama. So— no, honey, I'm definitely not sorry I got involved with you." Although he concluded by slanting her a knowing grin. "And if I'm concerned about *anything* . . . it's that we both want to be on top."

She bit her lip. "Not always," she whispered. "I've gotten a lot less bossy in bed than on the night we met, don't you think?"

He ran his palm lightly over her stomach in a soft caress. "Yeah, you have. The problem is . . . *I* feel bossier lately than I have in years."

"Because I opened up an old wound?" she asked.

He just shrugged. "Maybe. But *you* didn't do it. *I* did. I chose to tell you. And it's only fair that we both give a little, and we both take a little, when it comes to who's calling the shots. I just wish I was doing better at that, not feeling the need to control so much. Since I know when we get into these silent little struggles in bed that it's because we *both* need it."

"Is . . . my sometimes needing to control things . . . a big problem? For you?"

Jake thought it over. That *wasn't* actually the problem. It was only a symptom of the much bigger issue on his mind—that two people with their pasts would *always* struggle a little, would never be equipped to help the other forget, or completely get over it. But in reply, he simply said, "Doesn't matter one way or the other—because it's too late to stop it now."

"What do you mean?"

Then he told her the truth. The only truth he could come to in all of this. "The fact is, Carly, I think I'm falling in love with you."

Chapter 14

Carly sucked in her breath. Had she heard him correctly? She was pretty sure she had, but . . . she hadn't heard those words from a guy since she was eighteen years old. And that was her fault. All her fault.

But wait, no. It was . . . her father's fault. She was still getting used to that idea—that all her weirdness about sex had a reason, an explanation. One that didn't originate with her.

And now . . . she'd somehow begun letting go of all that and opening up to a man, a man who seemed almost too good to be true at moments. And who was . . . in love with her? Finally she said, "Really?" Because his words seemed too good to be true, too.

Next to her, Jake lowered his gaze, stilled his hand on her stomach. "Yeah." Then he sighed. "Maybe I shouldn't have told you. Maybe you don't want to know something like that."

Because all this was so new? Because he thought she didn't feel the same way? Whatever the case, he had it all wrong. "Jake, I'm in love with you, too."

He brought his eyes back to hers. "Yeah?"

She nodded against the pillow, a little nervous suddenly, her chest tightening. She was even less accustomed to a discussion like *this* than she was to good, normal sex. Or maybe it was because she suddenly *felt* how much she loved him. Maybe she was just now *letting* herself feel it because it was suddenly safe to do so. "How could I not be? I mean, you've been . . . so amazing. Patient. Kind. Understanding. And . . . perfect. I was . . . a total mess, and yet you've given me everything I could possibly want or need. *Of course* I love you." And that was when she hugged him to her, tight, realizing . . . she'd be lost without him now. He'd become such a pivotal force in her life. Every good change, every revelation, every desire to fix herself was all because of him. He was the foundation, the underpinning to all of it. "I love you like crazy, Jake Lockhart."

"Aw, baby," he murmured deeply in her ear, and she could feel the heat rising in him again, just from that—and they were soon lost in each other once more. And it was nearly midnight before either of them remembered that they'd never made it to Schubert's for burgers.

Life was good. Carly was busy planning Dana's shower for next month with Beth Anne, sales at Winterberry's were up—she couldn't make enough heart-shaped boxes to keep them on the shelves—and she had a lover. More than that. A man she was in love with. Who also loved her. For the first time ever, she was having sex on a regular basis. Really *great* sex. How could life *not* be good?

Everywhere she went, in everything she did, Carly continued feeling freer than ever in her life. And it wasn't that all the bad feelings had just disappeared—as Jake had told her, she knew they'd always exist. But she was processing them now, and she'd really begun letting go of the hurt, at least as much as possible. She was moving on from the things that had held her back for so long.

As she snuggled with Jake on his couch watching a movie, she wondered if he'd be surprised when he found out what she wore under her tank top and shorts. For the first time since getting together with him, she'd gone into the drawer of lingerie previously reserved for trips to Traverse City. Maybe he wouldn't even notice the lacy bra and panties more than any others she wore, but to her, it felt like . . . another turning point. She knew she'd been bold with Jake at times since he'd moved here, but putting on the lace bought strictly for a Desiree seduction felt daring to her in a different way. One more step toward leaving the past behind. And just having that lace against her skin for the past few hours had made her feel even more . . . powerful, a little like Desiree, but still more like Carly.

It probably shouldn't have surprised her to learn that movies about cops were at the top of his list. Sometimes, when he was so gentle and understanding, it was easy to forget he was an officer of the law. But the look in his eye as he watched the wide-screen TV reminded her. He was into the action-adventure story big-time, clearly more invested in seeing the downtrodden fictional cop catch the bad guys than she was. She liked that about him, though—how seriously he took his job, how important it was to him to help people, to save people. She'd meant it when she'd told him *he'd* saved *her*. And she thought he saved her a little bit more every single day.

When the credits began to roll, Jake muted the sound and said, "Now, *that's* the kind of cop I want to be." Then he pointed to her empty wineglass. As was often the case, they'd made a dinner of pizza and wine. "More to drink?"

She shook her head, then replied to his comment about the movie. "Because he was in danger and you miss that? Or because he got the bad guys? Or something else?"

Reaching for a piece of cold pizza, Jake leaned back on the leather couch and appeared to mull it over. "He had conviction," he finally said. "And . . . he made a difference in the world. Maybe that's the main thing—that he made a difference."

She tilted her head, thinking he looked a little bummed out. "You don't think you make a difference?"

He shrugged and offered a shallow grin, clearly trying to play it off. "Hard to make much of a difference in Turnbridge. That's the one factor I guess I didn't weigh when I made the decision to leave Detroit. I mean, don't get me wrong, I like it here. But there are just moments when I wonder if I'll ever really be satisfied doing nothing besides issuing speeding citations and writing up accident reports."

Wow. She hadn't realized he felt this strongly about it. "Accidents matter," she said.

"You're right, they do. But . . . hell, I even exaggerated *that* by making it plural. I've written up a total of one fender bender since I've gotten here. And it's not that I *want* people to have accidents, but damn, Carly—do you know what I did today?"

"What?" she asked.

"I was called to the intersection of Grant and Whitewood roads to help a family of ducks cross the road. Seriously," he added as if he couldn't quite believe it.

Carly didn't mean to laugh—but she couldn't help herself. "So we like ducks here. And you *helped* the ducks. And you helped the people who were *worried* about the ducks."

This drew a small, more playful smile onto his handsome face, tonight unshaven and sexy with stubble.

"And you like the people here, don't you?" she went on.

"Sure. I like Tommy and the other guys on the force." In fact, they'd gone to Tommy and Tina Gwynn's for lasagna last Friday night. "And I like *your* friends, too." They'd run into Dana and Hank just a few nights ago at Angelo's Pizza Parlor and the guys had ended up playing pool while the girls watched and chatted.

"Well, whenever there *is* trouble, you'll be extra glad you were here to help because you'll know the people you're helping."

He gave his head a tilt. "Tommy once told me something like that, too. I guess I just . . . feel ineffective as a police officer after the stuff I dealt with in Detroit on a daily basis. It was stressful, but . . . it mattered, you know?"

Carly considered insisting that his work here would matter, too, but since she couldn't know all he'd experienced in Detroit, she decided against it. And she almost reminded him once again of the ways he'd helped *her*, but she knew that wasn't what he was talking about. So instead, she dug deeper into the heart of the matter, to the question suddenly bothering her. "You aren't gonna leave, are you?"

She couldn't read his little smile—until he said, "I just packed up my whole life to come here—I'll give it a while longer before I throw in the towel. And besides, even if I wanted to, how could I leave *you*, sweetie pie?" His grin widened, so she smiled back.

And felt the tug of her new sexual freedom. "That's smart, because if you left me, you wouldn't get to see what I have on underneath my clothes right now."

As a familiar heat began to sizzle in his blue gaze, he leaned back and crossed his arms. "Why don't you show me, honey?"

She pursed her lips, hesitated. Usually, up to now, he'd undressed her. Now he wanted to *watch* her undress? She didn't really know how to do that—in a sexy way. And it seemed almost *un*sexy right now to simply go yanking her clothes off like when they were in a hurry. Her pussy tingled hotly and she wanted to make something more of the moment, something to show him anew just how far she'd come since the Fourth of July.

So she slowly rose from the couch and started down the hall away from him.

"Uh, where are you going?" he called after her.

"I'll be back in a minute."

Maybe this was taking the easy way out, but she ducked into his bedroom and only then slipped out of her clothes. The lingerie underneath was simple but potent in her estimation: lacy black boy-short panties and a matching demi bra that plumped her breasts up high.

Yet a quick glance in the mirror over Jake's dresser made her realize . . . it wasn't enough. She knew she felt different tonight, wearing Desiree's usual style of dressy, lacy undies, but she wanted to be sure *he* knew she felt different, too.

Taking a look around, she spotted Jake's policeman's hat hanging over one short bedpost. The stiff navy blue cap with the small, shiny black bill was close enough to black—so she picked it up, tried it on. A little big, dipping slightly to one side, but another peek in the mirror told her it worked—she was suddenly a naughty lady cop. Her cunt quivered slightly in response. *I can be a playful bad girl without being Desiree.* Somehow, for her, this made it official. And brought her a little closer to completing the transition than she'd been before.

But prior to revealing herself, she added one more thing—eyeing Jake's police belt, she detached and plucked up the open pair of handcuffs hanging from it. *Yeah. That was hot.* Or it would be soon anyway.

Rather than go back to the living room, she called, "Jake, why don't you join me in here." They usually hung out at her place, and she liked the idea of sharing Jake's bed tonight.

As his footsteps approached, she struck a pose, letting the handcuffs dangle from her index finger.

"Holy mother of God," Jake murmured upon stepping into the room. His eyes roamed her from head to toe. "You just made me hard as a rock."

"That's good. But I still have to . . . take you into custody, sir." She was trying this on for size, making it up as she went.

He cast a sexy, cocky grin. "Is that so? And just what are the charges, Officer Carly?"

"Um . . . indecent use of a pie?"

He tilted his head, recrossed his arms. "I think the statute of limitations has run out on that by now."

She touched her tongue to her upper lip, eyes still on him, thinking. "Then . . . let's just sum it up with . . . you've been a very bad boy. With me. Over and over again."

"Didn't know there was a law against that, ma'am," he teased her.

"Well, in a place like Turnbridge, there are probably some really old, outdated laws on the books like—no anal sex, or no having sex in a store on Main Street. I'm sure I can run you in for *something*." And with that, she finally took his hand to draw him forward, then pushed him to his back on the bed, crossways. She hadn't gone into this feeling so aggressive, but now she did. So she slid her body up the length of his, gave him a long, hot kiss, and grazed her palms up his arms, flung casually over his head. Then she began to slip one ring of the handcuffs around his wrist.

Jake reacted on gut instinct, yanking his arm free of the cuff before she'd fully encircled it. Clearly, he'd gotten spoiled lately. By how beautifully docile she'd become when they fucked. She was just as beautiful when she took control, too—but he wasn't ready for that tonight, and he sure as hell wasn't ready for fucking handcuffs. He knew she was only playing—but that was just too much control to relinquish.

Still working on raw impulse, he closed his hands around her wrists, tight, and held her there. Their eyes met—they'd been here before, even on that very first night in Traverse City, and that familiar struggle for control had just ensued once again. He didn't want to be a bastard and not let her have it; God knew he understood why she needed it—the same reason he did. But the handcuffs were simply more than he could handle. He'd never known that before this moment—he had, in fact, never played these kinds of cop games with any other women—but he'd felt it with clarity the instant the cool steel had touched his skin.

In some ways she was his perfect lover—they understood each other. But in others, she might be the *worst* possible girl for him; he couldn't deny that sex had been easier with women who didn't mind him taking charge. And tonight, as much as he wanted to be a good, generous partner, he couldn't let her have her way. So he made a move he'd made with her before—he rolled her to her back until his weight was on her.

She struggled slightly—it had become a common element of their strange mating dance, and it was partly playful, but also partly real. Her legs thrashed slightly until he trapped them to the bed with his own. And his heart beat a million miles an hour with the hot rush of the sex he liked best: the kind he controlled.

She sounded breathless when she peered up into his eyes to ask, "How did I end up on the bottom here?"

"Rookie mistake," he told her. "Underestimated your opponent. So now it looks like I'm the cop"—he freed one hand to take the hat still half on her head and plopped it onto his own—"and you're the one who's under arrest."

Her lace-adorned breasts heaved prettily beneath his chest. "And what are the charges against *me*?"

He gave her his most wicked smile. "Impersonating a police officer." Then he freed the same hand again to snatch away the handcuffs she still held clutched in one fist over her head. "Very sexily, I might add, but still— you do the crime, you gotta do the time."

"The time?"

"In this case, that means . . . letting me do what I want," he whispered deeply. And he knew she could feel the steel cuffs pressing against her flesh, the same way he had a minute ago. But he didn't want this to feel harsh, forceful—so he began to use one of the handcuffs to gently caress the tender skin on the underside of her arm. He stroked the edge of the steel there ever-so-lightly, as light as if it were nothing more than a feather. He wanted her to get used to it, wanted her to realize it was actually making her feel *good*.

"I *have* been letting you do what you want," she pointed out.

And it was true—she had. Most of the time. "I know. And I don't mean to be a selfish bastard. I want this to be okay with you. Is it?" he asked, giving her a sweet look as he kissed the tip of her nose, then her forehead—and then he gently slipped one cuff around her right wrist and clicked it shut. He wasn't sure why he wanted this so bad, why he would ask her to endure what he'd refused to, but he told her, softly, "I'd never hurt you. I just want you to play with me this way, Carly."

He couldn't quite read her expression as she peered up at him, her chest rising and falling visibly with each breath. "You didn't feel that way when it was *you* about to get handcuffed."

"You're right. But you're a tough chick, remember? Maybe tougher than me." He gave her a delicate kiss then—at the exact moment he used one hand to press her wrist into the remaining steel cuff, easing it shut. "I just want you to trust me. *Really* trust me."

"I do," she promised. "Surely you know that."

"I need to see it. Feel it. I don't know why." He gave his head a short shake. "Maybe it *is* about all these old feelings being stirred up. I just . . . want you to surrender to me completely, in every way."

The world seemed to stand still as they looked at each other for a long moment. They said nothing, yet the air was rife with the silent push/pull of trust, of strength, of lust.

"I'll undo the cuffs if you want—just say the word. But maybe I think," he rasped, "that you have the ability to heal. More than me. Maybe I think that even if I can't quite free *myself* that I can free *you*—that if you give it all up to me, that'll happen for you."

Her breathing was audible and he sensed such stark honesty surprising her. "You seemed so . . . cool and calm about the whole thing when you told me about it."

He let out a breath. "I thought I was. Now I'm realizing that maybe

I'd just gotten . . . lazy about it. I'd just picked girls who liked it however *I* liked it, and that made it easy. Maybe *too* easy." He lowered his voice to add, "Seems like I've still got some demons to conquer."

"What about *my* demons?" she reminded him.

What he'd just said wasn't bullshit—even though he was being selfish in one way, in another he really thought such surrender would ultimately help her. "You're stronger than you think, Carly. But like I said, I'll take the cuffs off if that's what you want."

She looked at him for another long stretch, during which he quietly caressed her wrists just above where the handcuffs held them—until she whispered, "All right."

"All right?"

"Do what you will, Officer Lockhart."

"Oh God, I love you," he told her, because it rushed through him like a river just then, how much the depth of her trust really meant to him. And it inspired him to want to pleasure her even more. He kissed her before she could even answer, finally letting his touch leave her wrists, up over her head, gliding them downward to firmly massage her breasts.

Her moan was like music to his ears. It meant her pleasure was greater than any discomfort she was feeling. And that was the simple key to it, he realized—make the pleasure greater than any negative gut reaction.

He couldn't remove her bra because of the cuffs, but he was perfectly happy just curling his fingers inside the lacy cups and pulling them down to put her sumptuous tits on display. He let out a low growl when he saw them—then eased his body down the length of hers until he could lick at one taut, lovely nipple and listen to her hot little gasp. Bestowing a kiss there, he lifted his eyes to hers. She bit her lower lip, her gaze all heat, tightening his erection.

After laving those perfect pink peaks—his knee pressed snugly between her thighs so she could grind against him—he slid further down her lithe body, grazing his fingertips along her skin as he went. "These panties are so fucking hot," he said on a groan when he found himself at eye level with them. Then he followed the impulse to close his teeth around the lace where it formed a V in front, sliding his palms beneath her ass to pull them down.

As usual, her delectable pussy was smooth, the way he loved it. And when he said, "Spread for me, baby," and she parted her legs, he suffered the urge to tie her that way, to secure one ankle to one bedpost and the other to the opposite one, to keep her hot, pink cunt on display, the flesh swollen and open, for as long as he wanted. But that urge would wait for another day. He'd indulged his desires enough here, and she'd let him—so the rest would be all about making her feel incredible.

Finally shedding his clothes, he didn't hesitate to sink his mouth into her wet, open flesh, loving the hot sob it tore from her throat. He ate her vigorously, licking, sucking, nibbling at her engorged clit. When he thrust two fingers into her pussy, another well-pleasured sound erupted from her and he finger-fucked her while he worked her over with his tongue and teeth. She moved against his hand, his mouth, in a hot, familiar grind, and he got lost in her pleasure, lost in the salty sweet taste of her.

But it was only when he took it a step further, when he reached beneath her with his other hand, slipping the tip of one finger into her ass, that she reached the pinnacle they'd been moving toward. "Oh God, fuck yes," she said through gritted teeth, exciting him all the more just before she began to sob her climax in earnest as it pumped through her body as wildly as if it were a living thing.

"God, fuck me, Jake. Please fuck me now," she begged as soon as the orgasm ended—and he loved it.

He loved her plea, and he loved the slow, tight, hugging entry of his cock into that tiny opening. He loved the hot rhythm they fell into automatically as he pounded into her, steady and deep. He loved how slick she felt and how hard her nipples stayed and how soft her neck was when he lowered a nibbling kiss there. And he loved when she looped her arms around his neck and the sharp edge of the handcuffs pressed against his upper back. She'd given him what he'd wanted—her trust and her surrender. And it hit him then that he'd *always* wanted that from her—as Desiree, and then after he'd met her here. Maybe because he'd sensed her resistance to that from the very start. And now he wanted to give her everything he could in return, every pleasure.

So he fucked her hard and made her cry out.

And he touched her, kissed her, worshipped her with his eyes.

But then came that inevitable time when the tide rose within him and for a little while his *own* pleasure took over, expanding through his body in hot pulses and a wild, wired sort of tension and heat—that finally burst free inside her.

They lay together afterward for only a moment before he got up and retrieved the key to his handcuffs. It was the least he could do.

After releasing her, he slowly drew her arms down from where they'd been raised overhead for so long; then he rolled her to her side, where he lay facing her, to gently rub her wrists in his hands. The cuffs hadn't been tight on her, but if her wrists were sore at all, he wanted to make them feel better. "Are you okay, honey?" he asked.

She nodded, looking a little astonished. "It was just . . . normal sex—only with handcuffs on."

"I know," he told her. He could have made it more than that, and maybe he would . . . someday. But not yet.

"It was . . . easier than I thought. To be cuffed. You should try it sometime," she added with a teasing, pointed look.

He ignored that part to say, "See? I didn't have anything *too* heinous in mind."

"Letting you fuck me in the ass was actually a lot more challenging than this when it came down to it."

"And you ended up *loving* that."

Her face flushed at the reminder—they'd indulged in that particular act a few times now. Then she said, "Maybe you would be stronger, too—if *you* surrendered to *me*."

He simply let out a sigh. It was a fair, sensible statement. "Maybe I would. But I'm just not quite there yet, honey."

She tilted her head against the bedcovers, looking inquisitive. "So how is it that I'm so much tougher than you, Mr. Tough Cop Guy?"

Not to detract from her strength—because she *was* damn strong—but ... "Maybe it's because I'm *pushing* you to be. Because I love you."

"Well, *I* love *you*, too—remember? And I'm not as good at being pushy—but I *will* push. Eventually. And you'll let me. And it'll be good."

Later, they lay in Jake's bed. Darkness had fallen, but moonlight streamed through the back window of his little house, still allowing Carly to see much of the room. It was simple in that "man way"—warm colors, old dark oak furniture that he'd told her had come from his grandparents. It was chipped up and could stand to be refinished, but Carly appreciated the quality and workmanship of the pieces and thought they suited Jake somehow. Solid, attractive, but just a little flawed.

Yet she could accept the flaws in him. Easily. Because—it turned out—they were so similar to her *own* flaws. She hated what had happened to him, but his past made it so much simpler for her to be with him, to open up with him. It was a rare thing in her life to feel as comfortable with someone as she did with Jake, even after knowing him only a short time.

When his cell phone buzzed next to the bed, he leaned over to grab it, and she listened to the one-sided conversation. "Dude, what's up?" he said merrily—then, "Well, yeah, actually, it *is* late and I'm kind of in the middle of something, so . . . feel free to get to the point."

After hanging up a few minutes later, he told Carly his friend Shane was borrowing his uncle's cabin cruiser, docked in Traverse City, for Labor Day weekend, just a week away, and inviting the guys from the H.O.T. program who lived nearby to come spend a couple of days on Lake Michigan. "Would you be up for going if I can get my shifts covered?" he asked.

Wow. Meeting his friends. And not just for a few hours, but a whole weekend. "Will, um, Colt be there?" she ventured.

"Naw," he said, swiping his hand through the air as if brushing the thought aside. "He's too far away—this'll only be a handful of fairly local guys, and a couple of their girlfriends."

She bit her lip. "But did . . . you or Colt tell your buddies about what happened after that night at the hotel?"

"It came up," he said quietly. "More from Colt than me—he has kind of a big mouth. But he told them about a girl named Desiree, not Carly. And I don't think they'd care anyway, even if they knew—but they never need to know I met you before coming to Turnbridge if that's how you want it."

"Um, yes please," she said, knowing it was the only way she could face his friends, and sort of hoping she'd never have to cross Colt's path again. She'd liked him, for that night, but all things considered, it would be difficult to face him as her mild-mannered, small-town self.

Jake grinned. "So does that mean you'll go?"

Carly's life had kept her so isolated in many ways—and socializing with a bunch of Jake's cop friends on a boat sounded a little stressful, just because she'd be so out of her element. But at the same time, it sounded kind of fun and exciting, too. She'd never actually *known* people who got invited on weekend trips on Lake Michigan. So she tried to sound perfectly cool and casual when she said, "Sure, that sounds nice. And it'll be nice to meet your friends. Besides Colt, I mean," she added, heat climbing her cheeks as she spoke.

"They're good guys—you'll like them. And they'll like you."

But she was no longer really thinking about the guys she'd soon meet—and because she felt so at ease with Jake, she didn't hold back the question that had just entered her mind. "Now that you and I have gotten close, does it bother you, what I—we—did with Colt?"

"It was the most exciting sex of my life," he said in reply. "Remember?"

"But . . . I mean, you didn't know me then. You didn't *expect* to know me. Now that you know the *real* me, does it make you think of me differently?"

She felt his look in the shadowy light. "Don't do this to yourself, Carly."

"How can I not?" she asked. "If I were really Desiree, I wouldn't care, but since I'm *not* her . . . I'm a girl who *does* care. And I'm pretty sure *that's* the girl you're in love with, right?"

She couldn't read his expression as he studied her, until finally he said, "The fact is, you might not like it, but you *are* Desiree. And you *are* Carly. And I'm in love with the whole package, honey, all of it. The only difference between you and most women is that you let yourself go that night, you let yourself do exactly what you felt like doing."

"And that's okay with you? Because even as Desiree, that was a big step, a first."

"I don't judge people too much on what they do sexually unless it hurts somebody—know what I mean?"

She did. But she also thought it might be different when it was someone you loved, that logic was one thing, but the built-in mores of our society usually ran deeper in most people. "I appreciate that—but to be honest, I'm still not sure how *I* feel about it. I mean, yeah, as Desiree, it was ultra exciting. As Carly, though . . . well, it's something I would never do. The *real* me."

"You keep talking about this real you, but what you don't seem to get is that the girl I met in Traverse City was just a different part of you. A part you're not comfortable with. But she's in there," he said, pointing his finger gently into her bare chest. "And that's okay with me."

She lowered her chin, still uncertain. "Yeah?"

He flashed a grin. "I *liked* Desiree. You act like she's the devil incarnate or something, but she's just the more confident, more daring side of you. And for your information, I was bummed out to wake up and see you were gone."

She drew in her breath, truly stunned. He'd never told her that before. And she wouldn't have appreciated it when in Desiree mode—because as Desiree, she'd forced herself to be so unemotional, so uncaring. But here, now, she appreciated it.

"I don't want to freak you out or anything," Jake went on, "but the truth is, that night excited me so much that . . . I wouldn't mind it happening again sometime. At first, I was a little uncomfortable with the idea, with another guy being involved, but I never realized until then how much it would turn me on to share a woman, to see the woman I was with being fucked, up close like that, to be with a woman bold enough to want two guys, two cocks, at once."

When she didn't reply, he said, "Shit, *did* I freak you out?"

Still snuggled against him, she shook her head against his chest. After all, it was hard to be *too* freaked-out given that she was the one who'd reminded him about their night with Colt. Maybe she truly *was* starting to accept that Desiree was a real part of her, and maybe hearing Jake's views on Desiree made that part seem . . . a lot less awful than she usually thought. She'd been consciously taking the pieces of Desiree she actually *liked*—that she was pretty and stylish and confident—and drawing them into her everyday life. But she'd never before thought about bringing the nastiest of Desiree's naughty sex into her life, too. Now, even as her stomach churned at the very idea, her pussy flared a bit beneath the covers.

"Then . . . do you think you'd ever want to do that again?" Jake went on. "Because . . . it would excite the hell out of me to see you experience that much pleasure."

Her heart beat faster at the very suggestion. "You wouldn't feel . . . jealous now?"

"You love me, right?" he asked.

"Madly."

"Then no, I wouldn't be. I mean, sex is different when you care about somebody. As long as I'm the one you care about, it would excite me to . . . to give you that. To give you more pleasure than I can on my own, you know?"

She glanced up at him, tilted her head. There was a lot to think about here. "I'm not saying I'd even consider this, but for the record—um, don't you have control issues? Worse than mine, it would appear? So . . . wouldn't something like this be a problem for you? I mean, even when I didn't *know* you had control issues—that night with Colt, you had control issues."

In response, he gave her a smile that conceded the point. "Yeah, if there's anything I could change about that night, I'd have been as pushy as you and Colt from the start, calling more of the shots. I was just . . . caught off guard by the whole situation. If it happened again, I'd know better."

"So you're saying if it happened again, you'd be the one in full control."

"Not necessarily *full* control. But I'd hold my own from the beginning this time. And if it was with *you, now*—well, I'd probably let the other guy know you're mine and that I'd have the final say on what does or doesn't happen."

She could have taken that in a lot of different ways. If she were in Desiree mode, she wouldn't have condoned his possessiveness—but the person she saw as her *real, true* self didn't mind, and even liked having a man who valued her that much.

Angling another grin her way in the dark room, he said, "You never answered my question, though, sweetie pie. Would you ever do it again? I mean . . . wouldn't that be the ultimate way to feel like you've conquered your problems? Last time, you were *all* Desiree, and you were fucking amazing— but I'd love to experience that with you as the complete woman you are, as Carly, with no pretenses this time."

Perhaps it was the first time since he'd asked her that she'd seriously tried to envision such a scenario. No slinky red dress or heavy makeup to hide behind. No fake name. It would also mean: no ability to turn off her emotions. She would feel it this time, inside her, as deeply as such a thing could be felt. She would be Carly Winters, Turnbridge town sweetheart gone wild. The thought brought another hot blush to her cheeks. "I . . . I don't know if I could, Jake."

"You want to," he teased her with a naughty little grin. "You loved having two cocks."

God, she *had* loved that. She might not be able to say it out loud, but the memory made her breasts ache with need as her pussy began to pulse. She'd never even *imagined* a feeling like that. Not only the physical part, but . . . what perhaps should have left her feeling at their mercy had instead instilled in her a sense of ultimate power and liberation.

Just then, Jake's words from earlier replayed in her head. *Maybe I think that even if I can't quite free myself that maybe I can free you—that if you give it all up to me, that'll happen for you.* Hmm. He'd just shown her with the handcuffs that sometimes surrender did make you stronger. Even if he couldn't surrender to certain things himself, maybe he knew what he was talking about.

Even so, she felt her blush intensify and bit her lower lip. The act had been outlandish *enough* when she'd been hiding behind a disguise, a whole different personality—when she'd thought there'd be no consequences because they were all strangers. What Jake was suggesting now would be much more complicated.

So finally she replied by saying, "I love *your* cock."

"Nice avoidance tactic," he answered on a laugh, clearly seeing right through her. "But if you want to tell me more about how great my cock is, I'll let it go."

Chapter 15

"About time, Lockhart," a muscular, dark-haired guy called from the shiny white boat's upper deck as Jake led Carly by the hand across the marina's dock. They each carried weekend bags, and Jake also held a beach tote and the small shopping bag containing the bikini he'd just bought for her after finding out her only swimsuit was old and worn.

"Sorry we're late," he said without explaining the reason why—which suited her fine. She didn't mind her boyfriend buying her a bikini, but she didn't necessarily want all his friends knowing she'd never even owned one before, which she'd confided in him while shopping together in the boutique up the street.

The day was bright and warm, the boat immense and beautiful, and Carly tried her darnedest not to feel overwhelmed as she stepped from the dock onto the lower deck to find herself surrounded by handsome men.

"Everybody, this is Carly Winters," Jake introduced her, then pointed out each of his friends as he said, "Carly, meet Shane Delacorte, Quinn Jamison, and Cameron Lynch—and the complainer up there is Rogan Wolfe."

"The pleasure's mine," said Shane, a clean-cut professional type who came across as confident and flirtatious as he took Carly's hand, then actually kissed it. The tiny kiss unexpectedly skittered right down her arm and into her breasts.

"Dude, she's already taken," said the less-clean-cut Quinn on a laugh. Both men wore their hair short and stylishly spiky on top, but Quinn's unshaven look, plus his whole general appearance, made him and Shane appear to be polar opposites.

"Hello," Cameron said with a light nod, and Carly instantly pegged him as being more reserved than the rest.

As Rogan descended the steps to join them, he lifted his hand in a wave. "Good to meet ya." He was slightly more muscular than his friends with coal black hair and a bad boy air about him.

"Uh, where are Ethan and Mira?" Jake asked. "Are we picking them up closer to Charlevoix or something?" Jake had told Carly that the couple lived in the lakeshore town about fifty miles up the coast from Traverse City.

"Nope—they had to cancel," Shane said. "Some big case he's working on—couldn't get away. Mira was pissed."

"Damn," Jake muttered. And Carly was disappointed, too. She'd learned that he considered Ethan—who'd gone from being a cop to being a lawyer—his closest friend in the group, and he'd thought Carly would hit it off with Ethan's live-in girlfriend, Mira.

"Yeah, sucks," Shane said.

"But Rogan doesn't mind—do ya?" Quinn chimed in.

Rogan simply made a face in reply. "You guys make a bigger deal of that than it is. Me and Ethan are cool. Hell, we play on the same softball team all damn summer long."

"Rogan used to date Mira," Jake explained to Carly, and she nodded.

"About a thousand years ago," Rogan added. "It's all good."

"So where's Tara?" Jake asked Shane then. Carly knew from Jake that Shane had mentioned bringing his girlfriend, too—though, as with Carly, this would be everyone's first time meeting her.

In response, however, Shane let out a discontented grumble. "She's in fucking Arizona."

When he said nothing more, Jake looked from Shane to the other guys. "Dumped him three days ago. Went back to the old fiancé in Phoenix," Quinn informed them.

"Shit," Jake muttered, shifting his gaze back to Shane. "Sorry, dude."

The previously oh-so-confident guy just shrugged, muttered something about her being a bitch, then bounced back to his more confident demeanor to say, "But whatever. We've got beer, we've got a boat, we've got beautiful weather—let's get this party started."

Carly had felt a little weird discovering that, as it turned out, she would be the only girl on the two-day excursion. Besides being intimidated by all that testosterone, she simply didn't consider herself adept in the social arts. It was one thing to chitchat with people she'd known all her life in Turnbridge, or to make conversation with strangers in Winterberry's about furniture, but it was another to comfortably hang out with a bunch of sexy cops who'd known each other for ten years.

Of course, when she'd confided this to Jake as they walked down the hall of the cabin cruiser—which she'd have classified more as a junior yacht—he'd told her not to worry about it, adding, "What's it matter?"

And maybe that was true, even if she'd been looking forward to meeting Mira.

As they unpacked in one of the small bedrooms belowdecks, he added, "We're just here for some relaxation in the sun, so you should try to do that—relax." His sweet smile reminded her that she *wasn't* the most relaxed person on the planet—and she decided it was good advice.

After Jake changed into swim trunks and left the room, however, she put on her zebra-striped bikini and her new notion of relaxation nearly fled the scene. And draping the short red sarong—an additional gift from Jake—around her hips didn't do much to make her feel any less on display. Though she'd been perfectly cool with the idea of trading in her old one-piece for a bikini, she'd have never picked out this particular one on her own—but Jake had practically insisted, especially once she'd tried it on.

Of course, a glance in the mirror—just like back at the boutique—confirmed that she did look good in it. Her breasts curved provocatively from the two triangles of fabric, making her feel sexy. And Carly was fairly sure Dana and Beth Anne would faint if they could see her right now. But then, they'd have done more than merely faint if they could have seen her during *previous* visits to Traverse City, so maybe this was nothing. Just one more change to get used to.

When she joined the guys on the expansive lower deck, sprinkled with various outdoor chairs, a table, and a padded seat that wrapped all the way around the front of the boat, she appreciated their admiring glances as they greeted her. And she wondered if they could see her nipples through the bikini top—since she was pretty certain those mere glances were making the two peaks hard. If nothing else, the glances were certainly making her aware of her own body—and in a good way.

The vessel meandered slowly through the central lane of the marina, and when a long, wolfish whistle came from above, she glanced up to see Shane at the helm. He flashed a flirtatious smile and called, "How am I supposed to concentrate on driving this thing with such a gorgeous woman distracting me?"

"Feel free to ignore him," Quinn said, lazing on a lounge chair, saving her from having to come up with a response.

"What—just because I let a woman know I appreciate her assets I should be ignored?" Shane said, still perfectly confident, almost arrogant.

"No," Rogan replied, digging beer from a cooler a few feet from Carly. "You should be ignored because you have a shitty habit of flirting with other guys' women." It seemed to be said half in truth, half in jest.

From the padded seat along the edge, Jake spoke too quietly for Shane to hear. "Eh, cut him some slack. He just got dumped. And I'm not worried he's gonna steal her away or anything." He concluded by sending a quick, sexy wink in her direction.

When she ventured another glance up toward Shane, he seemed entirely undaunted by it all, telling her, "Don't listen to 'em—I'm not that bad. I just think Jake's a lucky bastard."

"Hell," Rogan said, "I don't think that needs to be said. He's the only guy here with a chick. And a hot one, too."

"Who's flirting now?" Quinn asked, chin lowered derisively.

But Rogan didn't even look up from the cooler as he shrugged. "Not flirting. Just stating the facts." Only then did he turn to Carly. "Beer, hon? Or—I think Shane brought some wine coolers, too."

"Oh—not right now, too early in the day for me. But I'll take a pop or bottled water."

"Comin' up," Rogan said, dropping the cooler's lid and opening up a second one behind it.

Jake told Carly they'd saved her the best lounge chair, so she playfully said, "My, what gentlemen," and gladly took it. And from there the afternoon went on, full of snacking, sunning, and music from a boom box.

The occasional cottony cloud dotted a warm blue sky as they floated up the West Arm of Grand Traverse Bay, which then opened into the bay proper. Carly admired lovely houses tucked in among billowy green trees on the shore, as well as other stretches of coast where the water was edged strictly by forest, occasionally interrupted by small ribbony beaches of pale brown sand. Given that it was a holiday weekend, the bay teemed with boats of all sizes, but by the time they finally exited the bay into open water a couple of hours after departing, traffic was more scattered and Carly began to feel the great lake's vastness.

She liked listening to Jake and his friends chat—they clearly enjoyed each other's company, a fact that reminded her of the raucous laughter she'd heard from the group of H.O.T. cops that first night in the hotel bar.

She didn't add much to the conversation at first, but over time she grew more at ease, even asking questions when they occurred to her, and they seemed perfectly happy to include her. She found out that, like the absent Ethan, Shane was no longer a cop, either; he'd traded in his badge to be a private investigator instead. "Not the kind you see on TV or in old movies, though, with rinky-dink little offices and wearing bad suits. I've got a high-rise suite overlooking the Chicago River—and I only wear Armani," he told her, finishing with a wink.

"Being a cop came with too many rules for Shane," Cameron volunteered.

"Hell," Jake said, "being a cop came with too many rules for Rogan, too—but he finds a way around them."

They all laughed, Rogan included, even as he said, "Listen, those days are behind me. Mostly." And as more laughter erupted, Carly decided that she'd been right in pegging Rogan as a bad boy. There was something about him she found wholly intimidating—yet totally hot at the same time.

She also discovered that soon after graduating from the police academy, Quinn had elevated his law enforcement status by going through the training and selection process to become an FBI agent. Though when Rogan mentioned it, Quinn balked. "Dude, we don't just spout that out at will, remember? Shit."

"Don't worry," Carly instantly assured him. "I won't . . . rat you out or anything." And when they all chuckled at that, it built her confidence a little and put her still more at ease with Jake's friends.

Eventually Shane steered the boat in closer toward the shore, anchoring it and announcing he was ready for a swim. Since the hottest part of the day had arrived, everyone agreed it was a good idea, and when the guys all went piling into the water without a care, Carly realized they were great swimmers.

She herself hadn't swum much in recent years, so to be cautious she grabbed an old-fashioned inner tube from the deck before joining them.

Almost immediately, Jake swam toward her, dipped beneath the surface, and came up inside the rubber ring with her. And . . . mmm, it instantly felt *so* good to be back up against him, their legs mingling together underwater as she freed her hands from the inner tube to rest them wetly on his shoulders. "Hi," he said low and deep, casting a wicked little grin.

"Hi," she returned with her best playful, sexy smile. She'd never *had* a playful, sexy smile before Jake had come along—except maybe when in Traverse City—but it had developed very naturally along with their relationship.

She was a little surprised when he leaned in to give her a slow, sensual kiss—his friends were right there, after all—but she couldn't resist kissing him back anyway. It felt fun and a little naughty to be wet with him this way, to feel her sensitive breasts rub against his chest through her new zebra-striped top.

When his thigh pressed into her crotch, though, and she realized he was getting hard against her leg, she drew back slightly, wide-eyed even if teasing, and whispered, "*Stop.*"

He let out a low little growl in response, flashing a wholly seductive look. "I can't," he whispered back. "You're too fucking hot."

"Sure," Shane said off to their right, resting on a float now, "make out in front of the guy who just got dumped by the love of his life. I don't mind."

Carly knew he was kidding, but still felt a little bad for him—even when Rogan said, "She wasn't the fucking love of your life, dude. You met her a month ago."

"Well, I was getting serious about her anyway."

Jake told Carly quietly, "Shane can be kind of a drama king."

And Shane said, "I heard that, Lockhart."

After they got out of the water, Carly stretched back out in her chair, letting the warm rays of the sun dry her. "Mmm, this is heaven," she murmured, eyes shut.

"Just be careful you don't burn, sweetie pie," Jake told her.

"Sweetie pie?" Quinn asked critically.

"What can I say—I've got a way with words," Jake joked.

"So this guy can get a chick as hot as you," Rogan asked in Carly's direction, "with 'sweetie pie'?"

She was so relaxed by now that the conversation came to her as if through a haze, and she only responded with a light giggle, murmuring, "The 'sweetie pie' thing is silly, but he keeps me happy in lots of other ways."

She hadn't quite realized she'd said something suggestive until she heard the amused masculine snickers, but she merely let a lazy grin unfurl, no longer anxious about the situation. And she vaguely remembered Jake reminding her she needed to put on sunscreen—but she was in such a tranquil state she couldn't quite make herself exert the energy. She'd never have dreamed a few hours earlier that she'd succeed so quickly at relaxing so much.

A few serene minutes had passed when . . . mmm, a soft, moist caress warmed her shoulder.

Realizing Jake was putting the sunscreen on *for* her, she didn't even open her eyes. "That's nice," she heard herself say.

His voice came in a whisper near her ear. "Well, I don't want you to burn—and you look too good not to want to touch."

She bit her lip, merely letting out a languorous sigh in reply—then enjoyed the sensation as Jake smoothed the coconut-scented lotion sensually down her arms in a slow massage that resonated all through her. Next, he did her legs, starting at her ankles and working gradually upward. When his fingers dipped briefly to rub the sunscreen into both inner thighs, she emitted a tiny gasp—because she felt it in her pussy. And because she began to wonder if the other guys were watching.

The thought woke her up a little, made her want to open her eyes and check. But that would . . . break the spell. Maybe it was better she didn't know for sure. And yet . . . she thought she *felt* their gazes. Felt them thinking she was hot and feeling a little jealous of Jake—or maybe even a lot. And the fact that she was letting it happen—even if she *had* been edging near sleep at the start—made her feel a little wild, and utterly sensual. This was not something Carly Winters would ever do. Except . . . she was doing it. So maybe Jake was right—maybe Desiree was a bigger part of her than she wanted to believe.

But she could scarcely think anymore when Jake's warm touch descended from behind her again, this time to her chest. He smoothed the fragrant lotion in, working from her neck downward . . . onto the inner curves of her breasts. She drew in her breath and once more felt all those male eyes drinking her in as Jake worked slowly, thoroughly, even letting his fingertips ease inside the edges of her bikini top as if to make sure he covered every inch of skin. She knew her nipples jutted against the thin top now—her pussy tingled too much for her breasts not to be getting in on the act, showing Jake and his friends how aroused she was. She even heard another sigh of pleasure echo from her throat unbidden.

When finally Jake's hands moved lower, to her stomach, he dropped a soft kiss to the side of her neck. And when he'd covered that area, as he began to stand back upright, he skimmed his fingertips over her breasts. She felt it *everywhere*.

Carly barely knew who she was in this moment. She felt . . . like someone she didn't know—and yet she didn't really want to change a thing. She was a hot, vibrant, bold, sensual woman. And still, in her mind, she remained completely herself.

She murmured a soft "Thank you" to her lover, but kept her eyes closed. Because Desiree would have opened them, would have met all those hot, piercing male gazes, would have said something saucy or inviting or obscene. And she wasn't quite *there* yet—and wasn't sure she ever would be or even wanted to be. The truth was, she liked everything about who she was in this very moment. Sexy, bold—but still herself.

Finally, she heard Cameron say, perhaps a bit awkwardly, his voice low but breathy, "Um, anybody ready to eat? Maybe I should, uh, start getting the grill ready."

"Uh, yeah—good idea," Quinn answered, equally as uncomfortable.

And then everything changed—the awkwardness ended as the guys resumed going about their business, a couple of them getting the grill fired up as someone else said, "I'll grab the burgers and dogs from the fridge."

But it all confirmed Carly's suspicions that his buddies had indeed been as transfixed by Jake's sensual sunscreen application as she herself had been. She'd officially turned them on.

By the time darkness fell across Lake Michigan, dinner was over and the boat's passengers stood around the deck drinking, laughing, having fun. Everyone remained in their swimwear from earlier—there'd been no reason to change. While the guys all drank beer, Carly indulged in strawberry wine coolers.

Her mind kept drifting back to what she now thought of as "the sunscreen incident." It had been hours ago, and certainly no one had mentioned it nor treated her any differently, so it was almost as if it had never even happened— yet she couldn't forget it had. Now, as she stood at the railing, admiring the ribbon of sparkling light the moon cast on the rippling water, a pleasant lull of intoxication wafted over her and she found herself wondering . . . if she'd made them hard, all these manly men. Was it possible?

Of course, maybe she was blowing it out of proportion—maybe watching was just watching. It didn't necessarily equal a hard-on. But the very idea still made her feel sexy all over. *Sexual.* Hungry—and not just for the brownies and cookies and chips they'd all been nibbling since dinner.

Music still played, and she recognized the song just coming on—a very sexy older tune she remembered giggling about with Dana when they were kids, called "Naughty Naughty." The beat was intense and powerful, sensual in and of itself—and when a warm hand closed on her wrist and spun her around, she didn't expect it to be Shane. "Dance with me," he said, all confident smile and seductive eyes.

It caught her off guard as he pulled her into a rather close embrace, already moving to the music, but she laughed and went along with it, seeing no real reason not to. A couple of the other guys stood across the deck absorbed in conversation, and Jake had just headed off to the bathroom a minute before.

It felt strange now to be in another guy's arms. Shane was at once lean yet masculine, his arms and shoulders bulging with just the right amount of firm muscle, his chest peppered with only a smattering of pale brown hair. The way he moved to the song was nothing more than playful, yet she remained very aware of her body from the day's events. She let her palms rest high on his chest as his hands molded to her hips, making her cunt tense slightly.

"So tell me about this girl—Tara," she said.

His light grin seemed to chide her for asking, and it was laced with some sadness he couldn't quite hide. "Like Rogan said, probably not really the love of my life. But I cared about her. A lot. I saw it going somewhere. She was practically living with me already."

She liked that he was really answering her—not just joking through it or playing it off.

"What happened?"

He shook his handsome head. "Just came home the other day to find her stuff gone, and a note. Seriously. A note. Saying she'd gone back to Phoenix to her old fiancé. It felt like a kick in the teeth."

She nodded, truly sorry for his pain. "That stinks. I'm sorry." She slid her hands slightly upward, onto his shoulders. "But she doesn't sound like a very nice person if she'd leave you without even a word."

He shrugged softly. "Yeah, I've been thinking the same thing. But it still sucks. To find out she's not who I thought she was. I mean . . . I don't get . . ."

"What?"

His gaze narrowed slightly. "I don't get serious about girls. Not often anyway. So guess I'm just pissed this is the one I let myself really care about." His eyes told her he'd just confided in her, which touched her. "But enough about that," he went on, breaking the moment. "What did Jake the Snake do to get himself a sweet, sexy girl like you?"

She grinned, raising her eyebrows. "Jake the Snake, huh?"

Smiling back, he slanted her a conspiratorial glance. "Don't let his mature, upstanding demeanor fool ya—back in the day, he was a snake in the grass."

Carly weighed the information, trying to decide how seriously to take it. "Should I consider that fair warning?"

But then Shane shook his head. "Naw. He's a good guy, Jake. We were all young back then, all sowing our oats—and maybe not treating every girl as nice as they deserved. We were all about to be cops—we were full of ourselves and tomcattin' around to prove it. But we've all grown up since then. So no worries—Jake's a solid guy."

As if on cue, she looked up to see Jake moving in behind her just then, grabbing onto her still swaying hips, teasingly joining in their dance. "Still trying to steal my girl, huh, Delacorte?" he asked over her shoulder.

Shane just shrugged again, not letting go of her. "How can I resist? Pretty girl. Smokin' bikini. Moonlit night."

"And she's nice enough to dance with my drunk, lonely friend," Jake ribbed him.

Yet Shane only let out a good-natured laugh. "I'm not any drunker than you."

"But I'm cuter. And I give her what she needs," Jake said, rubbing against her from behind, the beginnings of a hard-on pressing into her ass. She couldn't help feeling a little embarrassed—clearly he *was* drunk, maybe they *all* were—but he felt so good it hardly mattered. In fact, it *all* felt good.

Jake's growing erection against her ass made her wiggle her hips a little—not a decision, just a reaction—and she found herself enjoying being sandwiched between two strong, hot men. Shades of that night with Colt echoed back to her—it was the only other time she'd ever been in such a position in her life. But like always with Jake these days, this felt very different from that. Because this was real. Not a one-night pretense. This was her real life now.

Ignoring Jake, Shane freed a hand from her waist, lifting her chin with one bent finger to draw her gaze to his. And with an arrogant glint in his eye, he said, "Well, honey, if you ever *need* anything this guy can't give you, I'm at your service." Then he winked and walked away.

Biting her lip to crush back the sensual little thrill he'd just delivered, she turned to wrap her arms around Jake's neck, shimmying up closer to him. Again, not a decision—just a response, made easier with alcohol.

"Kiss me, you sexy animal," he said, as playful and confident as his friend.

Her eyes widened. "Animal?"

He flicked a glance down at her bikini. "Zebra girl," he called her.

Yeah, he was drunk all right. But sexy as hell. So she kissed him for all she was worth, not giving a damn if the whole world was watching.

Within another hour, a day of drinking in the sun had begun to take its toll—Shane had conked out, then dragged himself off to bed, and a bleary-eyed Cameron had said good night soon after. Quinn and Rogan, however, both none the worse for wear, decided to try out the hot tub on the boat's rear deck, and they invited Jake and Carly to join them.

But as the pair sat cuddled in a lounge chair, Jake answered for them both. "No thanks—we're good here."

Once they were alone, Carly leaned back and looked up at the sky, dotted with a million shimmering stars. The night hadn't cooled as it usually did this time of year in northern Michigan, and the air hugged her skin like warm velvet. "This is nice," she said, leaning against her man.

"So you're having a good time?"

She nodded, curled in his lap, head against his shoulder. "Your friends are nice. I was silly to be nervous."

"Nah," he said, "it's cool. And even if they *are* good guys, I'm glad to finally get some time alone with you out here under the stars." And with that, he gently lifted his hand to her cheek and kissed her.

Jake kissed her in so many different ways depending upon his mood, and this one was soft, yet potent and sexy. She felt it spreading down through her like a warm drink. "Mmm . . . you were right earlier," she told him. "You do give me what I need."

His grin held a hint of mischief, those blue eyes sparkling. "When I heard myself say that, I was afraid you'd slug me. Glad it didn't freak you out the way . . . well, the way it could have."

"Lucky for you, I was a little drunk," she teased him, their faces close. "And besides, if something was going to freak me out, it probably would have been the sunscreen incident."

He didn't even pretend not to know what she was referring to. "Ah. Yeah. That." He nodded, his smile now half-naughty, half-guilty. "It started out totally innocent, I swear. And then . . . I guess instinct took over."

She swallowed, still both excited and embarrassed by the memory. "I, um, had a feeling your friends were all watching, but I couldn't make myself open my eyes to see."

"They were," he told her, his voice a hot whisper in the night. "And . . . it kinda turned me on. Did it kinda turn you on, too?"

The Carly of a couple of months ago—if she'd ever somehow found herself in such an unlikely situation—would have automatically lied, too uncomfortable with the truth. But now, with Jake, that didn't even occur to her. She'd gotten so used to honesty with him. "Yeah."

"Good," he murmured, and then he kissed her again—using his arms to shift her body until she was straddling him in the lounge chair. He let his kisses lengthen, deepen, until their tongues were twining and Carly's whole body tingled with the same hunger from earlier. But that hunger had been there, lingering in the background, for many hours, and now it became more consuming. She kissed him back just as hotly, and when his hands lifted to her breasts, a short moan escaped her.

She gasped upon remembering where they were—but Jake whispered, "It's okay—they'll never hear."

And that was likely true. Music still played low nearby, and the loud shushing noise of the churning hot tub could be heard from the front of the boat.

Clearly seeing she was appeased, Jake resumed caressing her tits, murmuring, "Mmm, baby, these are *so* hot," and soon pushing aside the two zebra-striped triangles like he was opening a curtain.

Fresh heat coursed all through her at having her breasts suddenly on display. She glanced down in the moonlight to see new tan lines seeming to highlight them, her skin still slick from old sunscreen, her nipples dark and fully pointed. "Unh," Jake groaned softly at the sight, then framed them with his hands as he leaned in to lick one.

He licked and swirled his tongue around the sensitive peak, and when he moved in to suckle the other deeply, she hissed in her breath, her pussy pulsing.

And then Jake did something he'd never done before. He backed off— just a little, just enough to gaze upon them again, his eyes lusty—before beginning to touch them once more, but this time with the softest, lightest, airiest caresses she'd ever felt.

From the start, it made her bite her lower lip to keep from gasping, moaning. He grazed his fingertips ever so gently across the soft, round flesh, at other moments raking delicately over the beaded nipples. No matter where on her breasts his touch roamed, it was featherlight and utterly exquisite. "That's . . . so nice," she managed between thready breaths. "So . . . so . . . good."

He said nothing, just remained squarely focused on his task, appearing committed to her heady pleasure. Sometimes they kissed as he touched her—other times they both just watched his skilled fingers play over her skin. And before long Carly realized her nipples weren't the only things that were erect—a long, hard column had grown in his swim trunks, so without forethought, she reached down between them, wrapping her hand around it through the fabric.

A low groan left him before he said, "You like that hard cock, baby?"

"Mmm, God, yes, I love it. You know I love it."

"Aw," he breathed. "Then why don't you rub that pretty pussy against it."

Without hesitation, she slid her torso closer to his until her crotch pressed to his gloriously stiffened length and they both emitted hot sighs. She began to grind then, her instincts taking over—and Jake's petal-soft touches deepened slightly.

That's when she caught something in her peripheral vision—a bit of movement—and she flicked her glance subtly to the right to see Rogan standing in the shadows at the side of the boat, watching them. Dear God. She was sure he'd appeared only now, and probably on accident, not knowing what he'd walk in on—but he stayed silent, unmoving.

Part of her wanted to cling to Jake, cover herself, hide. But another part experienced the urge to let herself stay on display for him. So few men had ever found her truly exciting. Desiree, sure—but Carly, no.

Still, she simply leaned in close to Jake, pressing herself against his chest and bringing her mouth to his ear. She whispered, "Rogan is here. Watching."

When he stayed quiet, she finally turned her head, looked into his eyes.

Their faces were but an inch apart and she could feel both their bodies practically pulsing from the heat she'd just tried to still. Finally, he whispered back, "We can stop if you want," but his voice sounded thick, throaty, from arousal.

"I . . . I'm not sure," she admitted. "What do *you* want?"

"Mostly I want to make you happy, turn you on."

"You always do. That's why . . . I want whatever *you* want right now."

His breath came labored in her ear as he said, "Then . . . hell, honey—if it's really up to me . . . please don't stop, please keep going."

The very words made her draw in her breath as their gazes stayed locked.

"I want him to see how hot you are," Jake breathed. "I want him to see how good you fuck me."

Chapter 16

Carly's heart beat so hard she could have sworn she could hear it. Old feelings warred inside her with new ones. What he'd just suggested felt unthinkable in one sense—until she reminded herself that she'd fucked both Jake and Colt together in a hotel room only a few short months ago. Short months that felt very long, though. Because she loved this man. And she was her true self with him. And that made everything she did with him mean so much more. Whether it turned out to be for the better—or for the worse.

And yet, he'd given her a choice and she'd responded by putting it back in his hands. And her breasts ached and her pussy yearned. She felt wild and sexy and beautifully dirty under Rogan's unexpected gaze. And she wanted to please Jake. She wanted it so much. She wanted to be everything he could ever want in a woman.

And the fact that she still floated in the sweet swirl of intoxication helped. Helped her to revel in wondering if Rogan liked her tits as much as Jake did. Helped her to decide the raging desire between her legs was more important than her old need to be a good girl. Helped her to lift her hands to Jake's face and kiss him with utter passionate abandon, her way of saying the word she couldn't quite get past her lips: *Yes*.

Jake delivered firm, hungry tongue kisses now that nearly buried her—in between stopping to suck on her nipples from time to time. He massaged her ass as she undulated against his erection, on the verge of losing control.

Until he murmured, "Slow down, baby. Don't you dare come yet. Don't you dare come until you're fucking me, riding me."

And oh God, she wanted to be doing that—*now*. Her lust had risen to a fever pitch quickly, almost from the second she'd resumed kissing him, the moment she'd known she was going to let the big, muscular, bad boy cop watch them.

As she rose to her knees, Jake tugged at the fabric molded to her rear, muttering, "Let's get these off you," then pulled the bikini bottoms to her thighs. A low growl echoed from Jake's throat, exciting her further—and her cunt practically oozed with the knowledge that Rogan could see it now, pale and smooth and shaven in the moonlight.

It was going to be awkward getting her bottoms the rest of the way off in this position, but she simply leaned back, *way* back, lowering her ass to the extended bottom of the chair between Jake's legs, and held her own legs up toward him, knees bent. He wasted no time removing her bottoms completely and tossing them away—and then she followed her naughtiest instinct without hesitation: Still leaning back, arms stretched out behind her to brace herself, she parted her legs. Wide. As wide as they would comfortably go. To let Jake look. To let Rogan look.

"Holy fuck," Jake murmured, eyes glued on her pussy, which she knew without even a glance was open and pink and glistening wet. Her whole body vibrated with lust. With being the willing *object* of lust. And she praised the heavens for a clear night with a large, bright moon that made her so visible right now.

"You're so fucking hot, baby," Jake said. "Come to me. Slide that sweet pink pussy onto my cock before I lose my mind."

Carly practically bounded forward to straddle him again, as eager as *he* was now, and they both struggled to free his erection from his swim trunks. Once it was within her sight, in her fist, she burned to have it inside her and felt empty without it. Balancing on her knees, with Jake gripping her ass, she smoothly impaled herself, taking him all the way to the hilt.

They both moaned at the deep entry and Carly's cheeks went hot.

"Always so tight, honey," Jake murmured.

"You feel so good and big," she told him, her inhibitions all but gone now.

"Fuck me," he said—and the deeply spoken command reverberated all the way down to her soul. She began to move, as fueled by Rogan's eyes as she was by Jake's. She fucked him with hot abandon, so turned on she could barely think—could only feel, react, follow her body's urges.

The orgasm wasn't long in coming. She felt as if she'd never been so wet, as if Jake had never been this big and rock-hard. He sucked her tits, and her clit connected with his body just above the base of his cock, and everything inside her moved in all the right, perfect ways until she felt herself reaching the precipice, pushed there all the harder by knowing an extra pair of male eyes watched her. "I'm coming, I'm coming," she whimpered as she rocked and rode him, sobbing softly as the pleasure tore through her in wild, throbbing waves that somehow made her feel all the more beautiful.

When the climax passed, she slumped against him, spent and clinging, needing his arms to fold around her after what she'd just done while letting another man watch them. But Jake held her tight and it made everything okay, even that sobering postorgasmic moment when it would have been so easy to suffer regret.

"You okay?" Jake whispered in her ear.

He meant about Rogan. Because he couldn't quite believe she'd gone along with it. And if she was gonna freak out, it would be now.

So relief poured through him when she nodded against his shoulder and murmured, "Yes. *Oh* yes." Relief and more hot lust.

"I want to fuck you hard now," he told her. "I want to fuck your pretty little brains out."

Slowly, she sat up, looked him in the eye. He liked the raw heat still residing in her gaze. "Then fuck me," she said.

And since he was still inside her—shit, that could have sent him blasting into orgasm right then and there, but he held himself together and said, "Stand up."

She looked a little surprised, but rose off him. Damn, she looked hot standing there in nothing but that pushed aside bikini top. And maybe he was a bastard, but in that moment he hoped Rogan was enjoying the view.

He wasn't quite sure why—he'd never really fucked a girl in front of his friends before. Although when they were young, there'd been occasions when he would be in one room with a girl while one of his buddies was in the next room with another, or other occasions when they would *hear* each other going at it. But this was different. Maybe he'd just taken pleasure in their jealousy all day and wanted to let Rogan see that it was well-founded, that they *should be* jealous. Or maybe this was about him telling her it would excite him to share her again. He'd been reasonably sure she'd never go for that— but this was a little *like* sharing. Or maybe it was about him wanting her to let go of all the old feelings that had always held her back, wanting her to make up for lost time and experience all the variations of sex he could give her.

Hell, though—didn't matter what it was. All that mattered right now was that, for whatever reason, Rogan's silent participation made this damn arousing. And Jake was going to push her now, a little more than usual.

Shrugging out of his trunks as he stood up as well, he said, "Go to the railing. Climb up on the bench, on your knees, facing the water."

He kept half-expecting her to balk at some point, since with Rogan's presence, maybe doing it in the chair, keeping it simple, should have been enough. But she didn't balk—just did as he said, her sweet round ass arching toward him now. As he approached her, he sought Rogan in the darkness using only his peripheral vision. Yeah, he wanted to share her, but he was afraid she'd get upset if he let his friend *know* they knew he was there, that they both condoned it.

After catching the glint in his friend's eyes, where he stood hidden in the shadows, Jake then turned his attention back to his gorgeous, naked girl. Moving up behind her, reveling in the view, he closed greedy splayed fingers over her ass and let his dick nestle at its center. "Are you ready for this cock?" he asked her. Yeah, he was feeling the urge to control, to dominate now, and he didn't even try to push it down.

"Please," she begged, sounding impatient. "Please fuck me."

Aw. Damn. Sometimes just that nearly undid him. His erection tightened even further as he slid it just once up the crease of her ass, listening to her moan; then he drew back his hand and slapped her rear. She let out a little moan. Then he finally took his shaft in hand and fed it into her waiting cunt.

This was one of the positions where she seemed to feel his cock more intensely, so it didn't surprise him when she leaned her head back to let out a sigh of pure, lusty pleasure. Damn, she was so fucking wet, and such a good, tight, hugging fit. "Oh God," she breathed. "Your cock is fucking huge."

Arrogant warmth settled over him. Because he was fucking huge. And because she didn't blurt out things that dirty all the time and it was damn exciting when she did.

"Hold on to that railing tight, because I'm gonna fuck you like a freight train," he promised her through gritted teeth—and then he began to pound into her as hard as he could. She cried out at each rough stroke—but quickly began biting her lip, trying to hold the sounds in. He didn't slow down; he didn't let up one bit—in fact, he smacked her ass a few more times, knowing she enjoyed some occasional spanking. He thrust so powerfully that the flesh of her ass jiggled with each commanding plunge into that tiny wet tunnel, and he heard her moans of pleasure coming through clenched teeth.

At one point, he hooked his arm around her waist to brace her and tangled his other hand into her long, loose hair, pulling back on it just slightly, not enough to hurt, just enough to make her scalp tingle. When her moans instantly dropped an octave, he knew the new pleasure was sifting down through her, making her all the more submissive to him in this moment. He'd never done the hair thing with her before—afraid it would be one dominant act too many—but tonight he'd plowed forward with the urge and wasn't sorry.

His loins began to ache from the position, but his cock and balls, which slapped against the outer flesh of her pussy with each drive, felt too damn good to stop. In fact . . . "Oh baby, baby . . . I'm gonna come. I'm gonna fucking come in you."

"Oh, do it," she sobbed hotly. "Come hard. I want you to come hard."

He continued pounding into her—again, again, again—overcome with pleasure and lust and everything about her, loving her naughty compliance, loving that Rogan was watching the whole thing, until finally—fuck yes—he erupted inside her, slamming his cock in as hard as he could with each last explosive stroke. He felt his come shoot violently, let his eyes shut, just rode it out until the end.

After which total exhaustion gripped him and he muttered, "Jesus Christ," slumping against her for a minute, hugging her from behind. "You're fucking amazing," he whispered against her back, aware of the sheen of sweat now covering them both.

After he finally withdrew, grabbed a napkin from a nearby table to help her clean up, then assisted her in turning around, they stood for a moment in a loose embrace, staring into each other's eyes, sharing it all: the submission, Rogan's presence, Jake's hand in her hair, the warm night, the stars up above. "I love you," he whispered. He didn't care if Rogan heard that part, either.

"I love you, too," she said. Music to his ears.

To Carly's surprise, it wasn't even yet midnight when they exited the small shower in their room a little while later—and she felt revived. "I wonder if your friends are still in the hot tub," she said, hoping they might be gone.

Jake, resting beautifully naked on the bed, raised his eyebrows. "Really? Aren't *you* the energetic little thing."

"I guess I'm feeling like making the most of this. I can sleep at home."

He grinned. "I like your attitude." Then he reached for his discarded trunks on the foot of the bed. "Although even if they're still there, I doubt they'd mind sharing it with us."

Yet she shook her head. "I'm not sure I'm ready to face Rogan just yet. And besides, I still haven't had much alone time with you."

"Look, woman," he said, giving his head a pointed tilt, "if you think we're gonna fuck again tonight, I've got bad news for ya. I don't like admitting this, but you wore me out."

"Me and all that beer," she teased. "But this isn't about sex—I'd just like to sit in the hot tub and cuddle. If they're gone, I mean."

Jake slipped into his shorts, gave her a wink, and said, "Let me go check."

A minute later he returned, reporting it was all clear, so she started to put back on her swimsuit. Yet when she picked up her top, Jake took it right back out of her hand to say, "If it's just you and me, no reason you need this."

She flashed him a suspicious look. "I thought you were too weak for sex."

"I am, but I can enjoy your tits just fine without fucking." Instead, he handed her the white tank top he'd worn onto the boat earlier. "This'll do. You can take it off when we get up there."

Five minutes later, the hot tub was roiling again, the water still quite warm from when Quinn and Rogan had used it. And, funny, as Carly stripped Jake's shirt off, leaving her topless, she didn't even give it a thought. *Who* was *this mysterious woman?*

You, she answered herself then. *The new you. A better you. Definitely a freer you. And a happier you.*

They'd grabbed the boom box from the front deck and now turned it back on, keeping the volume low, before easing into the hot water, bit by bit. Carly sat close to Jake's side, even lifting her left leg over his right. He settled his hand high on her thigh, then leaned over to give her a quiet kiss. They rested silently that way, eyes shut, just listening to the music, soaking up the night.

She wasn't sure how much time had passed when she heard a familiar voice say, "Sorry, you two lovebirds can't hog the hot tub all to yourselves," and looked up to see Shane. A glance down ensured her boobs were concealed beneath the bubbling water, so—all things considered—she didn't panic and, in fact, acted as if it were totally normal for a man she'd just met to come upon her without her top. Shane grinned. "If you guys are cool with me spoiling your privacy," he added.

She was actually kind of disappointed, but Shane was just too friendly— and even kind of sweet at times—to send away. And besides, she hadn't come here *expecting* alone time with Jake—it was a party, even if a small one. "Climb on in," she said.

When Jake flashed a look of mild surprise in her direction, she decided to tease Shane. "It's *his* boat."

Both men laughed and Shane said, "You really know how to make a guy feel wanted."

"Really, I don't mind," she said with an easy smile, repeating what she'd just reminded herself. "It's a party, after all."

As Shane descended into the tub, Jake said, "I thought you conked out. You looked wiped."

"Yeah. But a couple hours of sleep gave me a second wind. I really thought everybody else would be in bed by now—just figured I'd come out and soak in the tub a while."

The talk stayed light—Jake asked about Shane's work, and he shared a couple of cases he was investigating, and then Shane asked about life in Turnbridge. Jake shared his personal pros and cons—he'd found Carly there, and he liked the people, but the job was quieter than he'd expected. That still worried Carly a little—as horrible as it seemed, she almost hoped someone would commit a crime to give Jake some on-the-job excitement. Deep down, she feared that in the end it just wouldn't be enough for him and he'd leave.

After a while, she began to feel sleepy and announced she was ready for bed. Jake said, "You mind if I stay out here a few minutes more, keep catching up with Shane?"

"No," she said. "Take your time. I'll be asleep in five minutes."

And then, ready to get out, she remembered she was topless. "Um . . ." she began uncertainly without quite meaning to let her quandary show.

But Shane sensed the problem and said with his usual grin, "I promise I'll shut my eyes until you get your top on." Then he closed them—so she hurried from the tub, rushing to get the tank over her head even as an unavoidable question planted itself in her brain: *Okay, given that you just let Rogan see every private inch of you an hour ago, what does it really matter?*

Still, she felt better once Jake's shirt dropped around her hips and immediately said, "Okay, all set."

When Shane opened his eyes, though, she realized that he and Jake were both gaping at her. And Jake said, "Honey, you probably should have dried off first if you were feeling modest." She glanced down and—oh boy. She looked like an entry in a wet T-shirt contest—the thin white cotton hugged her every curve and left little to the imagination.

"No worries, though," Shane said quickly. "I consider myself lucky to get such a nice view."

"Um, thanks," she said, her cheeks flushing with warmth as she wrapped her arms around herself and bit her lip. Then she scurried off, still self-conscious but at the same time reminding herself once more that this was no big deal.

And again the question rose in her mind: *Who* was *this mysterious woman?* She barely recognized herself.

Though when she'd felt that way as Desiree, it had come with guilt.

And this, so far, came only with a sense of . . . liberation, freedom, and her own beauty.

Carly slept in Jake's arms, sated. Not only by the sex, but by the new sense of her sexual self she'd found just since yesterday. Add to that her relaxing day in the sun, the easy acceptance by his friends, and the comfort she felt in his embrace, and it was perhaps the best she'd slept . . . in years.

And yes, when she opened her eyes the next morning to the memory of fucking in front of Rogan, she suffered a little embarrassment, a little worry, over seeing him today. But in another way, it felt as if it had been nothing but a good, hot dream and she hoped it might feel that way to Jake's bad boy friend, as well.

"You okay this morning, sweetie pie?" Jake asked, as if reading her mind. His arm was tucked warmly around her waist beneath the sheet, where she wore only a cami and panties.

"Mmm hmm," she answered sleepily. "You?"

"Uh, I'm *way* more than just okay. Because—damn, you were amazing last night."

She turned to him in the bed, her pussy already tingling. "Yeah?" she whispered, smiling tenderly into his eyes. Maybe she just wanted to hear him say it some more, be reassured.

His gaze heated further. "Hell yes. Fucking me like that on the deck? And not freaking out in the hot tub? You're officially my dream woman."

Wow—she liked the sound of that. But the sex on the deck was starting to feel more real and less dreamlike. "So . . . you don't think Rogan will
act . . . weird or anything to me now."

He gave his head a short, sure shake. "He doesn't know we saw him. He
doesn't know we . . . got off on being watched." Then he brought his face
nearer, eyes narrowed. "That wasn't just me, was it? You got off on it, too,
right?"

She gave a gentle nod, trying to overcome her habitual shyness about
such things even as her cunt flared at the admission. "And Shane . . ." she
ventured.

Jake just offered a soft grin. "Shane's not the kind of guy to judge.
None of them are. I mean, I'm closer to some of them than others, but
we all share a bond that goes back a long way. Being at the academy was an
important time in all our lives. And even though not all of us are still cops,
in the H.O.T. program, we all saw each guy at his best, and sometimes at
his worst. And so . . . we've got each other's backs, in a big way. Despite how
we act sometimes, we have tremendous respect for each other. And no guy
on this boat would ever do anything to hurt any woman I'm with, or think
badly of her."

His words worked to assuage her fears—she could tell how much he
meant them, and that his relationship with these guys ran deeper than she'd
even understood until just now.

"And that's real convenient for me," he added, sliding right back into
naughty mode, "because I can't help it—it gets me hot when they see how
totally hot *you* are, honey."

Smiling over at him with his sexy blue eyes and sleep-mussed hair, she bit
her lip and said, "I'm trying to decide if I like how much you enjoy showing
me off to your friends."

"Take it as a compliment."

"I take it as you having a big ego and needing to feed it," she teased.

He arched one eyebrow in her direction, but then let a tiny grin spread across his unshaven face, as if in confession. "You make it easy to feed. When I see the way they look at you, it's hard not to . . . want them to know exactly how incredible you are."

Twining her arms around his neck, she gave him a kiss, unable to resist a man who made her feel so good about herself.

"You like them all, though, right?" Jake asked. "I mean, you're comfortable with them."

She nodded again. "Yeah—they're great. And . . ."

"And what?"

"And they're . . . pretty easy on the eyes, too," she admitted quietly. And when he let out a short laugh in response, she asked, "So you don't mind if I think they're good-looking?"

He tilted his head against the pillow. "I'm kinda used to it, since *most* women seem to feel that way. And trust me—I'm not the only one in the crowd with an ego."

She giggled lightly. "Don't worry—I already figured that out. It's just a good thing confident men appeal to me."

Jake's look turned more serious then. "Though I hope you know that if I'm showing you off, it's not only about *my* ego. It's that I want *you* to feel as sexy as you are. I want you to know that you don't have to be somebody else or put on an act for guys to find you attractive." He stopped, pushed a loose lock of hair back behind her ear. "I guess I . . . want to help you make up for lost time. In the sex department, I mean."

She gazed up at him. "Well, you're doing a good job of that so far. And I do . . . feel sexy. I mean, I'm starting to. It's very strange for me. And at moments, it would be easy to run away from that feeling. But then I just . . ."

"What?"

"Remember you're with me and that makes it okay. I really do trust you, Jake. Maybe more than I've ever trusted anyone."

The day was much like the previous one. It started with muffins and fruit enjoyed on the front deck in the sun. Then Shane pulled up anchor and they ventured away from shore out into the open water of Lake Michigan. They saw other boats, but there was also plenty of solitude, and at times it felt as if the serene body of water stretched forever. It reminded Carly how big the world was and that she'd never even seen the ocean. And that along with all the other changes she was making in her life, she should travel. To the ocean. And the mountains. And the desert. And beyond.

As the large cabin cruiser meandered slowly across the enormous lake, most of the guys seemed a little hungover. Quinn and Rogan indulged in some fishing off the back deck. But as the bright day revived them, they all eventually began laughing and telling stories about their police academy days.

Like yesterday, Carly enjoyed being surrounded by so many strong, attractive men and she could almost feel the testosterone wafting around her in the sun-soaked air. And as Jake had promised, neither Rogan nor Shane acted any differently toward her—although she might have noticed their admiring gazes on her even more often. Despite herself, she didn't mind. Each time she felt one of Jake's friends studying her, it made her pussy ache a little. On drives to Traverse City, she'd often felt very aware of her body—but that paled in comparison to this. Having so many men being sexually drawn to her—to Carly, no one else, no one she was pretending to be . . . well, it was a powerful and satisfying feeling.

Lunchtime brought cold cuts and snack chips—after which they found shallow water and anchored for more swimming. Somehow being wet with them all only heightened her physical response to all those muscles and that deep, masculine laughter. And when Rogan hung on the end of her air mattress, chatting about Charlevoix, the lake town where he lived and worked, it gave her a chance to notice just how warm and sexy his brown eyes were.

The day stretched on, languid and surprisingly sensual for Carly—and she found herself seeking Jake's touch more than yesterday when the other guys had been strangers to her. When she felt like kissing him, she kissed him. When she felt like curling up in his lap for a few minutes, she followed the impulse. And when she put sunscreen on his back, Shane said, "Damn, must be nice—guess the rest of us are gonna burn," his tone a flirty, playful hint.

So Carly said, "All right, all right—I'll do yours, too." And it truly was a matter of practicality, but when rubbing sunscreen into Shane's back led to doing the same for Quinn, Rogan, and even Cameron, her pussy literally hummed at having her hands on so many men one right after another.

It was after dinner, by which time the guys had been drinking for a while, that a speed boat pulled up alongside them. Quinn and Cameron stood at the railing, talking to the two girls inside it, and Carly glanced over to see a blonde and a brunette, both pretty and in smaller bikinis than hers. Before she knew it, the two guys were climbing down the swim ladder toward the other boat, Quinn tossing a wink at Shane and shouting, "Don't wait up for us."

Shane raised his eyebrows. "Seriously, dude?"

The cabin cruiser was anchored about a quarter mile offshore, and Quinn pointed to a small beach in the distance. "They're camped there. So if we don't come back, we'll catch up with you guys in the morning."

As the two guys disappeared over the edge of the mini-yacht, Shane and Rogan just looked at each other, clearly jealous of their friends' good fortune. "Damn," Shane muttered.

"Timing's everything," Rogan concluded with a shake of his head.

"Spare a hug for a lonely boat captain, honey?" Shane asked Carly as she walked past just then, adding a playful wink, as if in cahoots with her to make Jake jealous.

Of course, she complied, teasing both Shane and Rogan with, "Poor babies. I'm so sure you two have such a hard time getting girls."

"Well, in the middle of Lake Michigan," Shane said, "it's a challenge."

"Not for Quinn and Cameron," she pointed out.

And Rogan cracked a rare grin. "Touché."

As day turned to night, the mood on the boat was quieter. They still chatted and drank, but having the small party's numbers diminished by two made a difference, and the tone became more introspective as Rogan and Jake discussed their feelings about leaving a larger police force for that of a small town. Rogan, it turned out, had worked in Grand Rapids before relocating to Charlevoix.

As dusk stole across the lake, the four watched a stunning golden pink sunset over the western horizon. "To a damn nice weekend," Shane said, holding up a freshly opened can of beer. The other guys lifted theirs in the air and Carly raised her wine cooler, as well.

"Thank you guys for making me feel so welcome," she said after the toast.

And Shane gave her a you've-got-to-be-kidding look. "Trust me, honey, you've made this trip a hell of a lot more pleasant than it would have been without you—visually and otherwise." He finished with a wink that reminded her of her unwitting wet T-shirt display—and even as a customary blush warmed her cheeks, her pussy heated slightly, too.

Once darkness had fallen, they spotted a small fire on the beach that made them conclude Quinn and Cameron were indeed staying the night on the shore. But it surprised her when Rogan said, "Think I'm gonna turn in."

"Dude," Jake said, clearly surprised, as well. "What's the deal?"

The other dark-haired man shrugged. "Too much beer maybe. Sleepy."

"Hell—me, too," Shane chimed in. "About to fall asleep in my chair."

And within minutes, they were gone, disappearing belowdecks. Carly and Jake could still hear the light sounds of their voices from inside the boat, but being left alone with her man instantly revved her up. And the wine coolers she'd consumed over the past few hours had her in that pleasant lull of intoxication—the kind that took her inhibitions away.

Enough that she peered over at Jake, in the upright deck chair just a couple of feet from her lounge chair, and told him exactly what was on her mind. "My pussy's wet for you."

Like last night, a golden moon shone down—a bit smaller, dimmer, than last night's, but still providing enough shadowy light that she could easily see his expression pass almost instantly from shock to a deep, hungry heat. "Shit, babe. You drive me wild."

Carly's chest tightened, envisioning Jake's erection. Wanting to make him feel good. He'd given her everything, everything that felt so wonderful and new in her life. She wanted to show him how much she appreciated him.

So she lowered her nearly empty bottle to the deck beside her chair, got to her feet, walked to Jake, and knelt before him. The truth was, this went beyond appreciation—it was a gut-deep desire to have his cock filling her mouth, a desire that, like so many moments, took her back to the first night they'd met. And yet, as always, it was so very different now.

"Aw, baby," Jake murmured deeply, sweetly, peering down on her. And she knew his response was about more than what she was getting ready to do—it was because even when she was aggressive with him, it wasn't normally like *this*; it wasn't this raw.

As she pulled down his trunks with one hand, extracting his firm cock with the other, she let out a low moan. At just having it in her hand. So big. So long. Like a majestic stone pillar. She gave a tender squeeze that made him shudder lightly. Then she leaned in to drag a long, solitary lick up the whole length of him.

"Aw fuck, that's nice," he rasped hotly. Then he looked her in the eye, his shaft rising magnificently between their gazes, and whispered, "Now suck it. Suck my cock, baby."

She actually liked the command. She'd gotten so good at that, at enjoying the submissive role at times. And her position, plus his demand, had instantly changed this—from aggression to submission. Opening wide, she sank her lips over the staff of hard flesh, pleasured by simply having it inside her in some way, pleasured further by the idea of how she must look to him. Everything about the moment felt at once hot and dirty, loving and perfect.

She sucked him in earnest then, sliding her mouth wetly up and down in a leisurely rhythm, taking him as deep as she could, backing off until only the head remained within her lips, then repeating the descent again, again, again. Above her, Jake's low moans echoed upward and he began lifting his pelvis toward her, fucking her mouth. Another strange, powerful bit of pleasure.

His voice came in low, throaty whispers. "So good, baby. Yeah, suck me. Keep sucking me." The hot prodding at once entranced and excited her until she was lost to the motions of her mouth, moving mindlessly but lustfully, her lips stretched by his thickness.

"You're so fucking perfect," he murmured.

And that was when she suddenly heard Shane and Rogan exit the cabin, talking to each other as they rejoined Carly and Jake without warning—but then going instantly quiet.

Stunned, she released Jake's cock from her mouth, her cheeks going hot as his erection plopped heavy and firm against his abdomen. *God oh God oh God.* Tension weighted the still night air—and her stomach churned as she closed her eyes, mortified.

Until Rogan said, "You don't have to stop on our account, honey."

Chapter 17

"Rogan's right," Shane added. "You're beautiful doing that."

Carly sucked in her breath. She felt frozen in place, lost for what to do, what to say.

She tried to think. *Just stand up. Smile nervously. Say something sweet and cute like, "Oops, you weren't supposed to see that," and drag Jake to the privacy of your bedroom.* Except . . . while part of her certainly wanted to escape—not all of her did. So at a loss, confused, and with too many thoughts tumbling through her head, she simply looked to Jake. For rescue. Or whatever other guidance he might choose to give.

Their gazes met and she sensed him trying to see into her eyes, read her thoughts. And maybe what he witnessed there wasn't really a plea for rescue at all—maybe it was a question instead, the question she hadn't quite allowed to form in her mind. *Should I? Should I keep going? Should I let them watch?*

Finally, Jake's chin lowered slightly and their eyes connected still more deeply as he quietly said, "It's all right with me if it's all right with you."

Carly's cunt swelled instantly and her breasts ached with delicious need. Jake wanted to show his friends how hot she was. Like this. And in this surreal moment, *she* wanted to show them, too. She wanted to show them *everything*.

Pulling in her breath, she let her gaze drop back to Jake's big cock. She felt a little shy now—it was strange and jarring to suddenly feel as if she were *performing, entertaining*—so she simply reached up and gently ran two slightly trembling fingers down his hard, veined length. She was unsure whether it was the featherlight touch or the new circumstances that made him release a quivery hot breath in response.

She made the same move again, and then, very softly, leaned in to lick lightly at the side of his shaft. The deep sighs from all three guys moved through her like a warm caress.

And then Jake was taking her face in his hands, tenderly cupping her cheeks, whispering to her, "It's okay, baby. It's okay." *Okay to be scared? Okay to do this in front of his friends? Okay to go slow?* She wasn't sure—and yet it didn't really matter, because as always with Jake, the reassurance filled her up, and she believed him.

Enough to close her fist firmly around his erection once more, pulling it toward her as she looked into his eyes. Enough to keep her gaze locked on his as she parted her lips and sank them back down onto his perfect cock. Enough to relish the low groan from one of the men to her right. Enough to let that groan fuel her, thrill her, reignite the full measure of her lust.

And after that, it was more about urges and instincts than decisions. More about feeling than thinking. She loved feeling Jake's big dick in her mouth as she moved up and down on it, and the new eyes upon her made her still hotter, hungrier, naughtier inside than she'd been before. Her enthusiasm rose, her rhythm increased. She heard the sounds of herself sucking him.

And when Jake rasped, "That's so good, baby. Suck that big cock for me," she didn't mind.

And when at some point Rogan murmured, "Mmm, yeah, keep fucking him with that pretty mouth," it made her pussy weep with fresh lust. And it renewed her energy to keep doing just that, fucking him with her mouth, no matter how tired or sore her tender lips became.

Already, she was thoroughly aroused by their presence, by the very "performance" that had seemed so difficult just a few minutes ago. She'd delighted in being watched by Rogan last night, but now, to openly let them watch, to let them know she *welcomed* it, lifted the act of going down on Jake to an entirely different level of stimulation.

At one point, she gathered the courage to flick a glance in Rogan and Shane's direction—where she found they'd both taken a seat on the bench that lined the rail, and that Rogan lightly stroked himself through the khaki shorts he wore.

When finally she had to rest her well-worked mouth, she released Jake from its depths, but immediately lowered her breasts around his moistened cock. The bikini top made it easy and Jake let out a light moan. Then he used both hands to press her tits around his erection—and she leaned her head back and closed her eyes, instantly entranced by how hot and hard he felt in that soft valley.

Only a few seconds passed before Jake pushed the zebra print triangles aside to reveal her breasts, and their spectators moaned in unison.

"Such pretty titties," Shane echoed low and deep.

And Carly reacted by using them more vigorously on Jake, an impulse to show Shane and Rogan just how pretty, and *dirty*, they could be. Jake fucked her tits in earnest then, sliding the hard column of flesh between them in brisk strokes that filled her with pleasure. It amazed her, in fact, just how *much* pleasure she was able to reap with only her mouth and breasts at the moment.

And maybe it should have amazed her that she was reaping so much pleasure from this situation, period. Yet perhaps her past secret life made it so this wasn't such a big leap. Jake was right—the girl he'd met that first night really *was* a part of her.

From there, she alternated between sucking him and using her tits on him. Sometimes she stopped sucking to run her tongue over and around the head of his cock, licking away the salty pre-come—at others, she wiped the dot of white moisture away with her breasts, using it for warm, wet lubricant to give him a nice slick slide in between. At other instances, she took his saliva-dampened shaft in hand—hard as granite now—and rubbed the head or the length over her nipples, looking down to see the two body parts together, one so soft and the other so rigid, and to see the wetness left behind on the dark, pointed peak of her breast. The whole time Rogan and Shane appeared entranced by her every move, occasionally prodding her on with their soft, dirty words.

Finally, when she felt like nothing more than a mass of excited, jumbled nerve endings, she peered up at Jake over his dick, licked her upper lip, and sweetly asked, "Will you fuck me?"

Jake's jaw dropped—and she'd never seen him look so completely pole-axed. His voice came on another hot rasp. "Aw, baby—of course I'll fuck you. I'm *dying* to get in that wet, pink pussy."

With that, Jake pushed to his feet and moved behind her, dropping to his knees. She was on all fours now on the deck, waiting, desperate to have that part of her body filled with him. He wasted no time pulling her bikini bottoms to her thighs, then thrusting two fingers inside her. "Oh!" she cried at the hot little intrusion.

And Jake said, "You're fucking drenched."

"I know," she breathed. "Please. Fill me with your cock. I have to have it."

"Damn, honey," Jake growled through clenched teeth. He'd experienced a lot of excitement with this woman, but he wasn't sure he'd ever been quite as turned on as he was right now. Leaning back slightly, he watched where his fingers entered her, and the view of that hot cunt just below her lovely round ass made his dick stiffen a little more—if such a thing was even possible.

"*Please*," she begged in front of him. And his stomach contracted with an almost agonizing lust that made him extract his fingers, then lift his raging erection so that the head was poised at the hot little opening where she was so soaking wet.

"Here it comes," he warned, and then he rammed it into her, deep.

She cried out in pleasure as he emitted a groan that rose all the way from his gut. Aw, God. He was in her. So fucking tight, as always, and wrapped around every hard inch of his dick. He leaned back his head, tried to get used to the gripping squeeze her pussy had on him. *Whatever you do, don't come, not yet.* He wanted this to last a good long while.

The added arousal of having his friends there, of letting them see the bounty he had in her, fed his lust. Somehow this was easier than that night with Colt—probably because he was closer to these guys, just by virtue of them living within a few hours' distance; he saw them more often than just the annual H.O.T. reunion. And even though this had still caught him off guard in a way, he'd *wanted* this, *fantasized* about this. And now he was gonna fuck his sweet girl's brains out while they watched.

So after pushing back the urge to erupt—he began to pound into her, hard.

"Unh! Unh! Unh!" Her pretty little sobs filled the air as his fingers dug into her hips, and he thrust deep, deep into that waiting cunt. His whole world in that moment was the snug glove her pussy formed around his dick; nothing else mattered. His head fell back as he plunged into her over and over, just soaking up the hot pleasure.

A lusty sound from Rogan brought him back to himself, though, made him open his eyes. He caught a glimpse of his friends, their gazes glassy on him and Carly. He dropped a glance downward and caught sight of her sweetly puckered asshole just above where his prick entered. Hell, moments like this, when it was all he could do not to come in her pussy, he wondered how he'd ever managed to get in that super-tight ass.

She continued crying out with abandon at every firm stroke—and damn, that had become his favorite noise in the world: Carly losing all control, letting herself go in the pleasure.

When the time came for him to slow down, take a break, he drew back his hand and began smacking her ass. He liked the slapping sound it made, and the way her flesh jiggled, and he sure as hell liked the sexy whimpers she began to emit.

"Aw, you like to be spanked, don't you, baby?"

"Oh—yes. *Yes*. Spank me." No hesitation. No soft voice. Just raw passion.

And as he brought his palm down on her ass, he fucking *loved* that she was totally into this now, just like he was. And he realized they'd come full circle. From dirty Desiree to frightened Carly to the beautiful in-between: the hottest, nastiest version of Carly he could ever want. She could fuck with pure abandon now, no shame, no lies, no running—just a pure unadulterated surrender to pleasure.

He delivered that naughty spanking until her skin began to look a little pink in the moonlight, after which he stopped, then rubbed the spot gently, lovingly.

When she looked back over her shoulder at him, he nearly lost it. She was always a pretty girl, but something about the wild abandon in her eyes right now, the utter recklessness, made her more fucking beautiful to him than words could describe.

Without thought, he followed the urge to lift his hand toward her, to her mouth, to slip two fingers inside. The same two fingers he'd had in her pussy minutes ago. She began to suck on them, eagerly, and he nearly came.

So he fought it, held perilously still for a minute, until he'd regained control—and then resumed fucking that hot, moist little cunt as Carly met each hard stroke, still sucking his fingers and looking more thoroughly uninhibited than he'd ever seen her. Even as Desiree.

In front of him, Carly felt consumed. By every sensation. The warm night air wafting over her skin and teasing her clit. The hard cock filling her hungry pussy. The lusty male eyes that watched her. The fingers moving in and out of her mouth.

The Lycra fabric still framing her breasts added slightly more sensation when she moved against Jake, and she felt the bikini bottoms around her thighs, as well. Somehow even the hard material of the deck, biting into her knees, her palms, was welcome. Because she just wanted to *feel* things. *Anything. Everything.* Her entire body was alive, awash, with the need to be touched, caressed. There was no part of her that didn't yearn for more right now—she suffered the strange urge to be . . . overwhelmed by sensation from head to toe.

She moaned around Jake's fingertips as he fucked her—she arched her ass and pushed back against his erection every time he thrust so gloriously deep. And she sucked at his fingers still harder, harder—simply following the urge, strangely desperate for something more there.

It felt as if he'd read her mind—or maybe her body—when she heard him say, "Sweet baby—you want more?"

And her clit pulsed with new desire at the very question.

Because she knew what he meant—more cock.

Her heart beat faster as she released his fingers only to say, "Um . . ." But even as she hesitated, she knew she *did* want more—more of exactly what he was offering—she just couldn't quite say it. Her pussy knew, her breasts *ached* with knowing—but taking that last step eluded her.

That's when Jake leaned down over her, wrapping his arms around her waist, and whispered in her ear. "I want this for you, want you to have it."

She simply turned, met his gaze, now only an inch away. She still couldn't speak, her chest going tight, but maybe she didn't have to. Maybe it was all in her eyes. Because even in the moonlight, she could have sworn his expression darkened lustfully as he repeated, low and intense, "*I want this for you.*"

After which he raised back to his upright kneeling position, cock still buried deep inside her, and said to Rogan and Shane, "My hot girl here is too sweet to say she wants more cock in her mouth. Will one of you help her out, give her what she needs?" His voice came thicker, deeper, than usual, and yet he sounded very sure, totally at ease with the request.

Carly looked up from her hands-and-knees position to see Shane approaching, gazing down at her. Dear God. Her heart threatened to pound through her chest. Was that because this was more than a little awkward? Or because she wanted it so incredibly bad? The last one. Because she liked Shane, a lot. Because he had a nice body and was classically handsome even in the swim trunks he hadn't changed out of.

With smooth, fluid motions, he dropped the trunks to the deck and stepped free of them, then seated himself in the chair in front of Carly, left vacant by Jake. Pulling it a little closer to her, he reached down, closed warm hands smoothly around her upper arms, and helped her lift to balance her elbows on his thighs.

Thoughts swirled. His cock was wonderfully hard, stretching up toward his navel. *His pubic hair is pale, like the hair on his head.* Her arms were sore from having her weight on them for so long and it was a relief to resituate. *My tits are on display right in front of him.* Jake still fucked her from behind, but more slowly now during this unexpected transition. *I want to feel Shane's cock—I really do.*

And so she reached for it, took the weight of it in her fist. Holding it instantly fueled her lust. Holding a man's erect cock was like . . . holding his power. He still retained it, but he gave a little of it to you, too.

On instinct, she leaned forward—she wanted it between her tits.

He groaned as she used her hands to press her flesh around him.

And her face warmed at the splendor of having two male shafts pleasuring her at once. She knew what it felt like, from that night with Colt, yet it also felt brand-new. Letting herself experience this as the real, true person she was made it . . . more vivid, more impactful, more real. She let out a soft moan as she began to slide her breasts around his firm length.

"I need to be wet," he informed her throatily, and she agreed—some lubricant would help.

Remembering her wine cooler, sitting just within arm's reach, she leaned over, picked it up, and splashed a little strawberry alcohol down of the head of his cock and between her tits. Shane flinched, but as she returned the bottle to the deck, he took over, reaching for her breasts, hugging them around his penis, grazing his thumbs over her nipples at the same time.

Oh God, it felt good. Especially with Jake still driving into her slick pussy behind her. Together, she and Shane worked his erection between her now-moist breasts, and Jake groaned, fucking her harder at the sight.

And that's when using merely her tits on him wasn't enough. All shyness had fled. Finally. She simply wanted what she wanted, what her body yearned for. So she bent her head to lick at the tip of his erection—then she lowered her mouth full onto it.

"Sweet Jesus," he said on a moan.

And then her entire existence was only about . . . cock. Being filled with it. Relishing it. Taking all that she could and letting the wild sensations saturate her to overflowing. As she slid her lips up and down Shane's length while Jake slid *his* rigid length in and out of her, she felt as if, together, they created some wonderful and dirty machine where all the parts moved against each other at just the right intervals, delivering just the right friction.

She didn't know how much time had passed when she looked up, transferring Shane's erection from her mouth to her breasts, to see Rogan approaching as well, standing to Shane's left.

"Baby, why don't you suck Rogan's cock, too," Jake suggested deeply.

And even as a fresh wave of heat raced down her spine and into the small of her back, the very idea seemed easy now. She'd certainly had plenty of moments when she'd felt attracted to him—and it felt almost unfair to leave him out at this point anyway. So she peered up at him, one penis in her cunt, another between her tits, and quietly said, "All right."

His mouth went slack and she thought perhaps she'd surprised him. But she'd come so far now—what was there to fear? What was one more? Maybe advancing from two to three was significant, but somehow, in this strange, heady moment, it just felt closer to . . . natural.

She found herself watching with bated breath as Rogan unzipped his shorts, reached inside, and withdrew what struck her as a rather massive erection. The very sight made her suck in her breath. Maybe he looked bigger than the other guys due to her angle, below him.

Jake must have realized she would have a difficult time reaching Rogan's cock, so he leaned down over her, his hands coming to cover her breasts, and said, "Let's lift you up, honey." He raised them both upright on their knees, still inside her from behind, and the move gave her a much different perspective on her situation.

Mainly, she found herself resting on Jake's dick—which made it feel even bigger, stretching up inside her—and at eye level with Rogan's. And it wasn't an illusion—he *was* slightly larger, thicker, than she was used to. But her body felt so primed now that she was fearless, and she merely shifted her gaze from his shaft to his eyes, parting her lips. An invitation. *I'm ready.*

The man before her took his rigid cock in hand and held it down to her mouth. "Open wide," he whispered. And then he slowly fed it to her. Inch by inch.

Oh Lord! The difference in his size was enough to make her mouth feel fuller, her lips stretched even more taut. But her cunt flared around Jake's hard shaft and she willingly accepted what Rogan gave her as he began to gently fuck her mouth.

She moaned, starting to rock on Jake's erection, and as he kneaded her breasts, he murmured, "That's so hot, baby. Suck that cock. Suck it good. You're so fucking good."

Time became blurred. She didn't know if she sucked Rogan for two minutes or ten—she was too lost to it all. Male voices, dirty talk, sore lips but a hungry mouth, full pussy but an aching clit—and oh God, did it ache now. Her thighs were spread wide across Jake's, her bikini bottoms stretched around her upper thighs now, and she longed for Jake to lower a hand to the spot where she throbbed so wildly—but her mouth was too stuffed to tell him, and her hands were too busy on Rogan and Shane, as well, who knelt next to her, sliding his erection across her breast. As Rogan moved in short, steady strokes between her lips, she caressed his thighs, his balls, and used her other hand to grip the base of his hard-on. At other moments, she shifted her touch to Shane's cock, or his stomach.

Finally, Jake said, "Why don't we lay her down, on her back?" And she didn't care that she wasn't consulted—she didn't even want to be. She was happy to be a tool for their pleasure—because it pleasured *her* so very thoroughly, too.

Yet her legs felt like noodles as Jake pulled out of her and hauled her to her feet, so it was a good thing he kept his arms around her to guide her. After finally getting her bikini bottoms off, he lay her on her lounge chair, saying, "Tilt it all the way back, honey," so she adjusted the arms to make the chair recline. And she wasn't the least bit daunted to look up and see three naked men—Rogan had just shed his clothes, too—standing around her.

Jake sat on the foot of the chair and smoothly spread her legs. She bit her lip, aroused by just being on display that way. Rogan had seen her like this last night, but not this close, and a low groan echoed from his throat as Shane said, "What a pretty little pussy."

By now, though, she was on the verge of losing her mind, and blurted out, "Do something to it! Please—I'm going crazy!"

Jake gave her an *oops* sort of grin, saying, "Sorry, baby"—just as Shane said, "The girl's been damn generous. If you don't get her off, I will."

"Oh, don't worry, I'll get her off," Jake promised, then resituated himself on his knees beyond the end of the chair, bent down, and dragged his tongue through her needy, wet folds. She shivered despite the warm night as a high-pitched sigh left her. At last! Some attention to her desperately deprived clit! In response, she parted her thighs even wider and clamped her hands over her breasts.

That's when Shane knelt next to her and said, "I can help you with these," sliding his hands up under hers.

She bit her lip, let go, watched him caress her tits while Jake went down on her below.

"Still hungry, honey?" Rogan asked then, kneeling on the other side of her, near her face.

"Oh yes," she told him, because already her mouth felt empty after being filled so well for so long. "Let me have it, please."

And again, he held his cock down, feeding it between her parted lips, and it was like returning to sensual heaven. And when Jake thrust his fingers inside her as he mouthed her slit, that made it even better.

As the attention to her clit began to make her moan around Rogan's large shaft and buck at Jake's face, he stopped and looked up at her only long enough to rasp, "I'm gonna make you come *so* fucking hard now," before latching his mouth back around her swollen clit and sucking.

After that, it was dreamlike. She heard herself howling around Rogan's cock. She was aware of wild, permeating pleasure saturating the entire length of her body. She caught sight of Shane twirling, pinching her nipples just before bending to take one in his mouth, which he drew in deeply. And then Jake was suckling harder, and she was fucking his mouth, sobbing louder, louder, her entire being pulsing—until the orgasm rocked her body, jerking through her in wild spasms that felt like being tossed about on high, choppy waves she couldn't control.

She'd released Rogan from between her lips, gripping the arms of the chair tight as her body thrashed in thrilling pleasure that seemed to stretch on and on. Words left her mouth: "Oh!" "Yes." "Fuck." "God." And then at last a long, well-pleasured sigh as the climax finally waned and she felt herself sinking gently back against the chair, exhausted.

When Jake drew his face from her pussy to meet her gaze, his cheeks, nose, were slick with her moisture, and his eyes looked feral. "How was that?"

She tried to speak, but all she got out was an, "Unh."

"I think she liked it," Shane said, and as the guys' low, masculine laughter echoed around her, she bit her lip, her need for orgasm thoroughly met now, but her body still ready to keep going.

"Fuck me some more," she whispered.

Jake slanted her a wicked grin. "I'm planning on it, but I thought you might need a rest."

She just shook her head. With all these erect cocks around her, there could be no rest—their very presence provided too much stimulation.

"Well, what if *I* need a little rest?" He arched one brow, and the question reminded her exactly how long and hard he'd fucked her already, stopping only to lick and suck her to orgasm. He'd performed more than admirably.

Her first thought: *I have two other perfectly good penises here ready to serve me.* Her second: She didn't know if anyone had condoms, and maybe Jake's invitations to his friends didn't extend as far as actually fucking her. So she sat up and said, "I'll do the work." Then she stood up, even if her legs remained sore and a little wobbly, and pointed Jake toward the lounge. "Lie down. But stay where I can get on top of you without the arms of the chair getting in my way."

The amused look he gave her said she was suddenly back to being bossy—but that he'd let it slide right now. Then he followed her instructions. And she thought he looked pretty damn beautiful lying there naked and erect for her.

So she didn't waste another second before straddling the bottom of the chair and slowly lowering herself onto his lovely shaft. He groaned, and Rogan said, "Damn, baby, that was hot."

Well, if he thought that *was hot, this* will blow his mind. Having long abandoned the need to be sweet or cute or docile, she looked to Rogan and Shane. "I want your cocks. In my mouth. Or on my tits."

"Shit," Shane whispered, clearly turned on.

And then she reached out, one guy on each side of her, and boldly took an erection in each hand.

Oh Lord. Talk about feeling powerful. It felt as if she'd just reined in all these tough guys and had them at her very mercy.

She drew Shane's cock to her lips, took it inside. At the same time, she pulled Rogan's meaty rod to her right breast, running the thick head up and down over the sensitive nipple. And she began to move on Jake.

And on it went. Trading Shane's erection for Rogan's, over and over as she rode Jake's dick, bouncing on it for a while, then slowing down, undulating in hot circles. The whole time, the three men whispered dirty things, about their cocks, her mouth, her tits, her cunt. Jake watched her, no longer her blue-eyed stranger but her lover extraordinaire who was giving her an experience she could never have imagined and would certainly never forget.

They molded her breasts, fingered her clit. As Rogan stroked the top of her pussy, she realized she liked the idea of how close his fingers were to Jake's cock, liked looking down, seeing that they actually mingled in his dark pubic hair. Everything was pleasure, everything was stimulation. Nothing else existed.

And then she came again—from Rogan's fingertips strumming her while Jake fucked her—and she held tight to the other two hard-ons at her disposal as she screamed her way through the hot pulsing thrums of pleasure that vibrated from her cunt all the way out to the tips of her fingers and toes.

When it was over, she instantly felt a little more docile—that was her true nature most of the time and there was nothing wrong with that. So rather than draw one cock firmly back into her mouth, instead she tugged Shane's to her lips and gently licked at the side, almost as if it were an ice-cream cone. And Rogan's hot sigh filled the air around them.

"Will you lick the little slit, lick the pre-come off?" Shane asked.

The breathy request made fresh desire flare low in her belly and she gladly obliged him, being very thorough and making sure he felt it.

"Oh fuck, I'm gonna come," Rogan said, and then he began slapping his erection against her breast, almost as if spanking the hard nipple.

"Do it on her tits," Jake instructed.

They all watched, Carly continuing to nibble at the tip of Shane's dick, and moaning at the shock of pleasure she experienced as Rogan smacked his cock against her breast, finally saying, "Fuck, now." He aimed at her chest as spurts of white semen shot from the tip to leave jagged lines of it across her tits and stomach.

"Aw God," Jake said, voice thready, eyes on the two wet mounds, and she followed yet another impulse. Letting go of Shane for the moment, she licked her upper lip and used both hands to slowly begin rubbing the come into her skin. She met Jake's gaze, knowing that would do it for him, and his eyes fell half shut in pure lust. And when Rogan used one finger to scoop up a trail of white fluid just above her navel, then held it to her lips, she closed her mouth over the offering, sucking it off, tasting it, swallowing it, totally caught up in being a dirty dream girl for them all.

That's when Shane said, "Shit, here I go," and Jake followed with, "Aw hell—me, too."

And she found herself pushing her breasts together for Shane as his come spewed across her in three, then four long torrents at the very same moment Jake gripped her hips and thrust upward, groaning his orgasm as he literally lifted her from the chair with his cock.

And then all their hands were on her, rubbing in the sticky juices, caressing her breasts and stomach as she bit her lip and simply watched, drinking in the final moments of such wicked bliss.

Chapter 18

She and Jake lay naked in the lounge chair, alone. Moments after the sex had ended, Shane and Rogan had taken turns giving her a soft, tiny kiss, and Shane had said, "That was spectacular. Thank you for making this night far better than I thought it would be."

Rogan had followed with, "Good night, honey. Jake's a lucky guy."

And then they were gone and Jake was falling into postsex sleep as she rested quietly in his arms, thinking. *Oh God, I just took on three guys. Three.*

And it was amazing. And empowering. And brought me more pleasure than I knew I could feel.

And it made me dirty. In the good way. As dirty as Desiree.

Only it felt better, infinitely better, than anything I ever did as Desiree. It felt better as me.

And how the hell did this even happen? Apparently, Rogan and Shane had been unable to sleep after all and had decided to come back out for more socializing. And they'd ended up getting a whole different kind of social interaction than anyone could have anticipated.

Can something be wonderful and shameful at once? The truth was, despite her sense of elation, both emotions warred inside her—a familiar feeling from days past. She lay looking at the stars, still in a bit of disbelief.

"You okay, sweetie pie?"

She turned to see Jake's face next to hers in the moonlight. "I think."

"*You think*? I want you to *know*. Please don't tell me you feel bad about this."

She raised her eyebrows. "Jake, I think *most* girls would feel at least . . . *weird* about this. It's how we're wired."

He pressed his lips together and sighed. "That bums me out, though. I wanted you to *love* this."

"I did. I do. I'm just programmed to think things like—how can you possibly feel the same way about me now as before? Because when we fooled around with Colt, I was nobody important to you—but now I am. And how can your friends possibly not think I'm a slut?"

He lifted one hand to her cheek. "Honey, I love you, that's how. And . . . I thought of it sort of like . . . what you did with *them* you were really doing with *me*. Except that I don't have three cocks, so I needed help." He flashed a playful grin that made her smile. "I want to give you all the pleasure you can take, so when the opportunity came along, I went with it. And seeing you *take* all that pleasure excited me just as much as it did you. Seeing you take all that pleasure because *I* wanted you to have it sort of . . . gave me an even bigger sense of control than usual. Does that make sense?"

She nodded. She already understood very well the subtle ways control shifted between two people and how much of it was in their heads, in simply how they chose to view a situation.

"You know, I liked having control of everything as Desiree, yet . . . maybe I needed it more then—because there was no trust involved, and I had to *take* control to make sure things went as I wanted them to. But now there's you, and I trusted you to make it good—so in that way, doing what you wanted me to do was easy." She bit her lip, lowered her gaze, but then raised it back to him. "I can't *always* give up control to you, but I'm learning to more and more."

Jake's eyes sparkled warm and loving on her. "That's *so* good, baby. *You're* so good." He tilted his head then, trying to smile even though his expression flashed a hint of self-deprecation. "If I were half as good as you, I'd be more willing to give up control more often."

Yet Carly just shook her head. "I really don't mind. Giving it up. Submitting. Maybe I even like it. I want to make you happy, Jake."

The plan for Monday morning was to arrive back at Traverse City by noon—most everyone had work on Tuesday and some had a drive of several hours ahead of them.

Carly prepared to exit the bedroom with bags packed, wearing shorts and a beaded tank, her hair pulled back in a ponytail. A glance in the mirror reminded her who she was at heart—Carly Winters, furniture maker, pie baker—and made her wonder again if Jake's friends could really see her for the full person she was or just for the blow jobs she'd given them last night. At moments like this, it was still hard to believe she'd done such a thing. Still, she blew out a breath and climbed the stairs to the front deck with all the courage she could muster.

"Hey, how do you like your eggs?" Shane asked her first thing.

The question totally threw her off. "Huh?"

"Eggs—how do you like 'em? I'm making a big breakfast today before we take off." He sounded upbeat, energetic, ready to cook. And not at all as if he was addressing a woman who'd just serviced him and two of his friends last night.

"Um, scrambled or over hard—whatever's easiest."

He gave a concise nod, said, "Got it," and moved on.

A few steps more and she found Jake and Quinn sitting at the oblong table where the group had eaten all their meals. It was set with plates and silverware, and both guys drank orange juice. Apparently, she'd completely missed Quinn and Cameron's return. Cameron appeared to be consolidating the contents of two coolers; then he drained the empty one over the railing. Rogan came by just then and said, "Orange juice, hon?"

She met his gaze. And unlike with Shane, she saw the sex in his eyes, the memory of last night—but it was nothing judgmental, merely something . . . shared. "Um, sure—thanks," she managed, then took a seat next to Jake, who instantly lowered his hand to her leg under the table and gave her a quick kiss good morning.

When the whole group was gathered at the table half an hour later, digging into eggs, bacon, and hash browns, someone asked Cameron and Quinn about their night. The two handsome men exchanged glances and Cameron said, "They were real nice girls."

Shane just rolled his eyes, and Rogan asked, "The point is—did you get laid?"

"Damn straight we did," Quinn replied.

And after the guys pried a few more details from them, Quinn finally asked, "So, did we miss anything interesting *here?*"

Rogan shoveled some eggs in his mouth, ignoring the question, as Shane simply shrugged. "Nothing I can think of."

The payback for taking off work on his first Labor Day weekend in Turnbridge was that on the days following their return, Jake had to work double shifts. He'd agreed to that up front, of course, but now that he was actually doing it, it was—as usual—giving him too much time to think.

Damn, she'd been *so* astounding. Fucking remarkable. The truth was, when he'd suggested the idea of sharing her with his friends, it had been sincere, but he hadn't thought she'd really do it. At least not this soon.

And now . . . well, something in him felt . . . torn.

When he remembered it—any of it, from fucking her while Rogan watched to sharing her with both him and Shane—he got instantly hard. And it was easy, even almost a little addictive, to revisit those memories. They were so hot that it was just plain pleasurable to return there in his mind. And when he thought of the bravery it had taken on her part—of how far she'd come since they'd met—it blew him away. And then there was the moment when she'd told him how much she trusted him, and how that trust had enabled her to give up so much control to him—that had nearly turned him inside out. It made him feel . . . loved. And like a good man. And it made him love her back even more.

Problem was . . . three nights later, as he drove his cruiser slowly up Main Street, dimly lit by streetlamps, the peaceful solitude forced him to recognize that beneath all the heat of the memory, all the passion it had created inside him, something darker and more worrisome lurked.

The truth.

The harder, uglier truth you've been too fucking selfish to see up to now.

His chest tightened, and as he braked at Turnbridge's solitary stoplight, he shut his eyes for a second, tried to feel better. About what he'd done with Carly this past weekend.

That hard, ugly truth was: He'd gotten selfish, taken *too much* control.

What the hell were you thinking?

The things he'd encouraged her to do with Rogan and Shane had seemed like a damn fine arrangement on the boat—because he'd wanted it, for both of them. But now that they were back in the real world, their real lives, he had no choice but to face what he knew: This kind of extreme sex wasn't *really* good for either one of them.

For *other* people, people with normal pasts, maybe they could do this kind of thing and make it work. But Jake and Carly didn't have that luxury. Shit, he could almost hear Dr. Jim counseling him back when he was a teenager: "Victims of abuse generally go one of two ways—they either become sexually withdrawn or hypersexual. Neither end of the spectrum is healthy, Jake. Remember that. You'll need to find a happy, healthy medium in your sex life. You want to enjoy sex but not let it consume you."

Was he letting sex with her consume him? Was *she* letting their sex consume *her*?

He knew his desires had consumed him on that boat. When those moments had come, he'd conveniently blocked out everything Dr. Jim had ever taught him. And God knew Carly had been sexually withdrawn when he'd met her. So what was he doing about that? Prodding her into hypersexual behavior.

Odd, it had seemed so . . . almost beautiful to him at the time—because it was such a departure from the girl who couldn't even have sex with someone without wearing a disguise. But now he realized his thinking had been flawed.

Because *he* was flawed.

He'd thought he was so damn mindful and aware of his own issues, that he managed them so well. The truth was—he *had* managed them well, for a really long time, but he'd managed them *so* well that somewhere along the way he'd gotten lazy. He'd fallen into that pattern of dating submissive women. And then Carly had come along and changed *everything*. Fucking *everything*.

Somehow her issues had dredged up *his* issues, and her need for controlling the sex sometimes had amped up *his* need to control it *more*.

Now she doesn't mind you controlling the sex. She told you so. So maybe that means things are fine. Maybe it means you're back in another one of those comfortable situations where both you and she will be satisfied by letting you run the show.

Only what had he done when Carly had handed that control over to him? He felt like he'd abused it. He'd pushed her into places he shouldn't have, places that probably weren't very healthy for her. Shit—he'd seen Dr. Jim for ten years, his entire childhood. So had he truly thought it was a good idea to encourage Carly into a multiple-partner situation a few short weeks after she'd first faced her demons? *God, you're a piece of shit, Lockhart.*

And yet . . . other than momentary doubts, she'd seemed fine with what had happened. She'd told him on the ride home that she'd felt powerful and as if she'd been set free, let out of some invisible cage. So wasn't that good?

Fuck. He didn't know. He didn't know anything anymore.

Honest to God, if Dr. Jim was still alive, he'd call him, talk this through with him. But the man had passed away ten years ago after a heart attack at age fifty. And Jake had been pretty broken up about it, even gone to the funeral—but he'd never thought he'd actually *need* Dr. Jim again. And he wasn't in the mood to go talking to just any random corner shrink about his tragic past or his complicated present.

You just have to figure this out on your own. Damn, if ten years of therapy wasn't enough, probably no amount would be. So think this through. Figure it out.

The truth was, he wasn't nearly as concerned about what was best for *him* as he was about what was best for Carly. He was in love with her, after all. And he wanted to protect her from anything bad. But that very thought seemed to conflict with encouraging her to suck his friends' cocks while he fucked her. It seemed like . . . proof that he didn't *know* what was best for her, that he *wasn't* taking care of her, that he was instead just putting her in harm's way.

You're a selfish bastard, that's all. Sex could drive you to that, selfishness. He feared that somewhere along the way he'd forgotten about helping her heal, or he'd twisted it or something—he'd done what felt best to *him*, and had just talked himself into believing it was good for her, too.

Just then, his cell phone rang, and he looked down to see Carly's name on the screen. "Hey," he said, answering.

"Hey yourself. Are you coming over on your dinner break?" That had been the plan, and it was almost that time.

Shit. "Actually . . . I'm pretty wiped. If I stop moving for long, I'm afraid I'll just fall asleep. Trust me to make it up to you?"

"Sure," she said, sounding a little sad, but still like the sweet Carly he knew and loved. What he'd said about being wiped was true—and besides, he didn't think he'd be very good company right now. Maybe he just wasn't ready to face the girl he suddenly feared he wasn't any good for. "Love you," she said.

"Love you, too," he told her. That, too, was the truth. One truth among many. The question now was: Out of all those truths floating around inside his head, which one was the most important? Loving her? Or that loving her might also mean damaging her?

Jake was sleeping. And Carly officially missed him. But he'd worked super-long hours for three days straight, and now, on his first back-to-normal day, when he would pull only one eight-hour night shift, he was catching up on rest. So Carly missed him, but she understood.

As she set out toward Schubert's to pick up her lunch, she grabbed a sweater from the hook on the door—it was chilly out, the first day she could feel autumn blowing in. It made her sad in a way—she'd had probably the best summer of her life, and even though Jake wasn't going anywhere, she didn't like seeing the season end.

Walking up the street, she greeted people she knew, and she thought how shocked they'd all be if they had any knowledge of what she'd done with Jake and his friends. They'd be horrified. And that would be their right. And yet . . . the thought didn't make *her* feel horrified. Such things used to, back when Desiree was the only wild part of her. But now she saw things differently. Now she saw herself as a woman who was learning to accept her sexuality, her desires. She saw herself as someone who was more evolved, who could look beyond her small-town upbringing and the strange, twisted messages she'd gotten about sex and see that only *she* could weigh and choose her morals, only *she* could decide what was right and wrong for her.

Sure, she'd still be mortified if the people she knew ever found out the things she'd done. But that was because of how *they* felt about those things, not how *she* felt. She'd learned she could be a bad girl without feeling like a bad *person* inside.

And maybe that was why she missed Jake so much right now. Because he'd given her all this—he'd opened the whole world to her. And she burned to be with him.

"Howdy, Carly," Frank Schubert said as she stepped up to the counter.

"Hey, Frank," she replied with a smile.

As she paid Frank for her lunch, Tommy Gwynn sidled in and took a seat on a bar stool next to her. "Hey there, Carly."

"Hi, Tommy." The truth was, she'd never known Tommy well, and until Jake, they'd never been very friendly, despite him once asking her out when they were young. Yet he and his wife, Tina, had seemed very welcoming when they'd had Jake and Carly over.

"Not eating with Jake today?" he asked.

She shook her head. "He's still recovering from his double shifts."

He gave a short nod, then grinned. "That's what he gets for taking off on a holiday. And hey, that reminds me, I heard about your wild weekend with all of Jake's old buddies."

Oh, dear Lord. Carly's stomach plummeted as a sharp, stark panic paralyzed her, much like the awful, gut-wrenching fear she'd suffered in this very spot when Jake had first come to town—but even worse. Because—*what had Jake told him? Everything? Was it possible? How could that be?*

But just as quickly Tommy went on, saying, "Jake told me it turned out you were the only girl and you felt a little uncomfortable—guess I can understand that. But hell, sounds like it was a fun time anyway—fancy boat, swimming, great weather."

Oh. Okay. He didn't know. Thank God.

And . . . of course he didn't. What had she been thinking? Jake loved her—he would never share her secrets or do anything else to hurt her. She could breathe again. Sort of.

But she still felt light-headed.

"You okay?" Tommy asked. "You don't look good."

She got hold of herself—even though her body was still coming down from the fear—and climbed up on the stool beside him. "You know, I might be a little dehydrated, or need a little sugar in my system or something."

"Frank," Tommy called, since the older man had walked away, "can you get Carly a Coke, pronto?"

Frank complied, and Carly drank her Coke and, in fact, ended up eating her lunch there, too, chatting with Tommy the whole time. Once she got her head on straight about the conversation, she even managed to talk a bit about the boat, the nice scenery, and how nice Jake's old police academy friends were. And all was well.

As she walked back to Winterberry's, though, she still felt shaken by having been thrust so easily back into those old fears. She hadn't thought about those early days with Jake—those days when she'd been so sure he would destroy her—in what felt like a long time. Even remembering those old emotions felt a little like moving backward.

But the whole thing had been silly. She knew to the depths of her soul that Jake would never betray her.

The following evening, it was Carly who was working late. She'd started carving some intricate designs on her new heart-shaped boxes and had found herself not quite wanting to stop. So, with the door locked and the Closed sign in the window, Oliver sat curled lazily in the front sill watching over Main Street and Carly remained pleasantly surrounded by the smell of wood and sawdust, absorbed in her work—when Jake rang the buzzer.

She looked up with a smile—because she might be into her work, but she was more into her man. She eagerly set her tools aside, dusted off the thighs of her jeans, and went to answer.

And wow, after several long days apart, he looked delicious and good enough to eat. He wore a slightly rumpled long-sleeved button-down shirt with jeans, and she noticed his hair needed a trim and he was unshaven—but it all just made him seem even cuddlier. They greeted each other with a warm kiss, leaning over the pizza box he carried. "Hey, sweetie pie," he said, stepping in the door.

Funny, the silly endearment had become truly that now, an endearment, and she no longer heard the silly part—it had become his pet name for her. And that was a first for Carly—having a pet name.

Yet something in Jake's demeanor struck her as a little sullen. "You seem . . . down," she told him. "Is something wrong?"

His smile didn't quite reach his eyes. "No—just still tired. Thanks for not minding when I suggested we stay in."

She shook her head. "In or out, either way is fine with me."

After that, they headed up to her apartment, where they did what they'd done on their very first date—shared a pizza and a bottle of wine. But as he filled her in on his last few days at work and she did the same, things were so much more comfortable now.

The truth was—she was having a hard time keeping her hands off him, and by the time they were done eating, she knew he felt that way, too. Finally he grabbed her wrist and said, "I can't take it anymore—come here," pulling her on top of him on the couch.

And . . . God, what was it *about* this man? She never got any *less* turned on by him, it seemed—only *more*. As she ran her fingertips over the dark stubble on his jaw, his arms tightened around her waist, and they instantly sank into deep kisses that made her feel she was melting in his embrace. She tingled all over, especially when he started getting hard against her thigh. That very hardness, as always, tightened her chest and made her a little feral, not at all like the good girl people in Turnbridge knew. And she no longer tried to push that feeling away—it was just a part of her now, a *strong* and *welcome* part.

When he raised her shirt up over her bra, then let out a sigh merely at the sight, she said, "So you're not too tired to fuck me?"

He kissed her again, hard this time. "*Never* too tired to fuck you, baby," he said with a rasp, then lay her roughly back on the couch, angling his body over hers. His mood instantly seemed changed—he'd gone from tired to animalistic in a heartbeat, and her cunt swelled.

Within moments they were both naked and he was sucking her breasts with abandon as he thrust two fingers in her pussy. "Unh," she moaned.

And he said, "Damn, I thought I'd need to get you wet, but you're *already* wet."

Her stomach contracted as she confessed, "I'm wet every time I even think about you."

And as he parted her legs, then plunged his cock inside her, she didn't mind being under him, not one little bit. Control was truly the last thing she needed now, and she loved the dark heat in his eyes as he pounded into her, making her cry out over and over.

After a while, he put her on her hands and knees—one of his favorite positions—and drove into her from behind. As always like this, he felt bigger, his every stroke echoing all the way to her fingers and toes. Like that first night on the boat, he grabbed onto her hair and pulled just slightly, just enough to make her scalp tingle hotly as he rammed into her, and that along with the memory of Rogan's eyes on her heightened her arousal, made her feel dirty and beautiful all over again. She almost wished he were here watching now.

But when Jake's fingers snaked around her hip and between her legs to play with her clit, she forgot about anything except her *own* pleasure, all suddenly centered in that tiny, swollen nub. She heard herself whimper. Heard him tell her through gritted teeth that he was gonna make her come hot and hard. She automatically thrust her ass back against him with more power.

And that was when—oh Lord!—he began using his other hand at her anus . . . rubbing it. Words began to leave her unbidden. "Yes. God. Please."

And then the tip of his finger entered her, and then—oh fuck, yes—he pushed it in all the way. And that was it. The orgasm rushed over her almost without warning, burying her like a tidal wave, making her scream and sweat and flail about until she ended up collapsed on her stomach beneath him, finally going still.

"Aw damn, you're such a naughty girl for me," Jake said behind her, teeth still clenched, "and I love you so fucking much"—and he lifted her ass in his strong hands, just a little, then slammed his cock into her, again, again. They both moaned and sobbed and every pore of her body tingled when he said, "Oh God, yeah—I'm coming. I'm fucking coming deep in your tight little cunt."

After, they lay still for a minute, silent, until Jake reached for some tissues. And she turned over to face him, feeling as close to him as ever. Now she looked back on her nights as Desiree and thought: *How do you do something so very intimate and revealing with a man and* not *feel close to him?* How had she done that? She truly didn't know, since it was her very connection with Jake that allowed her to look into his eyes right now and feel nothing but happiness to have shared this with him, and so, so lucky to have his sweet love.

He kissed her lips, then one breast, before resting his head next to hers on a throw pillow. She loved being so covered by the very maleness of him, every corded muscle of his body seeming to press against her. She ran her fingertip over his tattoo.

"Tell me something," he said, voice low. "You still doing okay? About last weekend?"

She actually smiled in response. "Completely," she promised. "I've really never felt more alive, more in touch with my . . . womanhood or something." Her skin prickled at the memories.

And when he stayed quiet, she was swept up in *another* memory, part of the conversation they'd had on the drive home from Traverse City. He'd confided in her that as hot as it had been to watch her suck his friends' cocks, "there's a part of me that wants to see you fucked, too. If you ever wanted to take this a step further."

She'd bit her lip and said, "I can't deny the idea gets me hot. As long as it wouldn't change how you feel about me."

He'd acted as if she were crazy, like he was even getting a little fed up with it. "How many times do I have to tell you? Nothing you do is gonna change the way I feel. Sex is hot, but sex isn't love. If you do it with another guy, that's sex. But if you do it with another guy because we both want it, and if it makes us feel even closer afterward, that's love."

The idea had come back to her numerous times in the days they'd spent apart, and now that it was on her mind and they were talking about her being with his friends, she didn't hesitate to share what was in her head. Because she no longer *had* to hesitate. "I keep imagining you watching another guy fuck me," she whispered, her tone lower, sexier than usual—not by design; it just came out that way. "Just like you suggested on the way home. I'm still not sure I'm ready to take it that far, but the idea excites me. The same way it excited me when you shared me. I kind of . . . get worked up every time I remember being with all of you at the same time. Does it still excite you, too?"

She already knew the answer—she just wanted to hear him say it, wanted to let talking about it further arouse her.

He took a moment replying, though—and even shut his eyes. She watched his face carefully, trying to read it. And she thought he looked . . . unaccountably sad when he finally met her gaze and whispered, "Yeah, it does."

Carly swallowed past the lump that had just risen in her throat. What was wrong here? And why did she suddenly feel . . . bad inside? It wasn't shame, or guilt . . . but it was close. "What's going on, Jake? What's wrong?"

He shook his head, eyes closed again. "Nothing." It felt like he was shutting her out.

"Something," she insisted. And when he didn't respond, she got mad, and a little panicky, her heart beating too hard now, and said, "*Tell me.*"

Next to her, he sighed, opened his eyes, and said, "Don't get mad." But his expression still seemed weighted with sorrow. "It's just . . . what I said about wanting you to fuck another guy—I don't think we should do that. Okay?"

This did nothing to calm the pounding of her heart. And it wasn't that she really cared so much about fucking another guy—it was his sudden change in attitude. "Okay," she said quietly. Then, thinking this obviously required an explanation he wasn't giving her, she added, "Um, why?"

His answer came out slowly, and yet . . . he sounded very sure. "I think all of that is a mistake, *was* a mistake. We shouldn't have done it. I shouldn't have pushed you in that direction."

Jake had never said anything that had left her quite so deflated. Because it felt like a judgment. On her. "What are you saying?"

He sat up, then took a deep breath. So she sat up, too. She found herself reaching for the afghan she kept on the back of the couch, pulling it over her breasts, even though she wasn't the slightest bit cold.

He didn't look at her as he spoke, his gaze planted squarely on the pizza box on the coffee table. "I've been selfish, Carly. I've been selfish about pushing you to do things that get *me* off. And I've told us both I was doing it for *you*, but in reality, I think it was all about *me*, about letting sex *drive* me, *control* me. And now . . . shit—now I've got you sucking other guys' dicks just because *I* want it."

"What if I wanted it, too?" she whispered. Even though he was making it sound so awful now that, suddenly, she was almost loath to admit that.

Yet Jake just shook his head and she felt almost invisible, as if he was so lost in his own thoughts that she might as well not even be there. "I pushed you to it. I brought it up before we went, and I brought it up again at the time. I wanted you to do it so bad I could fucking taste it. And now . . ."

"Now what?" she snapped.

"Now I realize I'm just feeding the problem."

"The problem?"

"*Your* problem."

She blinked. "Exactly what *is* my problem?"

Now he looked at her, his blue eyes seeming to bore into her. "You know your problem. Your father abused you."

She drew in her breath, angry to be reminded. "You told me to let it go. Forgive. Move on. I did."

He let out a long sigh and reached for her hand, but something in his manner made her feel stupid, or maybe childish. "It doesn't just go away, Carly. It's always there. And healing takes time. And for me to push you to do the things I've pushed you to do was . . . just fucking insensitive and selfish."

She felt defensive. "But I thought it was good that I . . . you know, wanted to be . . . more adventurous."

"Honey, for a victim of abuse, being that wild isn't any healthier than being afraid of sex. It's just the opposite end of the spectrum."

She barely knew how to react, what to say. She felt shaky inside, and as if she'd been cheated somehow. Jake had told her over and over again that it was okay to do what felt good, and that he wanted her to have all that plea-sure, and that he would always love her the same afterward . . . but now that suddenly all felt like a lie. And she felt as if she was somehow being scolded. And with that came the familiar flood of shame, the gut-deep sense that she'd done something wrong. Dirty. The *bad* kind of dirty again.

Finally, she summoned words. "If it's all so awful, then why did you let me do it?"

His expression changed over to worry as he grabbed both her hands. "Honey, it's not awful—that's not what I'm saying. It's just probably not *healthy*. For you. At least right now. And as for why I let you do it . . ." He stopped, ran one hand back through his already-mussed hair. "Shit. It's like I told you. I was selfish. I . . . got caught up in my own old issues. I wanted that fucking control too damn much. I have no good excuse. I'm sorry."

He was sorry. "Sorry for what exactly?" she snapped. "Sorry you told me it would make me stronger? Or sorry you're telling me the exact opposite now? Sorry I was brave enough to do what felt good? Or sorry to be making me feel like I'm nothing but a huge slut now that it's too late to take it back?"

"Aw, damn me to hell," he wrenched out, eyes shutting as he bent forward, elbows on his knees, head in his hands. He looked as anguished as she felt. And when he sat back up, a tear rolled down one cheek. He sounded choked up as he slowly said, "I'm sorry for *all* those things." Then he shook his head. "But please, baby—please know you didn't do anything wrong. I would never see you that way."

Yet whether or not she believed him was only one piece of the big ugly can of worms he'd just opened. She'd never felt so . . . turned upon, or misled.

Well, once maybe. Her father had turned on her in a way, hadn't he? And, well, now that she thought about it . . . it had felt like her mother had turned on her, too, when it came to what had happened with that Kevin guy.

As a girl, as a woman, how did you possibly win? When faced with a whole damn life full of sexual situations and decisions, how did you possibly make all the right moves? And it wasn't Jake's fault that this horrid revelation had just hit her—but what was happening right this minute, *that* was his fault. And she couldn't help it—she finally just exploded.

"Who the hell ever put you in charge of my problems?" she shouted, rising to her feet. If she didn't stand up, she actually feared she might slap him. Her hands tightened into fists where she held the afghan in front of her. "Who the hell asked you to be my goddamn therapist? What gives you the right to tell me what I can and can't do? Should or shouldn't do? And to . . . God, after all this, to make me feel bad about it—how dare you!"

Jake pushed to his feet as well. "I never meant to make you feel bad, Carly, I swear."

"Well, you did, and it's one more thing that can't be taken back!" The rage inside her rose even higher as she yelled, "What the *fuck* gives you the *nerve* to take charge of my *problem*, as you called it? When you can't even handle your *own* fucking problems? You acted so smooth and smart about all this—when you're really just as messed up as me!"

At this, Jake sat back down. And answered very quietly. "I don't know. Because you're right. I'm . . . more screwed up than I thought. And now I've hurt you. And that's the last fucking thing I ever wanted to do."

She just swallowed again and said nothing, emotionally beat up and a little drained—the last way she'd expected to feel even a few short minutes ago. My God, he'd just had wildly intense sex with her. Like nothing was wrong.

Carly wrapped the blanket around her, feeling too naked, vulnerable. And still so, so angry. She slumped down into a chair near the couch, purposefully avoiding being next to him.

"This . . . has been on my mind for a few days, I guess," he admitted.

"Were you going to tell me about it if I hadn't brought it up or dragged it out of you?"

He lifted a glance her way. "Probably not. I was avoiding it. I knew . . . it probably wouldn't make either one of us feel very good."

"And yet it didn't stop you from fucking my brains out."

He nodded, looked grim. "That's part of the problem. Even as I want to control you, I can't control *myself, with* you. I knew I should talk to you about all this tonight, but when I got here, I couldn't quite do it. Because when I'm with you . . . hell, honey, when I'm with you I want to be *with* you. *In* you. *On* you. Especially after days of not seeing you."

Carly felt physically torn. His words aroused her against her will, made her pussy go liquid and warm. And yet that lust felt so wrong in this moment, almost offensive. Love and sex had gotten tangled together here in weird ways she couldn't decipher. And he was telling her it wasn't healthy. And she had no idea if she agreed or not—it was all so complicated.

But she knew she still loved him. She was mad as hell at him right now, but she loved the man.

And she knew she still wanted him. Her physical response had just told her so. And even rumpled and upset now, he looked no less than beautiful to her sitting on her couch naked.

I still love you. I forgive you. Or . . . I will soon. I'll work through this. I'll work through it all. And so will you.

All that was on the tip of her tongue—she was just trying to find the right way to say it—when Jake told her, "We shouldn't see each other anymore, Carly."

Chapter 19

God, he hated the look on her face. Pure torment. "What?" she said.

He just shut his eyes again. Because he hated hurting her so fucking much. And because this was so fucking hard. And he was a bigger asshole than he'd ever known he could be.

"I'm not the right man for you," he tried to explain. The words stung in his throat—because this hurt him, too. He loved her. He wanted her. He craved her. But this was too damn much, too consuming. It was everything Dr. Jim had ever warned him about and more. Almost from the moment they'd met—he just hadn't recognized it then.

"I'll never *be* the right man for you," he went on, each word more agonizing than the last. "Because people like us, with our pasts . . . we just aren't good for each other. Carly, you should be with somebody else."

When he met her gaze again she was simply gaping at him, clearly thunderstruck. "And just who on earth is it you think I should be with?"

He answered honestly. "Somebody normal. Somebody without all the baggage I have. Some nice, normal guy from Turnbridge, somebody like Tommy or your old boyfriend, Chuck."

Her eyes widened. "Are you serious? You think that's what I want? Now, after all this? You think some typical guy like that could ever really make me happy? Or satisfied? Or understand me, for God's sake?"

Did she mean after all the wild sex they'd shared? Or all the deep, abiding passion? In ways, they were two different things. He'd just let the passion lead them into the boundary-crossing sex.

But the answer wasn't important because no matter how he sliced it, the result remained the same. He hadn't come here planning to break up—this was ripping his heart out every fucking second—but he couldn't help speaking the ugly truth. "Two people who've been abused . . . are just never gonna be able to help each other heal. I'll always want to be in control of you. I'll always be a selfish lover, pushing you too far. And you'll always be . . . letting me, I'm afraid. And you deserve more than that. You deserve a guy who won't be so damn demanding. You deserve a guy who'll, I don't know, let you put him in handcuffs if you want."

"I don't care about handcuffs."

"I know you don't—that was just an example. You deserve a guy who'll let you be an equal partner in the bedroom. And I'm beginning to see that I'm probably never gonna be that guy. And I don't want you to be that girl— that girl who lets me get away with whatever I want. Because back when you weren't so crazy about giving up control—that's when I fell in love with you. Because *you* pushed *me*. Because you took what you wanted. The same way I do. But that didn't completely work, either," he said gloomily, thinking it through, "because we *both* wanted control."

An odd, sad smile took shape on her face. "I can't win, can I? You won't let me have control, but you don't want me to give it up, either. No matter what I do, you'll say it doesn't work between us. When . . . I actually thought it was working pretty damn well." A solitary tear rolled down her cheek and tore his heart to pieces.

"I love you, Carly. But . . . shit, this is about sex but so much more. By pushing you to be with Shane and Rogan—"

"*I wanted it!*" she screamed, leaning forward, fists clenched in the afghan. "*I wanted it just as much as you did! I wanted their cocks in my mouth! Between my tits! I wanted to feel that again, more than one cock! So there! It's not all on you! I wanted it! I fucking craved it! What do you think of that?*"

He swallowed, hard. Because tears streamed wildly down her face now and it was killing him. And it was as if she were confessing her sins to him or something, because *now*, under all the new circumstances, it clearly pained her to admit that—yet he sensed she somehow thought absolving *him* would fix everything. And it didn't even begin to.

He spoke quietly. "But you never would have done it if I hadn't asked you to. I know that about you."

"I did with you and Colt. That and more. I was even the one who suggested it then."

"That was different. You know that." He stopped, sighed, tried to clear his head, tried to make his point again—because it was important. "By pushing you to be with Shane and Rogan, I . . . I feel like I abused you all over again. Just in a different way."

"That's crap!" she snapped.

But it wasn't. So he just looked her in the eye and said, "I love you too much to keep hurting you in ways you can't even see right now."

And when she didn't answer—looking as exhausted and wrung out as he felt—he began putting on his clothes, even though his movements felt wooden, heavy, rushed. And as he stood up to go, he wanted desperately to pull the woman into his arms for one last, soul-stealing kiss—but he couldn't let himself do that, because if he did, they'd end up fucking like animals again, and he had to end this before he damaged her beyond repair.

So instead, he stopped next to the chair where she still sat, cupped her pretty face in one palm, and bent to lower a kiss to her forehead.

And shit—even *that* he felt in his groin.

Walk away. Now. You have to. You're not good for her.

And the even colder, harder truth? *She's not really good for you, either.*

In this case, neither one of them won.

Jake sat at his computer the next day, playing that amped-up version of Tetris again. Because he needed a distraction. From everything.

Not that it was working. His unpremeditated breakup with Carly kept repeating in his mind. If he'd planned any of it, maybe he could have somehow said it all better. But then, no matter *how* he'd said it, it wouldn't have been any easier for either of them.

And he didn't like recognizing the fact that she was, in a way, just as dangerous to his well-being as he was to hers, but it was undeniable now that he was finally forcing himself to face the truth. Because before her, even if he hadn't had much grand passion in his life—the deep, wild thing he felt with her—he'd been on a good even keel. He'd enjoyed sex; he'd been content with the romances that had come and gone in his life. But being with Carly had indeed dredged up his past, stirred up all those old feelings and issues— and he knew inherently that as long as she was in his life, those issues would remain front and center.

And yet . . . *she's the only woman you've ever loved this way.* Even after just a short time, he'd known the love was more intense, purer, deeper, than anything he'd experienced.

So maybe you'll never love anybody this much unless she challenges you, brings up those ugly old issues. Unless she breaks you out of that comfort zone. Hell, maybe he'd somehow loved her more because she was the only woman he'd been with who had a real understanding of where he'd been.

But either way . . . talk about your no-win situation. He'd rather be alone in life than be in a destructive relationship, hurting her, being selfish with her, over and over again. And it had indeed been escalating. At first, he'd been so careful—wanting her but also walking on eggshells with her. But the more she gave him, the more he took. And if he took much more, let his baser instincts drive him much further, that was when the real harm would occur—that was when it would all spiral out of control.

So he hated hurting her—fucking *hated* it—but better to hurt her like this, now, than to let a harmful relationship progress further. No matter how many times he turned it over in his head, that was how he saw it.

Just then, the Tetris blocks began piling up too rapidly, toward the top of the screen, and that quick, the game was over. But a glance down revealed he'd gotten far better at this game than when he'd started. And he realized that it wasn't much of a distraction, after all—as the puzzle pieces dropped into place on the screen, the thoughts seemed to drop into place in his head.

Rising from his desk, he walked into his kitchen, glanced out the back window. Between his house and the one behind him sat a small grove of young saplings and brush that he supposed would thin to nothing but gangly brown vines and branches when winter came. In fact, he'd thought about venturing in among the trees to plant some winterberry, let it naturalize there and provide some color during the more dreary Michigan months.

Only he couldn't do that now. Because if he did, every time he looked out his window he'd think of Carly.

But . . . hell, every time he patrolled Main Street he'd think of Carly. Every time he walked into Schubert's for a sandwich. Every time he drove across the railroad tracks on Maple and passed the bench where they'd eaten pie. His whole life here, he realized, was intrinsically tangled up with hers in a way he had no idea how to break free of.

Christ, he felt miserable. His chest ached. His eyes remained tired. Probably because he'd barely slept last night.

And he'd had plenty he'd planned to do today—there were leaves to rake, and his rusty old mailbox needed to be replaced—but dreary autumn skies had combined with his emotions to leave him feeling listless. He soon found himself lying on the couch, hugging a pillow to his stomach.

And wondering . . . *Should I even put the damn mailbox in?*

Or would it just make more sense to stick a For Sale sign back in the yard?

Because was he really going to stay here, make his life here, if Carly wasn't in it? The reality was that he felt useless here as a cop, and if he was honest with himself, Carly had probably been the only thing holding him here this long. He liked Turnbridge—but without her, and without a job he found satisfying, why stay?

He'd spent his whole career trying to save people, but there was no one here to save. And besides—how could he really save anyone after realizing that maybe he needed saving, too. Hell—maybe all of it, his entire life as a cop, had just been another way of . . . trying to save *himself*.

Maybe all his work in Detroit had only been a distraction—a *real* distraction, much better than any computer game—from what was still injured inside him. Maybe coming to this small town, this quieter place, had—along with meeting Carly—helped shine a light on that, given him time to look at it, think about it.

He thought back to Detroit and the inner-city neighborhood where he'd worked just before he'd left. It wasn't that he was bringing down bad guys every day, but he'd made a difference there. On a regular basis. He thought of the kids who'd hung out on a particularly bad corner that ran rampant with drug dealers and prostitutes—he'd earned their trust over time and had eventually gotten them to start spending some of their evenings at the rec center a block away. Were they still going to the rec center now? Or were they back with the dealers and pimps? And what about Crazy Manny, the homeless guy whom Jake had managed, more than once, to coerce into a homeless shelter for a few days or weeks at a time? Cold weather was coming, and Manny didn't quite have the mental capacities to understand he could freeze to death if he chose to sleep outside on the wrong night. Would some other cop know to look out for Manny? And how was old Mr. Bledsoe doing with his convenience store? Was some other officer keeping the thugs away for him, and keeping him safe and in business? Or was he, by now, back to fearing for his life every day when he went to work?

I'm not doing much good in Turnbridge. And God knows I'm no good for Carly. Maybe I should just blow this pop stand and get my ass back to the city where I can do some good.

What would Dr. Jim say about that? he wondered. Would he say that such a decision equaled denial, that to go back to Detroit would be nothing but running from the trouble still inside him? Hell. Maybe. But when he thought of those particular mean streets, where the troubles felt a lot bigger than his, it didn't seem to matter much. Yeah, he'd gotten stressed out there—he'd been called to one too many shootings and assaults the last year or two—but if he was gonna be stressed, it seemed better to have it be because he was helping people who needed him than because he was hurting a woman he loved with his sexual obsession with her.

Then he thought of Carly laughing, looking pretty and bright and cheerful as she'd ridden next to him on the way to Traverse City last weekend. He knew she *was* better off than she'd been when he'd met her. But now it had progressed into something that would be harmful to her in the end.

So . . . maybe this was all meant to be in a way. Maybe he *had* saved her, just a little.

Maybe you *can* save other people, even if you can't save yourself—maybe that was his lot in life.

But he'd saved her as much as he could. And his instincts were telling him it was time to go. Time to get back to saving *other* people in *other* ways.

Pushing back the pain that seared his chest when he thought about no longer being with her, he gathered himself up off the couch and returned to the desk in the corner of the room. But instead of playing another computer game, he picked up the phone and dialed the number of his old police chief in Detroit.

When the chief answered, Jake kept it simple and got to the point. "I was wondering if there's still a place for me on the force."

And ten minutes later, he had his old job back.

Carly tried her damnedest to work. Her heart-shaped boxes were flying off the shelves almost faster than she could make them. Yet as she fashioned another heart using her father's antique squirrel-handle circular plane, concentration was hard to come by.

It had been a week since Jake had broken up with her. A horrible, hideous week. Added to the fact that she feared she'd never be happy again, everyone in her life wanted to know *why*. Which, of course, she couldn't tell them. So she made up a vanilla version of the truth: *He thought we were getting too serious too fast, or something like that.* Then she'd roll her eyes and shake her head because she thought the whole thing was so stupid, and she'd try not to cry.

She'd been crying a *lot* lately. And she wasn't a woman who usually shed many tears. After all, until recently, she'd been pretty good at compartmentalizing things, turning off her feelings if she didn't like them. Her feelings for Jake, though, didn't seem to have an on/off button. Every time she thought of how happy he'd made her, how much he'd opened her up to living her life in a fuller, more vibrant way—and that she'd lost him now—her entire being simply ached.

And then yesterday, the worst news of all had come. From Dana. Tommy Gwynn had told Hank that Jake resigned from the Turnbridge Department and was moving back to Detroit. His last day was next week.

Every time she thought about that, she nearly couldn't breathe. Because now she knew she'd lost him *forever*. This thing was really ending, absolutely, without doubt. Deep inside, all summer, she'd feared his dissatisfaction with his job would make him leave, and now it had happened. Maybe breaking up with her had helped that decision, too. But the reason didn't matter—what mattered was that she'd never see him again.

Shit—she'd just dug the plane's blade too deeply into the wood. She stopped to look, ran her finger over the groove. She could sand the error away when she was done.

In the week since she'd seen Jake, she'd thought a lot about all he'd said, and she'd done a little more reading on sexual abuse. And now she almost saw his point of view, or at least understood it. But she still truly thought he was wrong. *Maybe* what she'd done on the boat *wasn't* entirely healthy for someone just coming to grips with her past abuse. But she'd been just as responsible for the decision as him. And it had felt *good*. Even afterward. She wasn't convinced that something that had made her feel so confident and empowered, so comfortable with her own desires, was *bad* for her, either.

And it was odd—before Jake, her longing to be with men had drawn her on her forays to Traverse City. And *with* Jake, the idea of being with other guys and him at the same time had aroused them both deeply. But after Jake . . . Carly couldn't even imagine being with a man who wasn't him. She couldn't imagine *wanting* another man. She couldn't imagine ever feeling so accepted and understood and loved by anyone else. She knew nothing she would ever experience from this point forward even stood a chance of being as good, as powerful, as profound as what she'd shared with Jake.

And damn it—she was mad at him. So mad that no words could describe it. For being stubborn. And for not believing her. For not believing she was strong enough to deal with her issues effectively. And for . . . for giving her his love, making her trust in it so much, and then snatching it away.

She was better off now than before she'd met him—she knew that. But there was a part of her that wished she'd never known a love so grand if it was going to be taken away from her so fast. Before, she hadn't known what she was missing—now she did. And already, she felt herself sinking back into old, familiar habits. The last few days, she'd once again ceased caring very much about how she looked, just grabbing an old T-shirt and a ratty pair of jeans from the closet. This morning she hadn't even brushed her hair—she'd just shoved on an old ball cap to hide it from view. Maybe she'd snap out of that soon. But then again, maybe she wouldn't. Right now, life was just about functioning—it was pretty much all she could do to get up in the morning, open the shop, make things from wood.

And somehow making these silly heart-shaped boxes seemed harder than it had just a week ago. The simple straight edges of the old designs felt so much easier, cleaner. Maybe she'd make this her last heart box for a while—no matter *how* well they were selling.

She stopped then, let out a sigh, tried to focus on perfecting that damn curve.

What if I'm truly never happy again? What if I've just experienced the most happiness, the most love, I'll ever know?

Chuck had been the great lost love of her youth. And it had taken *years* to get over him. But Jake would be the great lost love of her *life*. And she knew inherently that she wouldn't *ever* get over it. Over the things they'd shared. Over all he'd given her: the truth about herself, the sex, the laughter, the passion, the recovery, the love.

Just then, she dug the plane into the heart so deep that the wood cracked, right down the center of the heart. "Damn it!" she yelled, banging the old tool down on her workbench. Then she rose to her feet, picked up the heart-shaped lid, and slammed it down on the corner of her work table as hard as she could—over and over—until finally it splintered and shattered apart completely, jagged pieces and shards flying, most landing on the floor near her feet.

She stood staring down at the ruined wood then, her chest heaving, heart pounding.

Finally, she glanced at the window to ensure no one had been passing by to witness her outburst. But she'd seen the cat go darting from the front windowsill toward the back storage room when the heart had exploded into bits, so now she went to find him.

She spotted big, fluffy Oliver in a corner, perched atop a tall pile of oak beams. She called up softly to him. "Come here, Oliver. Here, kitty kitty."

The cat didn't move, and her heart ached. It shouldn't seem so important, but in that moment it did. "Please, Ollie, come to Mommy. I'm sorry I scared you. I just want to hold you a minute."

Oh God. Even her cat hated her.

Okay, that was stupid—the cat didn't hate her.

But she just needed him right now. Because she needed that comfort, that thing pets gave so freely to their owners. Unconditional love.

And it struck her then how rare that felt—love that came truly without conditions. Would the people in her life still love her if they knew the whole truth about her? Perhaps, but would they love her the *same*? Wouldn't her traditional, pure-at-heart friends at least feel differently about her? Wouldn't her mother be horrified? It dawned on her just now that maybe Jake was the only person she'd ever known who loved her in spite of—and maybe even more *because of*—the ways she'd explored her sexual nature. When he'd broken up with her, yeah, she'd felt as if maybe he was judging her—but now she knew that had only been *her* old emotions rearing up in the heat of the moment.

So no wonder she wanted Oliver so badly right now. Her cat was her only true source of unconditional love at the moment. How sad was that?

After a minute, Oliver finally made his way down from the pile of wood, and when he got within Carly's reach, she drew the big, hefty furball into her arms. Hugging and petting him until he began to purr, she soaked in the comfort it provided—and wished it were enough to heal her defeated soul.

Jake was going through the motions. It was his last day as a Turnbridge police officer.

And whatever he was feeling about that . . . well, he was trying to just turn it off. Yeah, he was figuring out now that he'd gotten a little attached to the people here. He'd been sincerely touched when Frank Schubert had made a big deal out of giving him his lunch on the house today and saying how much they were gonna miss him around town. And he'd wondered why Tommy was walking around the station acting pissy this morning—until finally his friend had stopped at his desk and said, "So you're really doing this, huh? You're really leaving?"

He'd already explained to Tommy most of the reasons why, just soft-pedaling the one that had to do with Carly. And he'd concluded with, "It just makes sense to me."

"Well, it doesn't make any damn sense to *me*," his friend said.

And Jake had actually felt a little bad—he cared about Tommy, too. "Look, it's not like you're never gonna see me again, dude," he'd reminded him. Tommy had consented to look after Jake's house until it sold. And he was helping him make the official move tomorrow, along with Ethan, who was driving down from Charlevoix. "We'll keep in touch."

"Won't be the same," Tommy said. "This place'll go back to being an old folks' home."

Jake just laughed. The other cops in the department weren't exactly senior citizens, but it was true—other than one young kid in his early twenties, most of the Turnbridge officers were older, and for the first time, Jake realized his arrival had probably added more to Tommy's life than he'd realized.

Now, as he patrolled the streets on an autumn afternoon, he noticed the small trees lining Main turning a warm red-gold from the change in the weather. People on the sidewalk whom he'd come to know lifted their hands in a wave as he drove slowly past. Hell, even Barlow Jones gave him a nod from behind the wheel of his big old Cadillac.

So yeah, maybe he'd miss it here a little more than he'd expected.

But none of that was a good enough reason to change his mind.

He'd just glanced toward the front window of Winterberry's, nabbing a shadowy glimpse of Carly that made his throat catch—when a voice came over his police radio: Patsy from local dispatch, where things worked a little more casually than they did in a big city.

"Just got a call from a little boy, Justin Webb, on his cell phone. Says he's hiding behind a tree along Red Mill Road. Apparently a fella in an old station wagon tried to give him a ride. Justin refused—he was just heading up to the fishing pond about a mile from his house—but now he says this fella keeps driving up and down the same stretch over and over, like he's looking for him. Justin tried to call home, but thinks his mom is working outside and didn't hear the phone. He sounds real scared. Not sure if there's anything to it, but Jake, Tommy, can one of you respond?"

With all his senses suddenly on red alert, Jake yanked up the receiver and said, "I'm on Main, just about a mile from Red Mill—I'm on my way." Then he switched on his blue lights and pressed on the gas, his heart pumping a mile a minute.

Everything else in his brain turned off instantly as he maneuvered quickly but safely through the scant Main Street traffic, flooring it as soon as he hit more open road. He threw gravel with the turn onto Red Mill and pressed on the gas again. He already knew where the Webb house was, and thanks to Tommy's thorough introductory tours, he even knew the pond down the road where locals went to fish.

He'd just passed the small body of water when a beat-up ancient blue station wagon came into view up ahead. He radioed both Patsy and Tommy, who was the only other officer on duty on a quiet weekday afternoon. "Got the wagon in my sights. Coming up on it from behind."

Over the radio, Tom replied, "I'm a few miles behind ya, but on my way, bud."

Jake slowed only slightly as he approached the vehicle's rear, waiting for the cruiser's lights to catch the guy's attention. The old car pulled immediately toward one side of the road—likely thinking Jake was only trying to pass.

Jake stopped behind him, got out, and walked toward the driver's-side door, his senses remaining on alert—his work in Detroit had instilled the good habit of always being ready for anything.

Before Jake spoke, a guy who looked to be in his fifties with longish, gray hair turned to peer up at him, asking innocently, "Is there a problem, Officer?"

And that voice—there was something about that voice. As Jake met the other man's green eyes, all the blood drained from his face. Because even more than twenty-five years later, he'd know the guy anywhere. It was Larry Downy, the man who had molested him when he was seven.

Chapter 20

For a second Jake froze in place. He felt all of seven years old again. Innocent. Victimized. Other than Downy's dark hair going gray and his face sporting the lines of age, he hadn't changed at all. He even wore his hair the same way and had kept the same out-of-style mustache. Or . . . maybe Jake had just gotten lucky—maybe the guy cycled through changes in his looks to appear different to his various victims and just happened to be back to the one Jake recognized so damn easily.

"Officer?" Larry Downy asked.

And that was when Jake's shock transformed into pure, unadulterated fury.

Without a word, he ripped open the car door and yanked Downy out, slamming his body face-first against the station wagon. With lightning-fast moves, he secured the man's wrists behind him and slapped on the cuffs, all while Downy muttered, "Wh-what's going on? What's this about? I haven't done nothin'."

God, that voice again. Something in it was slimy, shifty. Or maybe it just sounded that way to Jake, given what had happened the last time he'd heard it.

Jake snarled in the bastard's ear, "Not so tough with somebody your own size, are ya?"

"Wh-what?" The man looked over his shoulder, those memorable green eyes wide. "What are you talkin' about?"

Jake met his gaze, and hoped like hell the stark anger on his face put the fear of God into the man before him. He leaned near and said in a low, menacing voice, "I know you, Larry-fucking-Downy. I know exactly who the hell you are."

Downy blinked. "Well, *I* don't know *you.*"

Jake kept his gaze wide on his captive, and because it instantly felt very important to identify himself, he said through clenched teeth, "That's be- cause I was seven fucking years old the last time I saw you. *Seven,* you sick son of a bitch."

That was when the asshole finally began to catch on—and, starting to look alarmed, he shook his head. "You must be thinkin' of somebody else."

"No," Jake said definitively, rage vibrating through every word. "We both know what you did—what you *do*—to little kids. What you tried to do to a little kid *today.*"

"Like I said, I don't know what—"

"Shut up!" Jake yelled, then pulled back his fist and punched Larry Downy in the back.

The man cried out, buckling against the car, then went quiet.

Yet Jake's wrath was only just beginning to come out, and now it couldn't be stopped. Without warning, he spun Downy around and landed a right to his jaw. *"No more!"* Jake told him. *"No more kids get hurt by you!"* Then he delivered a left to the man's gut. *"No more lives get messed up!"* Grabbing the guy's shoul- ders, he slammed him back into the car once again, wanting to kill him, truly wanting to remove him from this earth, and trying his damnedest to get hold of himself so that *he* wouldn't be the one going to jail.

Now Larry Downy's eyes were wide, angry, even as his head tilted back, his face looking haggard from the pain Jake had just inflicted. "You don't have nothin' on me, pardner. I didn't hurt any kid today. I just offered him a ride, that's all. You got nothin' on me—but I got somethin' on you, and it's called police brutality!"

Jake simply looked at the man, shocked by his stunning audacity. *Don't kill him. Despite how much you want to strangle the life out of the son of a bitch, don't fucking kill him.*

"Joke's on you, buddy," Jake said, up in his face. "'Cause the way I see it, you resisted arrest. I had no choice but to defend myself." Jake had never once in his career roughed someone up without provocation, nor had he ever lied about anything. But he felt completely justified in *this. This* was personal. This was as fucking personal as it got. "And I have everything I need to send you away, pal. I have my *own* fucking testimony. And a few more I could probably scrape up from your past if I tried." Jake knew the statutes of limitations for various sex offenses were complicated, but that hardly mattered since his family had gone to the police immediately and the crime had simply stayed unsolved—until now.

"You should just be fucking *thankful!*" Jake told the prick, shoving him against the car once more. "Thankful that I'm gonna send you to prison, instead of straight to *hell*, where you fucking *belong!*"

That was when two hands pulled Jake back, and he looked up to see Tommy, clearly stunned. Shit, he hadn't even heard the other car pull up. "What the hell are you doin', man?" Tommy asked, voice low.

"Only what needs to be done."

Tommy kept his voice down to say, "Dude, we don't even know what this guy is guilty of. We—"

"Yes, we do," Jake told him quietly. "We do because . . . he hurt *me*. When I was a kid." He didn't particularly like telling Tommy, but at the moment, it seemed necessary. And he trusted him, as both a friend and fellow officer.

Tommy's jaw went slack with understanding. And then with the unlikelihood of it all. "Same guy?"

"Same guy," Jake said. "I don't know what he's doing in this town, but between me and you, it was all I could do not to fucking kill him." Even now, his whole body remained tensed, his hands still curled into fists.

"It's all right," Tommy said softly. "Why don't you just . . . let me take it from here. Let me take him in. Is that okay?"

Part of Jake felt compelled to do it himself, to make absolutely, one hundred percent sure it was accomplished, but what Tommy suggested made sense. "Just make sure the bastard gets there, and gets behind bars. And if anybody needs a reason to hold him before I get there, his name is Larry Downy and he's in the state database."

Tommy gave a short nod, then pointed up the road to where a young boy now stood next to a tree. "You think you're calm enough to help that kid get home, take his statement, explain to his mother what happened?"

"Yeah," Jake said. Actually, that sounded fine to him. It would *help* him calm down. And it was something that would actually do some *good*, some real good for the first time since he'd pinned on his Turnbridge badge.

He watched as his friend loaded Larry Downy into the back of his cruiser, pleased that Tom wasn't particularly gentle. Downy looked scared, a little broken, but that didn't even come close to appeasing Jake's need to make the man suffer. How many kids had spent a *lifetime*, as he had, suffering from what Downy had done to them?

His heart still pounded painfully, but he took a deep breath, remembered there was a frightened little boy waiting for him—and then turned calmly toward Justin Webb. "Justin, I'm Jake." Normally, he'd have introduced himself as Officer Lockhart, but at the moment using his first name felt right. "You okay?" He walked slowly toward the boy as he spoke.

Justin Webb appeared to be a typical kid—brown shaggy hair, lean build, freckles, jeans, and tennis shoes. He nodded, looking a little embarrassed. "Yeah."

Upon reaching him, Jake knelt down to put them on eye level. "Listen, the first thing I want you to know is—you did exactly the right thing calling 9-1-1."

"I wasn't sure," the boy said. "But it just seemed weird, him driving up and down the road over and over, even after I told him I didn't need a ride. And then he started going real slow, and looking off the side of the road, like he was trying to find me, and . . ." He trailed off, appearing frightened, and Jake well understood why.

He stood up and put his arm around the kid's scrawny shoulder. "You don't need to be afraid anymore. He's gone now and he's going to prison."

Justin peered up at him, surprised. "Just for trying to get me in his car? It's that easy?"

Jake shook his head, trying to decide how much to say. "No, but he's . . . hurt kids before. That's what he'll be going to jail for. He just always got away with it up to now. So you did a really good thing by helping us catch him. You should be proud of that."

"Yeah?"

"Yeah." Jake hoped the boy caught the gravity of his words—Jake was still trying to wrap his mind around what had just happened, how big it was in his *own* life, and he felt he owed the kid a profound debt of gratitude. "Think you'll be able to sit down with me and tell me exactly what happened again so I can write it up in an official report?"

Justin nodded. Then looked over to the side of the road. "I lost my fishing pole, though, when I got scared. Can I try to find it first?"

"Sure," Jake said. "Let's find your pole; then we'll get you home to your mom and work on that report."

In actuality, Jake was eager to get back to the station, to make sure Larry Downy was indeed under arrest and behind bars, and to tell the chief what he knew about the man. But right now, helping a little boy find his lost fishing pole seemed pretty important, too.

The first thing Jake did upon getting home was to call his parents and tell them the astonishing news: He had personally apprehended Larry

Downy. Both of them cried. And Jake felt very young again for a few minutes, thrust back into that place in time that had changed everything. But
after a moment, he resumed feeling every bit his age, and perhaps stronger
than ever. It wasn't as if he went around letting thoughts of his molestation consume him all the time—before Carly had entered his life, he hadn't
thought about it much in years. But on the other hand, it was something that
was always a part of him and always would be—and what had happened
today felt like probably the biggest victory of his life.

His reaction to the man clearly meant he hadn't ever *really* forgiven Larry
Downy like he'd told Carly he had. But maybe that wasn't such a surprise,
since he'd recently come to realize he still harbored more issues than he
wanted to acknowledge. The important part, he told himself, was that he felt
strong, in control of himself, and like a long, long nightmare was coming to
a close. He knew he'd healed a little more today, healed in a way nothing else
could have healed him. And he still wasn't sure if what he'd once told Carly
was true—that you could *beat* issues like this, truly get past them forever—
but today helped.

And along with everything else so personal about the day's events, he
was enjoying a familiar satisfaction—the knowledge that he'd saved kids
today. Not just Justin, who probably would have been all right, who probably
would have stayed hidden until Larry Downy had given up and gone away—
but he'd saved every kid Larry Downy would have abused from this day on.
Damn, that was a good feeling. Best feeling he'd had on the job . . . ever.

At the station, he'd told his boss and Tommy straight out what had
happened—even though he'd pretty much already told Tommy back at the
scene. "I was molested as a little kid and that's the guy who did it." He'd
really had no other option. Mostly, he didn't tell people—Dr. Jim had always
said it was his choice, that there was no right or wrong decision. He'd shared
it with a trusted friend or two along the way, including Ethan, and he'd told
a woman or two as well—like Carly—but mostly he kept it private. Now,

though, it was necessary in order to keep Downy behind bars and get him prosecuted, and he hadn't hesitated. He'd only asked them both to respect his privacy on the matter.

Afterward, Tommy had said, "Dude, I'm sorry you went through that."

"It's long in the past," he assured his friend. Some days, like with Carly, it didn't feel that way, but capturing Larry Downy made it seem a lot better, and a lot further away from the reality of who he was today.

Now he wanted desperately to go to Carly. He needed to see her, to tell her all this—after all, she was the only person in his life who would truly *get it*, really get how big it was, in a way even his parents couldn't. He sat in his living room, just itching to pick up the phone or drive down to Winterberry's. It was almost closing time at the shop.

But if I see her again . . . it will only make leaving all the harder for us both.

So he just sat there. He sat there on his couch, surrounded by boxes and empty walls, with not even a TV or computer to distract him, his only company the soft music from the iPod player he hadn't yet packed—tomorrow was moving day, and the rest of his life was unhooked, unplugged, and ready to roll. He sat there literally twiddling his thumbs, restless—because arresting his molester, and even helping out little Justin Webb, had sent a blast of adrenaline through him, a wild burst of energy, that still lingered. And the victory somehow felt incomplete without sharing it with her.

And like so many times lately, that was when he heard Dr. Jim's voice in his head. But this time he was saying something different: *If she's the person you most want to share the important moments of your life with, maybe that should be telling you something.*

Chapter 21

S he didn't know how to do this.

But it seemed important. Important enough to push her fears aside. That was something Jake had taught her to do.

So she took a deep breath, picked up the container holding the chocolate cream pie she'd baked for him, and got out of her RAV4. She was still miserable inside, and nervous as hell now—but she had to be brave.

Jake was leaving tomorrow. And even though she hadn't heard from him since their breakup, she felt she had to say goodbye. She had to tell him she loved him and that she hoped he'd be happy. She had to thank him for releasing her from the cage she'd somehow unwittingly built for herself over the course of her life.

He wasn't perfect; *they* weren't perfect together. But he was the best thing that had ever happened to her. And to let him leave without seeing him one last time would have felt like a sin—a sin far worse than others she'd committed, real or imagined.

She stood next to the car, hesitating, looking down at herself. She hadn't changed after working all day—she wore jeans and a navy blue tank top covered with a dark purple zip-up hoodie. Maybe she should have put on something prettier. Or maybe it didn't matter at all. She didn't know how to do this.

How do you say goodbye to the love of your life? Oh God, she *really* didn't know how to do this. But she had to try.

Another deep breath and she walked to his door, rang his bell. Tried to ignore the *boom, boom, boom* of her heartbeat, the nervous knot in her stomach.

When he opened the door, she nearly melted, right there on his front stoop. Because he looked so masculinely beautiful. Dark hair mussed. Face unshaven. Blue eyes sparkling on her in surprise. He wore a gray MSU hoodie and faded jeans, and soft music echoed from somewhere behind him. Every nerve in her body tingled.

"You're leaving tomorrow," she said, the words coming out more softly than intended.

"Yeah," he said, just as quietly. "I was gonna . . . come by then. On my way out of town. Say goodbye." His voice caught a little on the last word, and she actually believed him.

"Well, I saved you the stop. And I made you a pie." She held it out and he took it, glancing down through the container's clear lid.

"Thanks. That was sweet."

She just nodded. And felt a little stupid. "So . . . um . . ." She *so* didn't know how to do this, and she clearly should have come up with a more detailed plan. Maybe she should just go.

"Did you hear about what happened today?" he asked then.

She stood up a little straighter. "No. What?"

"I just thought maybe . . . well, news usually travels fast here." He shifted his weight from one foot to the other. "I was on patrol, and a call came over the radio that a boy needed help out on Red Mill Road." And then he proceeded to tell her an amazing story about rescuing little Justin Webb from a man who'd clearly been out to do him harm. Carly had gone to high school with Justin's mom, Sherry.

"Jake, that's amazing," she said. And she meant it. She knew he hadn't felt very valuable as a cop here, yet today he'd made a real difference.

"But that's not all," he told her, his cerulean eyes intense. "The guy in the car—it was him."

"Him who?"

"Larry Downy."

As Carly's jaw dropped, she lifted her hand, splaying fingers across her chest. Oh God. "Jake. Are you serious?"

He nodded. Then looked a little choked up for a moment until he said, "I nearly beat the shit out of him when I recognized him. Didn't mean to, but it just happened—and . . ." He stopped, sighed. "I can't say I regret it."

"Did you tell him?" she asked. "Who you were? How you knew him?"

He nodded, looking a little numb now. "He didn't really respond to that part much, but . . . it still felt good. To get it off my chest, you know?"

She nodded back, understanding.

"And . . . it's like a weight lifted. Just to know that bastard's finally locked up. And to know he can't hurt any more kids."

Carly could barely summon a response. This felt . . . far too big for mere words. "Oh, Jake." That was all she could come up with. And then she put her arms around him, pulled him into a hug. Because she just had to. And it wasn't about sex—it wasn't that kind of touching. It was about love, and comfort. It was about whatever remnants of that seven-year-old boy still existed inside the man Jake had become.

His arms closed around her, too—tight—and they stood that way a long time, silent, a soft autumn breeze wafting over them through Jake's front screen door. She became aware of the gentle strums of a guitar, recognizing it as the somber beginning of Jeff Buckley's "Hallelujah."

And at some point, Carly realized they were clutching at each other, holding on as if for dear life—her fingertips dug desperately into his back, shoulders, through his sweatshirt, and his hold on her possessed the same urgency, or maybe it was finality; she felt his warm breath on her neck, his fist twisted snug into the hair at her nape. Her eyes grew wet—but she tried her best not to cry. Not to cry for what they'd both been though in their youth, nor for the fact that he was leaving her, really leaving her.

And then she suffered a too-familiar pang—the wild wanting rushed through her, slow and consuming. Somewhere along the way, this had transformed into an entirely different kind of hug—and she bit her lip to try to keep from trembling when she felt Jake's cock hardening against her hip.

Her breasts ached and her cunt pulsed, empty and needful; her scalp began to tingle as desire rippled excruciatingly down her spine. Her chest went tight, as if she were starting to suffocate, and she let out a labored breath upon realizing she'd been holding it, trying not to feel all this. Then she heard Jake breathing heavy, too, felt the stark hunger rising between them like a wild, living thing, bubbling to the surface, like a volcano getting ready to erupt.

A short, hot sigh left him and then his face was against her neck, the rough stubble on his jaw scraping over the tender skin—and then his mouth, pressing there, but going agonizingly motionless, as if attempting to stop it.

The tiny sob of anguish left her unplanned—but it made Jake pull back, forced their eyes to meet. His were glassy, wet like hers, and filled with all the lust and desperation and need that surely shone in her own.

And she heard herself whisper, "Please Jake. Just take me. It's killing me."

"It's killing me, too," he told her, sounding breathless, weak. "But I've been trying so fucking hard not to let this happen. That's why I didn't come tell you myself that I was leaving. Why I didn't come tell you about what happened today. I didn't want to make my leaving any harder for either one of us."

A quivery sound left her. "*This* is hard. Being with you and not . . . Oh God, just please stop trying so hard to do the right thing, just for right now. How can it be the right thing when it's making us so miserable?"

His mouth came down on hers hard, almost violently—and yet her yearning was so great that it was the best thing she'd ever felt, like a sweet, soothing balm that spread, stretched all through her, to her breasts, her belly, the small of her back, her inner thighs. More rough, inelegant kisses grew from somewhere deep, someplace hidden and primal.

And then his fingers were fumbling at the zipper on her hoodie, and her body felt electrified with the need to hurry now as she clawed at his sweatshirt, trying to yank it upward. He stopped, tugged it off over his head, as she struggled out of her own sweatshirt and the top underneath. She reached for the button on his jeans, desperate now for his hard-on, desperate to have that empty, vacant part of her filled, as he frantically lowered her zipper, too, then jerked downward on the denim at her hips.

A low moan left him at the sight of her panties—they were simple, just white with lavender butterflies, to match the plain lavender bra she wore, but Jake always seemed turned on by *whatever* she wore under her clothes.

She stumbled trying to step free of her jeans, and Jake caught her in his arms, and they tumbled onto his soft leather couch just a few feet from the door. He pushed his boxer briefs off, and Carly sighed, feeling it in her breasts when she caught sight of his long, rigid cock, so big and stiff, just for her.

Instinct made her reach for it, but he was quicker—they sat facing each other, and he pulled her legs out from under her, then tugged her panties down and off. He roughly parted her thighs, then let out a low groan as his gaze dropped to where she was pink and wet and ready.

He pressed his hands to her shoulders, pushing her to lie down—but she got her knees back beneath her in time to push back. She didn't *want* to lie down right now; at this moment she didn't feel the least bit submissive. Her body was hungry—she needed to fuck as well as *be* fucked. And so it began—that familiar struggle they both knew so well.

She wasn't as strong as him, of course, but when she curled her hand snugly around his erection, she watched as the pleasure seemed to expand through his whole body, his eyes falling shut, giving her the chance she needed to rise up on her knees, then move to straddle his hips. With that powerful shaft still in her grip, it was easy to position herself over the engorged head and know heaven was just a heartbeat away.

She met his gaze, only inches from hers, and he grasped her hips with both hands and pressed down, impaling her sharply on his unyieldingly firm erection. They both let out small cries of bliss at finally having their bodies interlocked again. Oh God, at last! It seemed like so long since she'd felt him inside her this way.

Up until now, everything had happened fast, frantic, a little clumsy—but now they went still, both breathing heavily, peering into each other's eyes. They still didn't say a word, but Jake's jaw hung slack as his gaze drifted downward to where their flesh joined. He then lowered a hungry kiss to her right breast, through her bra, as he reached to lower the straps. When her tits tumbled free, he growled, dropped an anchoring arm around her ass, and hauled her up a little higher on him, bringing their torsos closer. He bent toward one taut nipple and she helped by lifting her breast toward him until his mouth closed over the tip.

That was when the purest pleasure came, spreading through Carly's body like hot liquid delight. She moved on him as he suckled her, latching firmly to the sensitive, aching peak, and her clit grazed the flesh just above the base of his cock as she fell into smooth, rhythmic undulations. Now it was *her* hand that fisted in *his* hair. She held him tightly in place, needed him to keep sucking her, hard, hard. She could almost feel her nipple getting longer and harder under the rough suction he applied.

She feared his need for control would make him try to pull back, but he didn't—despite his urge to be in charge, Jake was always generous about giving pleasure, and he clearly understood what she needed now and was going to deliver it.

And then—oh God—he delivered something she *hadn't* known she needed; shifting so that both hands cupped her bottom, he briskly slid one finger into her ass. A thready sob echoed from her throat as that one little additional penetration multiplied every sensation.

As always when that tiny fissure came into play, perspiration began to seep from every pore and sensation pulsed wildly outward to the tips of her fingers and toes. As intensely as she'd been feeling his mouth on her breast just seconds ago, she barely noticed now when he released it—she only realized that they were looking into each other's eyes again, that his burned a more vibrant blue than usual in the shady light of late day, and that they held her captive now.

She continued moving on him, the pleasure growing infinitely each second his finger fucked her ass—and then his other hand was pressing low on her abdomen, right above where his cock entered her. And . . . oh God—yes. It was her G-spot again. And though she'd been whimpering the whole time he'd been in her anus as well as her pussy, now the sounds leaving her echoed lower, louder, deeper. An almost unbearable pleasure permeated her, rocked her. "Oh Lord," she murmured. "Fuck me. Fuck me."

Her eyes began to fall shut, her head to drop back, but Jake said, "No—look at me."

And so she did. As the gut-deep orgasm burst through her like a tornado, she met his blue gaze. As it tore the screams from her throat, she still met those blue, blue eyes. When it jerked her body uncontrollably, again and again, whipping her head back, she returned her gaze to his afterward, moaning wildly even when the turbulent climax began to wane, leaving her drained.

They went still, her forehead pressing against his. Her breath remained labored as she came back to earth. His finger left her ass; the hand on her belly rose to cup her jaw.

And when their eyes met again, she said, "Now you can take me. Do whatever you want to me. Fuck me senseless." Not only for him, but because now that she'd reached that glorious release, she *wanted* to be at his mercy. She'd truly learned to love it both ways—both when the control was hers, and when she gave it up to him totally.

Jake was lost. Lost to sensation. To the warmth of her sweet cunt. He was lost in all of her.

And he was lost in himself, too. In what had happened today. In the power it had given him, combining with that old pain, and in the old needs that had resulted. In seeing her again and in the utter loss of control he'd known would come with that. He'd given up now, surrendered himself to what his body craved. And it craved something *hard* with her now.

He shouldn't give in so much—he shouldn't let his rough urges define this moment—but that was what she did to him; something about her made him into the beast he'd kept relatively well hidden and locked up until she'd come along. And if this was the last time he'd be inside her, he had to take what she was offering. *Fuck me senseless. Do whatever you want to me.*

So he wordlessly lifted her off him, turned her around to face away from him on the couch. "Arch your ass," he whispered. And then, finding himself face-to-face with her pussy, so pink and open for him, he buried his face there.

Hot, strangled-sounding moans left her as he licked, bit, slurped, sucked—not at her clit, but at her parted pink folds. He wanted her come in his mouth, on his face. He wanted to feel completely immersed in her, like he was drowning in her.

And when finally his cock wouldn't wait any longer, he rose up on his knees behind her, used his hand to position it at that perfect pink opening, and rammed it deep. She cried out as the thick pleasure blasted through him, her pussy bathing his dick in slick heat. "Fuck," he whispered, breathless. Then, gripping her round ass with both hands, fingertips digging in, he fucked her with every ounce of lust and energy inside him, thrusting hard and deep and wild, over and over. He needed them both to feel it in a way that would last a lifetime.

They both cried out—and still hotter, dirtier little sobs left her when he began spanking her as he plunged into her, *deep, deep, deep.*

He watched the soft sway of her back, the impassioned jerks of her head; his eyes dropped to the crease of her ass below him, to her puckered asshole, slightly swollen now from excitement.

Working on pure impulse and heat, he stroked one thumb over the fissure, recognizing the slight change it brought in her moans—and damn, he loved how crazy ass-play drove her. Then he began to massage her sexy little butt, thumbs and forefingers working at the skin near that tiny hole, using them to prod and tease the muscles around it, add to the stimulation there. Still fucking her below, he stroked his thumb outward around her anus, a fire growing low in his belly when it began to open slightly.

When he went still in her cunt, she whimpered, "Wh-what are you doing?"

He only said, "Shhh," his gaze focused squarely on that minuscule gap—aiming carefully from up above, he let a large drop of saliva drip from his mouth and watched as it hit dead-on, then slipped neatly into her ass. His stomach contracted. He wanted to be in there, too.

Almost weak with his growing lust now, he spit again. This time the saliva landed in the crease, just above her asshole, and he used his thumb to rub it in around the puckering entryway, moistening the skin there.

Her pussy was so wet on him, as always—his cock felt soaked in her juices—that it would be enough to lubricate her. And he didn't want to wait another second.

So he extracted his erection from her deep, hugging cunt and positioned it at that even tighter little tunnel. She didn't say a word now, only panted hotly in front of him—she clearly knew what was coming and wanted it, too.

And as always when he fucked her this way, when he saw his thick shaft preparing for entry, it looked impossible—but then he managed to slowly wedge the head inside. And then the length followed, gradual but smooth as it glided deep. Both of them emitted low, shaky groans.

"Tell me you love having me in your perfect little ass, baby," he rasped.

She sounded barely able to speak, but managed, "God, yes. I love it."

He bit his lip, tried not to explode. It was hard enough in her snug pussy sometimes, but in her ass—shit, he knew he wouldn't last long, not after them being apart for nearly two weeks, not after the full-on, consuming lust that had brought them this far. And he hated the idea of coming in a way, because he knew it would be the last time he'd be with her like this—but his body could only take so much excitement.

Clutching her ass, he began to deliver short but potent thrusts. His eyes fell shut as her ass squeezed him unbearably tight. "Jesus," he muttered. In front of him, she was whimpering, moaning—and he slipped one hand around her hip, pressed his fingers over the distended nub of her clit, and simply held it there as he fucked her. She cried out and almost immediately fell into the moans and spasms of orgasm, because that was how it was with her ass—it took her there fast. And as always, she was so fucking beautiful when she came, sobbing her pleasure, letting it all go, holding nothing back from him.

So fucking beautiful that just watching her climax and feeling the hot contractions of her ass around his dick pushed him over the edge, too, and with little warning, he was shooting his come into her, moaning, "Yeah, yeah, yeah," with each hot burst that left him.

After that, silence, and the gentle slumping together of bodies. He didn't pull out immediately—because he didn't ever want to not be inside her in some way.

As was sometimes the case, nothing about their sex here had been soft, or tender. And yet—he'd never experienced anything so intense. He'd truly been loving her with his body, and he'd felt her loving him in return. He'd felt their pain radiating through them both, but he'd sensed something else there, too. He wanted to believe it was healing. He wanted to believe it was the same healing he'd felt earlier today.

But a lifetime of dealing with this had taught him—you don't *ever* heal. Not *ever*. Maybe for a while, a long while, he'd tricked himself into believing you could. Now he knew that you might heal in bits and pieces, every now and then—but you never healed *completely*. And he never would. And neither would she.

And when all was said and done, that was why they'd still never be any good for each other.

Chapter 22

They lay on Jake's couch, naked, beneath a blanket he'd retrieved from the bed. And, resting in his arms, peering up at him, Carly realized she wasn't ready to let him go.

Of course, that wasn't much of a revelation—she'd known that painfully well all along. But perhaps the *true* revelation was: Just like in bed, she could take a stand for once in her life—she could engage in a struggle for a little control here. So she revised her thought: She wasn't ready to let him go *without a fight.*

"Do you realize how broken I was inside when I met you?" she asked him softly. Dusk had fallen now, filling the room with deeper shadows than before. "I didn't even realize quite how badly myself until you made me think about it, look at it. And I'm still not fully repaired, and maybe I never will be—but I'm a hell of a lot better off, a hell of a lot more happy, and normal, than I was before you."

"I'm glad," he said, sounding moved but somber, resigned.

And she went on. "So I'm not perfect. And you're not perfect. But most people *aren't.* I love you. And Jake, I don't see why we can't work through all this—together, the same way we've been doing so far."

He kept his gaze down for a moment before meeting her eyes. "The thing is, honey, I'm broken, too. Way more broken than I thought. And what good can two broken people possibly do each other?"

"You've done me a *lot* of good," she insisted.

He took a while before responding, finally saying, "Maybe, but . . . Carly, I've spent my whole life trying to save people—and I've come to the conclusion it's what I'm good at. And when I'm saving people . . . it keeps me busy enough, wrapped up enough in their troubles, not to shine a bright light on my own. And . . . maybe I like it that way, maybe I *need* it that way. Back in Detroit, I can have that. Every day."

"But then aren't you living the same way I was? Just running in place. Not moving forward, not solving anything?"

He let out a sigh. "Maybe. But maybe that's what works for me."

"Forever?"

"For my whole life up to now."

It pissed her off. He'd been so damn adamant about breaking down her walls, and *this* was the way he dealt with his *own* issues? So she shook her head and firmly said, "No. Just . . . no."

"What do you mean, no?"

"I guess I mean . . . if you're so busy saving the world, Jake, when are you ever gonna let someone save *you*?"

Another sigh echoed upward—and his gorgeous blue eyes shone on her sadly. "I'm not sure anyone can."

"I think *I* can," she told him. "Save you. Love you."

Her words took Jake's breath away—literally. He'd never thought about that—the idea of someone else saving *him*, from *anything*. He was a cop, a tough guy—*he* was the one who did the saving.

"I understand you like no one else ever will, and you understand me the same way," she went on. "Don't run from that, Jake. Don't run from *me*. Let me love you. Let me love you the same way you've loved me."

She made it sound so easy. And the truth was—they did understand each other. Other people he'd chosen to tell about his abuse—they were kind about it, caring, but they couldn't really *get* what he'd experienced and the way it had affected him like she could.

Damn, maybe that really *was* what had drawn him to her so much in the beginning. Not just the hot memories of Desiree. Not just the mystery surrounding her or the anger over being lied to. Maybe it had been that underlying feeling, that not quite acknowledged fear, that she'd come through something similar to him, that had made him so damn determined to be with her once he'd met her here in Turnbridge.

And still, nothing about it was easy or ever would be. In fact, it was complicated as hell. "Carly, you're about the sweetest woman on this planet. And I *want* it to be as simple as you're making it sound—but think about it. We turn each other into nymphomaniacs. And . . . two people who can't quite give up control in bed to the other? We'd want to kill each other before it was through."

To his surprise, she simply shrugged. "So we'll have one of those stormy relationships for a while. But Jake, I just think . . . if we can get through the storms *together*, things will be amazing on the other side."

"Blue, sunny skies?"

She smiled softly. "Like a perfect Turnbridge summer day."

He drew in his breath, let it back out. What she was saying—it was a damn nice idea. Damn appealing. But he was afraid she underestimated his need to feel valued when it came to his work, to make a difference, to do the thing he felt best—truly gifted—at doing. "What about my need to save people?" he asked her. "That's the only thing that gives me any real sense of power in this world, Carly—I need it."

"You'll be saving *me* a little more every day," she said, a sentiment that tore at his heart. Because yeah, he knew neither of them would ever be completely normal inside when it came to sex, but he hadn't thought his leaving could possibly . . . stop the changes that had started in her.

"You saved that little boy today," she went on, "and every other kid who Larry Downy might have hurt between now and the day he dies. And there are lots of ways to save people all around us, all the time, great and small. Maybe every act of kindness saves somebody a little, you know?"

He sighed. Again, she was simplifying things, big-time. But he got her point. In fact, today's victory had made him begin to wonder what else he could do to save kids from sexual predators. Maybe there was more to be done in that area, and God knew he'd find it satisfying. Maybe he didn't have to be on the streets of the inner city to do some good in this world.

And still . . . "What about sex? I'm not sure I can ever give up complete control there."

"You know I've come to accept that in you—and even like it a lot of the time."

"Yeah, well, I'm not sure that's especially healthy, either," he pointed out.

"Look," she said, sitting up a little more, beautiful and topless before him in the dusky air. "Everybody has a sexual hang-up or two. Or some little fear or kink or fetish. *All* that, in *every* person, had to come from *somewhere.* Meaning—*most* people probably aren't one hundred percent perfectly healthy in the sex department, right? So the way I see it is . . . sometimes I'm on top; sometimes you are. Just like the night we met. No big deal."

He raised his eyebrows, almost amused. "No big deal? We get into physical struggles over it, Carly."

And once again, his sweet girl only shrugged. "I'd rather struggle with you in bed a little sometimes than go through all these bigger struggles alone. Maybe there'll *always* be a little struggle, a little push/pull, but in the end, the sex is always good, right?"

He would never even bother trying to deny that. "The best. Ever. Always."

And then Carly lay back down, wrapping her arms around him, pressing her lovely body to his, and she whispered in his ear, "I want to love you. I want to fuck you. I want to heal you. And I want you to do all those things to me, too—every day. Don't leave me, Jake. Don't leave *us*."

Damn. Jake's skin tingled, all over. From her touch, from her words. From her unshakable faith that they could truly be good for each other, make a relationship work. He lay there, his arms folding around her, swept away by the utter closeness of their bodies, by all the things she made him feel. Almost . . . safe. Almost . . . saved. And damn, maybe she was right. Maybe sometimes . . . almost was enough. Maybe it was better to share the struggle than to run from it.

But mostly, his decision wasn't about anything logical. Mostly, it was about the simple comfort he felt with her in his arms, whispering sweet things in his ear. "How could I?" he finally whispered back to her. "How could I leave the most amazing woman I've ever known? How could I leave the woman I love?"

She lifted her head, surprise and joy and relief all mingling in her gaze. Even so, she pointed out, "You almost did."

He blinked—and said what suddenly seemed obvious. "I think that makes me a colossal idiot."

"Then what are you now?" she asked, giving her head a pretty, challenging tilt.

"I'm *ready*," he told her. And he meant it. "I'm ready to be the man you need, always. And to face everything together. Broken or not." Then he flipped back the blanket covering him and stood up.

"Where are you going?"

"Don't move. I'll be right back," he said. Because if he really was ready to do this, to face their struggles together, he had to start facing what was causing them, too.

He hadn't turned in his department-issued equipment yet, having planned to stop by the police station tomorrow morning. And as he walked down the hall to the bedroom and grabbed his handcuffs, it occurred to him that now he wouldn't even have to turn them back in. Returning to the couch, he handed her the open cuffs.

"Um, I'm good with the handcuff games," she said, "but right now?"

He grinned at her confusion. Then held his wrists out to her. "Consider it a symbolic act. To show you I can give up control. Or that I'm gonna learn to. I trust you to put me in cuffs—I can take it. So this is your big chance. Have your way with me."

A slow grin unfurled on her face as she slowly slipped one steel cuff around Jake's left wrist, snapping it shut—and then closed the other cuff around *her* right one. "This," she said, "is good enough for now. Just to know we'll get through all this stuff *together*."

Epilogue

Carly and Jake stood at his kitchen window, peering out at the falling snow that blanketed Turnbridge on a cold day the following January. Then she caught sight of the winterberry bushes they had decided to plant together in the thicket behind his house, which they'd managed to get in the ground before autumn had passed. Now, as she'd promised him, the red berries were the only dots of color among the white, a tiny cheerful reminder that life existed beyond winter and that spring would eventually come again.

Not that she needed a reminder that life was good. She was reminded of that every day lately, in lots of ways.

The Turnbridge Police Department had been more than happy to take Jake back when he'd decided to stay, especially given the Larry Downy arrest. It wasn't every day that a criminal wanted for nearly thirty years was apprehended in Turnbridge, and besides bringing the little town's PD lots of good press, everyone in the department understood the gravity of getting that kind of guy off the streets.

But better yet, she knew Jake was far more fulfilled by his work than he'd been back in the summer. Over recent months, the department had gotten the state to fund a local program that allowed him to visit schools and give talks about avoiding sexual predators. It had been so well received that other departments around the state wanted to implement something similar, and this spring Jake would be traveling around Michigan, giving training seminars.

Larry Downy was now in prison. Jake had had to testify, and it had been at once difficult but freeing for him, something Carly understood very well.

And Carly had moved in with Jake. Not a lot of people did that in Turnbridge—lived together without being married or at least engaged—but she was finally learning to quit worrying so much about what people thought.

So far, she loved sharing a home with him, and her biggest problems had been getting used to driving to the shop every day instead of just walking downstairs, and then deciding where Oliver lived. In the end, she'd packed up the big cat and brought him to Jake's with her, even though Tiffany and many of her other patrons missed Winterberry's mascot. But this was another case where she'd figured out that life wasn't always about pleasing other people—she couldn't reasonably tote a huge cat back and forth every day, and she didn't feel right leaving him alone every night from six p.m. until the next morning. And she was still wearing bright, cheerful colors and had resumed making heart-shaped boxes, which had continued to be a big seller, especially at Christmas.

Otherwise, life in Turnbridge went on. Dana had had her baby—a healthy girl named Hannah. Frank continued to man the bar at Schubert's, and Beth Anne still kept the town in sweet treats every day. And Carly . . . Carly felt like more of a participant in her own life, like it was no longer just passing her by through Winterberry's front window.

As for sex, sometimes it was easy—and other times there was indeed that struggle they'd grown used to. Some days the struggle was sincere, laced with the past abuses that would always be part of their existence—but other days they ended up laughing all the way through it. And sometimes Carly even *liked* the tussling and grappling a little bit—one more bit of kink she chose not to examine too closely. Because no matter how you sliced it, she'd been right—it was easier to struggle with someone you loved than to not have them at all. And thanks to Jake, Desiree was nothing but a distant memory, a part of her past now, a part she was glad to leave behind.

"Okay, the berries are pretty, but I'm bored," Jake announced, then flashed Carly a playfully seductive expression. "Want to break out the handcuffs?"

"Who's on top?" she asked, meaning the question more figuratively than literally.

He just shrugged in reply. "Whoever gets the other one locked up first, I guess. Race ya."

And with that, they both ran down the hall to the bedroom, soon indulging in a heated and mischievous little wrestling match that they both knew would lead to good, hot, naughty sex, no matter who ended up in control.

Read on for a peek at the next novel in
Lacey Alexander's H.O.T. Cops series,

Party of Three

Available from Signet Eclipse in March 2012

"Happy birthday, honey. Ready for your present?"

Mira lifted her head from where it lay resting on Ethan's shoulder in the hammock they shared. "My birthday's not until tomorrow," she reminded him with a playful smile.

"Yeah, but . . . don't you want your present *now?*" His blue eyes sparkled as he tilted his head to one side in the netting, and something in his look made the juncture of her thighs spasm, just lightly. Then again, it had been doing that a lot lately. In anticipation of this weekend.

"I thought my present was *this*," she said, motioning around them.

He'd brought her to a secluded cabin in the woods on the north shore of Michigan's upper peninsula for her thirty-second birthday. To make up for some things. To start treating their relationship differently. And, of course, for some hot sex, which her body currently hungered for.

"It is," he confirmed. "But . . . there's more."

Hmm. "More? Really?"

He nodded, yet added nothing.

So she leaned closer, lacing her voice with flirtation to ask, "Well, don't you want to save it until my actual birthday?"

"Can't," he told her simply.

And she narrowed her gaze on him. Her boyfriend wasn't usually a man of so few words, so this conversation was beginning to feel downright cryptic. "Um, why not?"

That's when he began to look more hesitant, his expression transforming into a mixture of hope . . . and uneasiness. It was the look someone wore when they'd worked hard to find you the perfect gift but were still waiting to see your reaction when it was opened. Only Mira didn't see any sort of gift bag or box anywhere. "I can't save it," he told her, "because it's sort of . . . *starting* tonight."

Her birthday present was *starting*? Okay, he must be talking about the sex portion of the gift. Yet . . . why would he need to announce it if he was just talking about sex? Because, yeah, she was good and ready for that, but . . . they'd had plenty of sex already during their four years together. "The sex, you mean," she said anyway to clarify, though she knew she sounded confused.

"Sort of," he said, and now he looked just as uncertain as she felt. Not nervous—Ethan was never nervous—but he'd slowed down on this present-giving thing and she sensed him wading through it gingerly now, and definitely holding something back.

She lowered her chin, met his gaze. "Sort of?"

"Okay, wait," he said, holding his hands out before him. "I should have thought through how to tell you about this, because now that it's time, I don't quite know how to say it. So . . . give me a minute to think about the best way."

Mira just looked at him. How complicated could this present be? He needed a "best way"? He sounded more like someone about to break bad news than a man giving a birthday gift to his girlfriend. "You're starting to make me worry," she admitted, still peering into his handsome face.

"The thing about your gift," he began, "is that I want you to love it, really love it. But . . . I'm not sure how you'll take it."

She blinked, thoroughly perplexed now, then finally laid her head back on his shoulder, drinking in his musky, masculine scent as she silently gave him that minute he'd requested. A bird twittered in a tree somewhere to her right and the late-afternoon sun warmed her face as she looked out over Lake Superior in the distance. Blue skies and unseasonably warm June temps in northern Michigan made the scene complete. And, up until a minute ago, she'd felt relaxed, happy, like he really *was* making up for the troubles they'd endured since last fall, and even before that. But right now she didn't know *what* to feel—and the uncertainty turned her thoughts unwittingly back to what had led them here, to this moment.

Ethan had been a workaholic since they'd started dating, and while she admired a strong work ethic—and particularly admired the pro bono legal work he'd embraced—over time she'd started feeling like she came in a distant second behind his career. And when he'd canceled their Labor Day weekend boating plans with friends at the very last minute, she'd realized her life with him was starting to be . . . well, not all she'd hoped.

He was hot. Sexy. And great in bed. He was a good guy, a sincerely good man. In fact, Ethan West was the man she wanted to marry, and she'd known that almost from their first kiss. But then things had changed. He'd left the Charlevoix Police Force to study for the bar exam around the same time she'd moved into his condo. And as soon as he'd passed the bar, he'd opened a small office not far from her shop, and business had been booming ever since for the quaint lakeside town's newest young lawyer. Life had bustled along, and they'd been fine. Until his work had started taking priority over *her*.

And things hadn't improved since Labor Day—and, in reality, they'd gotten worse. More late nights, more lost weekends. And the truth was, right up until two weeks ago, she'd been seriously considering moving out. The only thing preventing it was the fact that she loved him, and that when he *was* there for her, things were amazing and the chemistry between them—both physical and emotional—was intense. She connected with Ethan in a way she never had with anyone else. And yet lately she'd been asking herself: Can I give my life to a man who doesn't put me first? Is that what I want, forever?

And then—like some kind of miracle—he'd taken her to lunch at her favorite waterside bistro one day and told her he'd rented a cabin upstate for her birthday weekend. He'd said he knew he'd been neglecting her, and that he was going to change. Flashing a seductive grin, he'd told her he wanted to spend her birthday making it up to her by "Doing hot, nasty things to you in the sun. Then doing more hot, nasty things to you in the moonlight. With maybe a little sleep in between before we start over again."

She'd bitten her lip, given him a sexy smile across the table, and reached out to take his hand. This was the old Ethan, the Ethan who'd swept her off her feet.

And now here they were, alone in the woods, and she'd begun to think that maybe he really *could* repair what he'd broken between them. He hadn't so much as mentioned a case or a client since they'd left Charlevoix that morning. He'd even brought a few bottles of her favorite wine, one of which they'd opened to drink with dinner a little while ago. Ethan had grilled burgers—saving the steaks he'd brought for her birthday dinner tomorrow night—and they'd eaten at the picnic table just off the small cabin's porch a stone's throw from where they now lay. "I know wine doesn't really go with hamburgers," he'd said with a slightly sheepish grin, "but . . ."

She'd just replied with a happy laugh. "Who cares? I like wine and I like burgers. And I especially like how thoughtful you're being, Mr. West," she'd added teasingly.

Normally, she wouldn't have thought of renting a remote cabin as the way she wanted to spend her birthday, but the sentiment had touched her and now that they were there, she realized it was the perfect setting for a weekend of nonstop fucking. Since that was what she suddenly realized she wanted to do. Fuck him from now until Sunday, when it was time to leave. Their sex life was the one part of their relationship that hadn't suffered over the past year. She supposed it was the wine that now had her feeling amorous, and even though they were outdoors, no other house lay within sight, and the wooded landscape added to the sense of isolation, so it felt as private as their bedroom at home—just a little more exciting.

Of course, she wasn't the sort of girl who usually thought of their sex as *fucking*. A little dirty talk in the bedroom was fun, but it almost surprised her for that particular way of describing it to enter her mind. *I must really need this. I must really need to let go this weekend and just let my body have him the way I want him, with no inhibitions, nothing held back.* No, their sex life hadn't suffered because of his work, but . . . maybe she *had* held part of herself back lately, due to resentment, to not feeling totally connected to him anymore. *Well, this weekend, no holding back. This weekend, he gets all of me. Maybe even more than he's ever had before.* She bit her lip, feeling naughty, aggressive.

And as for this mysterious gift of his . . . well, it would just have to wait, because she'd just decided there was no time like the present to have her way with her man. She sat up boldy, turned, and straddled his thighs. "Uh, what's going on?" he asked, clearly jarred—but still a small, sexy smile reshaped his face as his hands came to rest on her denim-clad hips. She liked the feel of his eyes on her.

All of me. I want you to have all of me. The words echoed through her as she spontaneously stripped her tank top off over her head, revealing a pale yellow bra with peach polka dots. "I think I'm ready for some of that hot-and-nasty I was promised," she replied, assuming a sexy pout.

In response, Ethan's fingers splayed across her hips, then glided smoothly downward to stop high on her blue jean–covered thighs. She felt each fingertip like a pinprick of electric heat.

"Mmm, I like when you get aggressive," he said. "And I hope you still feel just as ready after I tell you about your present."

Oh, so he was back to the mystifying present again, huh? But she refused to let that get in the way of what she wanted right then, so she ran her palms up under his T-shirt, onto his muscled stomach, even as she asked, "Ever gonna end the suspense on that?"

When he squeezed both her thighs, she felt it between her legs. And his eyes twinkled warmly as he said, "Why don't you lie back down with me for a minute and I'll fill you in."

She lowered her chin, slanting a questioning look in his direction. This required lying back down? Stopping her midseduction?

A sigh left her, and yet—even as stopping killed a little of her arousal . . . the strange secrecy going on here kept the spot between her thighs humming with anticipation. Anticipation of sex mingling with anticipation of the unknown.

Ethan eased her back down beside him, soon cradling her in his arms, and then he said, "Do you remember that night last summer . . . that night when we had too much to drink and started talking about fantasies?"

She nodded. It had been an evening a lot like this one: warm weather, good wine, and a quiet dinner for two that had led them on a walk to a park, where they'd ended up cuddling on a bench. Intoxication had had them laughing at first, and then touching and kissing—and then Ethan had asked her what her most secret sexual fantasy was. "It's okay, whatever it is," he'd told her.

And she'd slowly, quietly admitted that in the darkest, most private parts of her mind . . . she sometimes wondered what it would be like to be with two men at the same time.

He'd asked her questions. "Do you want to have two cocks inside you at once?" "Do you want to be the one in control or do you want to have that taken away?" "How much have you thought about this?"

And she'd answered—with vague replies mostly, because her fantasies had been just that, vague. Not fully formed. Not detailed. The truth, she'd told him, was that it had started with a dream—she'd woken up remembering she'd dreamed about a threesome with two guys. "And sometimes I think about it because it turned me on, but at the same time, I'm not entirely sure I'm *comfortable* thinking about it. You know?"

He'd grinned, clearly pleased, aroused, by her sharing that. "Think you'd ever really want to do it?" he'd whispered.

"Only . . . under some perfect circumstances that I can't even really imagine," she'd told him honestly. And that had pretty much ended the conversation. Though they'd had really good sex afterward, back at home.

So now, after a long hesitation, she finally answered his question. "Um, yeah, I remember. Why?"

"Well, what if I told you," he answered slowly, reaching to skim his knuckles ever so lightly down her chest, between her breasts, "that for your birthday, I'm giving you your fantasy?"

Mira's mouth dropped open as the blood drained from her face. "You're what?" she whispered.

He spoke low, direct, but kindly. "You heard me."

Lying on her back on the thick netting, with Ethan peering down on her, she simply blinked, still not quite able to believe her ears. She felt like someone else, in some other place, time—her whole world transformed into something surreal she didn't quite recognize. "But . . . but . . ."

Yet her lover only smiled down at her. It was perhaps the surest, most confident and in-control smile she'd ever seen on his face. "Don't freak out, hon," he said softly. "Just trust me."

But Mira suddenly couldn't breathe. And the sun that had lulled and relaxed her all afternoon now began to make her sweat, even as it began to dip quietly toward the horizon through the trees to her left. Finally she managed three words. "I don't understand."

At this, Ethan bent to lower a kiss to her forehead. And despite everything, even just that one chaste little kiss made the juncture of her thighs tingle hotly. "Listen, relax," he told her. "Relax and let me explain."

He sounded so calm, so rational, that it *did* relax her. A little anyway.

Maybe she'd misunderstood what he was saying. Maybe he meant something else entirely.

"I know I haven't been a great boyfriend lately," he began. "And I know it's driven a wedge between us. I want to fix things, Mira. I want to make things right. I want to prove that making you happy is my top priority, starting now."

She still just blinked up at him, taking in his features, everything handsome and sexy about him. She'd always loved his olive skin, and his dark hair, as black as night, traits left over from an Italian ancestry that had faded in name a generation or two ago but showed up in his family's coloring. Now that dark hair stood out in bold contrast to the soft greens and browns above him, the trees that nestled their weekend hideaway and made it feel so deliciously remote. But the moment continued feeling utterly unreal—especially as he went on.

"I thought a lot about how to prove that—what I could give you to make up for how wrapped up in my practice I've been."

She felt the need to interrupt. "You don't have to give me anything more than this. Just spending time with—" But he pressed gentle fingers over her mouth, quieting her.

"I know that, but . . . I guess I wanted to make a grand gesture, something big. And so . . . I thought about your fantasy."

Yes, it had been vague, but she'd told him as much about it as she could that night—it *was* about having two cocks inside her at once. It was about being caressed by two pairs of male hands, having her body kissed by two men's mouths. It wasn't about control—keeping it or giving it away. But it *was* about . . . maybe being a little overwhelmed. In a good way. With masculine power. With sex itself.

"And I want to make it come true," he continued. "I want to give you that. I want you overcome with pleasure. I want you to have orgasm after orgasm in a way I could never make happen on my own."

Mira blew out her breath, poleaxed by the very idea. Strange how fear and stark desire could mix. And they both swirled inside her now as she tried to wrap her mind around the fact that he was offering this to her. Not as a fantasy, but as reality. Even though they weren't that kind of people. They were mainstream, middle of the road; they were dependable and responsible. Yes, a little dirty talk in the bedroom, but that was about as kinky as it got, and she'd always been perfectly pleased by what they shared. "We have great sex," she felt the need to remind him.

"I know we do," he told her, now cupping her cheek in his palm. "But I want this weekend to be . . . something beyond normal for us, beyond great. I want it to be something new, something extreme, something that'll bring you more pleasure than you can even imagine."

Okay. It was beginning to sink in that this was really happening, that he was really planning on this. But he didn't know her as well as he thought if he didn't realize . . . "Ethan, I can't have sex with just anybody. I mean, you know I haven't been with that many guys." She'd always been in serious relationships. She'd never had a one-night stand in her life. And she'd never been intimate with anyone she hadn't gotten to know first. For her, good sex was about trust, about knowing the person you were with. "So I can't imagine who on earth I'd really want us to—"

"Rogan," he said simply—and that's when her world changed once more.

Oh Lord. Rogan Wolfe was . . . Well, God, what *wasn't* he? Ex-boyfriend, tough cop, bad boy to the bone—and the man who had taught her to love sex. She'd never told Ethan that part about her relationship with Rogan, but while, before him, she'd liked sex just fine, *with Rogan* she'd found her true sexual being, and she'd loved how much he'd drawn that out of her. In fact, she credited her good sex life with Ethan in part to her time with Rogan.

Still, she was stunned to hear this was who Ethan had in mind. "Rogan? You don't even *like* Rogan."

At this, though, her boyfriend just shrugged. "We get along all right."

The fact was, Ethan and Rogan went back a long way, all the way to the police academy and the Hostage Ops Team on which they'd been placed and where they'd trained together. And she'd always been keenly aware that, in some aspects, the three of them were closely, weirdly intertwined.

She'd met Rogan when he'd joined the Charlevoix police force a little more than five years ago. She hadn't even known Ethan yet, but he and Rogan had worked together on the force and even now, they still played on the same summer softball team.

And what had led Rogan to Charlevoix in the first place? He'd been looking for a new position and, after reaching out to the other H.O.T. members, who'd kept in touch over the years, Ethan had let him know there was an opening there.

So she'd have never met or dated Rogan if not for Ethan's involvement in bringing him to town. And maybe she'd have never met Ethan—despite their both having been born and raised in the Charlevoix area—if she hadn't started coming to Rogan's softball games when she'd been dating him.

"Getting along isn't the same as liking," she pointed out to Ethan. Because, despite the things the two men had in common, they were very different. Almost like night and day, in a way. And despite their both being part of a tight-knit group of old friends who got together once or twice a year, apart from the H.O.T. affiliation, they weren't at all close. They might drink a beer together with the rest of the team after a game, but otherwise, they didn't socialize.

So the fact that Ethan was suggesting bringing Rogan into their relationship in such a radical way felt at once ironic and . . . almost fitting. Almost— dare she think—like a thing that made sense on some level, a thing that was supposed to happen?

"I can like him fine for a weekend," he told her. "And he was the only guy I know who I thought you'd be comfortable with. For this."

This. The mere word brought her back to the matter at hand, the threesome he'd suggested—and she swallowed sharply, the aftertaste of wine in her mouth now turning a bit stale. The fact was, if Ethan had gone so far as to select Rogan, her ex, to join them in his threesome plan, it meant that he'd really, seriously thought this through. It wasn't some off-the-cuff idea he'd concocted a few days ago. And it meant . . . "Um, about Rogan. Does he . . . know about this? I mean—"

"Of course he knows. He's on his way here right now."

"Holy crap," she whispered. Because this made it . . . real. *Really* real.

And he was already on his way? When there was so much to consider, so many questions to ask?

"Ethan," she began, "what if . . . what if you think of me differently afterward? I mean, how could you *not* think of me differently?" Because a woman who could do that, who could be with two men at once . . . Well, Mira had never seen herself as that woman. Even after her dream and the hazy fantasies. Doing it was different from dreaming it. If she did this, she would be changed forever. She *would* be different, a different person—at least in some way—than she was now.

"I won't," he told her. Again, as always with Ethan, all confidence. And it assured her once more that he really *had* thought this through, but . . .

"What if you're wrong? What if I do this and . . . and it kills something between us? What if somewhere deep down inside you, it . . . makes you think I'm slutty? In some ugly way. What if you can't help it? I mean, once we do this, we can't take it back."

He narrowed his blue gaze on hers and she realized that—Lord, the fear and desire from a few minutes ago . . . both ran deeper now, fuller. She could almost feel the two conflicting emotions consuming her at once. Was she really considering doing this? *Could* she? And not just from a morality standpoint, but . . . could she overcome her fear enough to pull it off? To be *that* sexual? *That* self-assured? When deep inside she was scared to death?

"Look, honey," he said, his voice going tender, "I understand what you're saying. But I've thought about this a lot. I thought about it for weeks. And the fact is . . . it'll be a gift *you're* giving *me* as much as a gift *I'm* giving *you*."

She blinked, and her voice came out light, high-pitched. "Huh?"

A solemn sigh left him as his eyes sparkled darkly on her while the sun shifted in the sky just enough to immerse them in shade. "The fact is, the more I thought about it, the more it excited me. The more I realized that *I* want it, too." His voice went deeper then. "I want to see you that way. With another man. And with both of us at once." Her skin flushed with warmth at his words. "And once we share that, it'll bring us even closer."

Mira's heartbeat pulsed all through her body. Her cheeks, fingers, breasts tingled with odd heat. She hadn't thought about it like that—that it could somehow pull the two of them closer together, that it could bond them in a whole new way.

And somehow . . . somehow *that* began to make it feel . . . possible. Like a thing she could maybe really do.

Just then, he leaned over her, the heat of his body warming hers, his palm curving around her neck, as he whispered in her ear, "Tell me you want this as much as I do."

She bit her lip, her pussy pulsing against her blue jeans. Did she? Did she want this? "M-maybe," she heard herself stutter. "I—I think," she went on. Then, "Yes. *Yes*."

She'd heard herself say it. So it must be true.

About the Author

Lacey Alexander's books have been called deliciously decadent, unbelievably erotic, exceptionally arousing, blazingly sexual, and downright sinful. In each book, Lacey strives to take her readers on the ultimate erotic adventure, and she hopes her stories will encourage women to embrace their sexual fantasies. Lacey resides in the Midwest with her husband, and when not penning romantic erotica, she enjoys studying history and traveling, often incorporating favorite destinations into her work.